THE INTIMATE DIARY

OF

POPE FRANCIS THE SECOND

a book by

VLAD BUNEA

The Intimate Diary of Pope Francis the Second
Copyright 2019 Vlad Bunea

All rights reserved. No part of this book may be reproduced, scanned, or distributed in any printed or electronic form without permission. Please do not participate in or encourage piracy of copyrighted materials in violation of the author's rights. Purchase only authorized editions. Thank you.

This is a work of fiction. Names, characters, places, and incidents either are the product of the author's imagination or are used fictitiously, and any resemblance to actual persons, business establishments, events, or locales is either coincidental or intentional. Smart readers will know which one.

Cover: *Pope Francis the Second* by Viorica Bunea (oil on wood)

ISBN: 9781724192097

EDITOR'S FOREWORD

These are the collected notebooks of Enyi Chebea, born in Nigeria in the late 1990s. He is known as Pope Francis the Second, the first and last Black-African Pope of the Roman Catholic Church. Enyi Chebea also remains the first and last Pope to come out as a gay man, and as an atheist. He is credited with initiating the Grand Reform of the Church, and is remembered as the father of the Council of Humanity.

Much effort has been made to procure all twelve handwritten notebooks. While the general chronological order has been preserved, there is an unknown number of missing pages which may contain, I believe, references to unremarkable events.

While it is obvious that the notebooks closely follow the structure of the biblical Book of Ecclesiastes, verse by verse, there are some disagreements about the meaning of the translations and references used by Pope Francis the Second. I elected not to cut, alter, or modify any of the original text, or to burden the reader with too many explanatory footnotes. It is unclear whether or not the Pope intended his intimate notebooks to resemble a commentary of the Book of Ecclesiastes, known to be the go-to book for skepticism and optimism in the entire Christian Bible.

The twelve notebooks, bound together in this volume under the title *The Intimate Diary of Pope Francis the Second*, have never been printed, copied, reproduced, distributed, transmitted, uploaded, downloaded, stored, or displayed in public. This is the first time they see the light of print, with the permission of Pope Francis the Second himself.

Our foundation hopes that by publishing the personal notebooks of Pope Francis the Second, the public will better understand the man Enyi Chebea, his life, his partner and best friend Nwanne Yinkaso, and the legacy of his papacy.

Vlad Bunea
Editor-in-Chief of the Pope Francis the Second Archives

NOTEBOOK ONE

O, my beloved angel, they elected me Pope, today! On my 50th birthday! I was not spared, I was thrust into the light of truth - my deepest, darkest fears exposed, my silence punished with the magnanimous sound of heavenly trumpets announcing my burning shame. If they only knew, if they knew that my heart is about to explode, that my entire being is screaming NO, if they knew that this is the gravest mistake they could make, they would realize the enormous danger that has befallen our Mother Church.

My dearest angel, you have been by my side all these years, and I need you now more than ever. A terrible journey is waiting ahead of us. I do not know if I can walk the path by myself. I do not know. After this very long day, I sit alone at my desk, I write thinking about you, thinking about this colossal appointment, thinking of duty and oath, hoping that God will remain by my side until the very end. I feel an end has already begun, as now, more than ever, I will not be able to hide my thoughts. My sensibility will emerge untainted by shadows and the monstrous thoughts that I carry will be revealed to the whole world. All of this will shatter the very foundations of the Church that I am entrusted to defend.

I have not told you until now, my angel, what these thoughts are, for I am not aware of them myself, yet I know they will be there, as a whip to my soul. Why have I let this happen? Why did I not speak the truth loudly? I am a fool, you know me. I am a fool to believe my modesty will keep me closer to the truth. Look what happened! I should have spoken to the conclave, "I am not the man you are looking for", I should have shown them the real me, but what is the real me, can you tell me, my angel? Who am I to challenge my Cardinal brothers in faith, or to undermine my very own reputation of a man of discipline, systematic faith, a champion of the poor, a crusader for justice? They were so determined, so adamant, so resolute to believe my outwardly persona, they elected me in a single ballot. One ballot! I didn't even get the chance to fully present my platform. "Oh, we know your platform," they said, "we know it quite well. You have lived it throughout your entire life." "True, I said." It is true, isn't it? Am I not the embodiment of what I believe? Have I not always done what is true to my faith? How could I have denied this? You know, dearest, that truth has always stood above anything else, that I equated truth with the source of my faith? I have spoken of these many times, everybody knows. From the slums of Abuja and the deep forests of Biafra, to the offices of the Vatican, this is well known.

1:2 On vanity

"Vanity of vanities," said the Preacher. Vanity of vanities, all is vanity. All these words come to my mind now and I cannot shake their weight off. It's the weight of my garments, the weight of my new crown, the large and beautiful Saint Peter's Square, the gardens that talk to me with pomp and adulation, as I am their master. It seems to be, so I must believe it myself, as I have no choice in the matter. Who am I to disobey the greatest blessing of this world? Who am I to question the wisdom of my peers? What good is it to question fate, when fate has clearly spoken? When divine providence has conspired, when everything came to be so I can be here, in this chair, toiling with the inevitable, with the most dreadful turn of events that I could not escape despite my numerous and long hours of prayer.

1:3 On profit and labor

What profit does man have from all his labour and toil under the sun? Tell me, my most fateful angel, what profit? Life becomes a burden to the soul when we carry the expectation of fulfillment, of realization, of creation without the necessary meaning attached to it. We walk aimlessly, disoriented, lost in an ocean of fog that we call life. We hail each other, we do not hear each other, we reach out for hands but we do not look at the body from whence they come, and we release them after we consumed their utility in full. Where are we going under the scorching sun? To the edge of the world where there are no winds, no shade, and no consolation? Are we working so hard to simply run away from the fangs of peril? From the claws of the unknown? We remember the sting of fear every day when we look at ourselves in the mirror, the fear of realizing terrible truths about ourselves, so we put on masks, paint, scarves, lenses of distortion and correction, shields of borrowed thought and explosive experiences. We hope this crushes the fear, the desolation, if only for a few moments, those of solitudes, until our beloved partners can rescue us, with their otherness, with their imagination, with the demands, to which we succumb gladly and make them part of who we are, without any shred of self-denial, without any need for additional compensation from the outside world, the world to which we remain strangers, because we are now characters in a skin of smoke, replaced day by day, recycled, refurbished, repackaged.

I kneel in prayer and ask for answers. I lay my soul open to be dissected and stuffed with the material of hope and understanding. Revelations are avoiding me. I feel impure and used. I walked the deserts, the mountains, the plains, and I arrived in a palace. Unlike the Messiah I was not on the back of a donkey, carrying an olive branch. They brought me in an airplane and offered me ice cubes and soft pillows and warm blankets, and the spectacular view of the creation from above the clouds. And there were no gates of heaven, there were no golden chariots and celestial trumpets, there was only a flatland of silky, white, expressionless clouds.

When I was born, my father told me before he went to war, "You are a man now, there comes a time when the son will leave the home where he was born to go on a quest, to discover the world, to learn the lesson of life, but it is the father himself who must leave for a duty that is higher than the perimeter of his family and his possessions, to fight a war of identity and self-determination." I then asked my father, "Why, father, is there such a duty, higher than the wellbeing of this home, higher than us, your family?" "Because," my father said, "it is God who made us a family and we must honor Him."

1:4 Change of generations, stillness of the sun

My father never came back, and we lost the war. Our nation was crushed. One generation passes away and another generation comes. But the Earth abides forever. I hope my deeds will soon become forgotten. I feel least worthy of them now. I tried to make good and help the helpless and I was raised on this mountain of earthly glory as a reward. The conclave told me, "You have earned the Holy See", but I am not sure if I have earned anything. How could I, when I did my deeds without the imagination of any reward, be it heavenly or material. Everything I did was from my deepest conviction of justice and rejection of suffering. It had to be done. I knew no other way.

"You are an Igbo," were my father's last words. "Never forget that, and be proud of it!" So I thought it must be pride that kept us united. I thought about it for many years. I spoke about pride with my mother, with my brothers and sisters, with the elders in my village, with all the men and women I have met during my pilgrimages across the continent, from the scorching deserts of the North, to the tumultuous South, from the Atlantic Ocean to the Horn of the East where all hopes seemed to be lost. All the peoples I have met had their own pride, worshiped their own traditions, respected their own elders, had their own codes of honor, had the same bouquet of emotions, had the same illnesses, faced the same troubles. They carried unique names and spoke numerous languages, many difficult to comprehend, yet their faces showed the same vibrations of life, "We are who we are and cannot be anything else," they said, "we want to live as we are."

They took me to the highest ground in their community and pointed at the sky.

1:5 The sun also rises

The sun also rises, and the sun goes down, and hastens to the place where it rose. The wisest among them understood this, it brought serenity in the way they spoke, not resignation, but simple calmness that inspired comfort for those who knew how to listen to them. I learned a lot from these wise men.

An angel stands near me. It is not you, my dearest, it is a simple angel - a dream, a fleeting sensation of a divine sanction. It gives me some courage, and I try to cling to it at this late hour. Yet soon it disappears, and all that remains is deafening silence. Foreign walls separate me from the tempest. Ah, but how easily walls fall, crushed by the most terrible armies! With the power vested in me and my well-known clumsiness, I fear I will shatter all the walls around me, from the thickest to the tallest, and no stone will remain unturned, no brick will remain untransformed into dust. I am a child, my dearest, you know me so well, you know that I am nothing but a child of the world, with millions of mothers and millions of fathers, never fully consoled, always restless, always awake, never careful where I lay my steps, never settling into one home.

I beg for your forgiveness, my dearest angel, as I have wronged you so many times whilst you have remained my truest companion. I have demanded so much of you and all of it pales when I look at what lies ahead. From the moment I met you at the seminary, until today, you were my lively inspiration, my truest confessor and friend. I talked to you in a commanding voice when urgent matters demanded it, and when peers surrounded us, for circumstances have thrust positions of authority upon me, when nobody else wanted them, and I had to carry the cross of power with sharp edges that scarred you occasionally, yet you never bled, you never complained, you always smiled, and offered yourself again and again. Now, I want to hear your voice and I cannot. This is my hour of solitude. This is me alone with myself, finding myself, rediscovering myself. Tomorrow, they expect me to shine and smile and sit on the throne and tell them what needs to be done. How can I tell them? What my heart tells me, my mind cannot embody! My angel, I need you by my side at this frightful hour.

1:6 Winds of change, talk of rivers

It is a new day. The wind goes toward the south, turns around to the north, the wind whirls about continually and completes its circuit. I have opened the windows of my room and I have felt the fresh air of roses animated by the bustling of Cardinals, guards, guests, worshippers, and admirers. The television crews, the congregations, the convulsions of words, the connivers, the champions of faith, all frolicking hither and thither, celebrating a new age that I apparently represent, without knowing it myself. With the consent of my heart, they themselves cannot believe it, I can hear it in the pitch of their joy, in the exuberance of their judgments and adjectives, they have unloaded their millions of hearts onto my shoulders and left me alone with them. Oh, but how they do not know that these mortal, frail shoulders, that once carried water in the muddy trenches of Darfur and delivered lost children to merciful receiving hands, these humble shoulders can carry no more - not even the golden garments of Papacy, not even a white sheet of linen - they are too battered by memories of the past, too battered, too battered, too battered...

I met officials, dignitaries, Cardinal friends, many of whose faces were not familiar. They congratulated me, I reiterated my boundless respect and gratitude for their friendship and confidence. I reassured them that I will try not to disappoint them, the Mother Church, and the millions of believers. They said they could not even imagine such an eventuality, given that my past constituted an irreproachable path of the deeds of a great man, some even whispered the words saint, how could they say saint?! How could they? They do not really know me, they did not hear my conversations with God, they did not hear my despair during the long treks in the desert, they know nothing about the darkness of my mind, how it haunts me at the peak of my prostrations, and they know nothing about you, my beloved angel!

How I met you at the seminary - remember the sunny day when I saw you walking with a bucket of roses? I smiled, I said nothing. You saw me and recognized my affection for flowers immediately. You said, "I see you love roses. These are for the office of the Dean." You were a boy then, your skin was of a river of Swiss chocolate, fine, pure, soft, innocent. You were a divine apparition, endearing and gracious. I will never forget that day. All the words you spoke to me, your kindness, your confidence that overshadowed mine. You had lost all of your family, but you had kept your smile. You had lost all possessions, but you had gained a purpose. You had no education, but you had the wisdom of an emperor. You thought of me as a king from the moment we saw each other. You told me that you valued our friendship more than your friendship with God. I scolded you for that. I replied, "Nothing ought to be grander than our love of God, not even our friendship." You said, "But *Enyi*, you are first to truly listen to me, even before God. When I pray, I have to wait for God's answer, but when I talk to you, you answer immediately, and my soul's thirst is quenched."

Your words are often ahead of my heart, my sluggish, immature heart that kept me awake during my youth, making me wonder what I am to do with my little life, how am I to serve those left debilitated and dismembered by the war, how am I to feed my brothers and sisters, my ailing mother, how am I to bring reparations to my village and my clan? I turned to God, as advised by elders and by the missionaries. I heard answers, guidance, assurance; I discovered exactly what I was meant to do: I had to serve, I had to learn forgiveness, I had to practice humility. But I did not truly believe all of this, with all my heart, with all my soul, with all my mind. These were words that were told to me in my teenage years. It was only later, after I met you, that I learned true faith. When you told me that you want to serve me, I realized that I had become a changed man. "You want to serve God, Enyi, and I want to serve you," you said. I remember the candour in your voice when you said those words. I remember the breeze from the forest that surrounded us. I remember the colours of the leaves and the sky, the length of your shadow on the ground, the openness of your eyes. You spoke with your whole being. I accepted you because of your infinite faith in me. I could not judge you. I did not have any choice. I could not fathom having choices. I embraced you like a little brother.

That evening I mustered up the courage and I asked you, "Why do you want to serve me, *Nwanne*?" You made me sit down, under the mango tree.

1:7 All the rivers run into the sea

You said, "All the rivers run into the sea, yet the sea is not full; to the place from which the rivers come, there they return again."

I said, "You know the Holy Book, Nwanne."

You said, "I know life, Enyi."

We were young, restless, and curious. I did not know life. I had seen war and death, I had seen our loved ones stolen from me, I had seen drought and famine, blood and swords. But I did not know life. I did not understand the meaning of people under the sun when their sense of attachment had been obliterated. You stood in front of me, with the sparkle in your eyes and you told me about life. What could I have taught you?

"I cannot teach you much, Nwanne."

"You can teach me everything, Enyi," you said.

We went together on a trip into the heart of the land, to find the most remote villages. We travelled for many days in carts pulled by oxen, in rusty buses without windows or roofs; we crossed rivers on rafts, and precipices on rope bridges. We found people of a very dark complexion, so dark that the night enveloped them in sheer mystery. I had no idea that these kinds of people existed in our country. We followed them and slept among them in their huts. They fed us their food, told us their names and the heroic tales of their ancestors. I told them about Our Savior and they said they knew about Him. They took us to see the old giraffe that died of natural causes. They said they had to release the giraffe's soul, so they cut open the giraffe neck from the head to the body, then opened the body so we could see the heart, which they took out and held upwards towards the sun so the giraffe's soul was free to return to the light. They thanked their gods and distributed the animal's body to the gathering so that they could feed their children. They said that the giraffe was their savior; just like Our Savior, whose soul returned to the light so that all of us can live.

I learned that day that despite what the prophet said, life is not always in vain. We can be reborn and live another day through the sacrifice of others.

Yet this is not enough, because life is frail and we are insatiable. We crave so much, that often there aren't enough heroes or giraffes to sate our hunger and desires. We lust for more, where there isn't enough, and the less it is, the more we want. Whereas in the lands of plenty, the lust has become warlike and devours entire herds, and wants to conquer entire tribes of people.

I knew my mission from the seminary days, but I had grown to feel it only during my first trips with you, Enyi. Often we had to rest for hours under the shade of mango trees, so I could catch my breath and regain my spirits after the overwhelming experiences of the day. You sat near me, with patience, as if you had known the lands and all people by heart, as if you were seeing them for the thousandth time. And you were a novice, just like me. You washed my tired feet, I washed yours. We prayed together.

After that summer I had to go back to school, because I wanted to become a priest, I wanted to serve in a church. "I cannot go to school with you, Enyi," you said. "You know I can barely read and write." "Now it is time to learn," I told you. "I will teach you."

We borrowed some books of literature, so you could see the letters on paper. I bought paper and a pen, and I told you I got the money from a wealthy peasant whom I helped in the garden. "That's not enough money to buy pen and paper!" you protested. "I tutored their children, as well," I said, which was half true, because I always tutored for free.

You were seven years younger than me. You learned fast, yet I couldn't finish teaching you everything you needed to know by the time I had to leave for school. I promised you we would continue the lesson. You promised we would go to school with the other kids in your village. I asked you to stop wandering and stay with your family. "Everybody is my family," you said. I knew that, of course. I think I cried a little - yes, I did - when I went back to school that September and I had to say goodbye to you. You didn't flinch; you knew that we had to pay with sorrow for longing. We both had to stay strong.

1:8 All things are wearisome

I am not a politician, I never was and I never can be. All that I can do is pretend and imitate. I do not dare to raise myself to the level of St. Augustine and further to St. Francis, who was the mentor of my predecessor and might as well be my mentor. I am nothing but a lowly insect compared to these holy men. The deeds I have done, my work, my travels and tribulations, have built this impression of me as a personable man, a good diplomat. Consequently, and somewhat naturally, my fellow cardinals found themselves believing that I am also a politician, capable of running this grand institution. Who am I to contradict them? Perhaps it's true. I cannot imagine the day when I will start to believe it myself.

Today I met some of the papal nuncios at a grand reception. My aides thought it was a good idea to invite some of our closest ambassadors and supporters as well. There were many voices and many opinions about the meaning of my new papacy. They kissed my ring and I thanked them. The Italian Ambassador was the most enthusiastic of them all; he spoke as if the entire population of Italy had crowded into his mouth and was cheering and singing. He proclaimed, "Holy Father, you are our greatest friend, your work is difficult, so I assure you of our unwavering support."

I said, " All things are wearisome." I paused. I was searching for something meaningful to add.

The Ambassador did not have patience for me and said, " More than one can say. That's for sure."

Then I knew exactly what to say, "The eye is not satisfied with the seeing."

And the Ambassador said, "Nor the ear filled with hearing."

Immediately I knew that he was my friend. A good fellow.

They asked me again why I chose my papal name. "Is it to honor the first Pope Francis?" Of course it is. Is it not obvious? Yet I felt they knew this and wanted to learn whether there was something deeper than that. I had not given a single second's thought to choosing my name. When the ballot was announced, I knew immediately what my name should be.

I walked among the poor my entire life. I lived with them, I cried with them, I laughed with them. My biography is not exactly that of my predecessor, but my philosophy is very close to his. I think the poor continue to be oppressed. I think their suffering is very present. I am friend of the poor, but not a friend of poverty. I had seen so much dignity, honor, wisdom, kindness, and poise among the poor, that I could not fathom anything aside from the divine that could raise me to such a state of exultation. Poverty is the shame, the agony, and the frustration that washes out the potential of universal magnificence of mankind. Poverty humiliates and crushes the body and the soul. Poverty is not the opposite nor the childhood of richness, poverty is a denial of participation in the fullest act of being alive, as creatures-creators of endurable meanings. It is not enough for the slum-dwellers to live just for today, even if their faces radiate with worriless joy, even if they say *I am happy I lived another day*, when others, who share their human makeup, can explore all the possibilities of nature, all the realms of imagination, all the joys of the senses, with the disposition of immortal all-powerful beings. This is why we must let poverty fade into the past, for good, and look forward to a world of few sorrows. This is the religion of the future.

1:9 There is nothing new under the sun

The hours of desolation have not left me. Dearest angel, even when I see your shadow passing by my door, I cannot regain the joy of innocence that I once had as a child, even when I know that if I called you, you would come immediately and talk softly to me. I am a man in a long line of men, anointed with the heaviest burden of mankind. I do not bring anything new, except that I am alive in a present that is not outstanding. This is what my heart tells me, that which has been is what will be, that which is done is what will be done.

Today they showed the books of activities of our *Istituto per le Opere di Religione*, which the people call the Vatican Bank. I saw many numbers and names, I understood little of it, and I felt a tremendous hole in my heart. Long-forgotten are the emotions associated with the detachment from the material world and the longing for transcendence. People know *of it*, but people do not *feel it* anymore, especially my fellow colleagues, especially those who tell me that those books of activities need to be balanced, need to be green, not red, need to have a vision, need to be cautious and well-guarded. "Who?" I asked, "the books or the activities?" They said both, especially the books. I told them, "Let everyone see them," "No Holy Father, we cannot do that, people will not understand." Oh, the arrogance of those who think people know less than they do. Is the Institute not supposed to work for the people? Of course, Holy Father, they said, but sometimes the ways of the Institute are not fully aligned with the sacred. Not fully aligned with the sacred?! You are right, they are not, by definition they are not, so we cannot dare to hide our works from the profane judgment of the people. Let God judge the sacred aspect of the Institute for the Works of Religion! Who chose that duplicitous name, anyway?!

I am so sorry, dear angel, I have lost my temper today. It's been only a few days and the exercise of power gives me shivers. The more I understand the burden and the honor, the more my body rejects the reality, like a rebel with so many causes on his plate he doesn't know which one to choose.

What a superfluous question it is: can we not live with the medium of money and all it represents? Philosophers and theologians have asked this for centuries, to no avail. There is no answer to this question. We are bound to our groundless nature; we are lost in the search of the divine, of the pastures of heaven that are always beyond reach. Always beyond reach! Our puny existence is the restlessness by which we long for these hidden pastures. We had a Savior and we forgot about Him. We barely remember the words in the Holy Book, let alone their meaning. How can we hope to get closer to God, when we forgot the origins, the path and the truth? We wake up every day with the same fear of loss, the same pressure of necessity, the same lack of imagination for options; every day, over and over again, like there is nothing new under the sun.

Perhaps there is nothing new under the sun. The struggle with the world is the same, except in new clothes. We are born in mothers' pain, we grow up with a mission instilled in us by our parents, a mission that we embrace or deny. Then we qualify as men and women, then we reproduce, then we die, many in oblivion, many unenlightened, many bored with themselves, many forgotten, many forgetful, many resigned. And there are those who embrace themselves, embrace life and embrace the world. They cherish the struggle, they welcome it, they defy it, they challenge it. They are the constructors and the saints. They are those men and women who refuse the sorrows of life and change them into bliss and accomplishments. To live without sorrow, for many of these men and women, is the greatest triumph.

Side thought: I tell them this Institute of ours is not in our control anymore. It doesn't mean that we don't have the records for this and that transaction, but that it's become a monster of its own volition. I told them: shut it down and in three days we will rebuild the truth afresh! They were stunned! They thought I was crazy! I felt it in their hearts, yet their faces remained true to the inertia of the profane. That's how strong these traditions have grown. They are stronger than us!

1:10 I try not to look back

We can never escape our memories.

I was not there when my father died in the war. I did not see his wounds. I did not see his body falling on the ground. But I have seen death with my eyes.

During my school years, I was helping a poor woman with house chores in a village where I was living. She had four children. Her husband was in hiding due to disagreements with a diamond trafficker. The woman came to my house screaming that the traffickers took her only son, who was only seven years old at the time. They accused the boy of stealing from them. I asked the woman, "Where did they take him?" She said to the village square, where he was going to be punished as a lesson for everybody. I ran to the square and saw a big gathering of villagers and the gang of traffickers who were holding the boy hostage at gun point. Their chief was brandishing an automatic weapon.

"Do you see what happens to a thief?" he shouted.

Nobody answered. I nudged my way through the crowd. The chief signaled to one of soldiers to bring a tree stump. He turned to the crowd and continued screaming, pointing his weapon at people and shooting bullets towards the sky. When the soldier brought the tree stump, he pushed the boy towards it with his boot. The boy fell on the ground, crying.

"Get him up!" the chief screamed.

Two soldiers brought the boy to his feet.

"To his knees!" the chief screamed.

The soldiers forced the boy to kneel.

"Put his head on the stump!"

The chief pulled his machete from its scabbard and brought the blade to the boy's neck.

"A thief does not deserve to live!" the chief screamed. There were many people crying. The boy's mother fainted.

I ran to the chief and pushed him back, away from the boy. I did not know what I was doing. He was startled.

"I know what hell is," I said.

The chief overcame his shock quickly, smiled and said calmly:

"I am hell."

"No, you are not. You are just a man. The boy is just a man. We all are just men."

"You are courageous, boy. I hear you are the village priest."

"I am not ordained yet."

"Work for me and I'll make you a priest."

"No." I said.

"No?" he laughed.

"Leave the boy alone. Set him free! He is innocent."

The chief said nothing. He signaled the soldiers and they pulled the boy's head up and put his right arm on the tree stump. The chief growled like a beast and sliced through the child's arm above the elbow.

"Nobody's innocent!" he screamed.

The soldiers relinquished the boy. Some villagers came and took him away.

The chief then turned to me, calm once again.

"Want to see how hell feels, son?" he said.

I said nothing.

"Take him to the pit."

The soldiers grabbed me and dragged me outside the village to their camp, where the desert meets the dirt road.

The chief trafficker said:

"Is there anything of which it may be said: see, this is new? I tell you boy, I am not a cruel man. What you have seen today has happened many times before. It's the law of nature. I obey it! So should you."

I never believed hell is a place or a gathering of evil people. Hell is the feeling that evil will never end.

They pushed me into a deep pit they had dug into the ground. A soldier climbed down with me and opened a trapdoor in the bottom of the pit. He pushed me down, into another pit, narrower and darker than the first. He jumped down with me into the second pit. He opened another trapdoor and pushed me down into a third pit, so narrow that I could not bend my knees. He closed the trapdoor over my head. I heard him closing the other trapdoors as well. The soldiers were shouting and cheering, their voices muffled.

They left after a while.

At nightfall you came, my dear angel, and you saved me.

1:11 Remembrance of things that are to be

When I was alone in the desert for the first time and the scorching heat was my only companion, I was not only bereft of the nearness of people, I was also bereft of the dialogue with myself, as I was a young man and had not yet prayed enough to understand the limitations of the human body. When the Savior went into the desert to pray for forty days, he went as a man, but he had his Father to talk to. Nobody spoke to me during my first days among the dunes. Nobody confirmed my existence, or my thoughts, or my pulse.

My water had run out after three days. I had not planned carefully. I had some bread left and some dry dates. I hoped to find answers, or at least I hoped I could learn to ask the right questions. I found only sand and the sensation that I was witnessing the infinite. Many moments I believed were pure serenity, as I watched the horizon blurred by the waves of heat, and the patterns in the undulating waves of sand, the various sizes of dunes that I thought were giants resting. I gazed at the scenery, amazed and numb. When I was able to walk again, as my body supplied me with energy in sporadic bursts, I lost the feeling of serenity and replaced it with the rationalization of what I had just experienced. How do I know when I suffer from a momentary lapse of reason and when I enjoy, even briefly, a blink of transcendence? These two sensations are painfully alike! I tried to remember the experience of saints, their dialogue with the divine, their recollections after returning to the reality of their mortal bodies; they all spoke of wonderful, surreal, feelings, powerful thoughts, reinforced convictions, ironclad faith, unwavering determination, all these splendid experiences of the mind and soul that I craved with desperation. Yet I received only sand in my eyes, and a plethora of erratic thoughts.

On the fifth day in the desert, I was livid. Thirsty and hungry. My powers had left me. I was barely trudging my feet when I saw the oasis ahead. Another hallucination, I thought. I was so sick that I thought God was talking to me. No, it was me talking to myself and not recognizing my own voice. I wanted to cry, so I could taste the water in my tears. My lips were dry like stone. When I came closer to the oasis, I knew it was not a hallucination. The shape and color of the trees and bushes become more clearly defined. Fast green; a green that wanted to flee the leaves and hide in the ground. I saw a group of men among the trees. Camel herders, dressed in white linen from head to toe. Some were standing, some were crouching around a fire. They were quiet.

They saw me. By their reaction they must have thought I was a hallucination too. They ignored me completely, until I was so close I could touch them.

They were eating a small-sized animal that looked like a rabbit. The skin was on the ground, drying in the sun. They offered me water to drink from a leather pouch. In their language, they said that I should slow down and not waste the water. They offered me a piece of that rabbit. Part of it was summarily fried, part of it was charred. I tried to take a bite, but the meat was so tough, I could not cut through it with my teeth. I struggled with the piece, I ground it with my teeth, I pulled hard. It was so salty, it tasted like a piece of fabric soaked in brine. The camel herders told me not to rush, that I had to chew it for a long time before I swallowed it. I failed with my first piece, I was that hungry. They encouraged me by trying to make me adjust my breathing. Slow down, they must have said. Breathe in. Breathe out. They showed me. After a while, and a few more attempts, I managed to relax. "Thank you," I said. They did not seem to acknowledge my gratitude. Instead, they asked me how I got there. I said I didn't know. I showed them that I came there to pray. I put my hands together and I pointed towards God. They understood. I showed them the little cross I was carrying around my neck. They nodded. They didn't have crosses around their necks, they had themselves, the pouches of water, the rabbits and the desert. That was their prayer.

Until sunset, I tried hard to remember how I found the oasis. All I could think of was that there is no remembrance of former things, nor will there be any remembrance of things that are to come by those who will come after. I slept with the camel herders that night.

1:12 The lamentations of a king

I cannot dare risk having weakness of heart or feebleness of mind in my position as the Vicar of Christ and Bishop of Rome, yet I can neither deny my own humanity, bestowed upon me at my birth, together with the duty to cherish it. So when I see the thousands gathered in the Square, when they reach out to touch my hand and my robe, when they fling forward their toddlers so they can be blessed by the Holy Father, or when they beg for a blessing, "Bless us Father for we have sinned", they say, I bet you did, I think, so have I, so do not talk to me like I am the Heavenly Father. Surely I do not say these things out loud, they would say that I had lost my mind, they would ask for my resignation, they would say that I am corrupting the faith, I know there are people out there who speak and write about such things, who never cease to criticize and attack. They prey on weakness and feast on scandal, real or imaginary, so I must ignore them and live with my thoughts, human as they are, dark as they can be, I am only one man.

Do not listen to my lamentations, my dear angel, I am not worthy of your attention, even when I know that I censor myself well enough, that when you come to my office and stand in front of me, I freeze and do not utter a word, and you wait patiently like you know what is inside me. You feel the fire burning behind my face, the entire volcano of unerupted words and declarations. You wait patiently and ask me, "You called me, Father?", which is your way of saying, "I am here, like I always have been, you do not need to call me, you do not need to utter your needs, I know them all, I feel them all."

I tell you something, whatever I could make up in the moment: fetch me this or that book, arrange this or that meeting, call this or that diocese for me, cancel dinner, postpone dinner, book dinner with cardinal W or X or Y, call in that reporter that has been waiting for hours just to talk to me for five minutes and thirty seconds, open the secret Vatican archives, no, no, that's a silly thing to say, since I just took office I cannot break with tradition, arrange a private visit for me at the tomb of St. Peter, whose bones I always wanted to see, tell me, which historians and archeologists have said that those are not the real bones of St. Peter, can you find me the names, my dear angel? Surely you can. You will have them for me by tomorrow morning, on my desk, next to the cup of tea and the biscuits, you will have them highlighted in pink. I know you could do that for me.

I was never a preacher or a king over Israel in Jerusalem. All my life I thought of myself as a priest with a mission and without a plan. Plans never stuck to me, you know. They never did, and now, more than ever, this seems to matter the least, given my position. Plans are for engineers, rocket scientists, space explorers, administrators of nations, not for me. Yet no man can truly live and prosper without the foresight of a result, without the projection of consequences, without the recreation of the future through reasoning and imagination into the present, using the language and knowledge of the present, with the aspirations and faults of the people living in the present. Since I always was a man of the present, I put all my faith in it, hoped for the best, prayed for strength of vision, trusted my friends and my family, walked one step at a time, whether in the night, or during the day, barefoot or clothed. I suppose this is how I survived the cruelties of life, the abominable atrocities that I had witnessed. My heart wants to say "Poor me" but my mind viciously denies it, and I revolt against these pitiful concoctions with determination and disgust for these weaknesses, and I try to forgive myself and I seldom cannot, because so many things depend on me now, and I cannot allow myself to fall into disgrace, not for the sake of my soul, but for the sake of millions who depend on my character and resilience, millions who judge an entire institution by my deeds and words.

I must always remain strong, cheerful, and sober at times, I could never, not even in my wildest dreams, allow these words written here to be found by God knows what eager, ambitious journalist, writer, reporter, jester, who will print them as his creation, just to gain fame, and to add more unnecessary harm and shame to the many believers and followers of our Church, whose faith will be scarred by the discovery of my intimate ruminations. My angel, I leave this up to you, in case these pages survive my death, to take care that this truth goes away with me, if only for the greater good of the faith. Burn these pages. Burn them! Leave me to meet my own judgment.

1:13 Wisdom, find me, if I do not find you first

When I finished my theological studies, I felt the greatest pride of my entire life. The dean asked me if I wanted to start my apprenticeship in a small parish on the shores of Lake Chad, out in the West of the country. I accepted with unrelenting enthusiasm. I rushed home that day, I searched for you, you were not there. I thought you must still be at school. I ran to your school and saw that the closing ceremony had ended. I wished I had been there for you, but when the dean summoned me to his office that day, I could not refuse. I knew you would understand. I did not see you in the courtyard. The pupils were scattering to their homes, accompanied by their families. My heart had shrunk a little and I had run out of ideas where to search for you. Yet even before I put my thoughts and hands together in prayer you appeared next to me and said, "You are here, Enyi." "I am here, Nwanne," I said. You kissed me and I blushed. We were both so happy but we didn't know what to say. You had your school graduation diploma in your hand and you were holding it there, like it was the least important thing. I had my assignment letter from the dean in my pocket and I was keeping it there, like it was the least important thing. We both knew that your diploma and my letter were the most important things in the world at that moment, and we both knew what the other wanted to say what joyous news we had to share. We both had a surprise for each other that our mouths were not quick enough to utter, since our hearts already had completed the mission. We embraced and shed a few tears.

"I have a school diploma, Enyi!" you said.

"I know, I know. I am so proud of you," I said.

"I am proud of you, too."

"Will you take me with you on your mission?"

"Of course I will take you with me."

"You know, Enyi, I can read and write now. I can add numbers. I know the history of our people. I can be your secretary."

"You can be anything you want, my dear Nwanne. Anything you want."

And we set our hearts to search and seek out by wisdom concerning all that is done under heaven; this burdensome task God has given to the sons of man, by which they may be exercised. We paid a last visit to our brothers and sisters and we told them they would always be in our prayers. Then we packed our bags and we took a train towards the West.

1:14 The wind was grasping for us

We were restless and cheerful when we arrived in the village by the great Lake Chad. The parish priest, Mr. Thomas, welcomed us with an open heart and great relief. He said almost immediately, "Boys, we sorely need your help here."

We were so excited, we couldn't care less where we would sleep. It could have been a treehouse for all I cared, or even under the open sky! Mr. Thomas arranged for us to rent two rooms in the house of a widow who lived alone. She had a big house, by local standards, built by her husband in the hope of having a large family, which didn't happen, "We were not blessed," the widow told us. One day her husband just dropped down on the floor, in the middle of the living room, and never woke up. "He left me all by myself," the widow said. "Now I have this huge house and nobody to talk to. I clean every room, every day. Maybe some lost souls will come and rest and keep me company." Later I understood that those souls she was talking about were those of her husband's and her unborn children. There were five unborn children, three boys and two girls, they had names, they were beautiful and healthy. They did all the house chores she asked, they were smart, they went to school, they were polite, well-behaved, and never late to go to bed.

When Mr. Thomas introduced us to the widow she thought we were her lost sons who were returning home from the hereafter. She didn't say it. I saw it in her moist eyes. She stood there with the door open, crying on her inside, for a good minute, nodding at Mr. Thomas, not hearing what he was saying. She was trying to remember our features. "How can you not remember anything, these are your sons," she said to herself, while her eyes were becoming dimmer and smaller, as she was trying to hide inside herself to run away from shame and shock. The widow was a strong woman, tall and burly, soft in gestures, her voice so mellow and frail, I could not believe that she was real when she finally spoke and told us to come in.

We headed straight to the kitchen and she had us sit down and taste the mango pie she had just made, especially for us. She wouldn't let us stand up until we finished everything. She offered us "fresh water collected this morning," which we couldn't refuse; it was not bad, I remember it had the taste of fish. "You'll get used to it," Mr. Thomas said.

The widow showed us our rooms, both had a view to the back of the house towards a small garden, a green pasture, the outdoor water closet. "See that hill?" the widow said. "Yes," we said. "Just on the other side there is Lake Chad. It's a beautiful lake. It shrinks in size, then it grows again, then it shrinks again. It's unpredictable and capricious, like people." I had nothing wise to say in response, and I didn't want to spoil the moment for her, as we were guests and she was already beginning to think of us as her family.

Then she looked at us and said we did not look much alike.

"He is my Enyi and I am his Nwanne," I said.

"Oh, that is lovely. You must take care of each other and you must always love each other, no matter what. Okay?" Her voice was fluffy as whipped cream.

"Yes madam," we said.

"Please, please call me Mama." For some reason I wanted to object: I have a mother and Enyi has a mother too, but I didn't say anything because I wanted to make the widow happy, and I was also happy that we had a place to stay and somebody to take care of us. We promised we would call her Mama.

Mr. Thomas said he could give us the day off so we could settle in and get to know Mama better. He left in a hurry, shouting from outside, "don't be late tomorrow, boys, we have a lot of work to do." I somehow felt that there was much more to discover in this little village than the appearance of calmness and standard poverty to which we were already accustomed.

When the night came I swear I heard hyenas giggling and crying and growling in the wild, sometimes so close it seemed they were just outside our windows, plotting to kidnap us and consume us methodically and leave our remains to other shrewder scavengers. Those were my night fears in strange new places, even if I knew I was still in my country and I was still able to understand most of what people spoke.

As if you heard my thoughts, again, Nwanne, you came to my room and you said, "I can't sleep, those hyenas are freaking me out, can I sleep with you?" I felt a rush of blood to my heart and withheld my emotion. "The bed is big, you can sleep here. We are stronger together," I said. "We are stronger together," you said and you fell asleep immediately. The hyenas continued laughing and making trouble. The shadows they had cast on the walls, in the light of the moon, I will never forget. Now, so many years later, I had seen all the works that are done under the sun, I had seen ugly and devious hyenas dying and suffering just like men, I had seen them grasping for the wind with obstinacy, day after day, in rain and in drought, prisoners of vanity, producers of vanity, just like men.

1:15 Pigs and ghosts: the making of men

Mr. Thomas, as he wanted to be called, had something special for us the next day. He said to me:

"I know the archbishop sent you here. You want to become a priest. I'll tell you one thing boy, being a priest is a hell of a job. We are not in the quiet, laidback, English countryside where parishioners sit on soft cushions. This is Africa! We have problems!"

Even though his words sounded harsh, he spoke them slowly and peacefully. And that terrified me more than if he had spoken them with a grave tone. That was my first lesson from Mr. Thomas - I had no idea what to expect.

Nwanne was as surprised as I was but he didn't show it. We obediently followed Mr. Thomas. He showed us around the church, he enumerated the names of the people who regularly attended mass, where they sat, how many children they had, how wealthy they were, and what their problems were. When we finished the tour, which was very short given the small size of the church, he turned to us and in the same calm voice, said:

"The problems are out there," as he pointed towards the outside. "Today we will meet the devil himself."

I thought he was pulling my leg. I was not schooled in local traditions. It could have been an inside joke on two naïve boys from the East. But Mr. Thomas seemed serious. We were actually going to meet the devil. I can't say I wasn't afraid, but I also can't say that I felt weak. I had my faith. I had Nwanne. Whatever happened, let it be the will of God, and let Him have mercy of our souls. Mr. Thomas is not a bad man, I thought to myself, and the Archbishop knew him well. I was sent there on a mission. I had to welcome whatever was thrown at me.

We went to the house of a man, that people said was possessed by demons. The man had destroyed all the things inside, banished his woman, and would not recognize his children. He was screaming when we arrived. The villagers gathered outside said he was possessed by the evil spirit of the departed pigs. The pigs that fell in the lake. I immediately remembered the story from the gospel of Mark, where Jesus allowed demons to leave a haunted man and enter a herd of swine, so Jesus approved, the demons moved, the man was saved, and the pigs ran berserk into the sea and drowned. It is a good story, a good parable, but I could never take it literally.

Our man's story was not biblical. He had been the driver of a truck that carried pigs from a farm to a slaughterhouse. He lost control of the truck on a narrow road. He skidded off the road and plunged into the lake. He survived, but he lost the cargo, and his mind.

That cargo was worth more than his life.

Not only did he lose his job, but he lost his dignity. There was nothing in the world that could bring his dignity back.

These were the man's demons. He would not accept forgiveness from anybody. Not from his wife, his children, or his community. He drove himself to despair and destroyed the little life he had left. He was swearing when we entered the house. He had been restrained on a chair with ropes, by the villagers. His eyes were red, bulging, and mad. He looked at me and said with a voice that sounded unearthly:

"What is crooked cannot be made straight."

I wanted to say that what is lacking can be numbered if that matters to anyone or to someone in particular. He did matter to his family and his tribe. But the pigs that drowned did not matter, because the deed was not on his account, but on account of nature. People, in their arrogance, think they are masters of nature, but they are not - nature is our master as nature commands our fate.

"Nothing else matters," the man said, and fell silent.

Nwanne helped me wash his feet and hands. We asked the villagers to untie him. They untied him and they put him on his bed. I washed his forehead. He grabbed my hand and smiled. I did not think of demons. I thought that angels descended upon him and brought him peace. I will never know, because soon he dropped my hand, lost his smile, and went silent again. This time, forever.

1:16 Pietà in a dormitory of bunk beds

I am coming to accept my fate with serenity as I am slowly learning that greatness is constructed brick by brick, with sweat and planning.

They already see me as a great pope, worthy of my predecessor, himself a revolutionary. I had never considered myself a revolutionary, I merely spoke and acted from my deepest convictions. You say, Nwanne, that I must produce encyclicals and forceful speeches because the human mind is forgetful and often needs reinforcements. I tend to agree with you. We must deliver more words in tandem with our deeds.

I washed the feet of the poor today. I told my aides they must organize a meeting with the needy in the great cathedral. As usual, they objected, for many reasons.

"I want you to go out and invite all the beggars and the homeless to our home. We will wash their feet, we will feed them, and they will sleep in our home."

"Do you mean in the great cathedral?"

"Yes, I mean in the great cathedral."

"Where, on the floor?"

"No, the floor is cold. They will have bunk beds."

"We don't have bunk beds, Holy Father."

"We are in times of peace. The army has bunk beds. You will talk to the military. They will give you bunk beds."

"How long will they stay with us?"

"As long as necessary."

"There are valuable things in the great cathedral. We can't guard them all."

"You do not worry about that."

"Great God, what about Michelangelo's Pietà?!"

"No need to raise your voice, my friends. Nothing will happen to Pietà. Gratefulness will never express itself through vandalism."

It took me more than an hour to convince them and to go over the logistics. At the end, I felt great about the whole thing and I couldn't wait to see it happen. Late that evening, alone in my chamber, I communed with my heart, saying:

"Look, I feel I have attained greatness, and have gained more wisdom than all who were before me in Rome. My heart has understood great wisdom and knowledge."

Then I stopped and reflected that the next step goodness takes is not that of self-adulation and joy, but that of seeking otherness and being determined to further the cause of the underprivileged.

At the same time, I felt enmity for the scornfulness of the rich and their perseverance in the contemptuous denial of the human condition: that we share a natural world of beings, beauty, and resources, that we share an origin, that we deserve equal rights to pursue our potentials, that we must prove that we had learned from the tragedies of the past. Why can enmity and kindness inhabit a heart at the same time? Is one nurtured by the presence of the other, or is it defined only by the absences of the other? Was kindness born because its birth was forced by a necessity, that of the presence of malice? Do we always need to live in a state of opposition to something, in the latent emergence of contrariness, to learn who we are and how we ought to behave? Is our nature so rotten from birth, that we would grow into beasts if we weren't corrected and adjusted by the adults?

I often ponder whether we will ever finish our mission or whether we will survive into the far future. I never told anyone this. I haven't told you, Nwanne. But I'm sure you know. That's why you keep asking me, "Why are you sad?", even when I'm chuckling at some silly joke. Yes, I worry, deep in my heart, that we failed to honor the Savior's sacrifice. I feel that the time of atonement has passed.

1:17 On madness and folly

Many days and nights were hot during our stay in the village by Lake Chad, in fact I remember more nights than days. More nights, because I was immobilized in my bed, alone with stars shining above me and the wild sounds of the nightly creatures. During the many hours when I couldn't sleep I thought more about you Nwanne. You were sleeping in the next room, so quietly that I couldn't tell if you were there at all, until some owl hooted for his mate. Then you moaned as if you wanted to fly. Then I became hotter and hotter from my toes to my forehead and felt like joining the flocks of creatures in the night and letting them take me wherever they were going. Going to feast or to mate or to quench their needs, to unite into a procession over long stretches of land across many countries, not caring that one day they may reach the end of the world where there is no escape and no return and no time for regrets, meeting the humans called hunters, the humans called poachers, and the humans called hungry. There was no escape.

When I went to see you when the night was the deepest, I had a pitcher of water with me at all times in case I needed an excuse. I never got the chance to pour water for you and you never heard me. I just sat there and watched over you, until the creatures got tired and went away to their business leaving me alone with the echoes in my mind.

After many nights I began to hear your voice. You were telling me about the chores you had accomplished and the passages from the Holy Book that you read and you found "most intriguing," or "unbelievably beautiful," or "indecipherable, foreign, strange." These were my words that you were learning from me, and rapidly using in your own sentences to show me what a good student you were. You disregarded my plea that you do not have to prove yourself to me as you have already gained a place in my heart and we were a family, we were brothers.

Then when I went to bed you were already there, waiting for me, I couldn't believe it!

"What are you doing here?" I asked.

You did not respond, but simply invited me to rest near you. I sat down and you were gone just like the wind. I thought I was going mad, I thought it was the heat and my ceaseless restlessness and anxiety with all things around me - you know I can't settle, I cannot be fully at peace when there is so much existence around me, so much pathos that pulls me insurmountably towards a shapeless void, that I knew I had to confront if I wanted to become a better man, closer to my mission. I did not want to lose my mind. I was longing to spend all the time with you, my oasis of peace, my faithful companion, while keeping my faculties and awareness, I did not want you to become a ghost in the heart of Africa. And I set my heart to know wisdom and to know madness and folly. I had to begin with the harsh realities of the village. By that time we had met a man that lost his mind, we had Mama, and we were beginning to learn the orphans' names. Then there were the names of demons, the spirits of the nights, the congregations of shadows. Everybody knew about them. These were the trials of folly, another way by which I was grasping for the wind.

1:18 Sound and fury in a slum of refugees

The time comes when a pope must shed his vestments and blend with the people again, under the guise of anonymity, the only way in which reality will not be blurred by the glitter of gold and the grandiosity of a clerical position. I did just that, I put aside my regalia and everything that I was wearing on my skin, and I clothed myself with the clothes of the poor people. I asked my barber to cut my hair very short, and Nwanne procured a wig and a moustache for me, which he applied very skillfully. When I watched myself in the mirror, I could not believe what I saw. It seemed that I was looking at a different person.

"You did great, Nwanne," I said.

"For you, anything, Holy Father," he said.

I called in a day of solitary prayer. The Curia was instructed not to bother me, pending further announcements from my personal secretary.

Nwanne and I, with the help of two trustworthy Swiss guards, left the Vatican City during the night and vanished into the streets of Rome. We had a car waiting for us and a driver that had specific instructions where to drop us off, what to say, and what not to say, when to pick us up, and how fast to drive.

After a few hours we arrived at the refugee camp. We went on foot for the last kilometer, as we didn't want to be seen coming in a car. The camp was a plateau of caravans, makeshift shanties, rudimentary barracks, and military tents. The place was bustling with activity, children hither and thither playing football, groups of men watching how others were playing checkers, backgammon, chess, card games, cheering and booing, women watching the watching men from afar, talking about what to have for dinner. Nobody seemed to have anything to do, there was an atmosphere of general waiting on somebody or something that would probably never arrive. We mingled through them and I told Nwanne to leave me by myself for a while. He reluctantly accepted, but beseeched me to allow him to follow me from a safe distance. I agreed.

I did not have to begin conversations. People already came to me and asked me where I was from, in what tent I was living, many swearing they saw me yesterday in line at the canteen. I confirmed their recollections to enforce my credibility. There was a woman who asked me if I had seen her husband, she showed me his picture taken with an instant camera, she said he went to apply for asylum three months ago and he has not yet returned. The poor woman was desperate, "I don't know what to do, I don't know what to do," she kept saying while her tears rolled down on her face and dropped on the ground and on her shoes. I wanted to kiss her forehead and bless her and tell her that everything was going to be fine.

"Where are you from?" I asked.

"I am from Libya," she said.

"I am from Nigeria," I said and I grabbed her hands and told her that everything is going to fine.

Then I saw a boy running from person to person with an old book in his hands, stopping people and asking them something. When people heard the boy's question they shook their heads and walked away. The boy kept trying and nobody could answer his question. The boy showed them the book he was carrying. Nobody tried to pick it up and open it, as if it was the most difficult book in the history of books. I was intrigued. I wanted to know the boy's question. I approached him. He didn't see me. He ran and ran in circles around me but did not stop me. Then I asked him:

"Little boy, what book do you have there?"

When he heard my voice, his face lit up and he was so surprised that he didn't realize where my voice was coming from.

"I'm over here, little boy."

He came to me confidently and showed me the book.

"Would you read me a story?" he asked.

"Of course. I would love to read you a story," I said.

I took the book from him, then I realized why the book was so unusual. There were no letters or text inside. There were just dots and holes. It was a book in Braille. The boy couldn't see. I told him a story about the adventures of a courageous little boy who climbed a magic mountain.

Then there was a man standing on the lid of a barrel talking to a group of people gathered around him. He was eloquent and neatly dressed. He said that the refugees must remain united and compassionate to each other. He said that we must not blame the developed countries. He said that they were all victims of circumstance and they must overcome their situations with resilience. He said the world can be a better place for everyone.

"I am a professor of mathematics, I am not a preacher. I refuse to give in!" he said.

I walked among the refugees and I listened to the mathematician. When bread is scarce you're left with hope. When hope wanes, you're left with each other. When you're alone, you're left with your faith. When faith leaves you, you're left with your stories. Those of the past and those you can imagine. And you earn the chance to discover more of the world and the others. There is never, never, an end to the potential of the world and of the others to pleasantly surprise you. Go out and meet them!

And also, in much wisdom there is much grief. And he who increases knowledge increases sorrow. This is a fact. All refugees know it and feel it. When they have each other, they will never lose the struggle with the world. We need to go out and meet them. They are my friends. They are my people!

NOTEBOOK TWO

2:1 Days of pleasure, bathing in mirth

One day, Mama came to us and said there were girls from the village who wanted to meet us. We should make friends and get to know them.

"But Mama," I said, "I am working to become a priest, you know, I cannot meet girls."

"Of course I know, you silly. We say here, never say no to a new friend. A friend is better than the sun. She can give you warmth and light during the night."

"I have Nwanne," I said.

"Do you boys know any girls?" Mama asked.

"Umm... no," I said.

"That ought to be fixed."

Nwanne said nothing. He was chuckling and playing along with Mama, teasing me, while knowing perfectly well that this was addressed to him too.

We had no choice but to accept Mama's plan to have a party at her house. She invited many girls our age, and a few boys. She lured them with mango cake and other delicacies she had made. By sundown, the house was full and my embarrassment was at its peak. Nwanne was having the time of his life, talking to everyone, shaking everyone's hands, showing interest in everything they were saying. I was not much of a talker in social contexts like this one. As a matter of fact, that party was the first occasion I was surrounded by so many girls. That night, I said in my heart, "Come now, I will test you with mirth; therefore enjoy pleasure."

There was no sadness on those girls' faces. They were as happy as they could get. They danced and pulled me into their midst and showed me the moves and taught me the songs. They said I was funny and that I had a kind face. A freckled girl, about my age, with long braided hair, took me aside at the end of the dance and whispered in my ear that she wanted to kiss me. At first, I did not understand what she said. Then she demonstrated. She kissed me on my cheeks. I blushed immediately, and stupidly said:

"No girl has ever kissed me!"

"Oh, that's a shame," the freckled girl said.

She stood there in front of me for a while.

"I'm going to get you a piece of cake," she said.

"Thank you," I said.

Nwanne came to me, while the girl was away and told me the girl was expecting me to kiss her back.

"Oh, really? But I do not kiss girls," I said, blushing even more.

We had each other. From that moment I felt a load had been lifted from my heart. When the girl came back, I thanked her for the cake and told her I couldn't kiss her back, but we could be friends if she wanted.

"Sure," she said with her mouth full, "I'd love to be your friend."

We both smiled and had much laughter for the rest of the night.

Surely, waves of mirth shared in a good company is not vanity. Or is it? Even when it passes, merriment shared brings people together. If not for happiness, then for an addition of meaning to life, we ought to allow ourselves to explore the sorrow and joy of others.

2:2 A Night at the Opera

There were thousands waiting for me in front of the opera, regardless of my insistence to keep the event as private as possible.

"Holy Father, you cannot go incognito to the Opera in Rome," Nwanne said.

Fair enough, I accepted it. "But no press release, please," I said.

"Of course."

Yet they knew. I don't know how they found out. I trusted Nwanne with my life. The people knew, they came, they cheered for me, "*Ti amiamo Papa*! We love you Papa!" "I love you too," I said and I waved at them. "You sing with me tonight, *Belle nuit, o nuit d'amour, souris à nos ivresses*," I said. "We will sing with you!" the people said.

I said of laughter "madness", and of mirth "what does it accomplish?" Why did I want to go to the opera like a ghost? Am I not the pope of the people, just like my predecessor? Yes, they know I am not him, I do not share his temperament, but I grew up among the people, just like him, I am a servant of the people, I should never hide from them, yet I wanted to. I am ashamed. I came to see *The Tales of Hoffman*, because I learned about this beautiful music from a film I love very much, called *Life is Beautiful*, made by Mister Roberto Benigni, a friend of my heart. In the film, Guido Orefice, a Jewish man held as prisoner in a Nazi concentration camp, signals to his wife, also imprisoned in the same camp, by playing la barcarolle *Belle nuit* through the loudspeakers that were left unattended by the guards. What a beautiful moment! In all that misery, he finds a moment to shed light on hope through music.

I came to the Opera to cry. I don't mind crying. Mama said crying builds character if you remember to wipe your tears.

"Do not let tears fall on the ground," she said.

"Pick them up after they leave your eyes, but always let them out."

The Opera director placed loudspeakers outside so the people could hear and sing along. The doors were also left open. The traffic stopped, the tourists sat down on sidewalks and listened. It was a beautiful night of patience and sensibility. I am not sure how many people were thinking that life is beautiful even when faced with death. Every moment lived with hope is a victory. We ought to remember this. I seldom forget this lesson myself.

Guido Orefice dies in the end, saving his son's life with stories and optimism. He refuses defeat. We do not see his last words before the guard takes him to be executed. We hear the bullets and remember his smile and his witty antics. The redemption that this story offers us is that evil and despair cannot defeat the intrinsic beauty of goodness. I know, it is strange to associate an aesthetic emotion with a moral sentiment, but that's how I feel. I have strong faith in the real power of deeds made in the name of goodness to create a more beautiful world; pleasant to the eyes, to the ears, to all our senses. I went to the Opera to remember how beautiful the world can be. I hope I can be forgiven for this indulgence.

2:3 Reflections on gratification of the flesh with wine

The pleasures obtained from wine are foreign to me. I am not a total stranger to them, but I never considered them part of me. I asked Nwanne to bring me some of the famous wine that Europeans drink. When he came back he showed me an old bottle that had the Romantic Nineteenth Century smell. He poured me a glass and I took a sip. It was as if rivers of honey flowed into my mouth, ridden by armies of dancing ants. My body shivered while I felt conquered by sensations that I could not master, could not understand.

"This is wonderful, Nwanne," I said.

"You can have more, Holy Father," Nwanne said.

"Only if you pour yourself a glass."

"I couldn't possibly."

"Nwanne, it's just liquid grapes. Have some."

I was already joyous and it showed in my demeanor. Nwanne poured himself a glass too, and we drank together.

"Sing a song, Nwanne," I said.

"Holy Father, you know my voice scares even the deafest birds."

"You are talking nonsense," I said. "You," I paused, "have," I paused, "have," I paused, "the voice of an," I sighed and gulped, "angel!"

I tried to stand up and couldn't. What was this invisible force that possessed my legs? Was it the consequence of inebriation? I had never experienced it with this strength. I had tasted Mama's mango fermentation, but it had never gotten down to my legs. I was a naïve adult. And they put me in this enormous public function? I don't know who was more insane. At my advanced age, I search my heart to know how to gratify my flesh with wine? Is this not a sign of folly? While I try to guide my heart with wisdom, how to restrain folly, will I ever learn what is good for the sons of men to do under heaven all the days of their lives? After all the terrible cruelties I had witnessed in my life, I was defeated by a small glass of sweet liquid grapes? How can this transform the human mind and soul? Under these words there is only darkness (and vanity?) and the sheer fact that we are nothing but talking overgrown grapes, elements of the same universe. We are no aliens to one another, how else could we communicate and transform each other? We humans boomerang our quests for pleasure by way of other living things, which become us as if it was their only purpose on this little planet - and it might as well be, for is it not true that we created some of them? Take this crimson liquid sitting still in a crystal glass on my desk - the vineyard that it comes from, is it not grown, cared for, and managed by crafty entrepreneurs whose hearts and minds are solely preoccupied with the distribution of silky sensation to the palates of mankind? How is this not a noble gesture? As noble as that of peacemakers who sit at negotiating tables for hours and hours, having only sparkling water or sugarless lemonade, and some hope that this will help them carry on the conversation with the opposing party for as long as necessary until an agreement is reached, hands are shaken, smiles smiled again and foreheads unfrowned, depending on the accumulated tension in their facial muscles.

We are only creatures of self-gratification. Some of us have developed an entire scheme; some are rudimentary in their endeavors. I drank my glass in full and cannot move.

"This happening cannot leave this room, Nwanne," I said.

He helped me go to bed and brought my notebook. "Stay with me," I said.

"Yes, Holy Father."

"I feel very hot," I said.

"You are sweating," Nwanne said.

"Give me something to wipe my forehead."

He brought me a silk towel. I used it. "Nwanne," I said. "Remember when we had only rags on us? We washed bare-chested in the river, we wiped ourselves with our shirts and we waited so they could dry before we wore them again. Remember that?"

"I remember."

"Now look at us," I said. "We are the Bishop of Rome and we are drunk. How did this happen? What did I do to deserve all this?"

"It's God's wish."

"Is it, Nwanne?"

"Do you think God cares about a pope drinking wine?"

"We are all judged by what we do?"

"Are we judged by all we do, are you sure? I am not sure anymore or perhaps I am. I don't know. There are so many people on this planet that do not share our faith. What does God have planned for them?"

"I don't know, Holy Father."

"I don't know either. I mean I have to say that God loves everybody, didn't I say that today at the mass?"

"You did."

"Very well, if I did. Truly I think I meant what I said but now these liquid grapes have put doubt in me."

"This doubt is not real," Nwanne said.

"How can you say that? I feel it, don't I? Why do you say it's not real when I can feel it right now? My heart is beating faster, I cannot walk, I am sweating profusely. We are not in the desert, Nwanne, and I am sweating profusely. It is in fact a chilly evening in Rome, you and I we had a good wine, what is it anyway? Don't tell me, I won't remember the name anyway, why do they have to have such sophisticated names?"

"They are elitist."

"Exactly! They want to be consumed by a few of men so they hide in words and price."

Nwanne looked at me with candor. He does that often.

"Why can't everything be for everybody? This is not how human nature is."

"No, Nwanne, it is not."

I paused and watched Nwanne's face. He has aged more beautifully than I did. He always was a handsome man. When I asked him to hold my hand, he said that I should better rest. He knew best. I often lose my time over silly ruminations.

2:4 Houses turned to dust

The village does not exist anymore. Its name is forgotten. Since Lake Chad has retreated from the shores of Nigeria, the land has become so dry that no one could live there anymore. It has already been many years since all the people left. Mr. Thomas was the last to leave, in a caravan, after he made sure that nobody was left behind. He sent me a picture of the deserted village. On its back, he wrote:

"I made my works great in the eyes of God, I built myself a house, and planted myself a small orchard. It's all turned to dust now. We cannot live here anymore. We have spoiled the creation and now we are reaping the punishment. I will tend to my flock, you tend to yours. That's all we have left. Make it a good life. Yours truly, Mister Thomas."

I still have the picture. It is my reminder that the poor have received an undeserved punishment. They continued to suffer, while those bathing in luxury have thrived. Maybe we failed at our revolution. Maybe we are on an irreversible course towards damnation. One thing is certain. There are billions still breathing and hoping and they have not given up.

Mama was a wise woman. She was not schooled much, but she knew the ways of life and people. She had watched the changes in shape and size of Lake Chad all her life, and while she considered herself a Christian, she always believed that regardless of Jesus's sacrifice, nature will have its own cycles and will not listen to anybody's prayers.

"I knew people praying for rain," she said. "I knew people praying for rain to stop. They all prayed at the same time. You think the lake listened? The lake did whatever it wanted. And it wanted to die slowly because it was tired of us and it deserved its peace."

In our first year in the village, Nwanne and I worked hard to keep the community together. It mattered less who came to the Sunday prayer, and mattered more who was not sick and who had enough food to put on their table. Our daily struggle was to be able to visit all the sick and watch over all children left alone at home, while their parents walked far, to fish on the lake, gather food, or trade merchandise in the closest town.

One day I asked Mr. Thomas, "Why do people make so many children if they cannot feed them?"

"It is the way of life," Mr. Thomas said.

I did not like that answer. I was never satisfied with it, with the inevitability of suffering, with the implacable reality of misery. Those many little children stood no chance whatsoever, to have a pleasant long life, even before they were born. Many died in my arms because we did not have medicine. I forgot how many graves I had to dig with shovels made of tree bark.

"Who determines who dies and who lives?" I asked Mr. Thomas.

"God."

"Does God want these children to die?" I insisted.

"I am Mister Thomas. How would I know what God wants? Nobody knows."

That shut my mouth for a while. Babies kept being born. Babies kept dying. Lake Chad kept shrinking. Mama got older. I could see her skin tightening by the month. I urged her not to stay outside in the heat too much. She wouldn't listen.

"I was born outside," she said.

"I will die outside and that's where I will meet my children."

She must have resigned herself to the idea that Nwanne and I were not her real children, that we were passengers and guests in her house, that one day we would leave, to carry on with our lives, and we would break her heart. Mama had little heart left. She gave us everything she had left after her husband passed.

"How can I live with no heart left?" she said out of the blue, while watching children playing with dirt in front of her house. She was talking to the ground and did not hear me coming towards her. I was bringing her a blanket, as the sun was preparing to set and the temperature was dropping fast. I put the blanket over her back. She felt its warmth.

"The sun is rising again. That was a short night," she said. She was beginning to lose her eyesight too. We had no eye doctors.

So we stayed outside that night, Mama, Nwanne, and I, and we watched the starry night. We felt that all the constellations were telling us stories. They were our friends.

2:5 No admittance into the garden of God

During the months that followed, the village was blessed with peace and stability. Mr. Thomas has managed to establish a regular supply of medicine from a charity. To this day I do not know how he managed that, since little can escape the vigilance of the traffickers and the mercenaries that roam the wilderness. Whatever he ordered, it was provided, and no bribes or protection fees were necessary. The villagers came to church in larger numbers. We even had a few conversions, though they were probably out of shame, since nobody in the village detested anything more than to be labelled an outcast.

When I raised this concern to Mr. Thomas, he simply said, "it really doesn't matter how you enter the garden of God, as long as you enter it and stay there."

Fair enough, I thought. I washed the new Christians, I helped baptize their newborns, I shared the Eucharist. The people came to me and praised my voice, praised Nwanne's voice, and thanked us again and again that we chose their community. I did not want to betray their expectations and enthusiasm, since it had not been my choice to go there, since the archbishop had sent me. After getting to know the people and their customs, I felt that it must have been my choice in the end, and the archbishop realized the wishes of my heart even before I did. Nwanne and I had become part of their family.

One day, nobody cried, nobody ached, and we heard only laughter in the village. Mama's house was clean. There was food in the pantry and the medicine cabinet was full. Since we had nothing to do, we set out to read under the mango trees. After a short while the schoolteacher came to us with a picnic basket and a joyous demeanor. She was a lovely lady. She always wore a red dress with white dots all over. She said the basket was a gift, from the villagers, for Nwanne and I. She suggested we should go on a picnic, outside the village, to relax and have fun, because we deserved it. Nwanne looked in my eyes, and I looked into his, and we could not refrain from our exultation. We thanked the lovely schoolteacher and we were gone from her sight.

Nwanne found a place on the shores of the lake, where he stretched out the picnic blanket in the shade of a tree. We ate fast and talked with our mouths full, washed our mouths with fresh water, sat on our backs and gazed at the clear sky. Then, all of a sudden, Nwanne jumped up and began to undress.

"What are you doing?"

"I am going to swim! What are *you* going to do?"

"But you can't swim."

"Yes. I can. Watch me!"

I watched him undress to his bare skin from top to bottom. Nwanne ran into the lake, cheering like a small boy, splashing the water as hard as he could, in all directions. That was the first time I saw his stately body, exposed in its fullness to the air. He was athletic, bound in a bouquet of grace that I had not seen in any other man, or girl for that matter.

Ah, the coy way he discarded his clothes and stood there in front of me, asking "Are you coming or not?" while blocking the sun with his body!

I was so full with food that my body was sending me signals of capitulation, while he was bursting with energy. And his audacity to tease me like that! I tried to make him come back and urge him not to go too far, but Nwanne had his own desires that day. I sat on my back on the blanket and looked at the sky again and I let myself become enraptured by warmth. In my daydreaming, bathed in sunrays, I made myself gardens and orchards, and I planted cucumbers and bananas, thousands of them in neat rows, equidistant across my field of vision. My awake-ego walked in those gardens and orchards and gathered a basketful of green cucumbers and ripe bananas. I made a salad with them and had it ready when Nwanne came back.

2:6 My water in the body of others, full of questions

Did I make ponds of water from which to irrigate a forest of growing trees? Did I spill water as if it were the voice of infinity, manifesting itself as the coat of God, in thunders and storms, in tears and sweat of slaves, of soldiers, of surgeons?

Was I the only man sitting at the last supper, in a corner, wiping off the corners of my mouth the excess of wine that I had ingurgitated while shouting from the bottom of my lungs that I want more of it, more from the blood of the Son of God, whom I already betrayed in my heart?

And who am I to think how my judgment day will be? Will I be punished with painful thirst for the rest of time, thinking that I could have avoided all this, by listening to a large number of phrases, stories, and sermons?

While other kings, barons and moguls, bathe their mortal skins in dew, did I sit on the shore craving attention, holding silver trays for the pleasure of simpletons, who needed only my frown or raised finger to bow their heads and worship me for the goodness of my heart, for my just and fair resoluteness, for my quick disposition to caress their wounded hearts, souls and bodies? What is the longest question that can be asked, that leaves the body alive, moments away from exhaustion, while nothing can save it except for a drop of water? Just water in any condition?

How can so many have so much laughter left in them, while the desert has incapacitated the imagination of the bravest and has crippled the hopes of many? How are angels not shrieking from the vast devastation that has neared their houses, leaving children with hands outstretched towards the sky, not calling for God, but calling for rain and mercy? Who can give them mercy, when there is nothing wet left on the horizon? Can I offer them my tears full of salt instead? When faucets are silent and rotten, will they not be poisoned by my words and the wasted beads of sweat?

How can they sit down when the earth is burning? How can they wash their faces when the pipes deliver them mud and illness? And we are surrounded by waters that have moved away from our lands into oceans and left us with the shame and the struggle with ourselves, and there is nothing we could do to reconcile ourselves with our previous generation? Have we not cried enough to feed the clouds? Have we not created enough dams and reservoirs? Have we failed in our anticipation of thirst?

I was a healthy man, wasn't I? Am I blessed and guarded because I was a bottomless sack of compassion, so they say, and did that pave my way to this high office? Is it true that when you run out of questions, you seal the fate of hope, and you will lose the sense of the ending and the sight of light?

What happened to the echoes whispered by lovers in caves and under bridges? Why is there no more singing in the rain and too much reporting from the storm? And who are those Olympian swimmers who break records, turning the swimming pools on their heads like they were floating through space, where there is no gravity? What are their thoughts? Their lives? What do they think about? How often do they clean their medals? How can they sleep and dream when the competition is never over, when there are infinite oceans out there that need to be crossed, that have unestablished records?

How do we know what is the right amount of things? How do we know when enough is enough and when not enough ought to make us cry and too much ought to make us laugh? How do you know that your body is your body and not somebody else's empire over you, trying to sell you their interpretation of what water ought to be, what thirst really is, what real *enough* ought to be, because it's good, because it is real and they say so loud and clear, over and over again, until their throats become dry, their voices become robotic, their heads enlarged and swollen, ready to explode from too much arrogance?

Who can tell me how to replace the thought of the inevitability of the end of things with the luminosity of a child's wonder? How much time do I have left to ask myself questions about time, questions about the meanings of metaphors? When will I find the courage to say what I really want so say, and lose the fear that has shackled my feet?

Is there a time for… everything? Must all bad and good happen before the end of time?

I know of no other way but to keep asking the questions, while thirsty and tired, feeling insatiable for life and fortunate that my love for the world has not vanished from my heart.

2:7 On meeting a rich man in the heart of Africa

There was a rich man in the heart of Africa, who came to the village in a convoy, and asked if we knew where he could shoot lions.

"There are no lions here," Mr. Thomas said.

"Who are you? Are you the priest?" the rich man asked.

"I am."

"Good. I am a Christian myself and I want to confess."

"Alright," Mr. Thomas said. "I'll get the church ready."

"No need," the rich man said. "I want to confess to him."

He pointed at me.

"He is not ordained yet, sir," Mr. Thomas said.

"Does he work at the church?"

"He does, but-"

"Then he is God's servant. That's good enough for me," the rich man said.

He stepped out of his limousine and came to me and asked my name.

"Do you think you can hear my confession, son?"

"Yes sir, I can."

"Very well. Show me the way."

We went inside the church. It was midday. There was nobody there. I grabbed two chairs and we sat in front of each other.

The rich man spoke immediately: "I have murdered. I have lied. I have been cruel. I have been ruthless. I have been a coward. I have been a devil. I told my parents that I will be home for dinner and I never came back. I told my cousin that he can rest while I watched his back, then I poisoned him with venom, I stole his wife, and his share of our business. I did not have remorse. Why? Because I am a psychopath, so they say. And what do I say in return? I say: do you want to work for me or against me. And they all work for me and do not say that anymore. Tell me, why do they work for me? Am I not just a man? Do you see all my soldiers outside? Half of them are stronger than I am. They could bury me in a pile of automatic weapons.

Do you want to see my pistol? No? Why not? I'm gonna show you my pistol. See? This is real gold, boy. Real gold. I have twenty of these. Do you want this one? You don't? Why not? Anyway. By the standards of Christianity I had been a bad person. Yes, but I brought so much order and progress for this country. Thousands, tens of thousands, millions have better lives because of me. So you want me to go to hell? Not you personally, but you know, this God of ours? He hasn't told me anything in person and He knows I asked, oh, but I asked so many questions. Such as: God, tell me is it wrong to blow this guy's brains out because he did not deliver my stuff on time? God said nothing. N-o-t-h-i-n-g. Fine, I said to myself. This is easy divine justice. That man was guilty so I applied the justice.

Moving on, I also asked God: Is it okay to buy this peasant's girls for half the price he's asking? God said nothing. So I paid the peasant half he was asking. The peasant protested and my men wanted to shoot him. I told my men: Wait, did you ask God first? They shrugged and lowered their guns. They totally missed the point of my question so I let it go, I let the peasant live, took the girls, and we went on our way, because we were already late. Was I not a fair man? You tell me. God certainly hasn't told me.

I know, I know what you want to say, that I should not tempt God or force Him to act. Who am I to dispense with God's will? How dare I? Yet I am a thinking man, I have ideas, I have desires, I have a strong will and I also have little to no opposition. I do not pretend to know the mind of God. I just ask questions and follow my heart. What is wrong with that? I do not make people suffer for no reason. I release them from suffering so they can go to heaven, while I take upon myself the burden of judgment, because some interpret my doings as against the teachings of Christ. So, I'm the one carrying the cross, I'm the one helping people reach heaven. How is this not making me the best man alive?

We are born into this world to seek power, to wield it and to overcome the human condition. We are born to become gods. This is not blasphemy. I'll tell you why. Jesus too was a man and became God. He was given choices and he made them. I was given choices and I am making them. I bowed my head to be baptized, so people could know I am one of them and not some fallen angel. I carry the cross with me all the time and I kiss it every time I have doubts. I do have many doubts and that's why the cross seems worn out. Do you want to hold it? No? That's fine, I don't mind. I see you have your own. You are a man of the Church, you have no excuse, you have to have one. But I don't have to. This is my salvation. I have chosen the path of the cross with pride.

I would like now to quote from the Book of Ecclesiastes. May I? This is one of my favorite passages. You know why? It is because it makes me feel so good about myself. The passage is: *I acquired male and female servants, and had servants born in my house. Yes, I had greater possessions of herd and flocks than all who were in this country before me.* Why does it make me feel good? See, that is the point. I have no idea why. It just does. It makes me feel that I can want anything, that I can defeat vanity, that I can defeat death. I hate death! It's such a nuisance. Always on my mind, always having to consider who deserves it and when, then I have all those bodies that I must discard, then all those cemeteries that occupy land.

My men are calling me. Our time is almost up. I see in you the spark of a great man. Listen to me. Do not give in, boy! You'll be somebody, someday. Get used to it. Move on. Do not look back. Carry on with your mission. I will let *you* be. So please, I beg you, let *me* be.

2:8 On meeting powerful men and women in Switzerland

I went to speak at a major conference in Switzerland invited by the world leaders who have praised my commitment to ending poverty and eliminating inequality between the rich and the poor. The president of the United States of America, Mr. Sanbard Renders, was the first to greet me. He made his way quickly across the large conference room, towards me. He shook my hand informally and said, "Holy Father, I am delighted to meet you in person." He is a young man, intelligent, determined, cultured. He speaks with the intonation and confidence of an old sage. He comes from a country that has begun its revolution. He is feared and respected by the other world leaders. He is a dangerous man for the rich money hoarders. He said that I can count on his support and that I must not be afraid to speak. "I also had to gather courage to come here," he said, "not because I am about to confront leaders who say the right words but do not act on them, but because of the many millions of my fellow citizens who have entrusted their vote in me." Then he told me how I represented a departure from tradition and an enormous opportunity to build a better world for the underprivileged.

What heavy words! I thought about what President Renders said for the entire day. Then I listened to his speech with attention and I noticed the petrified faces of some of the world leaders. The money hoarders, also present in the room, were frowning and smiling politely at the same time. There was terrible tension on their faces. They were shooting rockets from their eyes. The silver and gold rings on their fingers were burning.

"And the special treasures of our planet," President Renders said in his speech, "are not the trillions we move in capital and trade transactions, but the water, the flora and the fauna that make life possible. Without them we are dust. We are nothing."

The President got a standing ovation. It was a fine gesture from the audience, but their hearts were not in it.

Then the President of China spoke about cooperation and partnership.

The President of Russia spoke about energy equilibrium and stability.

Two European leaders spoke about the tragedy of refugees.

The kings of the Middle East spoke in generalities about helping the poor in their countries, and said they hoped the dialogue with the West would continue. They did not look up from the lectern.

A girl aged 14 spoke about the future of the planet with tears in her eyes.

A man of the Northern Canadian provinces spoke about how glaciers have retreated beyond his horizon. He said, "I acquired binoculars and cannot see the ice anymore."

When my turn came to speak, I was so shaken by the numbness of the audience, by their rolled eyes, by their cold mannerisms, that I screamed inside. I knew they would not hear my screams because of the thickness of my robe and the softness of my voice. I do not share the talents of singers, or the ability of actors and actresses who know how to delight our imagination with embodied stories. I stood at the lectern with the speech in front of me and I couldn't begin. They were watching me. Many of them were seeing through me, many of them had frozen smiles.

I cannot remember much of what I said.

I remember...

...men carrying their sons on their shoulders...

...drowning in the Mediterranean Sea...

There were musical reverberations in the echo of my voice carried by the speakers in the large conference hall. I wanted to tell them to open the windows and let rain wash over us.

...we are instruments for our primitive impulses...

They widened their eyes.

...we are essentially different in body at birth...

...yet destined for equality...

They applauded summarily.

…we are of all kinds and we are beautifully, inescapably, the same…

They applauded forcefully.

Back at the hotel, Nwanne told me the speech went very well and the press was talking about it. "What do they say?" I asked. "They say you will be the pope who will change everything."

I hope Nwanne is right, but I don't think I will change everything. Nobody really changes anything. It's the waves of people that vibrate in tandem that make change real. I am neither a storm, nor a cannon. I will say the necessary words and I will make the necessary decisions. I will tell the people they are not alone. I will tell them to keep looking for each other, to keep looking after each other, to keep meeting with each other. The world never ends as long as there are words.

2:9 Bees and bats were not created

"Bees and bats were not created, they became what they are," Mama told Nwanne and me, the day before she died. Mama had never tasted honey in her life. She had known the taste of sweetness but not the taste of honey. She had never seen bats, but she knew they were creatures of the night that lived through echoes. "When you are blind," Mama said, "you must learn to live through echoes. Your body will make echoes for his voice and his body will make echoes for your voice." She looked at Nwanne and me. She was happy to have us both by her bed, during her final moments. In her mind, she was ready to meet her husband and children. She was ready for peace.

She shuffled off this mortal coil the next day, without any last words.

Nwanne and I went outside the village to pray in silence.

I thought about how Mama found peace in the thought of the hereafter and not in life. She had entrusted her entire being, from soul to mind to living body, to the remembrance of her lost husband and unrealized children. She had committed herself to eternity before her time came, with a dedication worthy of the age of mountains. She continued to love strangers, she adopted me and Nwanne in her big heart, but nevertheless she did not abandon her commitments to the man she had chosen.

"It's just you and me, Enyi," Nwanne said after a while.

"We have the whole world around us," I said with my eyes closed.

"Are you not sad?"

"I am very sad Nwanne."

"But your face is so serene."

"Mama is at peace now. I am happy for that."

"We are not going to hear her voice anymore, or see her face, or taste her food, or feel her warmth. How are you going to replace that?"

"We cannot replace any of that, Nwanne. We are going to live with her memory and hear the voices and see the faces of those alive around us, and we will honor Mama by our deeds and encounters with other men and women. We will continue to feel alive, because we owe it to the world, we owe it to Mama's husband and her unborn children. We are responsible to realize others' dreams that were not realized."

Nwanne put his hand on my knee.

"You give me hope, Enyi," he said.

"I know of no other way, Nwanne."

"You will become great and excel more than all who were before you," Nwanne said.

"I am not a king of Jerusalem," I said.

"You are a king to me," Nwanne said.

I don't know if the wisdom of my youth has remained with me.

2:10 On abundance and the measurement of pleasure

A very rich man has asked for an audience with me. I was told he is one of the richest men in the world, and that it is advisable that I grant him an audience.

I asked them, "Why does he want to see me? Does he have questions that have not been answered? Does he have a request that cannot be fulfilled through the exercise of his wealth? Does he need a favor?"

They told me the rich man has made a substantial donation to the church.

"Oh, wait, does that oblige me?"

"Holy Father, it does not. However..."

"I know, I know, it is a question of good faith. Is it not always a question of good faith that we grant wishes to the lambs of God?"

They wanted to answer in the affirmative, but I told them it was not necessary. It was a rhetorical question. Whatever my heart desired I did not keep from them. I trust the Curia. I consider them my friends, even though I know they have the hearts of weasels and the shrewdness of wolves. I forgive easily.

The rich man came to my office. Nwanne, a translator, and an assistant were also present. The rich man, whose name was short and sharp like a blade, gave me a peculiar gift: a ceremonial pipe from the First Nations tribes of North America. I asked him how he obtained it, and he said it was from his ancestors.

"I do not withhold my heart from any pleasure," said the rich man. "Yet this does not enrich my life above the lives of any ordinary men and women. I seek pleasure because it exists and I can grab it easily. I am a sinful lowly man, Holy Father."

"I cannot truly cleanse your sins," I said. "I can say the words, I can perform the rituals, but the true judgment will come from God."

"I know that."

"Does it make you happy that you employ so many workers?"

"My heart rejoices in all my labor," the man said. "What I have created comes from my very essence."

"I see restlessness on your face, sir. They told me you came to me because you want to help us with a mission."

"I believe we can work together to change the world."

"It pleases me to hear this. The mission you want to help us with is the most difficult mission in the history of our existence. Do you know what the mission is?"

"I am not familiar with the details..."

"There are no details. Do you know why?"

"The devil is in the details?" the man giggled.

I smiled too and I agreed.

"It is a mission of belief," I said. "A mission to determine our future. There are as many details as people living in this world."

"I am not sure I understand." The rich man looked confused.

"There is terrible turmoil in the world. What I will ask of you will shake you from your foundations. Yet, this will not be sufficient. One man's sacrifice alone is not sufficient."

"I am ready for anything, Holy Father."

"I wish I shared your confidence and enthusiasm."

The entire room went silent. They did not expect these words from me, especially Nwanne. They all got to see a glimpse of the deepest corners of my mind.

"I see I have surprised you, sir. Do not worry. Sometimes faith dwindles, sometimes illness hits our minds and we fall into despair, but no matter what happens we must not give up before time expires. It's not about hope. It's about taking our lives to their fullest potential. And this will be the reward of all our labor."

The rich man relaxed. I am not sure if he made sense of any of my words. I do not know myself what I truly meant by what I said. Probably I will see this man again. Probably not.

2:11 On despair and hopelessness

After meeting the rich man, I had a free afternoon of prayer and paperwork. I don't like documents, so I had Nwanne sit with me and read me passages from what I had to sign.

I wish I could extract all my emotions like water is squeezed out of a sponge, and deposit them into a bucket, and leave the bucket out in the hot sun of the Sahara, until each molecule is absorbed by the grains of sand that get stuck in the turbans of desert nomads.

There are these news that come from all corners of the world: oil has reached the highest price in history, there is martial law in

Vienna because of the Schönbrunn riots, President Renders of the United States of America is thinking about declaring a state of emergency, floods have displaced another three million people, rockets have been fired by an unknown party, have landed in the Sea of China, have exploded underwater, and the subsequent wave has overturned a cruise ship of three thousand people, and nobody can get to them because of low visibility and other dire priorities, such as the Bangladeshi crisis and the fragile Kashmir ceasefire. Oh! I can't even remember them all.

Will I ever be able to visit Jerusalem again?

What is happening with the world, Nwanne? It doesn't look like it's ending, but it feels like an end. Is it the culmination of despair or is it just my wrecked heart?

Everybody thinks I am a strong man because I have seen suffering and I have endured pain, and despite all this I show strong resolve and utter the clearest and most just words, in their opinion. You are the man we need, the intellectuals say to me, while the most desperate cry to me: you are our last hope!

That is incredible! What happened to all the previous hopes? Were they not met with satisfaction? Did life not turn out for the better for anyone? Where are the happy choruses who sing Ave Maria? Where are the festivals of spring that celebrate the new crops? The snow falling over giant Christmas trees?

They show me pictures of these with colors that are unreal and transformed, taken from angles of eagles. Did they put cameras on eagles? Did they lift mirrors and viewfinders up in the sky? My old eyes are not used to these fabrications. People are alive in my mind, and they are trying to make them alive on flat pieces of glossy papers.

I reflected on the works that my hands had done, and they were not all soft works. In fact, I had worked more with shovels, crates, and buckets, than with paper and the Eucharist. It shows in my scars that slowly washed away with time, it can be felt in the rigidity of my joints and the slowness of my legs. I am only a reflection of the world.

They say something will happen.

Something always happens.

Millions have lived before Christ came to Earth. They had their times of despair, their lost hopes, their lost children and parents. They too starved and were beaten to death. So Christ came and gave some people an enormous load of hope, so much hope that many could not cope with it. They denied that this hope was even possible. They said the hope was the product of the devil, and that it was all an illusion. Worse, they believed that hope was trickery that lured them towards damnation. They wrote scriptures and gospels pretending to be the true word of God that must be obeyed under all circumstances. They instituted their own rule over mankind, without realizing that the labor after which they had toiled was all vanity, all grasping at the wind, because it was a shameless forgery! What was their profit under the sun, given that they had their short lives? What were they hoping to achieve?

Oh! But they left us with the trouble of faith and the struggle with the world, with a God that does not answer prayers, with miracles that are short of street magic?

What am I to make of all this?

How can I be a Pope and write these words? I feel finished and exhausted?

2:12 There is an end to all lines of kings

In the past week I have heard nothing but terrible international news, so I turned inwards to consider wisdom and madness and folly. It started in North Korea. Nobody knows exactly what happened, but it is clear that their leader is no more. Some say he died, some say he resigned, some say he was assassinated. He just vanished. The country is in complete disarray. There is news of violent internal fights for power. There is news of tens of thousands of soldiers deserting to neighboring countries. There is news of imminent nuclear attack, but who is going to attack whom?

The President of China said that these are grave developments. President Sanbard Renders of the United States said that as much as he is disturbed by the events in the Democratic People's Republic of Korea, he is also hopeful that change and democracy will prevail. Japan offered immediate aid that was flatly refused by one general and warmly welcomed by another.

South Korea reiterated their fraternity for the North Korean people, and their concern for the political leadership. Everybody cried for stability in the region, so loudly it was deafening. One North Korean general took to YouTube to announce that if one South Korean soldier crossed the border, he would unleash hell upon the South. Hours later, rumor has it that the general committed suicide. Many say this is propaganda and that none of it is true, yet some satellites show movement of troops in the North. Seemingly without sense, they are moving from East to West, they are moving towards the North, and from the North towards the South, as if they are restless and homeless and do not know where they belong.

Reports say that hundreds of thousands of people are fleeing cities, fearing atomic bombs from abroad; tens of thousands are approaching the border with China and tens of thousands are also moving from the South, but they don't yet know that a military blockade awaits them. Then I heard that the Chinese army is also approaching the North Korean border, in large numbers, purportedly to help assure the aforementioned stability, a movement that, "Concerns those of us in the West, very much," said President Renders, adding that Congress might very soon consider a similar move, despite the extreme negative reaction of the general public. But who is to listen to the general public, when they have no power but to vote and carry signs in demonstration, and march in large numbers, and occupy parks and boulevards, who is to listen to them?

Pundits say the region might as well fall into a generalized war.

Who are these pundits anyway? What are their credentials? Who made them prophets anyway?

What am I to make of this? For what can the man do, who succeeds a tyrant? Can he only do what he has already done? How can the minds of tyrants be changed?

There is a natural order of peoples that cannot diverge too far from the general order of life, meaning that there is a reaction to every action, that an eye for eye does not make the world blind but makes the world vision-impaired with a defective sense of depth perception. Thus, knowing this natural order, one must see that in the end order will follow chaos and chaos follows unnatural order. The unnatural order that has reigned in North Korea is coming to an end, so chaos ensues and there will be nothing but chaos. Who can say for how long, we can only hope that it will not last long. And I will pray that the people of North Korea find their peace soon, as it is not the deepest nature of men to live under oppression, to have their liberties obliterated, their minds writhing under the pressure of submission to the godlike leader, their imagination and hopes expunged, their bodies imploded with hunger and depression.

2:13 The illusions of infinity

Wisdom exceeds folly, as light excels darkness. When the human mind fails to comprehend the intricacies of large and complex events, it acts as if it was in the presence of infinity, and allows the emergence of irresponsible behavior. Our dependence on light has made us fear darkness, as if darkness were destroying life and was the ultimate annihilator. We came out of darkness, and to darkness we shall return.

The thought of heaven leaves me numb and tired. It is perhaps that I, a lowly creature in a high position, am no different than any of our ancient forefathers that have not met any of the prophets and have not understood anything from the world around their eyes.

I hear more terrible news from around the world. In the name of peace, great nations are moving armies and making grandiose declarations and commitments. President Sanbard Renders met with Prime Minister Fu Fushikuma of Japan, in Pearl Harbor of all places, and they decided they cannot remain passive vis-à-vis the North Korean crisis. Today their respective governments are debating whether to send peace troops to prevent a catastrophe. Prepare thy armies with steel to their teeth for the contingency of peace! How ironic: wars have turned into dances of threats. But I do hope this will be effective and I do fear that a bunch of lunatics with power could turn this in a world war that will doom us all.

In the Middle East, President Pavel Pushkin of Russia singlehandedly assumed control of the lands of Syria, Iraq, Lebanon - in the name of peace and for the stability of the region, certainly - noting carefully in his speech that stability is the first and best defense against an infinite circle of evil that "Must stop now and disappear".

President Pushkin is also a great writer of novels. He has enchanted us with his stories about the best possible world we can create and live in, he has shown us the lyricism of life in the plains of his country, through the voices of his characters Alexei Bogatyn, Dmitri Mudryy, Alyona Bogatyn-Mudryy, and Natasha

Gogoleevna, he has told us the story of the reconciliation of all people with planet Earth, by reinventing mankind under a vision of survival and prosperity. President Pushkin is a man of the future.

At the same time, President Mo Xi of China issued a state declaration about the intention of his country in the light of the crisis. He said, "The People's Republic of China has determined the necessity of peace at all costs in our region of Asia, and we will do everything in our power and legitimacy to make sure that peace is maintained. To this effect, the South Contingency of the Chinese Army is being deployed immediately to the border of the Democratic People's Republic of Korea." Soon after this declaration, we learned that the North Contingency of the Chinese Army is moving in the opposite direction, crossing into Russia. President Mo Xi has not issued any statements about this, nor has President Pushkin. This strikes me as peculiar.

Let me say a few things about President Mo Xi. He is a wealthy industrialist, and built a small fortune with textiles, plastics, vinegar, and microchips. When he entered politics he was well respected and admired. He promised a major change in Chinese politics, and change it he did. People say it's in his charming eyes, his powerful and solid voice, his strength of character and outstanding intelligence. Many Chinese see him as a prophet, despite the fact that the Chinese do not believe much in men of divine inspiration. Nevertheless, Mo Xi has that aura about him. He is a fierce believer in the sanctity of life and the benefits of prosperity.

I must make a note to myself here: today I had some very discomforting stomach pains. My temperature rose to 39 Celsius for about two hours, then it dropped again. I am also suffering from constipation. I hope I don't have those nasty intestinal worms again.

The Europeans were slow to respond. The President of the United Nations of Europe, Mr. Fred Kapiter, was very reserved in his statement. He used these words: concern, hope, our allies, commitment, foreseeable future, the dangers of nuclear warfare, catastrophic, refugees, hope, again, concern, will, determine, soon, we, will, show, assurance, and other words that I cannot remember now. One thing is certain, the UNE is not moving any armies. I don't know if this is the best idea. Since the UNE retreated from the Middle East, for the purpose of "Resetting our peace strategies" as President Kapiter put it, refugee migration has decreased and the Mediterranean waters have calmed down, implying that a European retreat into reconstructive passivity will have positive effects on the geographic region at large. It didn't take long, though, for the insurgence to resurface, events that forced President Pushkin to step in, since he had nothing else on his foreign agenda. In his own words: "We have nothing else on our foreign agenda, we might as well be messengers of peace. And we thank all those who are listening."

Well I listened, and I telegrammed President Pushkin at once to show my support.

This has been a busy day. I am too tired to continue. I hope I can catch some sleep before God knows what tomorrow will bring.

Nwanne brought me tea and sleeping pills, and rubbed my back.

2:14 Infinity revisited, recalibrated, revolutionized

I slept for about four hours and I do not feel tired at all. I prayed next to my bed in my nightgown, which made me feel very naked for some reason as I couldn't see any light with the eyes of my mind and no echoes of my whispered words reflected into my soul. I am barren like a slab of unused cement, conquered by weeds.

The wise man's eyes are in his head. But the fool walks in darkness. Yet I perceive that the same event happens to them all.

Stayingzento, the 15th Dalai Lama, sent me a telegram this morning. He is a wise person for someone so young, and seems to have a grasp on the world unparalleled by many grown men. There is something in the Buddhist Culture that is most intriguing. How do they know how to choose a new leader when he is a mere child? Truly, how do they do it? I am told the child is presented with artifacts of his predecessor, and the spirit will recognize and choose the objects that were owned by the previous bodily reincarnation. In other words, the spirit of the predecessor awakens in his infancy and tells the young body to present itself as the new reincarnation. Most intriguing indeed! However, there is a limited and small number of objects, and by mere consideration of permutations and chance, eventually, one child out of the many thousands of similar age, will make the right choice and will emerge as the new reincarnation. Poor me, I must be very ignorant, since I am certain that the Buddhists have a much more elaborate procedure than this, specifically to rule out mere chance. While a spirit is also young in a young body, it has the memories of a child and a previous reincarnation must have faded away. Curiously I have no memory of any previous lives, or of any ancient objects shared by my consciousness in a different body.

Despite these treacherous and disrespectful thoughts towards His Holiness Stayingzento, my admiration for him is not diminished but rather it is enhanced by the way he presents himself.

He wrote to me: "I am a pacifist in my mind, however as long as my body lives in a material world I cannot have but practical and actionable impulses. This means that I am not a pacifist in the material world, where bodies collide with bodies and nations collide with nations, and the natural world suffers as a cause of these interactions. I am a man of standing opposition towards violence and destruction. I will not engage in war, but I will not hide in undisclosed locations either. I will raise my fist against the rain of falling stones. I will advise my people to raise their fists against armies of illegitimate oppressors. I was born on the street, in a rickshaw. My life belongs on the street, with marching people. I live to save this world for all of us, from the worst of us."

How can I not love this young man!

On another note, my bowels still bother me to the point of exasperation. I asked to dine alone today, except for Nwanne, who as always was so kind as to ignore the effects of the severe bloating I felt after eating the most harmless of nourishments: Caesar salad and one baked potato. I could not believe my ears and especially my nose when it struck me. I couldn't help myself! Luckily, I was alone with Nwanne and nobody else heard. My embarrassment was so acute, I couldn't restrain myself from shedding a few tears. Nwanne looked at me and said, "Holy Father, it's me, you don't need to feel shame." Then right after he said this, I did it again. Louder and smellier! I looked away and thought of something to say, while Nwanne had the misguided idea to approach me, surely wanting to show his understanding by hugging me, not knowing that he was coming towards a dense cloud of unfriendly air that could anesthetize even the thickest-skinned Komodo dragon! He turned up his nose while grinning politely and compassionately, and with his cheeks smiling, with his nose pulling back, he looked like a funny running duck, inducing in me an urge to laugh and cry at the same time, simply because I too was numbed by the intake of air from my immediate vicinity. The mind works on many different levels, often in competition with each other, thus from all the impulses I felt at that moment, that is to beg for forgiveness, to move away, to giggle, what I chose to do was to reach my hand towards Nwanne and sternly say "Stop right there!" To his consternation, as he had not heard me use that voice in a long time, Nwanne stopped. I continued in a softer voice to diminish his surprise: "I need some moments alone, I don't feel well." Then I paused, gathered my thoughts, and searched for words in my mind. I said, "Nwanne my dear, be a lamb and bring me some carminative pills from the pharmacy. It seems that my body is in a state of sublimation."

2:15 Boxing with clouds wearing lovely iron gloves

Nwanne came back with the medicine so quickly, I barely had time to go to my bed and lay down, or perhaps in my mind the perception of time was so distorted, many minutes passed in reality while I felt only seconds. It took Nwanne more than thirty minutes to come back, judging by the position of a bundle of sunrays on the floor.

"Leave the pills on the table, please," I said.

"Certainly."

"Don't worry Nwanne, it'll pass, I must be stressed because of the international situation."

"I understand Holy Father."

He paused for a moment.

"Is there anything else?"

"The Prefect of the Congregation for the Doctrine of the Faith is here to see you," he said.

"Cardinal Thorsen Tchipcherish," I said to myself.

"Indeed."

I forgot to mention that, when Nwanne left to get the pills, he slightly opened the windows to let fresh air inside, and he also turned on the conditioned air from the thermostatic panel on the wall. Given his great attention to detail, Nwanne had made it possible for me to erase my embarrassment much quicker, and also to be able to receive guests, should it become necessary.

Nevertheless, I would not have minded receiving Cardinal Thorsen Tchipcherish in the atmosphere of the early moments, simply because I cannot stand his guts! I wanted him to feed on the air of my dislike towards him. I am not a man of low vocabulary and hateful sentiments, but Cardinal Thorsen Tchipcherish, with all the love I carry for human beings considered, is a despicable man, a foul character, a devilish fox, and a conniving weasel. He is a foxweasel! I had inherited him from my predecessor. What can I do about it? Maybe I'll do something about it.

"Let him come in," I said.

Cardinal Thorsen Tchipcherish was a very tall and heavyset man, though I wouldn't have called him obese. He had the appearance of a healthy and sturdy man. His voice sounded like it was soaked in a vat of whiskey, left hanging in the deep cold for a few months, and then taken to a blacksmith and pounded with a rusty hammer.

"Holy Father," the Cardinal said.

"Cardinal Thorsen Tchipcherish, how are you?"

"I come with urgent matters."

The pills have started to take effect. I was feeling cleansed. The Cardinal kept the customary distance.

"What is it?"

"We must discuss a possible radical reform within the Congregation for the Doctrine of the Faith."

"A reform?"

"Indeed. The attacks from the secularists against the Church have intensified beyond control."

"So I hear."

"We must defend the faith," the cardinal said.

"Defend it we must," I said passively.

"Your predecessor was a great champion of the faith. The Curia has high expectations that Your Holiness will continue this line."

Oh, how I wished he would just speak his mind. What he wanted to say was that I don't care about the faith as much I care about the people. For the Cardinal, faith comes first, before any consideration of the people. As he spoke, I suddenly felt another burst of pressure in my lower bowels, so I said in my heart, "As it happens to the fool, it also happens to me. So who am I to feel wiser? This is also vanity." I did not share any of these thoughts with the Cardinal, and the distance between us was sufficient to keep him far from my production.

The Cardinal said that the international crisis would deal a blow to the Church, indirectly through financial mechanisms and diversion from the preoccupation with salvation to preoccupation with political agendas. This sounded too vague to me, and I had no idea what the Cardinal was getting at, so I thought to reply that we are not facing the situation of the Second World War, where our predecessor Pope Pius XII was forced to turn a blind eye to the Nazi crimes, and, on top of that, to the crimes of Catholics against fellow citizens such as those of the Ustaše in Croatia under the iron fist of Ante Pavelić. What is the toll of human lives taken to ensure the survival of the Church? I think it is a difficult question to answer, and I fear that I will be forced to make that decision myself, very soon.

2:16 Remembering the future as it used to ought to be

The North Korean crisis is intensifying. Satellites are no longer able to grasp all the movements in the territory, because there are so many, and they so erratic and disorganized that the surveillance technology cannot keep up. It is worth saying that no fight has taken place and no invasion, yet. President Sanbard Renders and Prime Minister Fo Fushikuma have dispatched their respective armies, more specifically the Japanese divisions (of peace!) will be waiting for the American divisions (of peace, of course!) just off the Eastern coast of Japan, in the Sea of Japan, from where they will cross towards the coasts of North Korea and institute, not a military blockade, but a standing position of observation in the international waters, pending the necessity of disembarkation.

I have called for an urgent meeting of the Secretariat of State so we can properly address the position of the Holy See towards this new development. Everybody fears that the crisis will escalate and the entire region will be turned to ashes by a nuclear war. Cardinal Samuel Park-Ying from the Republic of Korea called me at an early hour this morning, and with a feeble voice, almost crying, he said he is a convinced pacifist and he will not betray his faith. I understood the man's anguish in that situation and I assured him, the Church stands by its principle and the Korean faithful will not be betrayed. Then Cardinal Park-Ying started crying in earnest and I couldn't understand much of what he was saying, and I felt obliged to share his concern with the Secretariat of State.

What the future will bring, I do not know. No one remembers the wise, and no one remembers fools. In days to come, we will all be forgotten. We must all die, wise and foolish alike. Men should not concern themselves too much with how the future will judge them, but should act in the present as judgment takes place while deeds are done and decisions made, since all that is now will be forgotten in the days to come.

The Secretariat of State suggested that we increase our missionary activity in the Republic of Korea, and prepare ourselves for a great influx of refugees from the North. I agreed that this is a great idea and we should immediately contact the *Istituto per le Opere di Religione,* so they transfer funds to the Korean Archdiocese of Seoul, should we need to establish refugee camps and mobile hospitals. The Secretariat's objection was that they should retain the control of what happens with the funds and we cannot let the weight fall solely on the shoulders of our brothers in Seoul. I told them I do not care for bureaucracy and that I trust Cardinal Park-Ying. He is a good soul and he will do a good job.

"But Holy Father," the Secretariat of State said.

"Zzzt! I will hear no more of this!" I said. Well, not in those words, but that's how I felt.

And if you're asking me, "How does a wise man die?", I will tell you that a wise man dies the same as the fool, and his body is buried, and it can be buried next to a fool's body, and no one will know.

2:17 The trivial, the ridiculous, and the futile

I cannot help thinking, while lying on the dentist's chair, that, first, everything is meant to decay eventually.

Second, all actions may seem noble to a certain group of people, whether as large as a nation or as small as a couple, and they may seem ridiculous and contemptible to another group of people, whether from the same time period or from a distant future.

Third, while we live our lives thinking mostly that there is a grand purpose to everything and that we must ride the arrow of time with alacrity and faith, we are doomed to a futile exercise when all our convictions are shattered to pieces when a Mr. Isaac Newton, and a Mr. Charles Darwin come along. And a Mr. Albert Einstein, and a Mr. Aloysius Smith with his mindblowing theory of the *chronochora* which explains the birth of the universe and everything else.

Moreover, in the social sphere, the futility that blasts our anchor to the material world when a hurricane levels houses to the ground, when the greed of a bunch of money hoarders erases the life savings of tens of millions, leaving them bereft of the right to exist with dignity.

While my mouth was wide open and the dentist was pulling on a molar like it was a rebellious dwarf, I felt an unexplained tug towards hating life because the work that was done under the sun by the great inventors and discoverers was distressing and alien to me, it was crumpling my soul, it was leaving me without any absolutes to pray for, to think about, to dream about, it was making the world seem too easy for me, thus making all life seem no more ordinary than the aggregation of minerals in rocks or the position of the planets around the sun, so when the dentist pulled hard on my molar, really hard, I thought right away that all is vanity and grasping for the wind.

After all the pain is gone, depending on how strong your memory is, you will retain the experience of suffering as if recalling an easy bedtime story. Or, if the suffering was indeed terrible beyond the comprehension of many, you will become a new man, possibly so different from the one you were before the event, that you will have no hope or chance of re-becoming that man with dreams of a brighter and better future. Whether these dreams were those of an ignoramus or those of a fantastic academic, it wouldn't matter, the transformation would have been complete, and perhaps not even a strong revelation could awaken such a man. I have seen people presented with miracles and the presence of saints who touched their very bodies, and the people have not budged in their convictions, they spat on the saints and walked away in disdain. Even God, who sent Himself in the form of a Son, did not succeed in convincing the entire populace of his message. How then, can I, a mere peasant from Africa, be of any value to the world?

2:18 A world of stretched extremes

does not make a good average

When one buttock sits on a hot frying pan and the other buttock sits on a block of ice, you cannot say that on average you are doing well.

There is tumult in the Middle East.

I have received letters through official channels from the following: King Sandal Alumnus Baad Al-Bizzi of Saudi Arabia, Mr. Moses Amisraeli, the Prime Minister of Israel, and Mr. Nadir Wadkirsch, the United Nations Secretary General. They are all concerned that the international situation is in danger of being destabilized and they all hope, that I, well known as I am as a peacemaker, will speak with the leaders of the Christian nations and plead with them to de-escalate the tensions. Believe me, as I told Nwanne today at lunch, I have no idea which Christian nations they are referring to. Diplomatically speaking, no specifics were given in the above mentioned letters, or precise directions, as one can interpret such directions and paths towards ultimatums, as inflexible positions, as reluctance to negotiate, as affront to non-enemy nations that could degenerate, or God-knows what presuppositions that often clog the dialogue of international diplomacy, except when this dialogue is not already clogged by getting lost in translation, or self-absorbed in impatience, or one's cultural habitudes being trampled upon by the idiosyncrasies of foreign governments with their respective democratic bureaucracies and democratic intelligence agencies, organized to serve the wellbeing of their respective citizens, often at the expense of the very same citizens, sidetracked by many business interests, strong interests that meander throughout the above mentioned bureaucracies, while all this process is essentially fueled by the fear of annihilation and the desperation to survive.

Mr. Nadir Wadkirsch, given his profession as an evolutionary psychologist, is an excellent diplomat doing credit paying tribute to his religion. As a moderate Muslim, he was an able academic and scientist before he entered the world of diplomacy in his native Kenya. He was assigned as an ambassador to the U.N. where he played a major role in the Middle East peace resolutions, the global recognition of the state of Palestine, and the isolation and final defeat of the fundamentalist armies in Nigeria and Syria. No wonder many say he will win the Nobel Peace Price very soon, if not this year.

In his bestseller, *Religion and Brain*, he wrote:

The evolution of religion is not only inevitable as a product of the evolution of the human psyche, but is also necessarily the biological evidence of extraneous intervention, or as many would say, the intervention of God.

How wonderful! Then he added:

How else could we explain such an intricate magisterium of thought and belief, the simplest of them all.

This book has changed many lives and encouraged peace worldwide!

I am a Muslim. Islam is one way of confirming our ancestry, one way of reaching God. Christianity is another way. Judaism is another way. We were given these many ways so we could learn from each other, not argue with each other. We must not hate all the labor in which we had toiled under the sun, because we must leave it to the men who will come after us. It is our sacred duty.

Splendid! I wish I were a diplomat. (Further in the chapter he mentions other religions and even the merits of nonbelief.) In his letter, he invited me to speak at the United Nations.

Mr. Moses Amisraeli, the Prime Minister of Israel, is an admirer of Secretary Wadkirsch. He said on several occasions that if it weren't for Secretary Wadkirsch, he would not have convinced the Knesset to ratify the U.N. Resolution P4ME (Peace For Middle East) that recognizes the state of Palestine. In his letter, Mr. Amisraeli underlined that the new Russian presence in the region is a benefit to the young peace and will certainly discourage any remnants of terrorist groups. Why did he write me? Why indeed.

"Your Holiness, you are more than just a broker of peace. You are the quintessential messenger of a new era of peace that can only bring a better future for all our children. By the way of this letter I would like to invite you to visit the City of Jerusalem and the Holy Lands."

Yes! This truly made my day.

Unfortunately, the last letter I read was that of King Sandal Alumnus Baad Al-Bizzi of Saudi Arabia. It was most intriguing and unusual, but I'm too tired to write about it now. Tomorrow.

2:19 A man with a frail memory must not have regrets

I do not have time to reminisce too much about my early days, even though I consider it necessary for the health of my soul.

Foreign armies entered North Korea at 5 a.m. this morning from the North and from the West.

This reminds me of the day Nwanne and I left Nigeria for the first time. It was not the best of times, it was the worst of times, surely it was not the age of wisdom but was the age of foolishness on my part. After the death of Mama and the departure of Mr. Thomas, we wandered the villages near Lake Chad for a while, seeking shelter. We could not find a place to stay and people were quite wary of strangers and were not looking for new priests. Many said they were not Christian, denying it while I could see the cross on the steeple in the middle of their village, so I asked them if they were afraid of something.

They said, "We are not afraid, what makes you say that? Go on your way, we don't need you here." Their eyes were telling a different story, that of resurrected ghosts that had known death and did not want to go through it again. I never found out what had happened to them.

We crossed into Cameroon at night, looking up at constellations. During that long walk I told Nwanne everything I knew about the stars and he told me everything he knew about the creation of the Universe. I had to correct him here and there, as he had read the Book of Genesis only once. For example he thought Adam and Eve ate a mango and were fooled by a talking lizard. I still think it's an acceptable approximation.

We crossed the border on foot on a dirt road and followed the stars. After a short while we saw a village in the distance, at least it looked like a village from afar, judging by the many little lights that were gathering to a central place. It must have been an entire sea of walking candles flowing, like rivulets, from every direction. As we came closer, we saw the lights entering a small house in the middle of the village. That must have been the church.

We stopped just outside the village and tried to find a higher vantage point so we could see what was going on. We found an old abandoned truck and we climbed onto its cabin. More and more people were gathering from everywhere, so many that after a few minutes Nwanne and I asked ourselves where all those people were going. The church was small, and they kept coming and entering in large numbers, as if they were stepping into an infinite black place from where nothing comes out. And why the church did not catch fire from all those candles? And why was there so much room when it was clear that there couldn't be? And who knows whether I will appear wise or foolish tomorrow after remembering what I saw? Nwanne wanted to go closer. I hesitated, I hid my fear by saying, "We don't have candles", while the real reason was the thought that those people were falling into a bottomless pit.

We left that place and the infinite church and found a place to sleep under the open sky that I knew had a limit.

The next day when we woke up, the mystery was revealed. We saw that the church was attached to a large hangar that had no windows. People were entering the church and moving into the hangar. From where we sat last night we could not see this capacious construction, as it was at an angle from us obscured by darkness. So I thought, how many mysteries in the world appear as they do because the eyes are not elevated to the proper heights and angles?

2:20 Circles of fire within circles of wind

within circles of despair

I had a delicious apple pie for breakfast and a glass of milk of exquisite creaminess. So mouth-watering was the milk that for a brief moment I forgot I was Pope, and all I could think of was the cow that had produced this milk, whether it had a name, and what breed it belonged to.

When I came to my senses I saw another telegram on my desk. It had just arrived from Ayatollah Ali Foolas of Iran. He must have found out that King Sandal Al-Bizzi also wrote me yesterday, and did not want to play the card of silence and be suspected of a lesser political value than the King. Had the Ayatollah known that I still had not read the King's letter, he would probably have felt a mixture of relief and of indignation, relief that he was not the last after all and indignation because I did not give immediate attention to note from important leaders of the world. Thus ignorance has its benefits.

King Sandal Al-Bizzi's letter was as intriguing as it was short. He wrote that he recognized and applauded my dedication to peace (etc. etc.) and considering my friendliness towards Islam, he invited me to visit the Holy City of Mecca, as his guest. Intriguing indeed!

Assuming that I decide to go, although at the first impression I don't see why I should not honor such a historic invitation, I will create such a precedent that it would be irreversible, long-lasting, and the undoing of this goodwill would be inconceivable. I don't want to regret that I had worked so hard. I can only hope that my successors will be conditioned by history to continue and enhance these gestures of goodwill between peoples of different faiths.

Ayatollah Ali Foolas' message was of a different nature. He spoke about the Armenian refugee crisis that was still occurring in Northern Iran, a situation that is contained, however that still needs some international attention.

"We showed our best support for the refugees, for our Armenian Christian Apostolic brothers, yet we feel we still come short when it comes to serving their spiritual needs."

Then he wrote he needed our help. I'm not sure why he wrote me, since the Holy See does not shepherd the Armenian Apostolic Church. I don't mean that I am not gladdened by this show of trust and that I wouldn't come to the rescue of our

Armenian brothers with all my heart, but should I not consider the passivity, apparent or not, of our Orthodox leaders, who by the simple fact that they are in closer proximity to Armenia should come to the rescue first? They have closer affinities to the region, don't they? Oh my, I hope this doesn't sound caustic or ironic! It's just a reflection I'm having while sipping this aromatic Italian espresso. Again, I must not forget that I am the Pope.

And what if our minds fall prey to the indulgences of the senses and to the raptness of architectural beauty, and we change as people, we forget our obligations, we forgo our moral compasses? Is this not also vanity? I think not, as I don't find anything unnatural with it. While alleviating suffering is my first preoccupation, once it is soothed, once it wanes, the soul will need to soar into the world and be connected to the world through the senses and through the workings of the mind.

2:21 The united tribulations of nations

The doctor said I need to wear a wristband for the pain in my carpal bones, just like professional tennis players. How can I be a presentable father of the church with my wrist wrapped? Don't they know this is not a customary appearance?

He said:

"Holy Father, you can conceal it under your garments."

"No," I said, "my hands need to be visible, including the wrists."

"But Holy Father-"

"I'm afraid I cannot accept that."

I saw the resignation on my doctor's face and I felt sorry for him. I did not need to remind him that Christ took nails through his wrists. I must be able to endure a puny carpal pain.

More international agitation.

Nadir Wadkirsch, the UN Secretary General, has called me.

He said: "Holy Father, I turned my heart. I'm despairing of all the fruits of the labor which I had toiled for under the sun."

I said: "What do you mean, Mr. Secretary General?"

He said: "I cannot reconcile the calling of my consciousness with the new reality."

I wish diplomats were more specific.

I said: "Our consciousness grows with the world."

He said: "The leaders of the nations are becoming nervous over the Korean crisis and the other realities."

Oddly, Mr. Wadkirsch was a man of great strength of intellect, and knew that well-tempered doubt is a necessary tool of all good scientists, let alone good diplomats. We spoke on the phone on several occasions, we briefly talked about his work, but he never mentioned changes of heart and insecurity. There must be something in my voice that invites confessions at the highest levels.

I said: "I see signs of peace everywhere, Mr. Secretary General. One must not lose hope."

He said: "It's not hope I'm talking about. It's faith."

This took me by surprise, as I knew he was not talking about losing faith, but about faith evolving in a direction that did not make him comfortable. I could not respond because he added that there will be a big conference at the United Nations, and I was invited. This is an invitation I must not refuse.

Then he finally made a clear plea to me.

"Holy Father, it would be a great benefit to international diplomacy if you could intervene with the President of Brazil and convince her not to escalate the situation in the Amazon."

The situation in the Amazon.

Margarita Bourbon-Renege, the President of Brazil, is a woman of impenetrable resoluteness. Compared to her, the Iron Lady of the UK seemed like a fluffy doll. She didn't share the coldness of the Iron Lady. She earned herself a peculiar nickname: The Compassion Tank. The journals have employed their sense of humor to concoct an oxymoron that is very effective and accurate. Since she took office she employed intelligent and powerful legislation to crack down on corruption. Moreover, she recognized the importance of the Amazon for the global ecosystemic equilibrium.

She said that the "mindless, criminal, and greedy deforestation of the Amazon is threating our own existence. We cannot allow it, we must stop it, and we must reverse it!"

How does she do that, when the corporations that have perpetrated it have become so powerful that nobody dares to stand up to them? She has declared a state of emergency in the Amazon and she has dispatched the army to take over the entire basin and stop the exploitation with a display of force.

How did the corporations respond? They issued statements and launched a public relations counter-campaign. The people are not on their side.

I've been tormenting myself over this news the entire morning. I prayed from 10:30 to 10:50, and then again, after lunch, from 13:45 to 13:56, when I found some free time amid my main duties. Returning to prayer usually rebalances my thoughts, but this time I found that when I prayed I merely heard the echo of my own voice bouncing around in my head.

2:21 (bis) Mousetrap: how poorly we see when the light is too bright

The are some voices in the Curia that think that our open support for Cardinal Park-Ying can be seen as an act of war by the North Koreans. Nonsense! Are they hearing themselves? We are helping the North Koreans, not fighting them. How some gentlemen obtained seats in the Curia is beyond my comprehension. I felt today I had to roust with a pitchfork!

The developments are the following:

The Chinese army has crossed the border over the Yalu River in several spots where geography permits, across the Shuifeng Reservoir, at Hyesan, at Heaven Lake (a strange choice indeed), and at Musan.

The Japanese-American contingencies have disembarked in more than ten locations on the North Korean shores, including Wonsan, Haean-Guyok, Seoho, Rakwon, Hongwon, and even as far North as Sonbong, which is most curious as it is so close to China and the Chinese peace troops. They may even meet each other soon!

The North Korean response is utter chaos. As far as the international press has communicated, there has been no immediate retaliation or opposition to the deployment of the peace troops. The North Korean armies continue to move about frantically inside the territory. Some generals issued threats of nuclear war. Other generals gave ultimatums to the "fascist invaders" to "retreat NOW or we will bomb Seoul so that no brick will remain standing!" without noticing that no South Korean soldier has crossed the border and no South Korean general has made war declarations, while tens of thousands of refugees are fleeing towards the South. On the Twitter program the most popular hashtag is #bordernomore following photographs with the deserted rooms in the barracks inside the Demilitarized Zone. Military sources have declared they are yet to encounter any North Korean troops.

What did not make headlines but was still in the news was that the Northern Chinese Army is progressing deeper into Russian territory. Curiouser and curiouser! President Mo Xi's press secretary has issued a statement explaining that the Northern moves are mere strategic exercises jointly with the Russian Federation. When President Pushkin was asked to confirm, he briefly said: "That is true. Next question, please."

There have been men in history whose labor was with wisdom, knowledge, and skill. And they died of natural expected deaths. And they left their heritage to other men who have not labored for it. Our prophets said this is also vanity and a great evil. Evil, I wonder? When I think of millions of lives saved due to the advancement of medicine, how is this evil? We are obligated to inherit knowledge, assume it, and build on it. How is this vanity?

We are on the verge of a new great war because nations want to preserve their legitimate state of mind. Must this happen, just because the rules of history command it? Fairness must evolve, like seeds, from ashes that turn into tulips, wheat, and forests. Nature deals the cards of our survival, we do not.

2:22 The proper attitude towards ladybugs

I must leave, I cannot stay here. There are too many other places I need to be.

Before I go, though, I will reflect for a brief moment about the dozen ladybugs that found their way inside my room. The first ladybug I saw was climbing the wall in front of my desk. It had three dots on each wing, thus it was a young specimen. I followed it with my eyes until it reached the corner of the wall near the window. The sudden change of geometry puzzled the ladybug for a moment. Then it got itself acquainted with the new surface and walked on it slowly. Then it continued its journey towards the edge of the glass window.

When the ladybug met the new surface of different consistency, friction, and temperature, it changed direction upward, continuing on the wall for a few centimeters, then it tried to step on the glass again. The ladybug put its two front legs on the glass, then retreated. Then it continued upwards towards the ceiling for another three or four centimeters, then it tried to walk on the glass again, this time moving its entire body onto the new surface.

I stood up and approached the ladybug and looked at it closely so it could feel my breath. The little insect increased its speed. The glass was warm. I placed a piece of paper in the ladybug's path. When it reached the paper, the ladybug slowed down for a moment and continued undisturbed on the paper. I took the paper away from the window, carefully, so I wouldn't lose the insect. I placed the paper on my desk, then I noticed another ladybug, an older one with five black dots on each wing, walking on my desk. I tried to make the two ladybugs meet so I placed the paper in front of the older ladybug so it could climb on it. It did, without much hesitation. The two ladybugs met on the paper and spent some time touching their bodies, exchanging information. In their world this must have taken years. In my world this took three seconds.

More ladybugs appeared around my room, on the flat surfaces of walls and photographs. They must have found a crack in the wall, a microtunnel under the window sill, a path through the ventilation tubes, or much simpler, when Nwanne opened the windows to let fresh air come in, the ladybugs grasped the wind and travelled inside.

I freed the five ladybugs that I had collected by the end of my experiment. Two of them flew away, while the other three clung to the paper with obstinacy. I shook the paper and I was not able to remove them. I shook hard and eventually the three dormant ladybugs fell off the paper. After a brief fall, one of them spread its wings and flew away. The other two continued to fall outside the field of my vision.

There are only so many adorable ladybugs I can save. The rest must be left to nature's ways and means of death and procreation.

There is no best way to handle ladybugs. They have always inspired my thoughts about blind trust and careless exploration. A ladybug's life is summarized by a collection of dots on its wing. When it crosses our eyes, a ladybug suddenly inherits the meanings we have carried with us in our own human lives. A ladybug sits on the frame of a painting: that painting becomes the strong reference of a new beautiful memory: *The Return of the Prodigal Son* by Rembrandt, as framed by the journey of a ladybug, *St. Francis in Ecstasy* by Bellini, as witnessed by a dying, hungry, ladybug.

I cannot think of a memorable morale for this little story. What does man derive from all of his labor, and for all the striving of his heart, for which he has toiled under the sun? There is a dark, quiet space outside this little world of painters and watchers of paintings, of timid ladybugs, of dead, dry ladybugs.

2:23 The quintessence of a lonely genius

I do not understand the work of Professor Aloysius Smith. The secretary of the Pontifical Academy of Sciences has explained it to me on two occasions and I remain befuddled. Aloysius Smith is a theoretical physicist and the discoverer of the unified theory of the chronochora. The word is his creation and it means, as far as I understand, that we live in a universe of time densities, and everything is a result of evolving densities of time, from the Big Bang to the present. The Universe was created by a vacuum fluctuation of enormous energy and will end up in a vacuum of the same nature, where time will end, because there will be nothing left. Then the cycle will begin again. The theory gives a solution to general relativity that explains gravity in terms of quantum mechanics. This means that physics is now unified. Hit me with an ivory cane in the back of my head, I still do not comprehend!

Aloysius Smith is a lonely professor who works in a small office crammed with papers and books. A photograph of him in his office has already appeared on the first page of all papers in the world. "We must honor him with the medal of the Pontifical Academy of Sciences", the secretary said, "he has brought us closer to understanding the mind of God."

I'm not so sure that Professor Aloysius Smith has brought us closer to God. In his only interview after the publication of the theory, which he gave over the phone, when asked exactly about knowing the mind of God, he answered tersely: "God? What is that? I don't know what you are talking about."

I like that the reporter pressed him afterwards. Professor Smith gave in, but said only this: "However you define this God for me, I can tell you only this - the unified theory of chronochora has no term for God in its equations and language. It uses only mathematics and chronochorics. I'm afraid this is my final and complete answer on this matter."

So be it. We ought to leave the man alone, albeit many pundits and dwellers on the electronic social media hail him as a prophet of a new age, forgetting that the weight of this metaphor carries with it attributes that poor Professor Aloysius Smith might not live up to, or care for at all, or even recognize as laudable attributes, such as a high moral character that is not exercised merely in seclusion, but on the contrary in the wide open world, amongst peers and suffering beings who need guidance and answers to their prayers. Such a man Professor Aloysius Smith is not, nor does he want to be. His days may all be sorrowful, for all we know, quiet and deprived of the presence of men. Or he may be a joyous, merry man, yet this is doubtful, as joy can only be a relation with the world. His work may be burdensome, engulfed by the claws of obsession; his heart may take no rest even in the night; thus for those who care only for the bliss of ignorance, this may look like vanity.

Aloysius Smith is unlike all the men I know. His passion for truth is not matched by any of the members of the Curia. He said: "My struggles with my own self, with my own preconceptions, with the limitations of my brain, have made me a weak and tired man. I'm not afraid to say it. But as I came closer to the truth, my spirit soared, and in my mind, I was reborn."

He will be remembered over the centuries. I, on the other hand, will be but a name on a list.

2:24 Notes on fear and pessimism, from the underground

Nwanne showed me a video on the Youtube about psychologist William James. He said: Happiness equals expectations over reality. Maintain reality, lower your expectations, your happiness increases.

We live in the underground of our potential. The crimes of the past, those left unscrutinized, unpunished, and unattended, are coming to the surface to torment us. We cannot rebuild the equation of happiness, as William James said, lest we know what variables to attach to it, because we are less and less capable of defining our expectations, less and less potent in exchanging values with reality. Our narrow sight is fragile and lenses cannot correct the distortions. Our crumbling memory leaves us anchored to the information feeds of the moment, and only of the moment. We discard words like old breadcrumbs and torn paper, into the dustbin of meaning. With great ambition, we climb the highest mountains to find ourselves engulfed in thick fog, with no sky above us, with no faces to see near us, with the knowledge of the precipice below us.

We fail to acknowledge fear when it appears and when it takes over our blood. We call it a momentary lapse of reason, we think it will pass, we drown it in the stimulations of the senses and in the numbness of the brain. We exit our body as if it were a suit, like those worn by astronauts. We leave it on the sofa, and we walk naked, bereft of ourselves, into the next room of nothingness. Random, repeated, regurgitated nothingness.

Angels: nowhere to see. Christ: nowhere to feel. God: nowhere to hear.

Then we reconstruct ourselves and become a new illusion. Probably, the best thing we can do is to enjoy eating, drinking, and working. And we labor, we labor, again and again, as if we were bathing in a bath of choices, sweet choices, that all of them, without exception, would allow us to construct the best imaginable and possible life for ourselves, from the hand of God, some say, from the benevolence of our parents, others say, towards the great wide-open future.

And when I say I feel less and less hope, I do not say my faith has dwindled in a way that I lost sight of the presence of God in this world, nor that mankind has failed again to see the light of Christ as the peoples of the age of Noah did, I say that my soul is drying up and I am pushed into shadowless, edgeless corners, where I cannot even muster the power to conceive the idea of escape, or even its necessity.

Often when the mirror shows me the face of a naïve, silly man, I ponder how inconsistent the voices in my head are, from wise to puerile, from well-tempered to tormented, from loud to mute. And when they vibrate all at the same time, and nothing but the ringing of their echoes bounces off in my head, I free myself from myself and all I want is everything to stop so I can hear the clear voice of God, His halcyon, eloquent voice that will enunciate his commands and explanations with impeccable grammar and efficacy. And I also know this is a heresy, born from fear and lack of discipline, and I include it in my prayers and in my diary.

Thus no man is spared from these qualms. Faith must unburden us, faith must recombine us, faith must paint the vision for us, as faith is canvas, brush, and stroke of color, all concurrently. And when all these things are not present, the path to despair must not seem inevitable, as other paths may appear from the same boundless corners.

We are bound to be reborn by negating the despotism of fear.

2:25 Uncanny conversation with the oxymoronic vituperator

Cardinal Thorsen Tchipcherish, the Prefect of the Congregation for the Doctrine of the Faith, is a master at making his wishes well known. He appears as an ox garbed in velvet, and he thunders the wisdom of our faith with the dexterity of St. Paul at the apex of his divine inspiration.

He insisted I shared a lunch with him, at my convenience, which actually means as early as possible, or in other words, at his earliest convenience. He managed to implant this in my head. How does he do it? Uhhh, I get shivers at night when I close my eyes and I see his face.

But he is a good man. He is a staunch defender of the faith, an encyclopedic scholar, a strong character, who must keep his post as a prefect. I know it and the Curia knows it. I must habituate myself with his demeanor. I have no choice.

At lunch:

"How do you like your chicken, Holy Father?" the Cardinal asked me with a broad smile and a furrowed grimace that could paralyze an entire battalion of poultry.

"I like my chicken crispy and well done, Cardinal. How about you?"

"I like it tossed, tender, fried or steamed, bloody or burned. As long as it doesn't fly away, I'll take it. For who can eat, or who can have more enjoyment, more than I?"

He laughed.

"Well, Cardinal, God has given us power over our food," I said.

"Indeed, Holy Father."

"The faith of many of those who are poor is not diminished by their hunger," I said.

"Indeed. And paradoxically, there are people of great luck and fortune whose insatiability is unquenchable, their peregrinations through life are solely to find enjoyment, and yet they claim strong faith and are great supporters of our Mother Church. Would you say you bless their hearts, Holy Father?"

"I bless everyone's hearts, Cardinal. Our benevolence is not diminished by the quality of people's ways of living."

"And the monsters, the criminals…"

"They will not be judged by me. I welcome them back to faith when they are ready to come back. I do sense, though, Cardinal Tchipcherish that this is not why you came to see me today."

"It is and it is not. I feel that our faith needs to be rescued. I think our Congregation needs a deep reform. I believe, Holy Father, that we are on the edge of an epoch of such radical tensions, that the decisions and prayers of today will mark the lives of many generations to come. And it falls on our shoulders to foster this reform."

"I completely agree, Cardinal. What are you suggesting?"

"Well, Holy Father, what I am about to say may sound so radical that it may seem beyond heresy. I am pleading that you bear with me and hear what I am about to say. This is a thought, and it remains so, as I have not given it any part of my heart, nor of my convictions. My faith in the Church remains strong and undiminished. In the same time, I cannot help myself to encounter in my prayers, over and over again, especially in the deepest and most reclusive prayers, the same thought that now pervades my readings of the doctrine, my meditations over the gospels and writings of early Church Fathers. This thought terrifies me and does not bring me any rest. I confirm it with the voice of the world, with the struggle of the many with life, with the tremors of the planet. This thought has to do with you, Holy Father, and with our institution, its traditions. This thought is an echo from the Doctrine of the Faith, as it came from Christ in my prayers."

While the Cardinal was talking I couldn't help feeling my pulse increasing and my ears throbbing with impatience. His deep voice was shaking the room, as Pontius Pilate himself had thundered in front of the crowd when he delivered his judgment. I did not know what to expect. When the Cardinal stopped and paused to breathe so he could deliver the apex of his talk, I was already tensed by his introduction and so wrong in my expectation, that my focus was on matters of faith having to do with the number of angels on a pin head and the rituals of prayer, of all things.

Then the Cardinal spoke again:

"Christ has spoken to me in my prayers. He said we ought to abolish the Papacy."

I heard the words but I was not able to tie them together. Did he say *abolish the Papacy*? Yes. He did. Was the Cardinal estranged from sanity? He did not seem so. His composure remained solid, contained, and self-assured. When he realized I had not answered anything after a long moment of silence, he spoke my papal title, to which I replied he made quite a statement, to which he apologized, to which I said there was no need to and that I have to reflect over his thoughts. Then I dismissed him and that was it.

2:26 Before everything had its time, chaos was a delightful order

We left the Republic of Cameroon and crossed into the Republic of Chad on a flatbed truck. We told the driver we were missionaries. He was happy to help. He asked us where we were going. "Towards the East," I said. "We want to see the Indian Ocean."

This was not a destination that we had in our minds. Nwanne and I were drawn towards sunset. We told ourselves we would continue towards the East until the Ocean stops us. Then we would turn towards the West and walk until the other ocean stops us.

The truck driver had to stop in a village in the heart of the Sahara. His vehicle had blown a gasket. He needed time for repairs. So he presented us the options: we wait until he fixes the truck, or we stay in the village until another vehicle comes along to take us farther. "Is this a Christian community?" I asked the driver. "These are peoples of the Sahel. They do not know your Christ."

We decided to stay in the village. The people were kind to us. They gave us a loaf of bread, mushrooms, and some fruit. We offered to pay. They refused.

We made camp in the shadows of a pack of trees overlooking the road and the village. We ate everything the villagers gave us and we began dreaming with our eyes open, while an eruption of joy filled our souls.

"Look Enyi, I see angels!" Nwanne shouted.

But they were no angels. There was a holy man, dressed in white linen, appearing from the heat waves. He had the glare of a star. His feet were barely touching the ground.

"He's flying, Enyi, he's flying!"

He had the head of a giraffe.

"No, Nwanne, he is not a man. He is Christ!"

I couldn't help myself laughing. At the same time I felt embarrassed, stupid and humble. I was seeing Christ and I was not in my best shape.

"Kneel Nwanne, kneel!"

Nwanne knelt and laughed out loud. "I'm kneeling Enyi! I'm kneeling!"

Then he laid down on his belly and rolled over several times shouting "I'm kneeling, I'm kneeling!", and laughing incessantly.

Christ came closer and opened his palms. We saw the holes from his crucifixion.

"Please Lord, forgive us!" I whispered.

Then I saw another figure emerging from the heat. Another man in white linen. Another Christ. He had the head of a tiger. He too was floating above the ground.

Nwanne stopped rolling on the ground and sat up. His face was covered in mud. His grin was wide and fully loaded with joy.

We both watched as Tiger Christ came closer and stopped near Giraffe Christ. Tiger Christ spoke:

"For God gives wisdom and knowledge and joy to a man who is good in His sight."

Nwanne was grinning happily and I was trying to recollect my composure. I was transfixed and couldn't speak. I wanted to express my enormous joy. My jaws were firmly paralyzed. Then Giraffe Christ spoke:

"But to the sinner He gives the work of gathering and collecting".

"No, he does not," Tiger Christ replied.

"Yes, he does," Giraffe Christ.

The two Christs were standing in front of us, watching us, and ordering us with their eyes, to listen to what they had come to say.

"Then tell me, what does the sinner do with what he has received from Him?" Tiger Christ pointed to His Father in heaven whose name was hallowed.

"The sinner must give to who is good before Him," Giraffe Christ replied and pointed towards the same heaven.

"No, no, no!" Tiger Christ said. "He must not give. He is a free man."

"Free men exist not," Giraffe Christ answered. "Free men are men who carry their own heads."

"We all carry our own heads!" Tiger Christ protested.

Their eyes were fixed on us. Nwanne and I, now both kneeling, we were grinning and standing still, like two boulders.

"Only saints carry their own heads!" Giraffe Christ replied.

"That is not true," Tiger Christ said calmly.

"I am the truth, the life, and the way," said Giraffe Christ.

"Me too."

Then they both said at the same time:

"No man cometh unto the Father, but by me."

"Yes, yes, yes!" Nwanne shouted happily and applauded.

A third Christ was emerging from the heat. His head was that of an Alligator. An animal that I always feared and respected.

Alligator Christ joined Giraffe Christ and Tiger Christ to form a trinity right in front of our very eyes. I felt the Sahel winds blowing in my face.

"Is this vanity?" Giraffe Christ asked.

"I think it is," Tiger Christ said.

Alligator Christ said nothing but stretched his holey hand towards me and said:

"Are you grasping for the wind?"

Then they all disappeared. Our joy had diminished and was soon replaced by fear and awe. We felt the presence of God and the Devil, near us, at the same time.

NOTEBOOK THREE

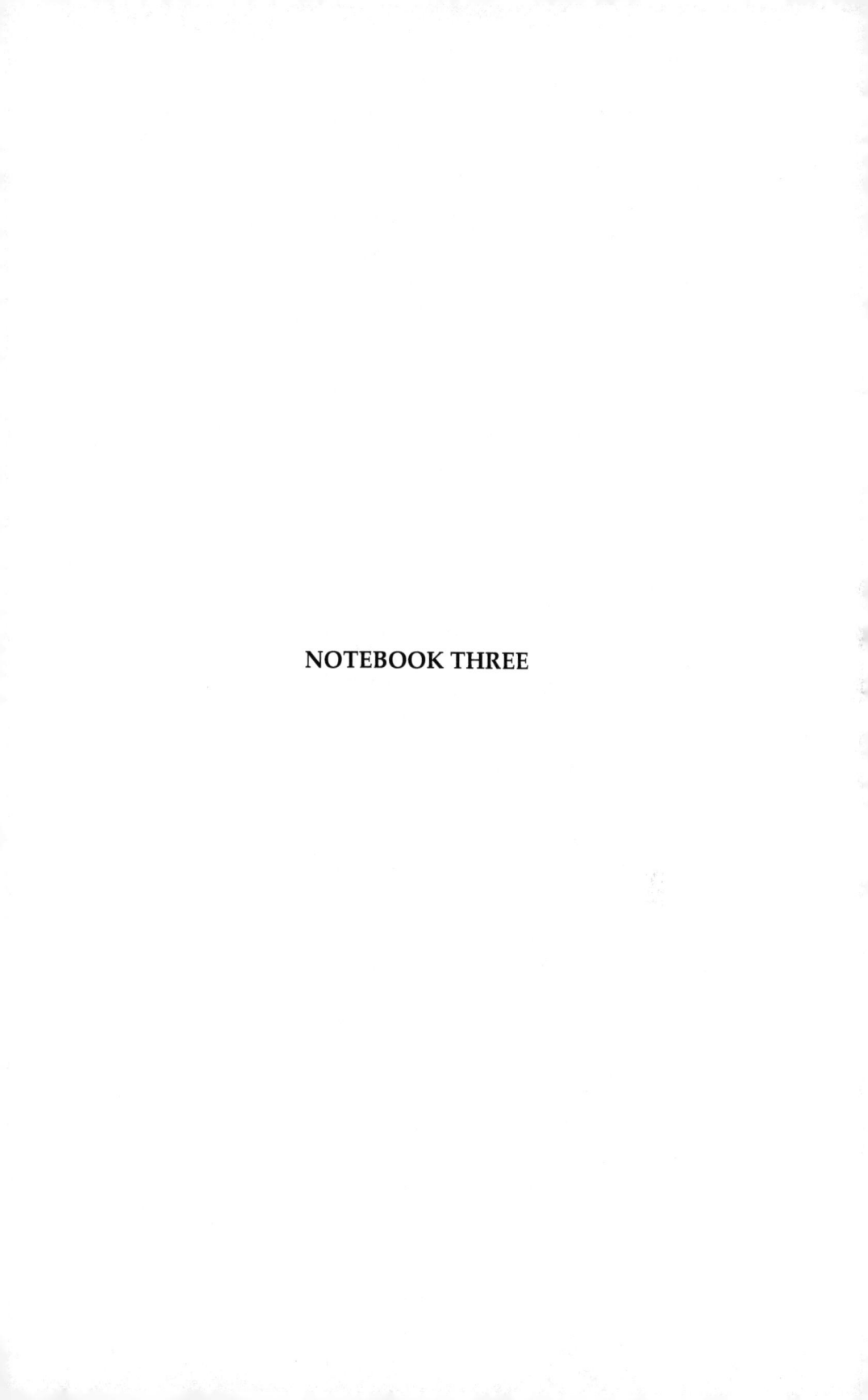

3:1 Stupefaction from Korea:

the beauty, the choreography, the war

A nuclear missile from the Yingbyan complex failed to launch. The release clamps on the launch pad malfunctioned. The rocket tilted to one side and fell to the ground before its engines were turned on. The damage was significant enough to prevent any other launches in the foreseeable future.

Another nuclear missile was launched from the Undongjang complex in the Myohyang-san Mountains and it was destroyed over the Sea of Japan by an American battleship. There were no victims.

There is much confusion in the North Korean army. Half of the generals have deserted, many fleeing in fisherman boats, to all directions in the East China Sea. Nobody knows what they expected to find. By now, surely the Chinese have captured them. Many have asked why they were not stopped in their homeland. Probably because many of these deserting generals were commanders of the North Korean Navy stationed on the Western shores of the country, while the commanders of the Navy stations on the shores of the Sea of Japan remained at their posts but were paralyzed by indecision and did not lift a finger to stop the so-called foreign invasion. The fleeing generals changed their attire for rags. The remaining generals blamed their indecision on the lack of orders from Pyongyang. The truth is that no information is coming out of or going into Pyongyang. The city is in total darkness. The leader was declared dead. However his body was not found. Several of his acolytes have committed suicide in their own offices. There is no next of kin claiming power. All propaganda radios in homes have gone silent. Nobody is seen on streets. No cab drivers, no workers, no police. Not even ghosts. When a satellite catches an ambulance rushing on the streets of Pyongyang, it becomes breaking news. A pack of lone wolves was sighted running through the streets in the outskirts of the city.

The peacekeeping armies are standing still. The world leaders are assessing the situation. The airwaves are frozen. The North Korean generals are posting contradictory videos on the Youtube. The official state television channel is closed. Its director and its key employees have most likely fled their posts. Where to?

This deafening silence is in peculiar contrast with the spectacle of peace in South Korea, where entire legions, no, not the right word, entire crowds of young people, fans of the K-Pop movement, are marching towards Seoul, wearing signs of peace, reunification, reconciliation. Their choreography is impeccable. Satellite images show a nationwide dance of crowds in rhythms of pop music. Stages have been assembled in all major public spaces and are filled with musicians and dancers and peace activists. There are thousands of donation pledges in support of the North Korean brothers and sisters. A million people prayed in a square where Cardinal Samuel Park-Ying came on stage dressed in a rainbow shirt, and called for the "great liberation of souls" of the Korean people. "We were One, and we shall be One again!" he said, and the crowd went wild.

I pray that this outpour of love will break through the blockade of silence in the North.

"They see us from the sky," Cardinal Park-Ying said to the crowd. "Let us show them our love. Make the peace sign!"

Within an hour, one million people made an enormous peace sign. They used social media and maps and they did it!

The satellites caught the image. It was a clear, multicolor peace sign, stretching over a few kilometers. It was spectacular!

To everything there is a season. Now the time has come when we ought to stop waiting for signs from above. It is time we show our signs to the sky. We have realized every purpose under heaven and we have chosen wrong paths and right paths. We must seize the oddities of history and break the cages of silence! Ah, what a great day!

3:2 I am he – the fruit of the corrupted garden[1]

I took a walk this afternoon, in the Vatican Gardens, looking for a space of serenity under the sun. And I found it in a place with no shade. There I met the Gardener.

He was a tall, heavyset man. His skin was darker than mine. He was Ethiopian.

"You must be our Ethiopian gardener. I heard your hands work miracles with roses."

"I hope my humility precedes my reputation, Holy Father."

"What is your name?"

"My name is Tekle, Holy Father."

"Tekle. Tekle. The name is familiar," I said.

"I was named after an Ethiopian saint."

"Indeed. Indeed. A Coptic saint."

"You probably wonder why I work in the Vatican, Holy Father."

"Oh, not at all. We need good gardeners. Are you a man of faith, Mr. Tekle?"

"I must confess, Holy Father, my faith rests in the seeds I plant and the flowers they produce. Then Christ is the witness to my garden. I pledged to Him that I will plant the gardens to keep Him alive."

---

[1] Divine Comedy, Inferno: Canto XXXIII by Dante Alighieri

"That is most peculiar, Mr. Tekle. What happens if your seeds are ill?"

"Seeds do not know illness. For them there is only time. A time to plant, and a time to pluck what is planted. When I load them with purpose to create a beautiful garden, then they become extensions of my body and the children of rain. But if I leave them on a slab of cement, they will desiccate and die, with no tears and no pain, they will return to ashes, like a candle that runs out of fire. This is how the faith of man wanes."

Mr. Tekle opened his fist and showed me a lump of soil mixed with seeds, ants, and larvae.

"I kept these seeds in a jar for a few days, in soil mixed with larvae and nutrients. I wanted to teach them that the struggle for life is fierce and ruthless, that they have to fight for food, so that when I release them into the garden where they will have no other competitor, they will do their best to thrive and produce the most beautiful flowers. I do not pretend that I am doing God's work, or that I am an extension of His will. The larvae, the ants, they have their own life, their own struggle. I am simply seeking to make beautiful roses, strong roses, that can please our eyes. I am not a pious man, Holy Father. I am an honest man and I'm trying to do honest work. And I tell you this because I know your life and your struggles. You have surpassed all the seeds that I have ever laid into the ground. Your life is a lesson to us all, and I grow roses to show recognition for what your life means to us. When the time comes to be born, we have no choice. When the time comes to die, we have no choice. I will say it and please forgive my impertinence, Holy Father, I feel I can open my heart, I have lost and regained my faith many times, my faith in our God and Christ that is, but I have never lost faith in my seeds, they have never betrayed me. I do not mean that God has betrayed me, no. I mean that my seeds have always been there, have always acted as I knew them."

I listened to Mr. Tekle carefully. Before I knew it he kneeled and kissed my hand.

"Nothing frightens me more, Holy Father, than the thought of a wasted garden and nothing exults me more than the thought of my life entwined with the life of thoughtless flowers. My sadness for all unbecomed seeds is only soothed by the sight of those who have become grown flowers. And the death of grown flowers, I do not have the time to mourn: as there is joy to find in this cycle renewed. I advance in life, carried forward by a fine balance of living and dead seeds, and when the end comes for me, I will take pride in my past and I will forget the future that will be for me no more. Will I end up in heaven, with its barren plots of earth? Or does hell await me, with gardens of fire where roses do grow? These thoughts are for theologians. For the wonderful truth that I had been, that I had seen, that I had heard, it will be enough for me to exit life as color exits the rose when the season comes."

3:3 Times to kill, times to heal

There is never a good time to kill and always a good time to heal. Since the Caliphate Wars in the Middle East, we are living through the first weeks of peace. President Pushkin's peace army stationed in Syria and the Mediterranean has assured the continuation of calmness, ironic as it sounds.

When President Pushkin said, "Russia is going to pay for peacekeeping troops as a sign and non-aggression", he was applauded worldwide. Even President Sanbard Renders saluted this gesture, knowing that Russia has taken up America's pledge to be a warden of international peace, an ambition that in my opinion is not yet matched by the large material commitments that America has made in the past, albeit in its own interest to a large extent. These are the new realities. We must live with them.

The Caliphate has stopped its offensive since the Cyprus Peace Accords. "The time to break down the West has ended," said the Caliph. "It is time to build up our new country." This is a country that does not exist *de jure*, however considering the peace accords the country exists *de facto*, at least until Secretary Nadir Wadkirsch convenes the United Nations to pass a new resolution. For this purpose, during this intermission of history, President Pushkin has set up camp in the Middle East, with the express acceptance of the Caliph.

I remember that beautiful scene from *Wisdom and Fleece* (the first book from Pavel Pushkin's Bogatyn-Mudryy trilogy) where Alexei Bogatyn comes home from his wool factory and tells Alyona about the worker's strike and the fire at the warehouse. Alyona tells Alexei: "Take my skin and graft it over the burned wounded, take my soul and wrap it around the children left orphaned, take my blood and give it to them. I can hear their cries from my room, through the thick forests of our estate. Their echoes reverberate in the rooms of our mansion. They get louder and louder by the minute. They haunt my day. They heat up my organs. I would give my life to save the lost finger or limb of any of our workers. But how many lives do I have Alexei? I am not an immortal dragon, Alexei. I am not an indestructible ziggurat! Oh, take this pain away from me and make me stone!"

One can say that the guilt Alyona felt, developed by Pushkin over three hundred pages, is only matched by Raskolnikov's dark tremors. But Alyona is no Dostoevsky's Raskolnikov. She committed no crime, yet she expected a great punishment.

I cannot help thinking of President Pushkin's work when I see what is happening in the Middle East. He is a man of great sensibility. He is a wise man, and just like his characters, his deeds on Earth reflect a moral duty so heavy that its foundation will endure for centuries to come.

3:4 Prostration of the prostate

Nwanne, my Nwanne, the fragile man he is when a butterfly stops on his hand, the strong man he is when in front of the devil he opens his bare chest and says "Come, take my soul, if you dare!", my Nwanne has fallen ill.

He complained of abdominal pain for the past few days. Darling and dedicated as he is, he refused my instructions to remain in bed, and continued to serve as he served me for decades. With unflinching tact and endearing attention to my every whim.

We, men, carry this little gland called the prostate. The Google explained that the prostate is the size of a walnut and inhabits a space between the bladder of urine and the long masculine organ that is precisely in front of the rear door of the human body. The canal of the urethra traverses the center of the prostate, originating in the bladder of urine, then goes into the large masculine organ, thus permitting the flow of discharge out of the body. God has designed it in such a way that the prostate secretes fluid that nourishes and safeguards the seminal fluid. During exultation, the prostate squeezes this fluid into the urethra, and it is expelled with the seminal fluid as male seed.

We, men, can become ill with cancer of the prostate. This is not a terrible illness. Even before we were elected to office, Nwanne and I had a good regimen for our health. From calisthenics to nutrition, we tried to conduct a respectable life honoring the bodies that God gave us in this world. When we learned of the existence of this illness, we thought we ought to do everything to protect ourselves. One day, Nwanne came home with an atlas of the human anatomy and opened it to the page of the prostate.

"Enyi, look, we both have this. It can catch disease." He pointed with his finger. "We have to check that it doesn't grow."

We learned how to check and we checked each other once in a while, with care and attention. Alas, this did not prevent the inevitable outcome! Nwanne has the symptoms of the cancer. The doctor told us we need not worry. He has performed the inspection, the tests, and despite the symptoms, the illness is curable. I have faith he will live a long life!

We, men, do not have much time to weep. This doesn't mean that we do not carry tears. We often carry more tears than we can bear and we often succumb under their weight when they remain inside us.

We, men, find odd times to laugh. We laugh in the face of death, we laugh in the face of danger, we laugh in the face of illegitimate authority. We laugh at clowns, we laugh at stupid deeds, we laugh for no reason.

We, men, often take a long time to mourn. Sometimes we take such a long time that those who have departed lose their patience with us. They appear in our dreams and tell us to leave them alone to rest, as they are in a better world. A world of complete forgetfulness.

We, men, crave for more time to dance, and when we get it we don't know how to enjoy it. We turn into buffoons, climb tables, blow the trumpets, and thump our chests. When big eyes turn toward us, and palms unite into applause, we jump high on the tables and the dance becomes a spectacle of dunces. What are we, men, without the attention of the crowds and the recognition that we are the greatest of hunters and the greatest of shepherds? Even the quietest man desires to dance, if only on imaginary tables.

We, men, are masters in the art of prostration. We knew it even before Christ showed us its purpose and sacredness. When He came, He was shocked by our zeal. He told us we forgot the meaning of prayer. Praying is to lose yourself in God, he said.

We, men, we invented the craft of submission. When we thought we were meant to submit to the will of God, we crumbled to the will of our bodies and we thought our souls remained intact. But I have seen too many men whose souls were destroyed by the illnesses and damages to their bodies. And I wonder if these men were mourned and prayed for. I do not see a more terrible illness for man other than to be forgotten.

I do not think we can escape the cycle of life. From dust into dust. From ashes into ashes. Time had a beginning. Time will have an end.

3:5 O heaven, in whose gyrations some appear[1]

Stately, bombastic, Prime Minister Pierluigi Pantalone entered bearing a leather binder on which the matte insignia of the republic lay crossed by elastic strings. He bowed diplomatically and offered to shake my hand, approximating the papal protocol, for which he knew well I myself had no high consideration. He replied to our prior invitation with much hastiness. In fact, that is how he opened:

"I come in such haste, Your Holiness."

It is unusual for an Italian head of state to pay me a visit of low pomp and minimal protocol. Heeding his appearance, I adopted my most jovial demeanor and did my best to reply with the same gusto.

"Your Holiness," Prime Minister Pantalone began. "There are matters in the South of my country that concern both the Catholic Church and the Republic."

I said "Yes, of course," and I moved my arms far from my body as I was trying to embrace all Italians.

---

[1] Divine Comedy, Purgatorio, Canto XX

"You must have heard the allegations of corruption-"

I had not. However, I said "Yes," and kept my arms wide.

"-surrounding some prelates," the Prime Minister said.

I brought my arms back and reached for my pockets. I did not have any, so I gently landed my palms on my cassock.

"Funds for the refugee camps have been mishandled."

I did not know that. Prime Minister Pantalone continued his sonorous presentation.

"The internal affairs of the Holy Church do not concern my government, but, umm, they do. Pardon my frankness. It is only justified by a motivation for justice. You are an athlete of justice, Your Holiness, we all know that-"

Athlete am I not, albeit Nwanne's protests.

"-State money, siphoned through muddy accounts, involved with the Mafia, the Mafia!, Your Holiness, the funds were supposed to help the refugees. The gratitude we show for your office and the policy of unprecedented openness shown by Your Holiness is mirrored by our concern for righteousness."

I nodded. Signor Pierluigi Pantalone was wearing a lilac-scented perfume.

"The State can only function properly by laic conduct. The Church has its transcendental attributions, of which you are the expert, and it also has the earthly functions that by definition happen on the territory of the State."

What was he trying to say?

"I am saying that the earthly functions of the Church must not derive into privileges. With all due respect, Your Holiness, the Church must pay its earthly dues."

"Ah, I see," I opened my eyes. He means not death, but taxes.

"We cannot exempt the Church for taxes, Your Holiness."

I completely agreed!

"Signore Prime Minister Pantalone, I am not sure if I can provide a statutory answer at this time. I am completely aligned with your feelings. I must consult the Roman Curia. The cardinals must weigh in. I'm sure you understand."

"Si, si, sure, sure, Your Holiness. Please consider that the State has attached a deadline to this policy. That is, the end of the year."

The end of the year?

"That is a reasonable deadline, Prime Minister."

"Also, Holy Father, I come to you with a personal matter. You have the reputation of a great listener."

"Are you a devout Catholic, Prime Minister?"

"Please, call me Pierluigi."

"I couldn't possibly…"

"Please Holy Father, please."

He waved his hand. His assistant and everyone else left the room. We were alone.

"I am not a Catholic," Pierluigi said. "In fact, I am not a believer."

I widened my eyes.

"I am not sure if I can hear your confession."

"You are a wise man, Your Holiness. Hear me as a man who seeks counsel."

"Of course. Please go ahead."

"I have a brother, Piermario Pantalone, whose mind is not very straight. He is in a mental institution. He has been there for almost five years now. Once in a while I visit him. He has this mania of collecting pebbles. When he sees me, he stands erect in front of me and says, "It's twelve o'clock, it's time to cast away stones." And he throws the stones on the floor. Then he says, "Don't just stay there, pick them up." And I have to pick them up, but not before I say, "It's twelve o'clock, it's time to gather the stones." Then he becomes another man, a normal man, the Piermario I once knew. I come to my brother, he says, "Where's my kiss?" So I kiss him on the left cheek, on the right cheek, on the left cheek, and I say, "It's time to embrace," and he says, "Of course it's time to embrace, who do you think I am, a moron?", and he laughs out loud and we embrace like real brothers and we pat each other's backs. He asks me how politics are, I tell him that they're fine. I ask him how the nurses treat him. He says they treat him fine. A nurse Ofelia cares for him every day. "She kisses me on the forehead, Pierluigi," he says. "You know who used to kiss me on the forehead? Our mother used to kiss us on the forehead," he says. "Ofelia kisses me on the forehead," he says again. And when nurse Ofelia enters the room, my brother becomes agitated because she came to change his clothes. Urinary incontinence. Piermario says, "It is time now to refrain from embracing." Nurse Ofelia changes him and leaves. Then my brother turns to me and says with a very sad voice, "You know Pierluigi, because of you God went away." I asked him many times, "What do you mean Piermario, where did God go to?" And he repeats, "God left." So I thought for some time, where did God go? And I think I found the answer. God went to

Palermo. God was our father Pierfranco Pantalone and he left us when I was five years old. He told us he was going to Palermo on business, and never came back. We have not heard from him since. My brother and I have been waiting for God to return ever since. Holy Father, what can I tell my brother next time I see him?"

"God is often so close to us that we cannot see Him. He never leaves. We move away from Him."

"Are you suggesting that I become Piermario's new God?"

"You already are. You just have to show yourself."

Poor Prime Minister. I don't know if I helped him much.

3:6 Heat on the Amur and the ice of Arabia

A large contingency of Chinese battleships is advancing on the Amur River that determines the border between Far East Russia and Northeastern China. In addition to the ground troops that already crossed into Russia, for bilateral exercise, according to bilateral declarations, this constitutes an unusual collaboration between Presidents Mo Xi and Pavel Pushkin, in the background of a riveting international situation. While everybody was expecting China to enforce their presence in North Korea, they acted to the contrary and are moving troops precisely in the opposite direction, for a trivial purpose. So it seems.

Then we have King Sandal Alumnus Baad Al-Bizzi of Saudi Arabia. He is a "good friend" of both Presidents Mo and Pushkin, not my words. It has to do with the "equilibrium of oil production and distribution spheres." Most Chinese battleships run on nuclear power, however there is plenty of military machinery that runs on conventional oil-derived products. What the Chinese cannot get from the Russians, they buy, in large part from the Saudis. This keeps everybody happy.

But it's all wrong. It's entirely different. The backchannel agreements are often in blatant contradiction with the official policy. And the same officials are making both the overt and the covert agreements. It's hard to make sense of all this. Christians shaking hands with Confucianists, who shake hands with Sunnis, and vice-vice-versa.

King Sandal has complained, officially, that the participation in the *hajj* is affected by the tensions in the regions. Less Muslims are making the pilgrimage to Mecca because the Russian presence in the region makes them uneasy. The "demographics are cooling down," King Sandal has said. Which coming from the King of the hot Arabian Desert makes it a noteworthy concatenation of dichotomic terms.

In short, King Sandal said, "I must warn our Russian friends that their footing in Syria is too strong."

President Pushkin immediately replied, "I assure our friend, King Sandal, that our presence is purely for peacekeeping and keeping the Caliphate on a short leash."

King Sandal officially doesn't like the Caliphate, even though they too are mainly Sunni with those flavors of Wahhabo-Salafism, which are "not entirely in the spirit of our Prophet," again his words, not mine.

The Chinese have issued a declaration that the fleet is intended for the Sea of Okhotsk. The risen water levels of the Amur River allow for quick progress.

King Sandal wields great military power also, yet he has not deployed any forces thus far. Satellites show the Saudi Army exercising within the confines of military bases: running around, outdoor exercises, many hours in shooting ranges, some strategic exercises in the desert with camouflaged tanks – apparently not camouflaged well enough, since they have been reported by the satellites (pictures published in the Foreign Affairs magazine, the Italian edition) – short naval movements in the Red Sea, back and forth, back and forth, and one brief incursion into Yemen with a squadron of 100 elite troops to neutralize a terrorist insurgent group that was planning an attack on a Saudi oil refinery.

[Reports of Saudi nuclear weapons remain unsubstantiated.]

While the Caliphate has not dared to deploy any new suicide attacks outside its self-determined territory, the ceasefire continues to work for the moment. The Caliph posted a video where he said there was a time to gain, there was a time to lose, there was a time to tie the shoelaces, then there was a time to untie them, take the shoes off, put the feet up on an ottoman, and relax in prayer for a while. Coming from the Caliph this is an unusual usage of poetic licenses, especially the word ottoman, that is Turkish at the origin. In all his videos the Caliph is surrounded by many ottomans. He seems to love them. Moreover, the prayers on which the Caliphate was born were far from relaxing since they involved the putative incitement of the Prophet to a holy war, for the preservation and dissemination of the true faith of Islam. The new incitements are now for deep relaxation, reflection, and for the "strengthening of the foundation," the Caliph's words, not mine.

I cannot help thinking that this play that is unfolding on the world's stage contains many elements of deception. I can't put my finger on it. Who is deceiving whom? What if I myself am the one deceived, thinking that the entire foreign relations fracas is supposed to have an underlying purpose? There is a time to keep the good ideas, nurture them and let them accumulate into the orthodoxy of peace. And – I can't stress this enough – there is also a time to throw away the nasty and deleterious ideas that can bring our civilization to its demise.

What will come of all this? I don't know.

3:7 The conference of the beards

A great conference of the Orthodox Patriarchs has been convened in Istanbul. Among the attendees: Patriarch Fyodor of Russia, Patriarch Pompiliu of Romania, Patriarch Aequilaterus I of Constantinople, Patriarch Philipilus III of Jerusalem, Patriarch Nestor of Serbia, and Patriarch Hieronymus IV of Greece. The other Orthodox bishops could not attend due to advanced age, or various forms of contagious flu.

I have been invited as a guest of honor.

Patriarch Aequilaterus began his allocution with a grave tone that echoed the grave times in which we live. He stressed the crucial importance of ecumenical cooperation. He said that all Christian brothers must be united, as we are haunted by the end of times.

Patriarch Fyodor added that we live in a demon-haunted world and we must brace ourselves against the armies of evil that threaten the pale blue dot named Earth.

"But who are these armies of evil?" asked Patriarch Philipilus.

"Let's look at the map," said Patriarch Nestor. "We have the caliphate, we have North Korea, we have the industrialist unbelievers of China."

"We cannot view our Chinese brothers as members of an army of evil," said Patriarch Hieronymus. "Surely, that is not what you meant, Patriarch Nestor."

"No, it is not, yet the thirst of their rich elite is driving millions of people into suffering."

"Not to mention, our Christian brothers in Saudi Arabia are still persecuted," Patriarch Philipilus said.

"Indeed," all the Patriarchs added.

"Dear brothers," I said, "let us work together on the peace process."

"That is a wonderful summation of our preliminary conversation, Holy Father," said Patriarch Aequilaterus.

Following the serving of roasted duck with a garnish of sweet baked potatoes and red wine for desert, our conference adopted a spontaneous decision to show support for the humanitarian effort to eradicate cancer. All the Patriarchs will shave their beards, save for a moustache, whose shape, thickness, and orientation will remain at the discretion of the wearer. I, not a beard wearer by nature, will grow a moustache to fraternize in appearance with the Patriarchs. This will last for the duration of the month of November. Our respective masses in our churches will contain explanations of our appearance and encouragement for all believers to donate their surplus finances to charities supporting cancer research.

Possibly when Patriarch Pompiliu felt an abdominal cramp during the consumption of the duck, he must have thought that there is time for the walls of the digestive tract to tear, a thought that lead him to think about cancer. He told us, "There is time to sew the wounds of the poor that cannot afford doctors. Let us unite to solve one of the greatest ailments of our generation."

That was the perfect time to speak. The Patriarchs recognized the effort of many organizations to cure cancer and the specific gesture of many men of North America to grow moustaches in solidarity. We decided to break with tradition and show ourselves to be men of the people.

After the delicious meal and long conversation, it was time to keep silence, reflect, and pray.

3:8 Into the Grand Bazaar of Istanbul

I told Nwanne I have no interest in spending the rest of the afternoon in my hotel room. I wanted to mingle with the people. He did not object at all. He simply asked, "Where would you like to go?"

"The Grand Bazaar," I said.

"We must go to the hotel and change you," Nwanne said with his customary delicate care.

We went to the hotel and he changed me to look like an Ethiopian merchant. He put upon me a white linen veil that covered my head. He glued onto my face a full beard. He painted freckles on my cheeks. He thickened my eyebrows. He painted around my eyes, so I looked a much younger man. He put tiny lenses on my eyes that changed their color. I did not look like myself.

He called for a taxi at the back of the hotel. He left word at the reception that our room was not to be disturbed under any circumstances.

At the end of our journey, after we got out of the taxi, Nwanne showed me a tiny object. It looked like a pill. He called it the Blue Tooth Bud.

"It's a beeteebee," he said. "I put it in your ear. You can hear my voice in it. You can speak to me with it. In case we get lost."

The wonders of technology and the wondrous Nwanne!

The Grand Bazaar is a very large covered market. If you are not well-grounded in reality, with a good sense of orientation, you can easily get lost.

Nwanne tested the beeteebee and asked me where I wanted to go. I told him, while covering my mouth so I wouldn't look silly, that I wanted to watch people and gauge their happiness.

We entered amongst a wave of people.

Soon the crowd got thicker and I lost sight of Nwanne. "I am right behind you, Holy Father. Do not worry."

I went from shop to shop and watched the merchants interact with their customers. It was a lively atmosphere. The merchants were proud of their shops. Their enthusiasm did not waver when a new customer approached.

Then I saw a beautiful woman in a textile shop not far from me. She had a candid and calm face, white and pious. She was wearing a headscarf. She reminded me of the Mary, the mother of Jesus. I felt the urge to follow her.

As I approached the textile shop, a beggar stopped me. "Spare a dollar, boss," he said. I did not have dollars on me. I did not intend to purchase anything, as I was not able to carry anything. I apologized that I did not have any money on me. The beggar did not believe me.

"You are a foreigner," he said.

"I am," I said.

"Where are you from?"

"I am from Ethiopia."

"What are you doing in the Bazaar?"

"I came to look at textiles."

"You are looking? You are not buying?"

"I am just looking."

"You saw the beautiful lady, didn't you?"

Now I looked closer at the beggar's face. I was starting to feel uneasy. His questions were distracting. There was something puckish and impertinent about this man. His complexion was so dark that I couldn't tell his features. And he was at my feet. On his knees.

I did not want to answer him. And when he met my eyes, he immediately grabbed my garments and said confidently: "I know you!"

I widened my eyes in surprise. I said: "I am a foreigner. You cannot know me."

"But I know you," the beggar said confidently. "You are Pope Francis the Second!"

I looked deeply into the beggar's eyes and I saw insanity and deception. He was a poor man, by his appearance, but by the shadows in his eyes, he was the devil. How could he know who I was? We had not told anyone of our incognito escapade. No one could have recognized me.

"You are mistaken," I said. "The Pope does not go into a bazaar."

"But you are here!" the beggar insisted.

"Listen, dear man, I can offer you no pittance, but I beg you to leave me alone and seek your fortune elsewhere. I wish you only peace and good health."

"By God, this is exactly what Pope Francis the Second would say! You are him. I can recognize your voice!"

Nwanne had told me to mask my voice be speaking slowly and whispering. I was not supposed to engage in long conversations with anyone. I must have forgotten all this. Now I found myself recognized.

The beggar seemed ready to stand on his feet and shout his discovery aloud. He was not as crippled as I previously imagined. He tightly grabbed my garment to pull himself up. When he was on his feet and his eyes met mine, Nwanne appeared from nowhere and put himself between us with the excuse that we wanted to enter the shop. The beggar was distracted and lost his grip on me. Nwanne turned towards him and said with a happy face: "Here sir, take this dollar from me as I am a happy man. My son was born last night and I want to honor his name with charity!"

The beggar mumbled *Teşekkürler* which means "Thank you" in Turkish. When he turned back to me, I was gone.

I had not lost sight of the beautiful woman from the shop. She carried on, deep into the labyrinth of streets and shops. I kept my distance. She stopped at anther textile stand. I stopped at a tea stand across from her. She carefully perused the fabrics with her fine hand.

When I raised my head from the tea stand, I saw the beggar again in front of me.

"It's time to love her, isn't it?" he said devilishly.

I said nothing.

"And it's time to hate me, isn't it?"

I said nothing.

"Do you hate me, Your Eminence?"

There was no escape now. He could scream at any time.

"I don't hate you," I said. "You are simply mistaken. Perhaps I will turn you in to the police for pestering me."

Then he vanished like a ghost.

Nwanne whispered in the beeteebee to meet him at the marble drinking fountain. I had to let the beautiful woman disappear back into the mystery she came from.

"This a time of war," Nwanne said when we met. "I just read in a paper that Turkey is in a state of unrest. They are determined to wage war against foreign aggression."

"This is also a time of peace," I said, thinking that I probably met an angel and the devil in the Grand Bazaar of Istanbul.

3:9 The tip of the Turkish iceberg

Yuriatin Topemkin was the Russian weapon systems officer shot down by Turkish artillery over one year ago. Why? The official Turkish version was that his Sukhoi Us-42 penetrated Turkish airspace and refused to leave it after multiple warnings. The Russian version is that the Sukhoi Us-42 never left Syrian airspace, and that the incident was an egregious act of aggression. This is the fourth similar event since the 2015 shooting down of a Sukhoi Su-24, an older model of the Sukhoi Us-42. All these events happened in the same region on the map, where the shape of Turkey puts a dent into Syria, like a flaccid banana. Sure, if you want to go in a straight line from Kepir to Al-Qunaya, it's impossible not to cross a stretch of Turkish territory. A detour could mean added fuel consumption and lengthier mission time. Nobody likes a waste of fuel and especially not a waste of time.

The pilot of the aircraft was shot and killed by Syrian Turkmen with ground fire.

Yuriatin Topemkin was thought dead for a while, however no confirmation was issued, and no rescue was ever attempted. Recently he appeared on the Youtube, dressed as a Turkish peasant. In fluent Turkish, he explained that he had survived and that he adopted a rural lifestyle among the locals whom he befriended. He learned the local cuisine, the local traditions, and he prided himself on being able to make a mean Baklava, his favorite dish. He does not want to be considered a traitor, because he has not shared any military secrets with the locals, who, by the way, have no interest whatsoever in the technical specs of the Sukhoi Us-42 or the details of the Russian peacekeeping mission. By being shot down, Yuriatin Topemkin ended his military service and earned a right to a life of his choosing. He did not have a wife or children. His parents were old and suffering from the Alzheimer disease and barely remembered who Yuriatin was, let alone the fact that he flew airplanes. Thus, Yuriatin did not have any emotional or social obligations to anyone, especially Mother Russia, a Mother that he continued to respect with all his heart, and a Mother that surely did not want to limit his free will. At the end of the video, Yuriatin Topemkin said: "What profit has the soldier from that in which he labors? Is it honor? Is it glory? Gravity's rainbow has taken my airplane down. I mourned the loss of my colleague. I regretted the decision of the rebels to shoot him while he was parachuting, unable to defend himself. Since the Cyprus Peace Accords, the rebels have shown their regrets as well. There is no honor in killing defenseless soldiers. The Turks are my friends. They have adopted me and think of me as one of their own. They respect President Pushkin as well, mainly for his Bogatyn-Mudryy books. We spent many nights, by camp fires, discussing the suffering of Alyona Bogatyn-Mudryy and the machinations of Natasha Gogoleevna. We even created a play based on these characters, to be played at the Christmas fair. As you can see around me, this is a peaceful and welcoming land where I live a carefree life. Do not come for me. Do not worry for me. Live your own lives, in peace."

I prayed for Yuriatin Topemkin today.

3:10 Raining with stars in Sudan

A week later, we crossed the border into war-torn Sudan, against the flow of refugees. It was during the second civil war, when Omar Al-Bashir had come to power after a successful military coup. When the border guard saw our passports and heard our reasons for entering Sudan he scoffed and uttered loudly and rhetorically:

"Good luck if you want to leave the country alive!"

He must have thought we were crazy.

"You want to help the war-wounded and the hungry? Ha, ha, you are out of your minds! The Americans don't give a damn, and you think you can get to them?!"

I said we would take our chances. He left us alone, shaking his head.

"What do we do now, Enyi?" Nwanne asked me.

"We just carry on. Do we fear death?"

"No."

"So be it. If we don't do what we are meant to do, what else is there to live for?"

"That sounds like fatalism."

"Does it, Nwanne? I'm not sure. I prefer not to think about that. I don't want to turn into a philosopher. I just want to do something in this world, but not God-given tasks with which the sons of men are to be occupied."

"Me too, Enyi, me too. I'm just worried that we aren't doing the right thing. I wonder if our journey is futile. I fear that our deeds will not matter in the end."

"Do you live for rewards or to be remembered?"

"I want to know that we did a good thing. I want to hear it from those whom we help. If they are silent or if we are forgotten, I cannot help feeling that all of this was in vain."

"Your heart will tell you that it was not in vain."

"The heart can be deceitful."

"Have faith, Nwanne. Have faith."

We travelled with a group of volunteers from the Red Cross. They were heading South. That is where most of the atrocities were happening. A former lawyer, now a peace activist, told us the complicated history of Sudan. There were close to 600 tribes in Sudan, that spoke over 130 languages. 70 percent of the people practiced Sunni Islam, 20 percent were Christians, and the remaining 10 percent belonged to traditional tribal religions. The period of joint Anglo-Egyptian rule (known as the condominium), that began in 1898 and ended in 1956, kept a tight administration of Sudan though a scheme of indirect rule, by forging alliances with tribal chiefs, sheiks, and clan elders. This allowed the British and the Egyptians to exert authority with minimal presence, unlike in the rest of the British Empire. Moreover, the Arabs considered the African Black population of the South as a God-given source of slaves. A mentality that continued and spawned the civil wars. Ask an Arab leader in the North that served under Omar Al-Bashir, and he would say that he had seen the God-given task with which the sons of men are to be occupied, that legitimizes the military incursions, as they are meant only to defend the faith and strengthen the country against godless rebels.

We didn't care about politics, the Arab rule, or wars in the name of God, whatever his name was. Nwanne and I recognized suffering, and that is all we cared about. We had to help those people. They shared our skin color and our faith, but this was not the reason. They were bleeding and they were aching.

The Red Cross took us on winding roads towards the South. We didn't hear gunfights.

When we approached the line, that decades later would become the border between two Sudans, we saw the devastation.

There were no painted birds, nor carcasses of wild animals left partly unconsumed by predators, nor rivers of blood. There was just destruction and shattered beings. Martin Luther said that man is like divine excrement: we aspire to be god-like, we rise only to appear as what God would discard as the refuse of creation. Is man not part of this filthy creation as well? One has to ask this question.

3:11 You have to believe it to see it:

a conversation about emptiness

I had a very interesting conversation, by hologram, with Mr. Stayingzento (Dalai Lama 15), about the spiritual crisis of the world; his opinion being that we are on the verge of a spiritual revolution, which is the underlying cause of the armed conflicts.

"Your Holiness," he said, "I am calling you with a tremor in my heart and deep worry for humanity. I have always felt, since you became the new Pope, that you are a great spirit and that you possess the proper determination."

"Thank you, Your Holiness, I feel the same about you."

"I would like to talk to you today about emptiness. We, Buddhists, call it *sunyata*. The objects in our physical reality do not have built-in and independent existence. They are essentially empty. The meaning we attach to them, such as shapes, colors, weights, structures and so on, originates in the activity of our minds. Thus, the world is a mere projection of the works of our minds, and nothing more, since, independently of our minds we cannot fully verify the true nature of reality. You may say that scientific apparatuses have measured many properties of the physical world, by the well employed scientific method, however, these results, regardless of their reproducibility and falsifiability, cannot have a value of truth, with our minds being present to attribute such value, to verbalize it, explain it, turn it into stories, to interpret it and use it to improve our lives. See, your Holiness, as John Milton wrote in Paradise Lost, the mind *can make a heaven of hell or a hell of heaven*. From these thoughts and beliefs, I came to realize that the world cannot escape this swirl of conflict without the realization not just of this emptiness, but of the fact that we humans share the same condition, within the boundaries of planet Earth. We must define a unifying and common denominator, a strong abstract bond for all mankind, if we want to survive the doom."

Powerful words.

While he was talking, I was attempting to fabricate a philosophical escape from the pliers of the doctrine of emptiness. I often felt the same futility in my relation to the world. Often, I felt dreamless sleep is indistinguishable from death, as all awareness of the world is severed. In dreamless sleep our existence is suspended. As if we become unborn, returned to the womb. We become a shell of meat without thoughts.

"Your Holiness," I said, "our Messiah has made everything beautiful in its time. He has also put eternity in people's hearts."

"Except that no one can observe the work that God does from beginning to end," Stayingzento said.

"True. However, the core of our very existence is to have faith in God's work and improve our knowledge of it, admitting that perfection will always be outside our reach."

"Indeed, Your Holiness."

There was a pause. Stayingzento seemed to rephrase an elaborate idea in his mind. His pursed lips suggested that he did not want to offend me. In the fullsize hologram I could clearly see how he dimmed his eyes and inhaled deeply. I, too, realized we came to the inevitable antagonism between our faiths: they say man can become God-like; we say we are created in the image of God, but we will never become God. But this is not what our conversation was about.

"Your Holiness," I said. "I too am very concerned about the world. In your opinion, how can we find this common ground? How can we triumph over divergences?"

"I think we have lost the joy of life. Joy is the celebration of life, through acceptance of the imperfections of our bodies, the randomness of chance, and the finiteness of life, while overcoming the destructive urges that place us against nature, in a causal self-perpetuating vortex."

"So, joy is accepting this emptiness?" I asked.

"Yes."

"But my body wants to feel things," I said. "My mind wants to believe in things. The emotions that come from my mind are real - they transform my body, my thoughts."

"Indeed, Your Holiness. Our rapport with the world is often through uncontrollable means: our emotions, another variant of emptiness. Don't you sense that, often, these emotions seem to come from somewhere outside you, hinting to the possibility that a much wider world exists? Was this not the message of Christ, that the kingdom of God is unimaginably richer than our earthly domain?"

"Precisely," I said.

"This is our common ground. The realization that we all possess a spirituality capable of grasping the parameters of the world that are not accessible to our senses. I am also referring to the philosophical extensions that become available to us only by employing reason. Only through these philosophical extensions did we create the concepts of freedom, beauty, happiness, prosperity, and peace. For all these, we struggled for millennia. It would be a pity to give up on them now."

The hologram flickered. We were both advised to give it a moment, as it might create a duplicate-effect, a common error of this new technology, where the holoprojector creates two projections of the same person, delayed in time and slightly superimposed, through a feedback loop. We stayed still and waited. When the communication was restored, Stayingzento said with the same warmth and passion:

"Your Holiness, let us create a Spiritual Council of Humanity. An organization for the spiritual unity of all people of Earth. A voice that builds on the positive and peaceful traditions of all religions and spiritual movements, and whose mission is to guide mankind in the dialogue of life."

"I like the idea, Your Holiness!" I said enthusiastically. "I will talk to the Curia, to the Orthodox Patriarchs, to everyone I know, and we will make this happen! Let us coordinate further."

"Fantastic!"

What a privilege is to be Pope!

3:12 Bathing with the master

In the South of Sudan, in those days, there were rumors that a naked hermit was baptizing Christians in the waters of a river, in a hidden place far from the eyes of the Janjaweed militia. We were not the first missionaries to arrive there, and our presence was scarcely noted as a novelty.

The baptizing was taking place entirely after sunset, under clear sky and moonlight. The naked hermit, whom people called the Master, chanted for an hour before he accepted the flocks of wannabe Christians. He was a very simple man and never wore clothes over his body. People thought he was crazy, but he always behaved piously. He began his chants with this verse: *I was born in flesh and skin, I will remain in flesh and skin*. Then he proceeded to sing about the virtues of faith and the suffering of Christ.

The tribes of South Sudan had been believing in one Supreme being before Christians came, and this prepared them for the news brought by Messiah. And when they came, the missionaries were kind and instituted medical care for the tribes. Kindness always molded the path to persuasion more effectively than war. When the tribes heard the story of the martyred prophet, sentenced by hated conquerors and executed by crucifixion, only to rise triumphantly from the dead, they found themselves redeemed, as they too suffered from the slave trade and wars of conquest. And the most tragic reason for the tribes to come to Christ was the fact that they were brutalized by the Arabs, who took the tribes into slavery while also pursuing their Islamisation. This pitted the tribes against the Islamic faith, and opened their hearts to Christianity. Needless to say, had the Arabs respected the culture of the tribes and treated them well, they might have succeeded in spreading their faith as well.

The Master was sitting in the middle of the shallow river and was washing his body. Nwanne was first to see his nakedness. I tried to look away, but soon I couldn't resist, as the moonlight was descending in front of the Master and drawing our eyes inexorably towards him.

A stranger came to me and whispered into my ear:

"I know that nothing is better for them than to rejoice, and to do good in their lives."

I turned and saw a peasant soaked wet as he had just been baptized. His face radiated joy and luminous peace. I understood then the power of faith. Those many people came there to bathe with the Master, to be reborn, to feel human again, by the effect of their restored dignity and hope.

It is then that I saw the absolute necessity of faith for those who have lost all hope, those who have been hunted and ostracized, those who have been stripped of their right to live peacefully and freely. "From whence comes this right?", someone might ask, feigning ignorance of the decrees of God. Let me say presumably that I abandon the necessity of God. I can still find a reason for wanting to carry life forward, as it is built into the very seed of life, and cannot be willingly extirpated by anyone, save for situations of self-sacrifice and bravery, leaving all of us, rich or poor, healthy or ill, powerful or powerless, with the drive to live.

Perhaps this is why God created us first, and then, sometime later gave us faith through Christ…

Nwanne and I stood in the queue of people, trudging our feet slowly through the river. When I came face to face with the Master, his male organ was elevated, by the rules of the body. He looked me in the eyes, and said:

"You are not a man like everybody else. You love him and he loves you," while flinging his finger at Nwanne. "Come on, there is no shame in this! Any confessed love is welcome in the eyes of God."

I simply couldn't hide my shame, and I kept telling myself in my mind that *Christ was also a man, Christ was also a man, his male organ must have been elevated as well at some point,* while begging for forgiveness for my unruly impiety.

The Master was smiling and insisting that there is no reason for my shame. He said:

"All these people came here to bathe with the Master, as Christ bathed with John the Baptist."

The naked master was right. This erased my shame, and I accepted the bath with gratitude.

After we dried off, Nwanne and I continued our journey further south.

3:13 The revolutions of the ordinary days

How can one live one's life, if not in a constant state of revolution? We are not born with the destiny of complacency and the sensibility of futility. We are not creatures of innate pernicious selfishness, we are not set upon the course of a banal life by any outside force. We are the makers of our days, the makers of our memories, the creators of hopes, the measurers of time.

Since President Sanbard Renders signed Universal Basic Income into law, the soul of the idea of revolution has changed in such a way, one cannot find a corner of American society that has remained in silence and rest. His fight was fierce and his enemies ruthless. The whole world watched in awe as the Grand American Revolution was unfolding under our eyes. If that can happen in America, there is true hope for mankind, many said. Lo and behold, it has happened now, and only God Almighty has the power to foresee the future.

…and I pondered for many days and weeks whether this was the doing of God, as the great majority of those who opposed President Renders were the most fervent believers, the most unshaken in their faith, the most ardent in the recitation of the doctrine, the loudest and the most vindictive.

And when their President said in their Congress:

"And also, that every man should eat and drink and enjoy the good of all his labor – it is the gift of God," they proclaimed against him: "No, we must not indulge the sinners and the slackers!" forgetting that President Renders was speaking their language, to sensitize them, to appeal to their deepest feelings, which they claimed were in the spirit of Christ.

What spirit is that? When in proclamations they are utterly against the modesty inspired by our faith, distorting and contorting everything that the Church supposedly taught them. I have strong doubts that their Churches, whether aligned or not with the Holy See, are nothing but self-aggrandizing business endeavors of their respective builders.

Here, now, I see myself taking the words *builders* in vain, and attribute it to men not worthy of our faith! That's a pity.

So when President Renders called himself my greatest supporter, he had little inkling that I considered myself his greatest supporter and admirer, even though I suspect, in my most intimate thoughts and intuitions, that the President is not truly a man of faith, as he infrequently declares, obviously constrained by circumstances and by the large expectations of the American public.

While, at the same time, a large number of believers endorsed the revolution inspired by President Renders, saying that the universal guaranteed income will free the spirit of inventors and creators, which will not be oppressed by the need to earn a living from jobs that do not inspire them. How about the entrepreneurs? What will motivate them? Will they not be tempted to idle? No. I know it, and they know it too. The motivation will be to improve the material existence of the entire society, for which they will earn their profits, certainly, but they will not be profits of greed, but profits of honor, as the work of anyone will be appreciated as a manifestation of dignity and honor. Idleness will carry the stigma of shame. And that will be its sanction.

We are revolutionaries... peaceful, loving, interconnected creatures.

...and this gives me a lot to think about.

3:14 Annoyed by Cardinal Tchipcherish

Not in stark contrast with President Renders, but abrupt antithetic tone, is my Cardinal Thorsen Tchipcherish. He presented himself in an audience today and reiterated his insolent idea about the abolition of the Papacy, now appended with a fundamental crucial reform of the entire Mother Church.

I made a wry face.

"Please hear me, Holy Father."

He is the Prefect of the Congregation for the Doctrine of the Faith after all.

"Holy Father," he said, "I come from a position of well-tempered, calculated, pious, and troubled pragmatism. I am The Prefect of the Congregation for the Doctrine of the Faith, after all, and my assignment is to ensure the preservation of the strength of our faith - its continuing mission, to explore the richness of the legacy of Christ, to seek out new ways of approaching the Creator, to boldly sow the seeds of truth where no one had sowed them before. I know that whatever God does, it shall be forever. This is the core of our faith. It's undisputable. And I feel that the growing complexity of the world is pushing us away from this truth, and the secular cohorts, the political agitations, the economic concerns of the people, have made us all quite foreign to the truth out there. People are simply forgetting, by an alarming rate, that there is something higher than the material world, that there is something well beyond our comprehension, and they misplace these thoughts with the thoughts of their immediate existence. They really care for what tomorrow brings more than they care for the Judgment Day. I know that you align yourself with your predecessors in declaiming that there is no actual hell, or heaven, or Judgment Day for that matter. So you may call me a traditionalist, I do not deny that, in fact I take pride in it and I carry it as the cross of my salvation. Perhaps it is the *true* cross of my salvation, who can tell, who knows for real? Nobody knows for real, Holy Father, let's be honest here, and pardon my insolence, I come with the humblest intentions. The entire world is in profound turmoil, we all see it, we are on the crest of a fantastic revolution, of which we can hardly make sense, perhaps we will never make sense, and perhaps even future historians will scratch their heads in consternation asking themselves what happened in the 21st century. All of this imposes a heavy burden on my heart, and despite my extensive theological studies, of which you Your Holiness are aware, I cannot find an inspired answer that could guide me into the right direction.

I am trying as hard as I can to be less verbose. Forgive me.

Neither still in my prayers have I found answers as to the position of our faith in the light of this revolution. Pilgrims flock less and less to the shrines of Fatima Our Lady of the Rosary, Our Lady of Lourdes, Our Lady of La Salette, Our Lady of Happy Meetings of Laus, Our Lady of the Miraculous Medal of Paris, Our Lady of Zion, the Virgin with the Golden Heart of Beauraing, the Virgin of the Poor of Banneux, Our Lady of Knock, Our Lady Help of Christians in Filppsdorf, Our Lady of Gietrzwald, Our Lady of Siluva, Our Lady of Lezajsk, and let us not forget Our Lady of Guadelupe in Mexico City, Our Lady of Superb Success of Quito, the Mother of the Word of Kibeho in Rwanda, and last but certainly not least Our Lady of Zaytun, how can we ignore or forget her? Pilgrims flock more and more to new shrines, many of which we cannot recognize or approve in accordance to the guidelines of our faith, which I found very troublesome, as they impinge on the authority of the Holy See over the administration of the books of saints, meaning that our faith is even more susceptible to detraction and defamation.

The incorruptibility of faith is absolute. Nothing can be added to it, and nothing taken from it. God does it, that men should fear before Him.

Thus, when I speak of the abolishment of the Papacy, pardon my insistence, I speak of a transformation that will answer the concerns of today's society. I mean that if we decentralize, if we depoliticize, if we loosen the tight grip of the doctrine, if we reform, rename, and remake ourselves, we will carry a chance of saving Mother Church, and the Holy See for that matter, and present ourselves as a new institution of charity, social communion, and moral reflection. We keep Christ, we keep Virgin Mary, but we drop the immaculate conception, we let women become Bishops and Cardinals, we drop the Trinity, we drop Heaven, Hell, Judgment Day, Angels, Seraphim, and Cherubim, and we simply come forth as a Church of everyday concrete charity and bonding, without borders and without miracles. How does this sound?"

"Cardinal," I said. "I am left speechless."

My arrhythmia was also acting up again.

I dismissed Cardinal Tchipcherish without further dialogue. There is only so much annoyance I can bear. Ah! And the pain in my chest and the disturbance in my stomach. Had I not eaten just before!?

While my blood was boiling, hearing the Cardinal, I could not sense insanity in his words and demeanor…

…and this gives me a lot to think about.

3:15 Of shame and its acceptance

In the past few days I have been feeling a tad apprehensive, since my medical check-up was due. And when I say medical check-up, I mean testicular examination.

Dr. Thaddeus Zhivago, my personal physician, reminds me of my Mama, because of his ability to sense my distress in the face of shame. Whenever Mama was knocking on the bathroom door, my heart started to pump, I felt hot in my stomach and couldn't find words, except for a squeak of panic, like a mouse cornered by a mischievous cat; oh God, I dislike cats so much! Ugh, I can't even begin to describe my displeasure, yet cats are creatures of God too, which is even more frustrating. Same with Dr. Zhivago, when he comes to my apartment with his leather bag I feel a heatwave rushing through my body, yet I have since learned to refrain from emitting mouse-sounds along with regular words. I gulp saliva profusely, though with discretion, and exercise breathing accordingly.

Dr. Zhivago gladly accepts jokes about his name. He offered to be nicknamed Boris, for the obvious reason. I politely declined, knowing that his humorous self-deprecating attitude was entirely for my benefit, as he is well aware of my psychological discomfort vis-à-vis medical checkups, especially those involving Adamic exposure.

The doctor acted professionally as always, he put on surgical gloves, chatted a bit before the examination, mostly about the recent developments in medical research, such as a procedure to create neurons form stem cells, which, in addition to gene therapy is very close to curing Alzheimer's disease and some other neuronal diseases, which I cannot remember right now. Suddenly, he grabbed my masculine bunch while maintaining eye contact.

He said, "that which is, has already been, and that which is to be has already been," referring obviously and indirectly to the construction of the human body. Hearing these words relaxed me.

After he concluded the verification and assured me that there are no signs of cancer, he accepted my blessing and left.

Now that I have habituated myself with the roles and roster of this office, I should better control my organic reactions of shame, shouldn't I? I don't find that my bursts of shame affect my judgments in any way, I think? No, I'm sure of it.

God requires an account of what is past, whether we remember our deeds or not, which makes me wonder if our culpability is diminished simply because we cannot remember it. Thus, I think that the persistence of shame, at least in my case, is a blessing for me, since it reminds me to remain humble and refrain from acts of vanity. So be it! Let me feel heat in my stomach and let my heart throb! I accept my condition, and I will accept the tremors next time Dr. Zhivago pays me a visit.

3:16 Chinese battleships vs stranded penguins

It is strange how the Chinese battleships have emerged from the Amur river into the Sea of Okhotsk, keeping close to the Russian shore, appearing to navigate in a parallel line with the land, all around the Sea towards the North. How long will they keep this maneuver, I do not know, as it is obvious from the maps that they can meet nothing but a dead-end. For days the battleships slowly followed the contour of the Sea until they met the full body of the Kamchatka Peninsula, and that's when they stopped. Some peasants from the shore posted a couple of photos on their respective social media profiles.

At the same time, at the Great Fair of Books and Culture in Beijing, President Mo Xi was launching his first book, titled simply *The Red Notebook*. This was an extraordinary event, given the popularity of President Xi worldwide. His affability was now paralleled by an extraordinary public relations campaign for the promotion of his book, which comes at a tense time, keeping in mind the large scale peace mission in North Korea, a communist country *par excellence*. Many commentators have called *The Red Notebook* an anti-Maoist communist manifesto with a strong new revolutionary flavor. President Xi actually introduced the philosophy of the new revolution in *The Red Notebook*, which attempts to reform the Chinese communist philosophy from the perspective of the *bottleneck of ages*.

What is the *bottleneck of ages?*

Well, as President Mo Xi explains, in his words: "We might say that we arrived at the end of history, as we know it, for the following reasons: population growth, climate change, and ideological social clashes. I call this the *bottleneck of ages*. If we don't change our ways, DRASTICALLY, we are going to overflow the bottle into perdition!"

The new revolution, of which President Xi writes with passion, is echoed by the voices of many other visionaries, whether they hold political office or not. I think they are all right. I watched the folly of men reach new heights of evil during my lifetime, and now we have these new problems that added new tensions. Moreover, I see under the sun: in the place of judgment, wickedness is there, and in the place of righteousness, iniquity is there. I have also seen how many times wickedness wears the clothes of justice and marches triumphantly under the ignorant applause of the masses.

The battleships travelled south along the Kamchatka Peninsula and then out into the Pacific. Not long afterwards, their heading changed North, they encountered sparse islets of icebergs that were travelling on a cold current. For a fleet of steel machines, a few blocks of ice should not pose a problem. The battleships continued unperturbed towards the North.

How do we know this? Who was the keen eye that observed these naval movements and reported them to the international press, accompanied by photographs? How can the angle of the pictures be explained, since it clearly showed a convoy of many battleships, so long they could not be entirely contained within the frame that had a wide angle to begin with?

Soon we learned that the source of the report and the pictures was a small crew of green activists that were monitoring the migration of ice and penguins across the North Pacific currents. The climax of this report was that the Chinese fleet of battleships suddenly came to a complete halt when they encountered a larger iceberg. It was not the size of the iceberg that determined the Admiral-in-charge to order Halt, it was the fact that the iceberg was inhabited by people and penguins, and while the penguins had crowded into one corner of the iceberg, the people had camped in the other corner, for the simple reason of not scaring the adorable aquatic birds. Men and penguins were floating on the ocean.

When meeting the Chinese armada, the people displayed a large banner, on the side of the iceberg facing the ships. The banner said: "We are penguins. Did you come here to save us?" It seemed to be a sign made ad-hoc, on a pre-used roll of frost-resistant light white material, written with a thick brush or marker of some sort.

The picture of the banner hanging on the iceberg, and the armada facing them, has made the front page of the National Geographic magazine.

The Chinese government quickly issued a statement: "We wholeheartedly support the activity of green activists, we are travelling through international waters in peace, we offered the people stranded on the iceberg all our support." And the media, the social media, the world at large, accepted these words, as other concerns probably quickly overtook the minds of the people.

By the end of the week the Chinese fleet will enter Bering Sea, and then it will be closer than ever to the United States of America. I know, I have no reason to worry, and yet…

3:17 Nwanne's wet dreams

Nwanne has just brought a cup of tea, and he insisted that I drink it.

"It has the touch of angels," he said, promoting the tea with heartfelt conviction.

He had something on his mind, and I could easily tell that he was burning to talk to me about it.

"What is it, Nwanne? You can talk to me."

"Forgive me, Holy Father. Sometimes I forget you are the Pope, and I can barely contain the urge to speak my heart."

"You know you can talk me, anytime, about anything. I am more than your confessor. We are friends, Nwanne."

"I know."

"Talk to me."

While I sipped my tea, he spoke.

"I said in my heart," he said, "God shall judge the righteous and the wicked. God shall appreciate the good-hearted, the good intentions, the good thoughts, and He will punish the evil-doers and the evil-thinkers. But I do not know what God shall do where my soul is tormented by the ghost of strange dreams that come to me without my power, leaving me writhing in agony, in puddles of sweat, at the earliest hours of the day, before the sun has shined its first light. These dreams, Holy Father, they cut my breath and agitate my heart. They bring me questions that I cannot answer, that linger in my thoughts for many days.

In my dreams, I see the children we have met in our travels. I run to them. I want to hug them. And when I am about to grab them in my arms, they pop just like a balloon, they disappear into thin air, as if they were hollow, as if their skin was made of vanishing colors, as if they had no substance.

Then this fear grows in me, that if I touch anything else, I myself will pop right into nothingness, and there will be no trace of my life, and no echoes for my voice.

I travel in my dreams to the Basilica of Saint Peter, where more children welcome me with hands stretched out to meet me. They are smiling. They are happy. They are poor. And I remember the other vanished children, so yet again I am afraid to touch them. So I decide instead to drop a fresh and sweet clementine into their hands. When the fruit is about to touch the palms of the first child, it goes right through his body, and falls to the floor, and the child pops - poof! - like a balloon, and there is nothing left of him. I look around, and see many other children receiving clementines from others priests without vanishing.

And I meet you, Holy Father, in my dreams, and I am afraid to shake your hand or lay your garments over your shoulders, because I think you are going to vanish too.

I turn to my rosary and try to pray. I pop each marble into thin air. One by one.

I looked up at Christ on the cross and I try to pray with eyes closed. When I open my eyes again, Christ has vanished. There was an empty cross in front of me, with nails sticking out from the places where His hands and feet once were.

The dreams took me outside, on a sunny day, and I looked up at the sun, for there is the certainty of time in its rigorous positions in the sky, and this certainty works for every purpose and for every work. I thought, what if I blinked and the sun disappeared? I would be responsible for an eternity of darkness for all creatures.

I tried to keep my eyes open and I couldn't. I fell asleep in my dreams and I woke up in my real life. I grabbed the rosary from the nightstand and it stayed real. Immediately I had a revelation. That all the children I had dreamed about were angels, and that I had banished them away from me.

I have carried that fear with me in my waking hours since then."

3:18 Hollowness lances at me from the Amazon River

I saw on the television that there is a military crisis of some sort in the Amazon River. My media secretary told me that an activist filmed a scene with an amateur 3D camera. The footage has reached one hundred million views on the Youtube. It is a scene of unusual and harsh confrontation between the Brazilian army and a convoy of mercenaries. I put on the hologlasses and I watched it. It was a nightmare!

It opens with a wide angle, shot from a treetop, of three large cargo ships navigating the Amazon River. The convoy is flanked by smaller armed ships, carrying both long-range and short-range guns, high caliber machine-guns, and personnel in military gear. The video zooms in on the personnel and we clearly see the logo of Blackadler Inc., the infamous private security company. Then it zooms out right when a helicopter bearing the same logo flies over the treetops, almost knocking the cameraman down. The cameraman drops the camera to the ground, where it's picked up by a collaborator. We can hear a man shouting: "I dropped the camera, I dropped the camera! Take it and carry on!" The video keeps rolling while the new cameraman takes the camera to the riverbank to see the convoy approaching.

From the opposite direction, we see a Brazilian battle cruiser accompanied by a flotilla of smaller ships, all armed.

Within a minute, the two sides come to a complete standstill.

"Oh my!" the cameraman screams. "They are going to war!"

We hear rustlings in the forest, growing quickly into thudding, shouting, and heavy machinery moving.

"Over there, to your right!" the man on the treetop shouts.

The image turns towards the noise, and we see vegetation falling to the ground, a path opening in the wake of an advancing military convoy. We soon realize this is the ground support for the cargo ships.

The cameraman moves in closer.

We see a group of tribesmen and activists in a line facing the advancing troops. They carry signs saying Over Our Dead Bodies, This Is It, and We Are Amazon. They force the troops into a standstill.

Loudspeakers are brought out on both sides.

"You will not steal our forest!" "Please move away!" "You are criminals!" "We have a legal right to export this wood!" "You do not!" "Yes we do!" "Over our dead bodies!" "Do not make us remove you by force!" "You destroy us but you cannot shut up the world!"

Then we hear machinegun bullets shot in the air from an off-screen source.

As the cameraman moves in closer to the scene, we hear the ground shaking. We are right in the middle of the confrontation.

A delegation from the mercenaries steps forward. And now the horror! In the middle of them I see a man wearing a black amaranth-piped cassock with a pellegrina, a purple fascia, and a gold gilt pectoral cross. I screamed No! I wanted to take off the hologlasses, but I forced myself to see the scene to the end.

Who was that man? I did not know. He surely seemed a man of Our Mother Church.

He raises a loudspeaker: "I am father João Rodrigues. I come in peace. We all come in peace. We are helping you move this old wood off these lands, and plant food instead. We are here to help a hungry world."

From the line of activists another man in a black cassock appears. In lieu of buttons, he has a fly fastened with hooks at the collar and bound at the waist with a cincture knotted on the right side.

"I am father João Borges. You are a charlatan! You are a criminal!"

To be honest, I felt good hearing those words. The scene was so real! It felt like I was right there, in the middle of it.

The two fathers spoke over each other: "I am not a charlatan, you are a charlatan. You do not respect the law!" "You have no right to be here. No right! This is sacred land. We will defend it with our souls and bodies." "In the name of Christ, you do not have to sacrifice yourselves here!" "Don't talk to me about Christ. You are a charlatan! Who are you anyway? I don't know any Father João Rodrigues. You stole that name! You disgrace Our Mother Church." "Please don't make this difficult."

More shouts and agitation as the Blackadler ground troops begin advancing. People start screaming.

"Hey, you! Stop filming!" we hear an off-screen voice.

We hear a gunshot. The camera falls on the ground.

More screams. Somebody picks up the camera, and runs away with it for a while.

Then the video ends.

I took off the hologlasses. I was in shock. I sighed and said out loud to those around me: "My friends, I say in my heart concerning the condition of the sons of men, God tests them, that they may see that they themselves are like animals."

On TV, Margarita Bourbon-Renege, the President of Brazil, is issuing a statement: "We are at war with Worldsanto Inc. and Blackadler Inc."

3:19 The biggest question of them all comes from a little girl

...it may be Nwanne's dreams and fears, or the hollowness in my heart, I do not know, and I cannot put it aside. I cannot find rest and peace in my own skin. My thoughts are getting ahead of me and my will and faith cannot keep up. Heatwaves and chills pound me unexpectedly. I need to get out into the world of people. I need to see the face of believers, the image of God on their faces. I want them to tell me that they feel God, I want them to remind me what the feeling of God in their hearts is like, that soothing velvety warm feeling. That calming thought that someone is out there, watching, caring, relieving the burden of loss, explaining the necessity of suffering, really explaining and not just hulahooping the name of Christ and our original sin. I truly want to hear this voice of God mirrored in the self-assured calmness on people's faces.

Look at me, writing nonsense to myself, words that would have appeared blasphemy to my predecessors. I think these words with the full faculties of my mind intact, with full awareness.

I am on pastoral a visit to the City of Zagreb. I have met many courteous people and a large welcoming crowd. I was honored at a state dinner, and I have heard only laudatory words vis-à-vis our Papacy. I have asked our honored hosts what is the refugee situation in Croatia. "It is perfectly under control, Your Holiness," they said leaving no room for disbelief.

The next morning, I had a couple of hours for myself, to rest and to receive private audiences. On the visitor list I saw a group of schoolchildren. "They are all refugee children," Nwanne said. I asked Nwanne to send them in first.

They were nicely dressed and well behaved. They brought me a present: a basket with vegetables from the school garden. They were so excited to see me that they forgot to stand in line. Their teacher fretted around them, very embarrassed that she had lost control.

In the middle of the group I saw a little Syrian girl with long hair, freckles on her cheeks, and wide candid eyes. She was calm, in contrast with her colleagues. She did not push forward towards me. In her eyes there was a fire burning. I could tell she came here with something really important to ask me. As my gaze met hers, she became so nervous that I feared she would faint. The struggle within her was keeping her standing. Hoping that she would accomplish her mission, I smiled at her and waved gently for her to come forward.

"What is your name?" I asked.

"My name is Amira."

Before I could draw another breath, she asked:

"Why did God allow my brother to drown in the sea?"

That was the burning question she wanted to ask me. Bless her heart. She looked so innocent, so naïve. As I took a moment to find my words, I could not escape her eyes locked onto my face, as if her life depended on what I would answer.

There was nothing wise I could tell her. Immediately I felt that if I answered with established formulae like "We don't know the mind of God" or "Through suffering we find salvation" or "The innocent always go to heaven", I would betray her expectations, I would tell her a lie, even though in my heart I knew of nothing else to say in line with my faith and echoing the teachings of Christ.

"You deserve the truth, Amira," I said. "I do not know why your brother's life was taken away. For what happens to the sons of men also happens to animals. One thing befalls them: as one dies, so dies another. Surely, they all have one breath. Man has no advantage over animals. For all is vanity. When we lose a loved one, for reasons we will never understand, we ought to honor them by living a just life, honoring their name, and helping others overcome suffering. This is the only true meaning we can give for the unjust departure of your little brother."

When I finished these words I was a changed man. I did not realize it then, but I feel it fully now. Amira understood what I said. She shed a tear and found her inner peace.

The children left. I asked to remain alone for a while. When the room was empty, there was a void in me, and around me. There was no God left, no Christ, no glimpse of salvation. I was by myself, completely by myself. Faith had left me.

3:20 All are from dust, and all return to dust

Memories of our time in East Africa rush at me with the force of all Crusades put together.

We had heard rumors, Nwanne and I, that there was a humanitarian crisis of an unknown nature. We immediately thought that we could be of some help.

As soon as we crossed the border, our guide gave us fake identification with Rwandan names, and he insisted that we declare ourselves Hutu, "No matter what, do you understand me?" he said.

Our guide called himself Mr. John. He said he did not understand why we wanted to put our lives in danger. However, since we insisted, he could take us where we were needed the most, in deserted villages where many people fell victim to the civil war.

So we went to the first village on an absolutely magnificent day. As we approached the village, the gentle breeze waned away and was replaced by the pungent smell of rotting corpses. I was not prepared for this, so I stopped for a few moments and regurgitated my breakfast. "You'll get used to it, Father," Mr. John said.

Then we saw the tragedy.

A little boy was crouching on the ground, in the mud. He was staring through us, towards the void of the horizon. He was skinny and severely malnourished. We approached him and covered him with our shadows. He blinked once, stood up, and turned around. He did not acknowledge us in any way. He just reacted to us blocking the sunlight that was bathing his face. He walked slowly, trudging his feet towards a house across the street. The door of the house had a very high threshold, so it seemed from far away. The boy climbed over it with some difficulty, stirring a swarm of flies in the process. As we approached the house, we realized the threshold was the body of a man in an advanced state of decomposition. He must have been dead for some weeks.

We stepped over the body in horror and we were immediately stormed by a cloud of flies that sought to enter our noses and mouths. Before we could see anything in the dark interior, we inhaled the stench. Our vision adjusted shortly and we saw a communal bedroom and another space that served as a kitchen and living room. Two rough windows had been cut into the mud-and-stick wall. On the ground there were more decayed bodies: a man, a woman, two children. Their porcelain white bones were poking through the remains of paper-thin skin that was flaking off. The little boy crouched near the remains of his mother and was sucking his thumb, still looking deeply through us, into the void of the horizon.

Nwanne carried the boy outside and sat him down.

I kneeled next to him and washed his feet. I tried to feed him water, straight from my bottle. The boy blinked, but did not acknowledge the bottle. I could tell by his cracked lips that he was severely dehydrated.

I mumbled a prayer and Nwanne joined me. Mr. John stood near us, scouting the surroundings. He let us finish. "There's nothing more you can do here," he said.

The boy looked up at us, blinked again, then he closed his eyes for good. We settled him on the ground, as there was nothing else we could do.

All go to one place.

All are from dust.

And all return to dust.

3:21 Loud cries for Christ, faith in shambles

Oh no, again this hollowness! I have lost the warmth of faith in my heart. The voice of God has completely disappeared. I cannot find him anywhere! He is gone. Gone in darkness. I uttered the words of prayer loudly, I clenched my fists, I pierced the flesh with my fingernails, I read the psalms over again, from early in the morning until the sun had risen, and no shadow of comfort had descended upon me, no reassurance from the Heavens that my faith is restored. These thoughts of pestilence, of bodies washed from the ocean on the beaches of Europe, the voice of Amira unbearably loud and uncomfortably close, repeating over and over again, Why did God allow my brother to drown in the sea? Why? Why? Why! Pounding my ears like an indestructible, relentless hammer. And my confidence gone, completely gone, with nothing left but the thoughts, Where is God?, Where is Christ?, why don't they just say something? While my weaker thoughts attempt to answer, But it's in the Holy Book, it is your life's work to deal with the question of suffering and death in the world, it is precisely Christ's mission, the very reason he came down to Earth, to answer these questions! Then the weaker thoughts pale in submission to the hammering thunders, But why an innocent child?, How does the death of an innocent child teach us anything?, and needles burrowing deep into my mind, hunting for all slivers of faith, plucking them out, one by one.

What if it's all a lie? Life is truly nothing but vanity. Our doings are nothing but concoctions of our minds and the forceful voices of our ancestors. What if we live a story made true by the strong wishful hopes, abnegations, and ignorance of our ancient forefathers?

Oh, truly I have gone insane, and hell awaits me! But what hell?! What other devious invention is hell? A masterful lie to keep the unruly masses in obedience? A lowly dogma to create morality? And what about the glorious heaven? A future of eternal bliss? But what is bliss if not punctuated by the passing of time? How can bliss be eternal, when it's only a product of our struggles with the world? For the first time in my life, I am frightened by the thought of eternity.

In my prayers today I begged Christ to tell me if he recognizes the spirit of the sons of men, which goes upward. And he said nothing. Nothing! He said nothing because I feel he is not there. I saw with the eyes of my mind a skeleton scattered in the sands of Israel of two thousand years ago, and I knew that was Christ himself, a regular man whose body entered earth just like anybody's. There was nothing godlike about those white bones. Nothing... Just a man...

...I tried hard, oh so hard, to reinstate the good feeling of faith, yet my reason continues to fail me, continues to push forward the blasphemous, irreverent thoughts of an errant believer...

...and it's all lies, my faith tainted with so many lies... They spring at me from the words of the Holy Book, they spring at me from the memories of my days past, from the teachings of saints and theologians. No one can satisfy me with an answer. The world is cruel, too cruel for a godly plan. Nobody knows the spirit of the sons of men, which goes upward, and the spirit of the animal, which goes down to the earth, simply because there are no distinctions in spirit between men and animal, as I have seen that man is wolf to man, and animals can be kinder than men, and regardless of our advancement in reason and morals we have not yet found a communion in spirit among ourselves, we have not found the grand peace with the entire community of life on Mother Earth.

My heart is broken by the words of Amira, the words that transformed me into a ghostlike creature with no faith. I cry for the return of God in me. The harder I cry, the less room I find for Him in my thoughts. There is nothing out there, nothing above us, nothing below us, that can reestablish my pulse.

Suffering has pushed God and His Christ away from me. I dare not write anymore today, for I fear this will be the end of my days.

3:22 First high-detailed vision of Virgin Mary

(as if she was flesh of light)

I woke up in the middle of the night, sweating on all sides of my body, not just underneath me, as it usually happens. All this moisture around me, embedded in my bed sheets, in my pillow, in the creases of my nightgown, made me feel worried that I had caught another illness. Soon after, I caught glimpses of light from the clear night sky through the curtains, as awareness took over my entire body, I realized that I had emerged from a profound dream that was all about the Virgin Mary. I was there, with Her, on the shores of a small lake. Soothing scents of lemon trees were descending upon us. Birds were chanting in their love nests. There was nobody around. The Virgin was washing her feet in the lake and was unaware of my presence. She was wearing a simple cloth of linen, wrapped around her in a single piece. Her dark long hair was reaching the ground. She stood up and stretched her arms towards the sky, to receive the warmth of the sun. She closed her eyes and prayed for a while, still calling out to the sun, then slightly leaning her head on one ear, then on the other, then leaning her whole body gently to her right, then to her left, like a willow tree in the wind. She spun on her naked heels a few times, slowly clockwise, not minding my presence, how could she, as her eyes continued to be closed, radiating with the self-assuredness of a wise old man, who has seen and known it all, who had no need of keeping the eyes open.

The Virgin danced, danced, danced, danced, danced, mutely, no noise, no fear, full freedom, with immense love, and carafes of honey flowing in my mind, stirring the sky, the day, the light. She was pure, she was exquisite, she made me think of life, real life, the joy and its qualities.

Then she pulled the cloth down from her body, so she remained naked to my eyes, while dancing, dancing, dancing. Her skin appeared brown and splendid, not white and milky as I was taught by Raphael Sanzio. So what dawns on me, stupid of me, is to undress from my own garments, to be naked as the Virgin, in all equality, in all-natural making, not to position myself below Her, on a scale of shame, even though such a scale is of human production and not divine inspiration, if you're asking me. In my dreamy asininity, it did not occur to me that I might impose upon the Virgin Mary, that she might consider my appearance in such an unclad state as the culmination of impropriety and the manifestation of the greatest of all blasphemies, punishable by the harshest damnations. What if I had copulated with the Virgin there? I would have left her bereft of her very essence, (that is the virginity itself), and moreover I would have cheated even God Himself of the right of the first and only inseminator, perhaps causing the entire chain of Christianity to be severely altered, considering that I would have fathered Christ! Me, a lowly African creature of no divine nature whatsoever! My goodness! These afterthoughts I have now are terrible.

In the dream, I had no such indecent musings, I felt only awe and admiration for the Virgin. Her skin akin to mine made me feel liberated. I approached her. She heard me. She opened her eyes and slowed down the rotations of her dancing, dancing, dancing.

"Hello, how are you?" she said.

"I am fine. How are you?"

"I am dancing. Dancing. Dancing," she said.

"That's fantastic!" I said, and instantly felt like an idiot.

"Don't be shy," she said, "dance with me, dance."

"Very well," I said and started dancing clumsily, with my five limbs in all directions, flapping and bobbing erratically.

She splashed me with water, (hence the moisture in my bed sheets), as science shows that reality transfers into the imagery of dreaming. Certainly, it's unlikely that it's vice versa. When she splashed me with water, she said "Splash me back", to which I said "Alright", thinking that it's the same as a baptism, and I wouldn't mind baptizing the Virgin Mary. Who would say no to that, right? I splashed back, she laughed, she palmed more lake water and tossed it at me with great precision and no waste of droplets. Back and forth more splashing, until we heard a young voice from afar, shouting "Mother, mother, where are you?" We stopped. I woke up. That's it.

I.am.defiling.the.core.of.purity!

I went to my desk to scribble these words, to recollect my scattered mind. It has been many, many hours, perhaps days, since I lost sight of God. All I feel is futility and a history of lies. I emptied a glass of water, looked out the window towards the moon, and I perceived that nothing is better than that a man should rejoice in his own works, for that is his heritage. For who can bring him to see what will happen after him? Who can? Can anybody reach out to the netherworld? Can anybody? Please, I really want to know.

NOTEBOOK FOUR

4:1 Convulsions in Europe before the ratification of UBI

I am on a tour of Europe's capitals to meet with local clerics and people of goodwill. I attempted to avoid publicity as much as possible, and as usual I have failed, since in every city big crowds were waiting for me at airports and in the squares of presidential and governmental palaces. On the seventh day I met the President of the United Nations of Europe, Mr. Fred Kapiter, at his office in Brussels. Mr. Kapiter, a former Olympic gymnast, with a statuesque appearance, greeted me with the most gracious words and affability.

Nothing is more pressing on his agenda than the rollout of Universal Basic Income in all member states of the UN of E. "We are having big problems, Your Holiness," he said candidly, "as many state parliaments have major friction with the ratification of UBI. While the majority of member states have accepted UBI on general principles, agreed on its utmost urgency and necessity for the preservation of the Union, the strengthening of liberties and of solidarity, when it comes to the fine-tuning of regional-specific policies they seem to falter, fallback, and lose their momentum. Why is that? What can I do to rekindle the original enthusiasm about UBI? You know me; I'm a strong believer in this project. I think it's our only chance for a profound transformation of our society for the better."

"I believe, Mr. President, that your heart is in the right place," I said.

What do I know about economic policy and European federal politics? I know all about UBI, what it is, what it means, how vital and important it is, but how to implement it, to draw lines and numbers, to schedule milestones and juggle with political pressure, election cycles, ideologies, cultural inertia, detractors, pundits, and scholars, to bring them to the same table and make them speak the same language, oh no! This is a madman's job, this is a task for a 21st century Hercules, a task Christ himself wouldn't have tried to undertake. As in our time, it is not enough to climb up a hill and preach, or flip over tables in a temple, or defy a King with silence, or endure a bestial beating by some moronic Roman soldiers, no, no, that was a child's play, ha! And dying on a cross, what a fulgurous moment of pain, compared to the agony of carrying the burden of the destiny of hundreds of millions of people and having to think about a legacy that might transform the peoples of Europe for generations to come, if not for the rest of HISTORY, now that's what I call the real struggle with the world! Mr. President knows all of this, he is a good man, so I wish him well.

I dared not offer him my blessings, since I am certainly not capable of offering them anymore. Fred Kapiter is not a man of faith, as he openly admitted. Incredible, I thought to myself, while listening to his educated description of the situation and elegant use of language that conveyed the entire gamut of emotions attached to the idea of UBI.

I returned to my hotel and considered all the oppression that is done under the sun. I turned on the holovision, I put on the hologlasses, and I let myself submerge into the frightening reality of a holocast of the today's news. I walked on the streets with the reporters; I looked behind me and I saw the camera crew. They were in the slums of Palermo. Thousands of tents filled with refugees. I looked at the tears of the oppressed. They had no comforter. They saw the light of day as a burden descending upon them from the sky. I saw power on the side of their oppressors. In the eyes of the oppressed I could see that they knew their fate, but they did not understand it. They are the survivors, but they have no comforter. What good is this, to outlive the martyrs and the heroes and the weak, but to be bereft of peace?

4:2 Love between man and man, woman and woman

My European trip has been intense enough until now, leaving me no hope that it might get any easier. On the first day of my visit to Prague I met the Orthodox Patriarchs again, to discuss, above anything else, the future of the idea of family and the intimate communion of men and women. The entire afternoon was dedicated to this meeting, with esteemed members from the civil society present, including our host, the Czech President.

Present at the table, in order, were: Fyodor (Russia), Pompiliu (Romania), Aequilaterus (Constantinople), Philipilus (Jerusalem), Nestor (Serbia), Hieronymus (Greece), and, lo and behold, expected by no one given his advanced age and his reclusive character, Patriarch Neophyte of Bulgaria, wearing an eyepatch due to a recent cataract operation that rendered him visually semi-incapacitated. Still missing, were the following patriarchs: Ulianus of Alexandria (just had his kidney stones removed and deeply regrets he could not attend, however he has sent his position in a long letter that I did not have the chance to read), John XII of Antioch, Syria (still recovering from a shrapnel wound, has not sent a letter but has sent an emissary whom I have not seen, which makes me think he is lost in the Prague traffic) and Ilia IV of Georgia (is not sick and not that old but prefers to attend to matters of urgency in his own church, which I know means consolidation of his power).

The Patriarchs' beards have grown back nicely since our last encounter. I envy them so much. I always wanted to have a wide, thick, long beard of my own, but I was not endowed with such quality of follicles.

Off we went, straight into the conversation, dispensing rather quickly with the greetings and initial pleasantries.

Patriarch Fyodor stated that a man cannot copulate with a man, and a woman cannot copulate with a woman, because, in his words, not mine, "A protuberance cannot enter a protuberance, and a hole cannot envelop a hole". Patriarch Pompiliu said that God has placed us on Earth to grow and multiply, and by allowing the aforementioned copulatory relations, we disobey God flagrantly. Patriarch Aequilaterus said that we are nothing without our history, we have no identity without our traditions, and the traditions clearly say that sodomy is a sin, period. That family comprises a man and a woman, and that is the end of the debate. Immediately Patriarch Nestor jumped in and said there is no debate, since a fact is a fact, no man can ever conceive with a man, no woman can ever impregnate another woman, and all the alternative practices are nothing but cheating and defiling the dignity of life, to which all Patriarchs cheered "Hear! Hear!" after waiting patiently for their respective translators to do their jobs. Last to voice his opinion was Patriarch Hieronymus, who had waited patiently for his turn, and said mildly, "I am somewhat puzzled by this notion of limiting personal liberty when trying to regulate sexual behavior. We know that liberty itself is God-given, and it was meant in such a way as not to infringe with the natural order of things, including the propagation of life." The Patriarchs nodded in feigned understanding.

The jocular Patriarch Nestor, extremely excited to attend this holy ecumenical roundtable, eloquently extemporized a long presentation, which can be summarized by the idea that, yes, all the above is true, yes, people have the right to be happy on Earth and to exercise their freedoms, however - and he raised his finger to enforce the conclusion - however, the treasures of heaven are much greater than, and supplant the earthly ones, and we must do everything in our capacity to live our lives for the promises of a greater, truer, afterlife. "If we were not created with the purpose of following God's dictum on Earth, to trust and love Him, and to receive eternal gratitude after we leave this life, well then, I see no other purpose in this existence. Thus, these acts of same-gender communion, or whatever you want to call them, are nothing but deleterious and regrettable deviations from the true and recognized purpose of mankind!"

Great gestures of approval ensued from all Patriarchs.

While they were talking, what really bothered me was that I developed a sudden itch on the interior of my upper thigh, right under the seam of my underpants, and my goodness, it grew to be unbearable and it was impossible to scratch! Perhaps if I stood up? Yes, then I would have rubbed my thighs against each other and addressed the problem! But what reason would I have to stand up in a meeting of equals? Therefore I praised the dead who were already dead, more so than the living who are still alive, for the dead do not know the unbearable torture of an unscratchable itch.

I couldn't help myself, and I stood up! Ahhhh, what relief!

"Yes, Your Holiness?" Fyodor asked, visibly surprised that I broke protocol.

"Umm, pardon me Your Holinesses," I said, embarrassed, searching for my words. "I see and understand your opinions, which I used to share myself. Not to be contrary to them, I would like to raise to the attention of Your Holinesses that I have had a recent divine inspiration that made me believe that times are a-changing, and, in the light of the spirit of the new age, we ought to look closely at our traditions to see if they are not telling us something else."

Rub, rub, itch gone!

"What do you mean, Your Holiness?" Pompiliu asked.

"Your Holiness Pompiliu. I mean that tradition has always evolved; it has changed along with the morals of the ages. Do you know what has not changed? What still keeps us together as living beings? It is the desire to connect with one another, the desire to love, the need to belong, and the calling of freedom. That is what the Virgin Mary has revealed to me in a dream."

"That is incredible, Your Holiness!" said Nestor, bewildered.

I was still standing, feeling proud of the words I had just uttered, except for the last sentence, which was, well, quite a lie, since the Virgin asked me to splash her with water, and did not mention anything about love, connection, or freedom.

The Patriarchs seemed taken aback, yet none of them showed overt signs of outrage. They had even forgotten my breach of protocol, since they started talking amongst themselves, each to his neighbors, in pairs, bypassing the translators, for whom they had lost their patience. Finally, Philipilus suggested we take a break for lunch, since we were promised roasted duck and baked potatoes, thus we all agreed and the meeting was adjourned.

4:3 When a lion wants to play with chickens

The nasty dictator of North Korea, the rotund, minionic, punk-haired fugitive, mysterious Kim Kim-Un, has been found! And where was he, above all places? He was way up high in the mountains of his country, at a chicken farm, disguised as a chicken farmer.

"I am the apprentice of a chicken farmer!" he loudly protested, when the elite forces stormed the old farmer's house, spilling two crates of fresh eggs, two bales of hay, one handmade wooden table, one pot of fresh milk, and one pot of hot soup on the mud floor, over the protests of a skeletal housedog that was summarily silenced by being captured and placed in a bag.

"I am Kim Kim-Un! I am the great chicken farmer of North Korea!"

The leader of the taskforce, a sturdy captain named Kim, according to the press release, tried to reason with the great leader, explaining that he would be in good hands. He is now rescued and is badly needed to save the country from peril, given that the evil invaders are now approaching Pyongyang from three sides - the Chinese communist traitors from the North; the established traditional enemies Japan and the United States from the West; and from the South, the despicable capitalist pigs, the South Koreans!

"And who's coming from the East? Haha!" Kim Kim-Un scoffed at the report and took an attack position, holding a pitchfork at arm's length. "You don't get it, you scoundrels; I am a chicken farmer now! You can't touch me!" And he pushed the pitchfork towards Captain Kim.

Realizing that the Great Leader cannot be reasoned with, and might be victim of a severe delusional episode, perhaps due to inadequate nourishment, Captain Kim pulled out the ace from his sleeve. He ordered his troops to bring forward a soldier with a ski mask covering his face, into the tiny house.

"Who is this?!" Kim Kim-Un yelled, still in a defense position.

"Don't you recognize me, darling?" the soldier said, and uncovered her face. It was his significant other, the young, beautiful, dancer Barbie Kim-Ono, who was used by the desperate state apparatuses as bait to bring back the Supreme Leader.

Kim Kim-Un did not budge, but softened his grip on the pitchfork.

"Yes, yes, I know you, Barbie Kim-Ono. You used to fornicate with Supreme Leader Kim Kim-Un. Then you betrayed him with the choreographer! I know everything! I know all the lies. I will have him executed. Do you understand?!"

"Come back with me, Kim," Barbie Kim-Ono said.

"No!"

"Please," she said, softly trying to make her way onto one side of the pitchfork.

"No."

"Please."

"No."

Kim Kim-Un's hand was shaking. Barbie Kim-Ono helped him lower the pitchfork and he started crying. Captain Kim pulled the pitchfork away from Kim Kim-Un and signaled the troops to secure the surroundings for a quick exit.

Sighing and crying, Kim Kim-Un said softly:

"Better is he who has never existed, who has not seen the evil work that is done under the sun."

"Yes, darling," Barbie Kim-Ono said.

"I will not come with you. I will be a chicken farmer."

"Okay, darling."

"That is my final answer."

Obviously, the press release did not detail the encounter with the runaway Kim as I imagined it here. The conclusions are nevertheless obvious. The dictator Kim Kim-Un is not returning to power, citing grave health issues, thus North Korea remains in shambles, invaded, very close to being completely overrun by a coalition of international forces that have promptly reacted to a power vacuum and to the threat of nuclear disaster.

In addition to this tragedy for the North Koreans, another pack of admirals, generals, and colonels have simultaneously conditionally surrendered to various equivalent invading officers, asking for political asylum in return.

Who knows what will happen? What matters is that a general war has been successfully averted by the unexpected, and very fortunate, outburst of insanity in the brain of a godlike dictator.

4:4 Froth of lies and tears

Why am I deluding myself, thinking that I am adulated by the masses, when it's certain that in all crowds there is a devil hiding, a detractor?

My motorcade was advancing slowly on the streets of Warsaw. People cheered, raising their babies to be blessed, so I blessed them with air-crosses, flowers flying from all directions to land on the pavement in front of my Popemobile. Many were flung at me but were fortunately stopped by the glass shield, without which I would have been clothed with tulips, there were so many. Abruptly, in the shower of flowers, an egg splashed against the window in front of me, and glided down slowly, leaving a smudgy thick trail of yolk, definitely not of a hen's provenance. The strength and the precision with which this egg was tossed towards me quickly erased the smile from my face and determined my driver to accelerate hastily, forcing me to lose my balance and fall back into my seat, while Nwanne and a Swiss guard covered me with their bodies. What an unnecessary drama! It was just an egg - albeit a large one.

When we came to a secluded, well protected space, I immediately began thinking about the uncontrollable fantasy I had about the North Korean Supreme Leader. I began to feel uneasy, and the whole world began to collapse in on me again.

It was not that I indulged in wishful daydreaming, as I used to do when I was young. It was more a sensation of being enveloped in layer upon layer of conjuring, intricate lies, lies that have no head and no tail, lies that make themselves present by the sheer sensation they imprint upon your subconscious, with that perturbation of your humors, the blockage of your mind, into a net of strangling thoughts closing in on your respiration, while your body is heating up towards an unknowable climax.

That's when I felt, strongly, that I am so alone, bereft of God and Christ. This echo in my mind was drowning out all other thoughts and lashing out at me with insurmountable might, saying loudly, "There is no God! There is no God! And you know it!" As if the echo was not coming from inside my mind, but from another man's mind transplanted into mine, splitting my body and my personality. It hurt so much it made me cringe and squint my eyes. My aides assumed it was an effect of the earlier upset, and scolded the driver. I asked to be taken somewhere to rest. They drove to the hotel. I lay in the bed and asked to be left alone, except for Nwanne, who could stay, but quietly, in a corner, watching over me.

The throbbing of my veins intensified. Now, my eyes hurt, my temples, my ears. My breathing was raspy, erratic. My throat was closing and opening as if a stone was trapped inside. More thoughts of desperation. Anxiety. Fatalism. There was simply no escape. The truth was hammering me without mercy. THERE IS NO GOD. The voices I had heard in my prayers, the soothing feeling of faith, was a self-deception. I saw this truth perfectly and clearly.

The wars, the crimes, the deceptions, the struggle for power perpetrated in the name of God and Christ, all came to me at once, with the vivid image of the little girl Amira asking me over and over again why God allows suffering and injustice in the world, while the answer is so obvious, so transparent, so befitting the real world.

From the depths of my heart I was fighting my mind, crossing the memory of the feelings of elations I had when I prayed, and the joy of hearing God's voice, and the comfort of having known that above this world there exists only love, caring, and certitude. But these feelings are mere memories now, and they are waning, slowly being taken over by this incredible presence in my mind that I cannot dispel.

And I'm looking at the multitudinous iniquities of the selfish and the tyranny of evil men and I cannot see any other emollient for the souls of men but the stark truth, from which an honest life can be built, away from a history of lies and deception. There are no blessings I can offer for those who shepherd the weak through the valley of darkness; there are no virtuous words I can say in the name of faith to soothe the lost children and the ingenuous believers and members of our Mother Church.

I see that for all toil, and every skillful work, a man is envied by his neighbor, whether the neighbor is a man of faith or not. How is this too not vanity and grasping for the wind? How is it not obvious that faith is placed in the neighbor by his parents, his church, and the continuance of tradition?

A God that strikes down his alleged creation with great vengeance and furious anger is foreign and malignant to me. Such a God is the image of man who created Him, while it should be the contrary.

So I lay here in agony.

4:5 Of Cardinal nuisance, or Papal Bull in a china shop

Cardinal Thorsen Tchipcherish called me by regular telephone at my hotel in Berlin. He was agitated and forthcoming, as usual. Why does he always give me the impression that he has no piety whatsoever? Am I a superficial judge of character? Is it his herculean body, or his thundering hoarse voice that instills in me this uneasiness around him? He has these earth-shattering ideas that stagger me, yet I lack the capacity to retort with the same majesty. I am the Pope, for God's sake!

"Your Holiness," Cardinal Tchipcherish said, "your meeting with the Patriarchs is having huge echoes and reverberations with the general public and the media. I mean huuuge! The world is picking up on your revolutionary ideas. If we go ahead and issue an apostolic constitution proclaiming that the union between same-gender people is as sacred as the union between a man and a woman, that would be great! It would be a fantastic achievement for your papacy, your Holiness!"

"Cardinal... I... I appreciate your... umm... support. I had not expected it. You are the Prefect of the Congregation for the Doctrine of the Faith. I am particularly surprised that this comes from you. You are asking no less than a papal bull from us, a major shift in the history of our Church, in fact, a profound revolution in our faith. Isn't that too shocking for our brothers and sisters? Our doctrine had a divine mandate of immutability. What about this? We can't just play willy nilly with what was given to us by Our Holy Father through Christ."

"I sense, Your Holiness, that you are not speaking from your heart..."

How dare he!

"...because what you said to the Patriarchs came from your heart. I sensed that. My learned opinion is that the doctrine must evolve with the times. We have evolved from other creatures, as Mr. Darwin established. Granted, this took our Church some time to recognize, true, but we recognized it in the end, without in any way diminishing the symbolic truth of the biblical creation story. Thus, in this vein, as we change both in body and spirit, our relation with the environment and each other evolves as well, and compels us also to evolve morally using Christ's original message as an inspiration and as a symbolic philosophical framework of reference."

Ugh, what a mouthful. No escape from it.

"By this logic, Cardinal", I said, "soon Our Church will have little say and authority in matters of morals. Christ's message will become a story, no different from the repertoire of legends and myths that have survived from our ancient history. We will leave the administration, the sanction, and the objective character of moral laws to the discretion of politicians, legal systems, moral philosophers, public discourse, and deliberation. People will start believing that they are the masters of their moral domain, that they are in charge of all moral realities. Can you image that, Cardinal? This is inconceivable for hundreds of millions of people. That there is no moral authority outside the material realm of society? That we are the creators of our own rules of conduct? That we are the sole judges of good and evil? That the laws of morality precede the establishment of Our Church by millennia? That, in fact, religion has borrowed the golden rule from ancient history, and that the rule was not invented by Moses or Christ, but merely reproclaimed by the prophets and carried forward to become scripture!?"

"If this is how it must be, then it must be. The transformations of society are inevitable, Your Holiness."

"Cardinal, the Church must survive. The Church is the organic institution at the heart of all communities. The Church binds people together, unifies and codifies, the Church brings order, purpose, and solace, embodies the elevation of life from body into spirit and into law. The Church must survive!"

"I agree, Your Holiness", the Cardinal said.

"And what is the price of this transformation? The abolition of our papacy? The dissolution of our faith? The inclusion of women in the administration of the Church? A female pope? Are we not the bearers of the divine truth, of Christ's legacy, the heirs of Saint Peter's establishment?"

"Christ spoke for the people of his time and the message carried with it the necessity of evolution. Your Holiness, the fool folds his hands and consumes his own flesh when he is hungry. Hence the need of a teacher to show the fool how to feed himself. Not all men and women are created equal in capacity, but we are all created equal in rights and liberties."

"I must agree with you, Cardinal. I have nothing further to say."

"I will help draft the papal bull, Your Holiness."

"Very well, Cardinal."

Then he hung up and left me in turmoil.

4:6 The thawing Arctic relations

I've tried to ignore my predicament over the past few days, to find an escape where I can find some solace, lest I burst into a frenzy in the middle of St. Peter's Basilica and become restrained like a madman in a straitjacket. As a distraction, I turned to my love of geography and maps.

Nobody in the Curia seems preoccupied with the military maneuvers of the Chinese fleet in the Bering Sea. The newscasts have barely mentioned the new developments, since the theatre of attention in the Far East is solely in North Korea. This morning I learned that the Chinese fleet has crossed the Bering Strait, on the Russian side of the Diomede Islands into the Chukchi Sea, and is advancing into the Arctic Ocean, bearing left towards the East Siberian Sea. Curiouser and curiouser. At the lunchtime news, I learned that the fleet has split into three subfleets, one heading East, one heading North-East towards Wrangel Island, and one heading precisely in the direction of the Geographic

North Pole. The oddest thing is that there is no international reaction, except for a brief declaration by the Prime Minister of Canada, Mr. Dante Beaujolais, who said: "We are somewhat concerned about the presence of the Chinese fleet in the Arctic Ocean, however we are assured by our Chinese partners that they are merely conducting exercises in the Russian territorial waters, according to the Chinese-Russian Bilateral Arctic Treaty. Nothing to be worried about. Next question, please." That was all from Canada.

When the oceans are too calm and the ice too thin. The passing of ships will not leave the waters unstirred.

I went to bed extremely tired. The thought of a late prayer did not cross my mind, not even remotely.

I woke up well before the break of dawn and went straight to the TV. I turned it on and could not believe my eyes.

Overnight, the Chinese subfleet that was advancing towards the North Pole changed course after crossing the 80 degrees North latitude. It veered towards the Canadian Arctic Archipelago. The subfleet that was heading North-East changed course towards the North Pole. The subfleet that was heading towards the East Siberian Sea has now passed Wrangel Island, heading back East. What is going on? Their speeds, according to satellite information, are at maximum, in stark contradiction with the speeds of exercise.

The Canadians are alarmed. Prime Minister Beaujolais came on live 3D-television and warned the Chinese fleet not to enter Canadian waters, especially during the mating season of whales that recklessly flock in groups through long stretches of ocean, making their respective mating calls and obviously not expecting a hoard of steel ships to collide with them, transforming the mating dances into carnage.

"Whales cannot defend themselves! And there are just a few of them left!" protested Prime Minister Beaujolais.

Due to the warm weather, the Arctic Ocean presented no hurdles for the Chinese whatsoever. Suddenly, around 3:45 AM while I slept, the satellite signals that were observing the fleet in high details went completely silent as if the entire fleet had vanished. Now the Americans began to pay attention. Finally, their news outlets have started mentioning the Arctic story. The headlines were "Where did the fleet go?" "Mystery in the North" "The Bermuda triangle of the North", et cetera. The Chinese government declined to give any details except for what they stated before, President Mo Xi's recorded video statement that "We are conducting military exercises with our Russian allies".

And I think to myself, are we not living in a wonderful world? It's better to have one handful of tranquility than to have two handfuls of trouble and to chase after the wind.

Now, some answers on the news.

Nwanne caught me undressed and unready for my morning duties.

"Your Holiness?" he asked, still holding the breakfast tray.

"Sit with me Nwanne, let us watch the news."

"Your 8 AM audience is here."

"Cancel it, please."

We sat and watched the news. The satellites have been hacked and shut down. No one can tell where the Chinese fleet is now. It has been a few good hours since their last sighting. By now, they may well be deep in Canadian waters, perhaps near the shores of Banks Island, rushing towards the Northwest Territories. For what purpose? Analysts have duly noted that based on the iGPS data collected, the Chinese fleet has carefully avoided the American territorial waters by the "width of a boat", as one popular hashtag described. Now what?

I feel for poor Mr. Beaujolais, who, for the past two hours, has been desperately calling for answers from his Chinese counterpart.

By 9 AM he has still had no answer, and the satellites are still down.

As Canada is waking up, the internet is being flooded with shock and awe. To add to the mystery, no inhabitants of the Northern regions were able to be contacted. It seems that ground communications have been affected as well.

4:7 Eastern promises

In the aftermath of my meeting with the Orthodox Patriarchs, I have been receiving messages from one of them in particular: Patriarch Pompiliu of Romania. He insisted on having a private conversation with me on a matter of significant importance.

Today, finally I gave him his chance.

He called me on the holophone. The image was so crisp, I could see the fine details of the embroidery on his garments, and the impeccable geometry of the golden cross he was wearing. I had no idea what he wanted to tell me.

"Holy Father," he began.

His English accent was much better than mine. Pompiliu is an intelligent man, well adapted to the 21st century.

"Our meeting in Prague still resonates with me. I have since had many meetings with the Holy Synod on the matter Your Holiness raised, that of the union of same-gender couples. We are all servants of God, the holy Christian tradition, and of our

Holy Church. We must also listen to our parishioners, their confessions, their demands, their needs, their cries."

What was he getting at?

"As you probably know," Pompiliu continued, "my country has suffered terribly during half a century under a communist regime. Many assets of the Orthodox Church, as well as of the Catholic Church, both the Greek and Roman rites, have been seized by the communists through nationalization. Some of these assets have been returned either in kind or in monetary equivalents."

He was losing me...

"To abbreviate: the Catholic Church continues to have unadjudicated claims on assets, buildings, and land holdings that are currently considered owned by the state. You know the demographics of our country: 80% of people are Orthodox, and not more than 10% are Catholic. Naturally we recognize that some of our parishioners have changed denomination and become Catholic, after the scandal surrounding my predecessor - needless to say this is not worthy of our time here, we do not deny it - yet in addition to this, we would like to underline another truth: the Romanian government has no intention of resolving the claims of the Catholic Church. They will delay it as much as they can, over as many electoral cycles as necessary, the bottom line being that they will not give back those buildings that number in the dozens, if not hundreds, nor will they offer the customary monetary compensation, no, no, indeed, I know them, they are politicians, they will not budge on this, the main reason being the political capital of the Orthodox conservative base that has grown in size."

Now he was starting to make some sense. Or was he?

"-Which brings me to the purpose of my call, Holy Father. We can help promote your ecumenical proposals of acknowledging the communion of same-gender couples, from a liturgical and scriptural point of view, in conjunction with the renouncement of Catholic claims on the aforementioned real estate assets (and their subsequent transition into the patronage of the Romanian Orthodox Church). Thus, these houses of God, that are currently not at their full capacity, will become more useful. Many are sitting empty. Some are in ruin, or half-finished, and are now being used as an entertainment facility with laser shows, dance floors, and haute couture fashion shows. It is outrageous! It is defiling our faith! But what can we, the Orthodox Church, do!? We do not own it. If we did, we would surely put an end to this debauchery!"

"If I understand correctly, Your Holiness, your proposal seems to be of a material and political nature."

"Your Holiness, the categorization and qualification of our proposal is beyond our scope. We are merely looking for a mutually beneficial agreement."

Patriarch Pompiliu is quite an astute man. He impressed me. He commanded the holophone perfectly. He paused to let me digest his proposal. Not once did he lose his smile, or stress a syllable too hard, or sound too harsh. I certainly needed time to reflect on his proposal. His manner of speaking was too confusing for me.

After we detailed the background of the Prague meeting to some extent, and its implications for the world at large, we both agreed that both our institutions needed to change to keep pace with the evolving beliefs of the population.

"We live for one purpose, Holy Father," Pompiliu concluded. "That is the preservation of our Church far into the future. We have to fight for it with our blood and souls, even if this means anchoring ourselves deeper into the material world."

Somehow I knew he was about to say that. I had read it in the self-assuredness of his elocution. We ended the conversation in warm, fraternal terms, promising each other dedication to the tasks at hand, after which I returned to my room, looked outside over the obelisk in St Peter's Square, and I saw vanity under the sun. Sheer vanity.

4:8 Deprived of faith, I battle with emptiness

The believer says that without faith, a man is nothing but an empty shell, with a poor soul, a narrow field of vision, a desiccated prospect of enrichment with the eternal grace and gratitude of God in the afterlife.

The believer accepts with fortitude that creation extends much farther than what the senses can inform and the intellect can fathom, insofar as this expanded reality can only be accessed by revelation and faith, as it carries an enormous complexity that man, given his frailty and lowly character, cannot grasp by any other means at his disposal, except through the means given by God, through direct messages and scriptural instructions, through the passion of Christ, through the exemplary lives of the Virgin Mary and the many prophets who lived before and after her.

The believer sees faith as immutable and invincible. There is nothing in this world that can shatter it, shake it, or spoil it. The believer's faith is so powerful that it feeds him the strongest nourishment available to man: the certitude of the end of suffering. In this life or after the death of the body, the believer knows he will find what he is looking for: atonement, companionship, exultation, peace, love. What else can the believer hope for? What else is there to gain from the dedication to God and His Christ? How else can submission to the greatness of God be rewarded? The believer cannot ask for anything, except for what he knows to articulate with the language acquired from his parents and from his pastors.

The intelligent believer sees nature as it is, then paints his faith over it, so it appears as a canvas of miracles and many layers of mysteries that lead only towards the reconfirmation of his faith in the great origin of everything: God. There is no other path for the believer than that of returning and finding God in all nooks and crannies of life. Everything connects to his faith, everything explains it, everything is explained by it.

In order to live his life as a mortal creature, the believer indulges in the benefits of his free will. He eats it for breakfast, he munches it at lunch, he dances with it in the evening, and embraces it late in the night. Free will speaks to the believer's earthly needs for freedom and connection to others. His freewill is also a gift from God. His freewill is also the source of evil, so the believer blames the freewill of others when it misfires and causes harm, as if God was entirely absent in the exercise of evil, which He is, of course. The believer returns to God and asks for reparations for the damages caused by the faulty freewill of others. He prays to God to amend the freewill of others. He beseeches God to alter the laws of nature to overcome life's shortcomings.

In his quest to balance the scales of justice, the believer struggles with the world. He often feels blind and helpless.

Then one day, the believer hits the wall of suffering. He becomes estranged from the world and overwhelmed with questions. There he is one day, a lone weak believer, without companions: he has neither son nor brother. There are no answers from his family, no answers from his friends, no answers from his peers. He sees no fortunate end to his qualms. He deeply regrets his sins, and people he has lost, and there is no end to all of his labors. He lives through days and nights in a terrifying routine of breathing, bathing, feeding, and sleep. Nothing can soothe him, nor is his eye satisfied with riches. But he never asks, "For whom do I toil and deprive myself of good?" He insists on praying to

God and craving answers. He demands the answers! And now, when the struggle is most intense for him, the believer is deafened by SILENCE. There is nothing out there. There is no world beyond. The hopes, the pangs, the cries, are his, and his alone. This is also vanity and a grave misfortune.

And one day, perhaps, a new light will shine, a new freedom.

There will be a new man. There will be a new life.

4:9 Two are better than one

(because they have a good reward for their labor)

The one-year anniversary of the Cyprus Peace Accord approaches.

One of its stipulations was that at the first anniversary, the parties concerned will meet again to review what has happened during the year, how effective the peace-keeping mission was, and what adjustments need to be made to secure the peace in the region.

I was invited to attend.

At the roundtable: President Pushkin; President Renders; a Mr. Burj Al-Caliph, the Caliphate emissary; President Kapiter; President Amisraeli; and President Siri Al-Bashad of Syria.

On the table: San Pellegrino mineral water and soft tea biscuits that do not leave crumbs when you bite them. My favorites!

On the agenda: free travel within the Caliphate; open borders with Syria and Turkey; the establishment of an Institute for the Preservation of Antique Treasures (IPAT) with a secular leader; ending rebel fighting in the North; the extension of the Russian peace-keeping mission; and the addition of American troops.

Positions:

- Russia wants to do whatever is necessary for the preservation of peace for the benefit of the region.
- The United States want fair treatment of all ethnicities, and a path towards democratic elections.
- Europe wants guarantees from the Caliphate that refugees can safely return.
- The Caliphate wants statehood recognition.
- Israel wants exchanges of prisoners of war.
- Syria wants a significant aid supply of penicillin, bottled water, and blankets.

Objections:

Russia doesn't want elections to be held too soon because "Certain political elements cannot be trusted for fairness." "But your military presence has kept the region relatively peaceful," the Caliphate said. "We all know how many subversive groups are still active, many dressed as women, posing with shaved legs on the streets, and misleading the authorities," Russia said. Europe objected that the cause of the millions of refugees has been forgotten and there is a strong desire for them to return to their homeland, however this does not mean that they are not still welcome in Europe. Syria said that the hacking of its internet connections and satellite access rights must stop at once.

My allocution:

Gentlemen, I have considered all your positions, meaning that I have listened carefully with my heart and mind wide open. Let us settle on the universal human values of freedom and happiness. When the expansion of one's pursuit of freedom and happiness trespasses onto the space of one's neighbor, then we ought to pause and turn to introspection. Devout people are not people of destruction. Merry people are not people of selfishness; they are people of openness and camaraderie. We do not need to be friends to each other. Friends are those faces who populate our memories. We can be decent strangers to each other and partners in sharing the planet. That is the one true thing that exists above us and has existed long before us.

We have a duty to honor this home of ours with reverence and respect. And I have one more thing to say: forget fear as you would forget a bad dream. Truly, I say to you, is that simple.

They all applauded me joyfully and turned to each other and shook each other's hands.

There was one man I watched carefully, Mr. Burj Al-Caliph. After he smiled his smile and shook the hands around him, his face became dark for a second. He closed his eyes and prayed in his mind. I can tell when a man prays in his mind with all his heart. Immediately after he opened his eyes, his smiles resumed, and he continued his political stance.

There was a thin scent of absolution in the room. Thin, very thin.

And grins of hubris mixed with exhaustion. Chuckles at the gates of heaven, hoarse post-apocalyptic promises of friendship.

The day was long and hard! I fell asleep within seconds, face down on the pillow.

4:10 On being alone for the rest of your life

On this day I have felt so alone.

I woke up with a blasting migraine that would not go away, not even after Dr. Zhivago administered a substance by intravenous injection. Nwanne brought me fresh cold wet towels and wrapped them around my head. It didn't help. Not even his soothing voice could help me. He offered to read to me passages from the Book of Psalms. It sounded like a sawmill cutting stumps of tinfoil. He tried some Shakespearian Sonnets. Same effect. He opened the Divine Comedy and I put my hand over his wrists and shook my head. I couldn't hear any of that. How about a Mozart quartet? No. It was stirring my brain. Then he left.

I saw myself as an old man, a very old man, forgotten and anonymous, barely able to hold a spoon to my mouth. Ah, the desolation around me, the stillness. I was in a small room, in a hospice somewhere, possibly in Switzerland, on the top of a mountain, far from the bustling towns. I was wearing a nightgown. My hair was all white. My skin looked like worn-out parchment. I looked at myself in a tiny mirror on the wall. I could barely remember my name, who I was, or what I did in my life, the people I loved, or the people who loved me the most. Where is everybody? I said to myself. My face was wet. Was I crying? Why is this nurse wiping my face and my mouth? I was crying. She was feeding me a puree of something from a porcelain bowl. I automatically opened my mouth and accepted the food. She wiped my mouth again. Did she know who I was? She must know. Her nametag says: NYANDENG. She was black, very black, blacker than I was. I felt safe around her. She exuded an air of familiarity. Did I know her? NYANDENG. Name sounded familiar. Perhaps I had met her once, in the distant past, during one of my trips. I must have had an important job, I must have met a lot of people. Where was everybody? Why was nobody asking me anything? NYANDENG asked me how I was feeling when she entered the room. I said I am a voice inside the face of an old man. She laughed and helped me change my nightgown.

What is a man if he does not have companions when he is old? Why do we crave each other's company? Why can't we live with ourselves and the beauty nature offers us? Why do we need anything else but total silence?

I must have had lots of friends. I must have! I know I did. All I can gather is the feeling of having needed the closeness of somebody. And there was an angel in my life. Yes, an angel.

With wings! No, not literal wings, God no. He made me feel lighter. He made me feel I could fly on a cloud with him. Yes, I remember him.

Where was he? What was he doing? Was he well? Was he wearing a nightgown of his own? What if he was in the next room? I asked NYANDENG if there was an angel in the next room. She laughed. She said, no, there wasn't. In the next room there was the former president of an international bank, who did not have a family. She said the banker was fired from the bank and nobody wanted to have anything to do with him anymore. The banker was so poor that he had nothing else but lots of money. So he came to the top of the mountain to hide his poverty.

My angel surely remembered who I was. And since he was not here but elsewhere in the world, he either had something much more important to do, or he was not in this world anymore. He stopped existing.

I know clearly why two are better than one. For if they fall, one will lift up his companion. Like NYANDENG when she changed my nightgown. But woe is he who is alone when he falls, for he has no one to help him up from the floor where he would lie for many, many hours until the night falls or a nurse starts her shift.

Then the silence will be so deafening that man will surely feel he is no longer of this world.

4:11 The Korean division bell is now a peace gazelle

Cardinal Adriano Mutella, director of the Holy See Press Office, and the one and only Cardinal Tchipcherish, stormed into my office this morning, announcing of course the important news of the final liberation of North Korea. I said:

"I beg your pardon? What do you mean liberation?"

Cardinal Mutella said:

"Your Holiness, it is exactly what it looks like. The Democratic People's Republic of Korea is now declared, and I quote, *A country dedicated to the advancement of modern forms of government for the benefit of the loyal Korean peoples*, end quote."

"Who said that?" I said.

"The leader of the interim government, a Mr. Kim Ni-Moy."

"Well then it's wonderful news," I said.

"Not so fast, Your Holiness," Tchipcherish said.

"What is the problem, Cardinal?" I said.

"We have been overwhelmed with messages from South Korea, and surprisingly from North Korea as well, of well wishes, hope, joy, etc. That included over one million holo-messages."

"I see no trouble in this," I said.

"However, Your Holiness," Tchipcherish continued. "The messages also request the establishment of a North Korean Catholic Archdiocese with headquarters in no other place but Pyongyang. Some of the most daring messages even request the extension of the patronage of Cardinal Park-Ying over this new archdiocese, suggesting, as you may have guessed, the imminent unification of the two countries under the blessing of the Holy See."

"I see."

"Which presents us with the indubitable concerns about logistics, administration, costs, political theology, and humanitarian action."

"What is it to be done, Cardinals?"

"We need to be engaged with the Koreans," Mutella said.

"We need to dispatch a nuncio to help Cardinal Park-Ying address both nations," Tchipcherish said.

"Cardinals, please, I think we need some time for reflection. These changes affect us-"

"Your Holiness," Tchipcherish jumped in, "times are changing too fast for pensive reflection. We need to be on top of our game, as the saying goes."

"Cardinal Tchipcherish, my dear Thorsen, I understand your eagerness. The unification of Korea is great news indeed. I'm just thinking that it is wiser to-"

"Your Holiness, pardon my candor," Tchipcherish said. "This is a lifetime unique opportunity. This can define your Papacy."

"Papacy shmaypacy!" I said, losing my temper. "I'm not feeling well! I need some time to reflect."

"Your Holiness!" Tchipcherish started.

I couldn't say anything anymore. Mutella pulled Tchipcherish's sleeve until he understood that he had to stop. I saw the frustration on Tchipcherish's face and the shame on Mutella's, who simply wanted to convey a message. I bet Tchipcherish seized this occasion and piggybacked on Mutella to deliver his agenda. What does he want from me? Abolish the papacy? Extend the papacy? Holy See Incorporated? I don't get it.

I hate politics! Oh, my goodness. I said "hate". I absolutely wrote that with my own hand. A disturbing feeling that has resurfaced in my thoughts since... that happened. My goodness! I can't even say it. Every time the struggle of the world comes to my ears I feel these waves of discontent boiling in my veins. I don't know what to do with them. I even tried to drown them in some tasty Tuscany wine, until Nwanne saw that I was being cheerful for no objective reason and pulled the glass away from me.

And now this. Two Koreas want to be one Korea. Truth be told, if two lie down together, they will keep warm; but how can one be warm alone?

Let the Koreans be warm again together. Under one sun. Under one language. Under one border. Let their spirits roam free.

And when I say free, I cannot view the hand of the Holy See shepherding that freedom. Freedom is freedom. Spirits must soar by themselves under the effulgence of peace and unification. I shall be an applauding spectator and let the course of history invite me wherever I am needed. I am no disturber or thief of joy.

So, Cardinal Tchipcherish ought to leave me alone for now. I truly hope he understands this.

4:12 The past speaks to me with the power of a bullhorn

I remember where I met Nyandeng, the nurse from my dream! It was in South Sudan. This was some time ago, but I remember it clearly. It was the summer of 2015, a hot summer in South Sudan, just like any other. Nwanne and I were in the city of Agok. We had just escaped from a terrible danger in the North that almost cost us our lives - but more on that later, when I feel better to write about it.

We were visiting a hospital where thousands of refugees fleeing from the North were seeking treatment. On the day when we arrived, carrying some boxes with medicine that we were able to rescue from the robbery of a United Nations truck, a nurse came straight to me and grabbed me with determination. She said to me:

"Father, you must come immediately!"

I had no idea why she could possibly need my services, since I had no medical training. I was only capable of telling stories and inspiring some hope, often with a weak heart, since there was no real hope of deliverance for the thousands I had seen. Only the benefit of rapidly flowing time can sometimes be a comfort.

The nurse took me to a salon full of children where she was called to attend to a little girl that was just brought in by her parents. The girl was so weak and thin, she barely raised the white sheets over her body. When the nurse lifted the cover, I saw a malnourished, feverish little girl. She had fresh scars and a cut that was bleeding.

"Talk to her," the nurse said.

I didn't know what to say. It was so unexpected. I was not new to this much suffering, yet I was frozen.

"Tell her she is going to be alright," the nurse continued.

I leaned over the little girl's head and I began murmurs of a prayer.

The nurse attached the feeble girl to an IV.

"What is the girl's name?" I asked.

"Nyandeng," said the nurse.

That was a real memory.

Nyandeng is a grown woman now. I am an old man overpowered by loneliness and demons. Nyandeng helped me withstand the struggle, as a threefold cord is not quickly broken… I am not broken because she remembered me.

4:13 Proclamation of unification

Over five million Koreans have taken to the streets in South Korea, and another five million have gathered in squares in North Korea, singing and shouting "WE ARE BROTHERS AND

SISTERS, THERE IS ONE KOREA, BORDER NO MORE", bearing white flags of peace, crying and embracing one another.

Cardinal Park-Ying holophoned me. He was ecstatic! He was so agitated that his image suffered a few noticeable holodelays: his glasses remained frozen while his face moved into another position, his left arm remained raised and hung in the air detached from his body, meanwhile his actual arm continued to gesticulate, and the beautiful cross he was wearing made a copy of itself that bounced around. These minor technical glitches were only a sign that technology cannot keep up with the enormous outpour of enthusiasm from the Korean Peninsula.

"It is crucial, Your Holiness, that we help the unified Korea find its new spiritual purpose. We must play a role in shepherding the faith of this newly born nation," the Cardinal said.

While I listened carefully to the Cardinal's report, I wondered what happens to a nation that has suffered decades of Orwellian spiritual suffocation. Have they lost the sense of wonder? Have they lost the will to embrace the world? Has the forced worship of the chain of despotic Big Brothers warped their imagination, their hopes, their perception of the large spectrum of liberties? I know that the human mind can be obliterated into submission. I know that the sense of self-worth, the sense of dignity, the love of life, can be deleted from a man, leaving nothing but an empty shell behind. I know, because I have seen it many times. I also know that a man, or a woman, whose spirit has been destroyed, can be reborn and see the rainbows again, can understand and recognize beauty again, can come back to the willingness to live a normal life and spread joy around them, can choose to leave the tragedies of the past in the past, and think forward about doing something with their presents and futures. I know because I have seen it many times.

I saw hundreds of thousands of soldiers crying while they disassembled the fences along the 250-kilometer-long demilitarized zone. Long caravans of trucks on both sides of the former DMZ carried loads of guns and ammunition to be destroyed and recycled. A spectacle of fireworks continued to light the sky and set a colorful background for the celebration. The roads were packed with cars moving from the South towards the North, and thousands of self-driven trucks loaded with goods, programmed to be delivered to many North Korean cities. North Koreans have flocked to the underground tunnels, under the DMZ, to enter South Korea, as there is not enough room on the roads for the massive migration. The entire fleet of airplanes from Korean Air has been dedicated to transporting people from the North to the South and vice versa, free of charge, as a sign of solidarity.

Whereto for the soul of the liberated man? Whereto for the millions whose minds have been shackled by the insanity of despots? What guilt to unload onto these people, for sitting in silence, for obeying mechanically, for faking submission and glee at the feet of giant statues?

There is no clear resolution to the question of man versus history. Man is victim of history inasmuch as history is the creation of man. When the millions can be controlled with iron fists and fear by a small number of bureaucrats and plutocrats, what is their only salvation? It is a random happening of history that sets loose a chain of events that implodes the head of the dragon and withers its body into chaos.

That was the doom of the despot Kim Kim-Un: his insanity was not confronted, his divinity was taken beyond religion and doctrine, his infallibility was beyond the rule of law. The liberation came not because evil was challenged, but because evil had disrupted itself from within. It was inevitable. It is always inevitable.

What comes next?

I must go to Korea and help the two nations coalesce spiritually. And who am I? A godless messenger of peace and faith!

I'm tasting a soft Tuscany wine. Nwanne just brought it.

11:33pm You may be poor and young, but if you are wise, you are better off than a foolish old king who won't listen to advice. Amen.

I will do whatever is necessary. Peace and joy always come before faith.

4:14 On meeting Mr. Desmond Tutu, and talk of forgiveness

Sometime after leaving Rwanda, Nwanne and I travelled further South to a congregation where we heard we could meet Mr. Desmond Tutu.

We met him just outside the church, as he was leaving the sermon. At first, we were shy and did not dare approach him. I still don't know how we ended up in front of him, shaking his hand. We told him we came a long way to meet him. He graciously offered to take us to his home, and offered us a cup of tea.

"What is forgiveness?" I asked Archbishop Tutu.

"Forgiveness is recognizing the interconnectedness of humanity. In South Africa, Ubuntu is our way of making sense of the world. The word literally means humanity. It is the philosophy and belief that a person is only a person through other people. In other words, we are human only in relation to other humans. Our humanity is bound up in one another, and any tear in the fabric of connection between us must be repaired for us all to be made whole. This interconnectedness is the very root of who we are. Forgiveness is not weakness, forgiveness is not a subversion of justice, forgiveness is not forgetting, forgiveness is not easy.[1]"

I had pledged to God in those days to forgive everyone who has harmed me, and everyone who was going to harm me. I pledged to not let myself be changed by evil and to not carry revenge. I pledged to never forget my part in the Ubuntu.

Then I turned to see my thoughts from the outside and I couldn't see a way to overcome the predispositions of my temperament. What about the trespassers of my feelings who never sought my forgiveness? What about the pride that didn't let them come to me? What about their blindness and lack of compassion? Can I forgive them in spite of their continued adversity?

I realized I could not. And I did not think then, nor do I think now, that it is a weakness of character or a strength of character not to be able to forgive. I do not believe that the fundamentals of the Christian faith, that of vicarious redemption through the passion of the Christ, have a great moral altitude. On the contrary, I think that placing the burden of guilt on the shoulders of somebody else is a lowly position, that does not elevate the believer to a higher moral standard, nor does it absolve the perpetrator from the crime. It is only by the honest supplication from the perpetrator and the willingness of the victim to listen, that inflicted suffering can be overcome, at least psychologically, if not also by material reparation.

Justice is not enough. Dialogue is not enough. We must not accept defeat when forgiveness is not offered; we must not exercise revenge, we must conduct ourselves with dignity.

Even if you were not born into the royal family and have been a prisoner and poor, you can still be king over the Kingdom of Forgiveness.

---

[1] Desmond Tutu, *The Book of Forgiving*, 2014

4:15 First in Seoul, then in Pyongyang

We landed in Seoul three days after the outburst of enthusiasm in the Korean Peninsula. We were greeted at the airport by a crowd so huge, I couldn't see the end of it. So much joy was in the air, my portrait appeared everywhere, on holosigns, on flags, and banners. I thought I saw all the living who walk under the sun gathered there in Seoul.

We were taken straight to the Olympic Stadium where 100,000 people were waiting for us, and many more waited outside in the overflow space, where gigantic screens had been installed, where images from Pyongyang were being broadcast, where soon my face would be shown, an incredible spectacle of mass engagement and technology. Why did they want to see me? Why me? How was I so important for a country where barely 5% of the population formally declared themselves Catholic?

Soon I realized that my ego had gotten ahead of me. The entire gathering was not there only to greet me. While they were certainly ecstatic to see me, they were there to celebrate in dance and public displays of solidarity by listening to concerts and public speeches. I was about to speak for half an hour, yet I wanted a bit more. Fair enough. I swallowed my ridiculous little outburst of pride.

Still, one thought could not leave me alone. They did invite me; they did want me to speak. They did know I was a religious leader. Cardinal Park-Ying guessed my worries and tactfully explained to me in the limousine that the people of Korea see me as man of peace, as a man of the future. I asked why.

"It's because of your revolutionary ideas," the cardinal said.

While the motorcade was approaching the stadium, I could only wonder if my recent novel thoughts, my loss of faith in God, had somehow shown through in my character and my words, despite the fact that I am struggling to choose them carefully out of respect for the many believers who still honor their faith in the Mother Church.

I delivered my speech inspired by the joy of the Korean people. I spoke from my heart of a simple human being. I even forgot to mention God, or religion, or salvation. I went beyond hope. I spoke the truth: You are one!

That was it. The Koreans do not need me anymore. They never needed me. I am extremely grateful for that. I respect them for that. They did it themselves.

They took me back to the airport.

Later in the afternoon we arrived in Pyongyang. Same large crowds. There were no holosigns, no zeppelins with large screens, there were just people waving flags, and my picture visibly glued over the pictures of the dictator in the old frames. Much simpler, closer to my tastes.

The protocol was the same. We were taken to the Rungrado 1st of May Stadium. Cardinal Park-Ying was still with us in the car. The entire way to the stadium, people were cheering at us, tossing flowers in the air. Their joy was identical with their brothers in Seoul and it had something more. It had symmetry, it had some sort of inner structure and calculation, it had inertia and a sad wisdom weaved into its undertones, no less genuine than the exuberance of their Southern brothers. I realized it was the stamp of history.

I was politely seated in the chair of the former dictator in the Rungrado Stadium. Before I got the chance to speak, rest assured I will get all the time in the world, the hosts invited me to watch a welcome presentation on behalf of the Korean people.

I saw my face composed of thousands of colored rectangles held by people in perfect synchronicity. I was flabbergasted. Huge letters displayed my name and the words WELCOME POPE FRANCIS SECOND, WE LOVE YOU, WE ARE YOUR FRIENDS. I must have said Holy Ghost out loud. I felt Cardinal Park-Ying's hand on my shoulder and his soft voice:

"Are you alright Your Holiness?"

I suppose old habits die hard. But humor always conquers tyranny, so I took the liberty to crack a joke with the 150,000 people listening to me. I said:

"You made the giant face of your dictator. Now you showed me my enormous face that stands in his place. Can you make the face of Mickey Mouse?"

And they did! My goodness, they did! Instantly! They had it ready! How did they know I would ask? I thought of it on the spur of the moment. I had told no one. No one!

Roaring applause and cheers ensued. The wounds of the North Korean people were beginning to heal. I cried without knowing that this was being broadcast all over the world.

4:16 My own private Jerusalem

As we flew from Pyongyang back to Rome on the non-stop X-Jet, I received a message from Prime Minister Moses Amisraeli of Israel with a heartfelt invitation to visit the great city of Jerusalem.

I was so excited to hear this, I jumped to my feet, knocked the tea tray onto the floor, and said loudly into the phone:

"Thank you, Prime Minister, I will be right there!"

We were over Tajikistan at the time.

I called Nwanne and Cardinal Mutella, shared my decision with them, urged them to alert the captain and announce a press conference in the next five minutes, so we could tell the world that Pope Francis 2 will visit Jerusalem today. To my surprise, Prime Minister Amisraeli, Nwanne, and Cardinal Mutella had no objections to my sudden decision. Perhaps Amisraeli had been prepared for this, perhaps he was banking on the positive wave of enthusiasm in the world that expanded from the Korean epicenter. I'm sure there is some political motivation around this, but I do not care, I simply wanted to see Jerusalem with my own eyes. I hoped there might be some answers for me there.

About two hours later, I got another call, this time from King Sandal Alumnus Baad Al-Bizzi of Saudi Arabia. And what did he say? He invited me to Mecca, to visit the Kaaba, to address the crowds, to talk about peace. He was euphoric! I asked when he would like me to visit? He said as soon as possible, right now, if I'm available. I had to disclose that I was already committed to a visit to Jerusalem. He paused. I could hear him breathing and grinding his teeth. He conceded. Whenever I can, preferably in the immediate future, he would be more than happy to have me as his honored guest. The timing of his call was uncanny.

Jerusalem. Holiest of the holies.

Exquisite organization from Prime Minister Amisraeli. They took me from the airport to the Knesset, where I read the allocution that Nwanne was so kind to write for me. Then a quick stop for lunch with the Prime Minister.

"I want to walk on the Via Dolorosa, to walk the steps of Christ," I told him.

"Certainly," said Prime Minister Amisraeli, "it has already been arranged."

I barely had time for my after-lunch ablutions. The crowds have already gathered and the security detail was already in place. The reporters were in front of us. I asked to walk alone.

Everybody, including the Prime Minister, was walking behind me.

I walked on the stone slabs. There was silence. Feeble sounds from our steps. The reporters were well-behaved. They kept their distance. My black face against the background of stone. Thoughts rushing through my mind. Trying to connect to something, trying to distill imagination from history. I told no one why I wanted to walk on Via Dolorosa. From station to station I followed the passion of the Christ. There was no end to all the people over whom he was made king. He had no idea, no desire to become a king. He didn't say he was king in heaven. People made that up. He was a righteous man, yet those who came afterward would not fully rejoice in him. I wondered why. I placed my hand on the walls of Via Dolorosa. Photo reporters, holo reporters were ready. Indeed, all this too is vanity and grasping for the wind.

If we strip ourselves of history, what is left of us? Legends. Imagination. We simply have to create realities where there are none. It's the instinct in our veins. Some were on Via Dolorosa when Christ carried his cross. Many were not. Many were a few houses away, making dinner for their children, doing laundry, repairing broken wheels. They did not pay attention to the noise on the street. There is always some agitation since the Roman occupation began. So what, they condemned another criminal, another charlatan? There are plenty of those around.

What is this itch that bothered me again when I arrived at the ninth station where Christ fell for the third time? It started on my left calf. I put my hands against the wall and I rubbed the itch with my other leg. Nobody could see under my robe. Then it spread devilishly to my thighs and to the jock area. A forbidden zone that I could not scratch. Had I still felt the power of prayer I would have asked for an instant gratification from God. And it would have come. Probably. Now, I was left with the crude reality of unbearable distress. Think of Christ. Think of his beaten, broken body. His open wounds. His protruding bones.

The Church of the Holy Sepulcher is in sight. I bite my tongue. I clench my fists. The church is empty. It has had been reserved for me. They signal me that I can go inside alone, so I can pray in peace. Little do they know... I enter. It's cold. A small place. Inside, the last four stations. Number 10: where Christ was stripped of His garments (entrance to Calvary), I am alone so I take care of the itch. Number 11: Christ is nailed to the cross (Roman Catholic side altar). Number 12: Christ dies on the cross (main Greek Orthodox altar). Number 13: Christ's body is removed from the cross (to the left of the main altar). I can hear the echoes of my breathing. I kneel in front of the altar. Hard stone. It hurts. I stay for a while and meditate.

How can I purge these creeping sentiments of revolt from my soul? How can I silence my heart? How can I give God and His Son another chance to speak? If not now, then when? If not here, then where? I never knew anything. I believed everything. I believed and I felt at ease. Now I am broken and I need my peace. I cannot find it. Not where Christ died. Not anywhere. Perhaps I never will.

NOTEBOOK FIVE

5:1 Disguise in Jerusalem

I could not help myself. I needed to feel the real city unencumbered by pomp and attention.

Nwanne's advice before I went out was:

"Your Holiness, walk prudently when you go to the house of God. And draw near to hear rather than to give the sacrifice of fools, for they do not know that they do evil."

I asked him to dress me like a Hasidic Jew, with the appropriate beard attachments and a *shtreimel*, because it would better disguise the shape of my head.

"A black Jew, Your Holiness?"

"Why not? They exist."

"You will still raise eyebrows. Someone will recognize you."

"Very well, Nwanne. Lighten my face a little bit with your magic powder. And give me a large white beard. Nobody will tell."

I went out on the streets of Jerusalem. There was a stark, flowery scent of olive trees in the air. Nwanne had sent the map of the city to my watch. All I had to do was imitate the movement of the red dot on the map. The red dot was me. On my way to the wailing wall I was not questioned by anybody. There were no beggars and no garbage on the streets. Everything was very clean and friendly to the tourists.

I blended in with the crowd at the entrance to the Western wall. There were Jews from all over the world, as I could tell from their garments and the languages they spoke. I was nothing special to them. I saw other black Jews as well, wearing *yarmulkes* with pride. I could hear Nwanne's breathing in the earwig he made me wear as a minimal precaution.

The queue of people carried me slowly towards the wall. What a humbling sensation, to be one with a community of faith, yet to be so different. Had anyone asked me what my name was, where I came from, I would have told them everything, the whole truth, and nothing but the truth.

I found a spot by the wall with a large crack level with my eyes. The crack was filled with paper notes. I wished I had brought one. I never thought of bringing pen and paper with me. In that moment I completely lost the purpose of my being there. I had forgotten why I wanted to touch the Western Wall. It is a wall of stone, nothing more. Had I been subconsciously predetermined by a calculation of my mind to touch the wall? For what purpose? I had learned the Wall's entire history from books. What else was there to learn? Why do people feel so drawn to the magic of places? Why do they want to experience them with their own eyes, touch them with their own feet and hands? Now, when we have all these holovisions, all these virtual devices that are so real, why do we still need to travel?

And how does the mind remember the old days when the experience was of the whole five senses, not just of the eyes?

For a brief moment, I developed a profound longing for times past, as I was caressing the wall, trying not to touch the paper notes. The times past, with their simplicity.

The wall had been cleaned of weeds.

So, during my last moments at the wall, a sudden rush of love for everybody there, men and women, filled my heart. I wanted to embrace everyone and tell them there is so much more to life than stones and dry shrubberies. I looked at people's faces and I saw pure inner peace. There was nothing else - no secrets, no dark lives, no deception. That was good enough for me. If we see this light in people, it is good enough. When we tell them, when we show it, it becomes real. There will be no more walls to divide us.

5:2 The Black Rubik's Cube of Mecca

Somehow King Sandal learned of my last day in Jerusalem and he managed to squeeze a holocall out of me. I could not refuse, since the negligence of my media staff was slyly exploited. I don't mean to disparage my wonderful staff, they were simply overwhelmed by the past few days.

I said to myself, while the link with King Sandal was being established: Do not be rash with your mouth and let not your heart utter anything hastily before God, because God is in heaven and you on earth, therefore let your words be few.

It's something that stuck with me from the scripture days. Moments later I regretted thinking this, since King Sandal was a mere earthly ruler, much less a god.

King Sandal also had the latest technology, so his hologram was crisp and clear. He was terse, very courteous, and friendly. He said I must honor his invitation at once, since the people of Saudi Arabia were extremely eager to see me, the messenger of peace.

I gladly accepted the invitation.

On the X-Jet again, this time a short 2-hour trip. A tuna sandwich, peppermint tea, 30 minutes of meditation.

From the air, the tarmac in Mecca seemed to be plated with a film of gold. In reality, natural light and the heat perturbed my vision and blurred the ground. The pomp was even greater than in Jerusalem, as if King Sandal had learned the minutiae of my visit in Israel and challenged himself to overimpress me. Red carpet and everything. A limousine that I could not refuse, as the words were escaping me, a loquacious translator that overly interpreted King Sandal's kind words, even though the King himself spoke a decent English. Lots of press following us. Many women with beautiful *hijabs* showing their beautiful faces, waving flags of the United Nations and of the Vatican.

"Perhaps, Your Holiness would like a refreshment?" King Sandal asked me in English.

"I would love one," I said thirstily, not knowing that the refreshment would not be offered right now, as I couldn't see a proper dispenser in the limousine, but at the King's palace where the reception was organized.

I did enjoy a lemonade as soon as we arrived, greeted most of the ministers, and ten minutes later I was invited to retreat to my chambers to rest for a while, not for long though, as our agenda was quite full.

One hour later, on the dot, Nwanne came into my room and declared that we must promptly descend as we are scheduled to visit the Great Kaaba of Mecca, where a crowd is patiently waiting for our arrival. Through the streets of Mecca, a disciplined crowd contained by the fences and security forces, welcomed our convoy and shouted "Peace" in Arabic and "We love you" in English and sometimes in Italian, I even saw a couple of signs in Igbo, correctly written, which pleased my heart. At the Kaaba, we walked on foot from the parking area through the crowd inside the compound in a sea of white garments. We approached the black cube, King Sandal stopped to kiss the *al-Ḥajar al-Aswad* and instructed me to do the same. I was honored to do so, as few Muslims even get the chance to come close to it, let alone touch it. We entered into the Kaaba, King Sandal and I, the two of us alone. We sat on a bench and exchanged a few polite words. There was much warmth and impatience coming from King Sandal, which threw me off a bit. I was not clear of his intentions, except that they were only the kindest and most friendly, however the way in which King Sandal expressed them made me feel put in the limelight. We meditated and prayed, barely moving our lips. I called out to the strength of my willpower not to ruin the moment.

Then we climbed some narrow stairs inside the Kaaba to reach the top, where one Royal Guard bowed his head. A microphone had been installed.

King Sandal spoke to the crowd in Arabic to elicit cheers of joy in unison from the tens of thousands present, and millions probably watching. Then it was my turn.

I widened my eyes, visibly perturbed by the overwhelming situation, and walked slowly to the microphone. I read my emergency speech that I keep in my pocket at all times, courtesy of my dearest Nwanne. The regular speech I had prepared for the occasion proved to be inadequate. I made the decision, on top of the Kaaba, to speak from my heart, so I knitted words from the little piece of paper with what came to me at the moment. It was just fine. It pleased the crowd. They felt good about themselves, how could they not? Since their faith is no less genuine than any other, hence the bridge towards peace is all equal. That is why King Sandal invited me there. That is why the Saudis are craving to be part of this new global resurrection.

Somehow, flowers rained down upon us from up-high in the sky. An escadrille of drones had timed the delivery with my speech, certainly aided by technology.

I had also looked at the sun, by mistake, for a second or so, and got a glimpse of its corona. Or it might have been an illusion, as no one can stare into the sun. I teared up immediately. I felt so happy.

5:3 Searching for the prophet

Nwanne already knew what I wanted to tell him when we got back to my room at the palace:

"No, Your Holiness, I most respectfully do not recommend this endeavor."

Nevertheless, his love and dedication for me demonstrated itself promptly. Before the time of the Maghrib prayer, the fourth prayer of the day, I was dressed as a devout Muslim, ready to join the pilgrims. Nwanne found a passage through the palace kitchens, to the back entrance, where a Jeep vehicle was waiting for us. There were three men in the Jeep.

"I thought we'd be alone," I told Nwanne.

"Don't worry Your Holiness, they are friends. They work for the King," Nwanne explained.

I realized I had to accept the situation and, albeit being less incognito this time around. The three men assured me that they were bound to silence and they would take the truth of tonight's events to their graves. They would not even tell the King, as they were my humble servants for the duration of my visit. They asked me where I wanted to go. I said I wanted to go to the Maghrib prayer.

"Would you like to visit a Christian church?" they asked.

I could not believe my ears. A Christian church in Mecca!?

"Certainly," the King's men confirmed.

There were many Christian churches in Mecca. Everyone was free to practice their faith. But the King had said nothing about this. The King's men explained that this had been going on for some years and the King did not allow publicity as he wanted this to occur naturally by the word of mouth, as faith once originated. King Sandal never ceases to surprise me.

The King's men took me to a very busy street. Men and women crowded, all going to the prayer at precisely the time announced by the muezzins whose calls to prayer were overlapping from adjacent mosques.

"Let us join them in that mosque over there," I said.

The King's men had something better for me. They advised me to follow them across the street to a Catholic church. I was so hypnotized by the flow of Muslims going to pray that I had missed a beautiful church directly opposite the mosque. It was beautiful, white, covered with marble and adornments, quite tall and majestic. Statues of apostles and Christ populated the façade. The bell tower housed a solid bronze bell with the expected inscriptions.

As I mingled with the pedestrians and walked towards the church, I closely watched the Muslims rushing to not be late for their prayers. They made fulgurant eye contact with me, smiled, greeted me with *As-salamu alaykum*. I responded in kind, they moved on undisturbed. The King's men were following me a few steps behind.

I entered the church as casually as I could, and found many Saudis and foreigners praying, meditating, whispering, looking around. I felt peace. Nobody recognized me, how could they? With this powder on my face, this beard, these clothes, I could barely remember who I was. I walked to the altar and did what people did, I knelt and pretended to pray, with my eyes half-closed and peeking at the architecture around me. I could not concentrate on anything in particular. I could only feel serenity now, and hear imaginary celebrations in my mind, of Christian Saudis and Muslim Saudis dancing and embracing, passing bricks and buckets of mortar to each other to build this church, praying together to Christ in Arabic and explaining history to each other and laughing about it. The scent of incense surely helped my mood. The singing of the muezzin from across the street was muffled, but it could still be heard and did not bother me at all, or anyone else for that matter. The muezzin was part of the acoustics of the church, and I was quite sure that the bell ringing and the organ music could also be heard across the street, in a nonoverlapping schedule that worked perfectly for both congregations.

Any words on my part to anyone at that moment would have been superfluous. For a dream comes through much activity, and a fool's voice is known by his many words. So I kept silent, while in my heart I wanted to tell the world. Cunning King Sandal, I wonder what else he has up his sleeve. Surely there is much more.

5:4 Visit to the U.S. of A.

Holocall, the evening I returned to the Vatican, from President Sanbard Renders.

"You must visit us at the White House, Your Holiness," he said.

Oh my, oh my! What is happening? Everybody is looking at me, wanting me to seal their inner conviction that we are truly on a path towards peace. Or so it seems. President Renders has made progress in his country with the Grand Reforms for All Americans Living, also known informally as GRAAL, very popular with the young generation, not quite so with the traditionalists. Since America has been formally secularized by the introduction of a new amendment to their Constitution that clearly separates religion from the affairs of the state, and moreover forbids the involvement of the Church into said affairs, there has been a surge of progressive upheavals in the country. Since I am perceived as a very progressive Pontiff, I am a symbol of evolution for the American public, and President Renders would like to recognize me as such.

The next day, I landed in Washington. There was a rally at the National Mall that was celebrating reason and progress. The President asked me if I wanted to make a speech there.

"Absolutely," I said.

We both went there, straight from the airport. I did not need a personal break. I was too excited to feel the need for anything for the functioning of my body.

There were tens of thousands of people at this Reason Rally, that has been going on now for many years. I was certainly not ready to address such a big crowd. Well then, I am never ready to address big crowds, as the love for so many people overwhelms me and tends to dry my throat. Luckily, Nwanne has remedies for this: warm humidifying mints that I can hold in my mouth, and a bottle of water. I always carry them with me when I need to make speeches.

I knew very well in my heart that the people gathered there were *my kind of people*, those who have been awakened. Yet nobody there knew what I was holding back in my mind, nobody truly knew me as not a man of faith. Thus, I spoke what has been expected, and, truth being told, I still cannot fully speak my mind, not even to myself.

"I am a man of God," I said to the crowd. "You can tell by looking at me and by the place where I work." There was laughter in the crowd. They got my joke! "And I am also a man of reason, who is trying his best to uphold tradition and to recognize the evolution of the spirit, at the same time." Heartfelt applause. "I would like to say that from the standpoint of justice, when you make a vow to God, do not delay to pay it, for he has no pleasure in fools. Pay what you have vowed. That is what the Church teaches. While these words have God in them, they might as well not have Him, as justice and honor can be learnt and taught outside the Church." Splendorous applause. "Thus, we are brothers in defining our lives from different angles yet towards a common goal. Of righteousness, of comradery, of respect for one another. God is my witness to my allegiance. Reason is yours. I applaud you, my fellow humans."

The crowd went crazy and shouted my name and declared that they loved me. I was touched, knowing that on the same, spot many decades ago, Martin Luther King had had a dream. I was no longer certain if all this was real or if I was dreaming. I was lost for words. I had much more to say. I struggled for a few more words, then I allowed President Renders to address the crowd as well. He had no less of a positive reaction from the crowd.

Such a full day. And it was the first time I was visiting the United States of America. Truly overwhelming.

Only at sunset, after more protocol at the White House, was I allowed to rest at my hotel. The sky was ablaze with fireworks. I hoped they were not in my honor, and when I learned they were not, I was finally able to settle my mind and go to sleep.

5:5 Incognito in Washington

This time there we no objections, in principle, from Nwanne.

"We go to the suburbs of this great capital," I told him.

How I really wanted to be alone this time, truly alone, no security detail in disguise, no worrying from my angel, just me and the unknown world, at the mercy of chance and human encounters. I beseeched Nwanne to let me go free. He said he couldn't live with his conscience if he did that.

"How about you give me one of those alarm-bracelets and if I get into trouble I call you? You can be just around the corner."

I saw him wavering. He conceded after he tested the alarm-bracelet three times. He explained everything to the security detail. They agreed, but they added a microwave microdrone just in case.

We stopped at the intersection of 45th and Capitol. I got out of the car and ventured into the neighborhood. I was wearing the hoodie, the khaki pants, the snickers, the glasses (so I've been told they are necessary), the nice fake black beard. So local, I was completely inconspicuous. I didn't even have to alter my Nigerian accent.

I went inside the first building I encountered, called "Brother Chuck's Ribs'n'Wings". Inside were only black people, and a white police officer that was getting ready to leave. The police officer had a riot-helmet on, but he seemed friendly. He sized me up and said "Goodday" to me, so I said "Goodday" back. Then he left. I went to the bar and talked to the bartender. His name was Brother Chuck.

"You army?" he said.

"Yessir," I said.

"What deployment?"

"Yemen. I was Airborne and Peace Corps," I said.

"Respect," Brother Chuck said. "You talk African. You outpatriated to the States?"

"Yessir. They gave me a card and temporary benefits to settle."

"Man, this government does things. No offense." Brother Chuck was upset.

"Not at all. I like it here," I said.

"Man, just don't get yourself blown up."

"I will pay attention," I said.

"What can I get you?" Brother Chuck said.

"A full rack with fries and a fresh pint of Yosemite."

"Have a seat. Coming right up. I make the meanest ribs in town. Soldier's honor."

When Brother Chuck walked towards the kitchen to deploy the order with the cook, I saw he was wearing a leg prosthesis, exposed. It was shoed with army-issue boots. Brother Chuck was also a veteran. Moments after I sat down at a table and got used to the stickiness of the table, a man with a mask over his face entered the restaurant and waved a pistol at everybody inside: five clients, Brother Chuck, and a cook.

The man with the pistol yelled something in an accent I could not understand. He was very agitated, he pointed the gun at a person then quickly moved to another person, screaming something that we were supposed to do. I have seen violence in my life. Guns have been pointed at my face many times. Somehow, I felt this was different. The man's hand was shaking. He could not hold the pistol steady.

"Relax man," Brother Chuck spoke calmly. "You want money? Money you want?"

"Ya, gimme your monies all of you!" the man shouted, not looking anyone in their eyes.

"It's okay, man," Brother Chuck said. "It's gonna be fine. Just fine. I'll give it to you, man. You like ribs, man? Juicy ribs. You like 'em?"

"Yeah, I like ribs," the man said.

"You know what I'm gonna give you?" Brother Chuck said calmly. "I'm gonna give you all my money and I'm gonna give you a box of ribs. That sit well with you?"

"Yeah," the man with the pistol said. His face was sweating under his mask.

"Just point the gun at the floor, okay?" Brother Chuck said.

He opened the register and collected all his cash. He made it into a wad and put it on the counter. He backed up slowly with his hands in the air.

The man with the pistol took the money and waited for the box of ribs. He looked at me.

"You veteran?" he asked.

"Yessir," I said.

Better not to vow than to vow and not pay, I thought.

"Your ribs are ready," Brother Chuck said, and put them on the counter.

The man with the pistol grabbed the bag and backed off slowly towards the door without saying anything. When he was outside he ran into a dark alley.

All this time I had my hands on the table. I had not touched my alarm-bracelet. My heart was pumping normally. Brother Chuck did not look scared at all. He was sorrowful and sad, like he had seen worse in his life, been to hell and back, and a mere robbery was a child's play for him. When he met my eyes and saw I was not scared either, he spoke:

"Do I know you, mister?"

"You do not, sir."

"You look familiar."

"All brothers' faces who have served look familiar."

"That is true," Brother Chuck said. "Why were you not afraid?"

"He was just scared. He forgot to take anything from me and these clients over here."

Brother Chuck realized I knew how to read people and I was somebody special. He brought me the ribs. I asked him to pack them for me so I could take them out. I paid and tipped generously.

"Take care Mr. Chuck," I said.

"Good days to you too, brother," Brother Chuck said.

I walked out.

5:6 The confession of President Renders

Official visit at the White House. There was a state dinner and a reception with less pomp, precisely what I would have expected from President Renders. After the mandatory meet and greet, the numerous selfies and benedictions I offered with great pleasure, President Renders asked me if I wanted to have a private conversation in his office. Just the two of us.

"Now that we are alone, Your Holiness, there something on my heart I would like to share with you," the President said.

"Certainly Mr. President," I said.

"There is a recent tradition in my country that its politicians must be men of faith. Well, I have broken with that tradition. I am not a believer, Your Holiness, in the vicarious redemption offered by Christ, nor in any form of absolution and prolonged existence in the hereafter. I have never declared this publicly, nor have I clearly stated my faith. My spiritual strength comes only from my belief in the potential of mankind, in our resoluteness to do good, in our love for life and for each other. There is no mysterious warmth from outside nature that envelops me or inspires me. I do not pray to anyone. I do not know how to. I only meditate about the state of my country and how I can do my best to serve. So why do I tell you all these things? Because I have felt, Your Holiness, that you can understand me."

"I understand you well, Mr. President," I said.

At the same time, I felt unprepared to answer the President. Somehow, he was reading into my heart and was about to expose me, not out of malice, but through his caring for truth.

"Am I lying if I do not talk about God to people who expect me to talk about God and my faith? Am I being dishonest if I talk about my spirituality as confidence in the good potential of mankind, instead of invoking religious narratives? I do not mean to cause you offense, Your Holiness-."

"Oh no, not at all, Mr. President. See, you put me in a difficult position. I can only speak the truth. I too have to consider my words very carefully, all the time, perhaps even more cautiously since my mandate is for life, while yours is only for four years. I see greater value in the deeds of a man than in the strength of his faith, greater value in real caring for the poor and the disadvantaged than in endless prayer, greater value in doing than in thinking about doing. I see more good in the actions of people who take to the streets to protest against oppression, than in a monk who spends his life in a monastery, praying to the sky. You will be surprised to hear me say this, Mr. President: one does not need God to do good."

"This is indeed a surprise to hear, Your Holiness. It makes me feel much more at ease."

"I have seen it in politics many times, Mr. President, leaders using fear to pull support from the distressed population. Spoken evil and spoken division is half way to the realization of evil and division. I would say to those who claim to be inspired by God: do not let your mouth cause your flesh to sin, nor say before the messenger of God that it was an error."

"I agree, Your Holiness. Why should God be angry at your excuse and destroy the work of your hands?"

"Exactly. Many would say you would make a true good Christian."

We both laughed.

"I am not one. I am sorry to say, Your Holiness."

"That is just fine, Mr. President. Often, I feel I am not one either, and I forget what a true Christian would look like. While I shepherd an ancient institution, I would like to think of us as people, and nothing else."

"I trust, Your Holiness, that one day we would see each other as mere neighboring people."

"I would like that very much too, Mr. President."

"Please allow me to seek your council more often. I would appreciate it very much."

"By all means, Mr. President. By all means."

5:7 Nwanne's sin and his departure to a monastery

We are home, we are finally home.

I am extremely tired. The changing world is spinning around me, is pulling me in all directions. I enjoy the work, the struggle, and I wish my body would do more for what my mind would want to achieve. Perhaps this is the true cross we need to carry: knowing that with your mind you could move mountains, while in reality your frail body can only move stones. I let my mind wander in my meditations, listen to peoples, hear endless stories, watch terrible newscasts, see movements and revolutions, grand parades and sporting events, inspiring speeches and millions of people hashtagging truths. I see people's hopes and dreams declared to the world. And it all saddens me, for in the multitude of dreams and many words there is also vanity.

And the scriptures tell us: But fear God, and you will live forever, you will feel better, happiness will rain on you, guilt will disappear. So we go out, fear God, and nothing happens. Life just goes on, as if there was no fear at all in the first place. Things will just happen, whether we dread them or not. We will be happy or sad when we least expect it. We will be angry or peaceful for reasons coming from the people around us. We will perhaps feel alone in a crowd, or crowded when our mind is loaded with many troubles. And that's just life, I suppose, for us to make something out of it.

Nwanne was invited by Cardinal Justinian Rechtsman (I don't know him very well) to go to a reception at a private residence in Rome. It appeared to be for some charity symposium.

At 9 o'clock in the evening Nwanne came to my apartment. He was pale and was breathing heavily.

"I have sinned Holy Father."

"What happened, dear Nwanne?"

"I was invited by Cardinal Rechtsman to one of the Vatican's social outreach apartments. I was not very familiar with them. He told me we were meeting a group of promising young talents who want to help us with missionary work in New Korea. When we arrived, I did not expect anything out of the ordinary. However, as soon as I entered, there was an unusual scent in the air, quite pleasant, and a raised temperature that made me think of our outdoor walks in Africa. Cardinal Rechtsman took off his jacket. For as much as I thought I would see the upper part of his cassock, I saw only a white shirt, tight to his body, and nothing underneath. The bottom of the cassock was therefore a fake cassock, resembling a woman's dress. Cardinal Rechtsman invited me to unload my jacket and remain in my shirt. Most unusual, but I followed his recommendation. It was quite hot, indeed. In the living room, there was a bishop whose name escapes me for the moment. The bishop had his shirt unbuttoned. I could see his chest. There were six other nonclerical men, who were wearing loose shirts over their belts and loose linen pants. These six men were very friendly. They were serving cold beverages on silver trays and various sweets. There was jam, honey tarts, mini cheese cakelettes, chocolate dipped raspberries. They offered whipped cream on everything. One server was talking to the bishop and asked if the bishop wanted whipped cream, the bishop said yes, and the server sprayed whipped cream on the cakelette but did not stop, and the whipped cream overflowed from the saucer onto the poor bishop's pants and exposed chest. I wanted to help, so I rushed to the bishop. Soon, I realized there was no need. The server knelt and collected the extra whipped cream with his mouth and left the bishop stark clean as before, perhaps a bit more humid. In response, the bishop thanked the server by kissing him on the cheeks, then moments later directly on the mouth. I was flummoxed. Then the bishop asked me if I wanted to be served. I said I can help myself, as I did not want to inconvenience the servers. We all sat down on couches. I thought we were about to interview these men. That is not what happened. Cardinal Rechtsman received the attention of another two servers who purposely sprayed whipped cream on the cardinal's shirt. I was petrified. Before I could open my mouth, another two servers came to me, one from behind to rub my shoulders and one in front to attempt to remove my shirt and to spray me with whipped cream. I tried to decline, politely, but the man in front of me pushed a chocolate-dipped raspberry into my mouth so I couldn't speak. I tried to eat the raspberry fast, so I could express my position in words. I failed to do that, since as soon as I swallowed, the man in front of me knelt and kissed me on the mouth, attempting to further prevent me from speaking. I thought on the spur of the moment if I returned the kind gesture, perhaps the man will retreat and allow me to speak. It did not last more than ten seconds, maybe fifteen, but at most twenty seconds, when I realized that the man had no intention of letting me speak. Moreover, the man in the back almost succeeded in removing my shirt. I decided to stand up and show physical force, by pushing the man in front of me. This indeed succeeded and both men removed themselves away from me. I was shaken and did not know what to say. Cardinal Rechtsman was surprised at my reaction. He said he thought I would like this friendly meeting, as he thought I enjoyed the company of men. I begged his pardon and I excused myself, as I had realized I had sinned, from an amorous point of view. I felt I had betrayed Your Holiness, and Mother Church. The encounter obviously had another purpose. Please forgive me."

I listened to my dear Nwanne with much attention. Then he said:

"I would like to go away for a while, to pray for forgiveness and for a strong mind."

There is nothing else for me to say.

5:8 If you see the oppression of the poor

When emptiness is bereft of concepts and the potential of any creation, we fall back into pure absence of mind with all the consequences, from emotional links to life, to serene reflections about the purpose of everything. Lingering in us will be the notion of permanent change which we name time, without a soul, without sensations, while we are still awake, placing us in a state of absurd contradiction with the notions of cause and effect, with the notions of being and non-being.

But I cannot find more justifications for the existence of mankind. The arbitrary laws are created with motivations and they degenerate in utensils for limited interests. The Leviathan of corruption, with its many arms and daggers, does not discriminate around, but it carries forward its self-proclaimed mission, slashes and dismembers all opposition in its vicinity, while minding its purpose.

Those who have survived in trenches raise their heads to see the incoming armies, and see nothing but the fumes of caravans approaching on continuous iron tracks that flatten the Earth. The survivors eat what was left and drink what has rained and write their memories on parchments made of tree bark. They are barefoot, they are half-naked. Their hair is broken, their bodies are weak.

If you see the oppression of the poor, soon there will be a painting of it in an art gallery, and the King will buy it for his own private collection. If you see the violent perversion of justice and righteousness in a province, there will be a crowd who will riot and a cohort of riot-police that will respond, but do not marvel at the matter, there will come a time for change, there will come a time to forget, there will be a written history. People will remember.

When we built these pyramids of power, from the bottom on up, and we created doors and elevators, we left room for earthquakes and the works of falling rain. When pyramids became gargantuan, we tried to call down the high officials, and many would not come down, as other high officials watched over high officials, and higher officials are over them. Some pyramids end in the clouds.

5:9 The drafting of the Great Papal Bull

I have sat down with Cardinal Tchipcherish for the past three days. We have begun to draft the Great Papal Bull of reformation, the first in a series of bulls that I would like to write during my papacy.

We began by studying the problem of poverty and we concluded that the one major cure for poverty is the emancipation of women. Self-evidently, by allowing women to control their bodies, by allowing them equal rights with men in the binding of procreation, they will become more aware of themselves as carriers of life and builders of families.

"I have to be frank, Your Holiness," Tchipcherish said, "I do not see an alternative, other that accepting women into the clerical ranks."

"Yes Thorsen, yes, I've been thinking the same thing for a while already."

"This is how we show that we truly value women, by making them equal to men. It doesn't mean we clericalize them."

"No, it certainly doesn't mean that."

I have found myself agreeing a lot with Cardinal Tchipcherish lately. He doesn't get on my nerves that much anymore. Perhaps it was his way of speaking and his abrasive character that stood between his ideas and our camaraderie. That being said, I still feel uneasy around him. Probably he smells my loss of faith, not in my words, but in my liturgical intonations. And I wonder what his true agenda is. He is the most progressive Cardinal I have ever met.

"Before you say anything, Thorsen," I said. "I would like to lay my thoughts. I do have the equality of women within our ranks in mind. And I would like to take things a little further. I am prepared to make a woman Cardinal. I am prepared to open the path for a woman to become Pope, some day."

"Your Holiness!"

"Tell me you were not thinking the same thing. Be honest, Thorsen."

"I am always forthcoming with you. Yes, I was thinking the same thing."

"Was there anything else you had in mind?"

"No, not about this subject."

"I do have something else in mind. I have the name of a candidate in mind, that I would like to elevate to Cardinal, very soon."

Tchipcherish was genuinely surprised.

"Who is it? If I may ask."

"Allegra Maria Yolanda Coccinella."

"Who?"

"An Italian Mother Superior from Naples. She has travelled around the world as a doctor, chef, and educator. She sometimes works in the Santa Croce della Sofferenza monastery on the Amalfi Coast. Her humanitarian work is outstanding."

"I dare not doubt. I wish I had heard of her."

"Soon, you will hear more. I want to feature her in the Great Papal Bull. She has been contacted privately and has agreed to the appointment in principle, on the condition that it will enhance her humanitarian work. I promised her that that is exactly the reason I want to appoint her. We will both meet her soon."

Tchipcherish was speechless. I felt the need to emboss my joy with a saying:

"Moreover, the profit of the land is for all-"

"-even the king is served from the field," Tchipcherish replied softly.

"Thank you Thorsen for your support," I said with a friendly tone.

"Your Holiness, I am here to serve you and Mother Church."

He left it at that. I found it very peculiar, since he always used to mention at least Christ, if not God in his closing. I still wonder what the Cardinal is hiding.

Off now to important work.

5:10 Of Chino-Canadian Arctic relations

It has become clear that the purpose of the Chinese fleet was to infiltrate the Canadian soil. Heavy airplane-carriers have deployed hundreds of armored trucks in various strategic points in the provinces of Alberta and in the Northwest Territories. President Mo Xi came on holovisions to declare that this deployment is nothing like an invasion, and it is a simple exercise to secure the transport of Canadian oil into oil tankers stationed in the Arctic Ocean. Why the military intervention? Of course, it's a security precaution against potential activists who have threatened to boycott the Chino-Canadian Arctic pipeline.

I've seen the work of these activists. They are fierce. They are armed. They are well trained. Since the climate wars began, here and there, one season in the Amazon, as we have seen in the Brazilian Papers, another season in Middle East, another season in the Pacific Wind Complex, these relentless activists have not ceased to fight any attempt to ransack the fossil entrails of Planet Earth. If they want war, war they will get.

I must to say I do not condone war of any kind, yet the work of these many activists makes me pause. They said: he who loves silver will not be satisfied with silver. Which is true of these hungry oil drinkers. They said: nor will he who loves abundance be satisfied with increase. True again, as this is also vanity.

Then President Mo Xi said:

"The Chinese people have partaken in the economic growth of the 21st century. We have grown at par with the Western world. The needs of our people are similar of those of our Western partners. We need to sustain our life style, just like you need to sustain your life style. We are all hungry together, we are all thirsty together. We mean no harm, we mean no war. We simply want to protect our investment. We deplore the meanness of the activist groups. We promise them we shall remain friends of Planet Earth."

Pretty convincing, isn't it?

Prime Minister Dante Beaujolais was of a different opinion. He said:

"We welcome our Chinese trade partners, friends, and sharers of Planet Earth. We are proud to assure them that our end of the Arctic Partnership is holding strong. Lest we forget the dangers of war, we shudder slightly at the sight of foreign military convoys on our soil. We the Canadian people are positively against acts of violence, we do not support the activist warmongers and we understand the importance of conducting business peacefully."

This Canadian message was not holovised and was broadcasted in 2D, therefore appeared flat to the audience. Perhaps it was intended that way. What could the Prime Minister have said otherwise, faced with an almighty Chinese fleet in his backyard? He said what he could to save face. I would probably have done the same thing. Plus, no rockets were launched, no bullets have been shot. It is simply about business.

Naïve nonsense! It's not just about business. Mo Xi knows it, Dante Beaujolais knows it, everybody knows it. It's the game of vanity. It's us against the patience of nature.

Oh… I miss Nwanne already…

5:11 Seeing my angel

I had to see Nwanne, I had to! What better excuse to tell the Curia other than one week of prayer and reflection away from the Vatican at a monastery none other than Santa Croce della Sofferenza on the Amalfi Coast, the same monastery where Nwanne chose to go.

The motorcade dropped me off at the main gate. The Swiss Guard insisted they remain with me for the duration of the visit. I accepted on the condition that they keep their distance.

Mother Superior Allegra Maria Yolanda Coccinella greeted me with a loaf of bread, salt, and a glass of red wine, according to tradition. She was a beautiful middle-aged woman. She looked me in the eyes the whole time, with passion, conviction, and respect. I sensed her strong will and her warm heart.

"Signora Coccinella," I said. "I bring you great news and I bring you my tired soul."

"Your Holiness, please call me Mother Allegra. Santa Croce della Sofferenza is our home and now it is your home. You can rest your body and mind here, while we welcome you any news that you bring."

I followed Mother Allegra to my room. I could only think of Nwanne. Where was he? How long until I meet him? Certainly, I could not tell Mother Allegra any of this. When unexpectedly she said:

"Your Holiness, I am very honored that your personal secretary has recommended our humble monastery to you!"

Nwanne had no idea I came to visit!

"I hope we have not disappointed him," Mother Allegra said.

"Surely you have not," I said politely. "I will meet with him later."

I asked the attending sister to call Nwanne to my room to help me settle in. The sister asked me how long I would stay at Santa Croce della Sofferenza. I said that it will be seven days. She said that if there was anything I needed I could ask for her at any time of the day or of the night.

Nwanne came after sunset. He was wearing the garments of a monk. He had cut his hair short and had a clean-shaven face. He smelled of lavender. His hands were soft and creamy. He seemed at peace with himself. He spoke as if he had unburdened himself of a heavy cross and was in the company of lightweight angels.

"Your Holiness, you came," he said.

"Nwanne, look around, there is nobody. It is just you and me in a small, simple room, at an Italian monastery. We don't need to pretend anymore. I am your partner in life. We will never be strangers to each other."

"I have never forgotten, Enyi."

Nwanne was always the tender one. While his heart was never closed on itself, mine had often struggled with dark thoughts and the fear of judgment.

"What is a fearless heart," Nwanne said, "if not one that speaks the truth at all times."

"What about the suffering of others, Nwanne? How do we know that we don't hurt others when we speak our heart?"

"No heart should feel oppressed when truth is spoken."

There was no need for more words. The night was upon us together with the silence of reflection. Santa Croce della Sofferenza does not make use of bells in the evening. "The bells are inside us," Mother Allegra had told me. We dimmed the lights in the room and we remembered the nights when we were young in Africa. Sleeping outside under the clear sky, watching constellations and shooting stars, while we held our hands and spoke about holy things. Now, I am the Pope of the Catholic Church. We had come a long way. We had strengthened the union of our souls while our bodies have aged. There were no secrets between us, even though I had not told Nwanne that I had lost my faith. But he knows. I'm sure he knows. He can see it in my eyes. There will be a time for this conversation, soon, I hope. Until then, what we have is a week of companionship, far from the goods of the world. Later in the night, Nwanne whispered to me:

"When the goods of the world increase, so do those who consume them. And what benefit are they to the owners except to feast their eyes on them?"

5:12 Mother Allegra

Before sunset, in my sleep, I heard the chirping of birds quenching their thirst with dew droplets. Then I smelled the scent of brewed coffee, the one that only Nwanne knows how to make.

I opened my eyes to find Nwanne near me, tending to my needs.

"Mother Allegra is here to see you," Nwanne said.

"Oh my goodness! Does she know you have been here with me?"

"Of course she knows, Enyi. She understands the true connections of souls."

I had to get dressed quickly, comb my hair, brush my teeth and shave with the laser razor.

I met Mother Allegra in the beautiful gardens of Santa Croce della Sofferenza. She was waiting for me, reading a book on an old bench.

"Your Holiness," Mother Allegra said. "You seem to be in good spirits today."

I blushed.

"The sleep of a laboring man is sweet—" I said, "—whether he eats little or much, but the abundance of the rich will not permit him to sleep. I am rested and tired at the same time, Mother Allegra. My body is rested. My soul is rested. Yet my mind toils over great worries."

"I was told you came here to see me," Mother Allegra said.

"It is true."

We walked together in the serene gardens of the monastery. The perfume from the lemon tree orchard elated my spirits while the gentle breeze caressed my skin. Why did I deserve so much beauty and so much comfort to my body, while millions wither in squalor?

I must say that Mother Allegra had no idea why I came to see her. I was left with no option but to lay out the words to her plainly and without hesitation. I came to Santa Croce della Sofferenza to offer her the office of a Cardinal. She will be the first woman to be confirmed as Cardinal since my predecessor introduced the canon law reform for the ordination of women in the Catholic Church.

Mother Allegra did not take the news lightly. At first, she stopped walking and looking directly into my eyes, for a long time. She grabbed my hands into her hands and was reading straight from my soul. I felt so embarrassed, I felt the urge to pull my hands back, yet I could not do it. Her grip was much stronger than my embarrassment.

"You have the soul of a woman, Your Holiness," Mother Allegra spoke first.

There are not many people who can truly interpret my sensibility and equate it to that of a woman. Only Nwanne knows me that well, and he does because he has been a lifetime companion. Never in my life I had met somebody who reached so deeply into me, to find the core of my being. A tiny woman, with strong tiny hands and the disposition of a warrior, has told me I was aching and feeling with the soul of a woman.

"Forgive me, Your Holiness," Mother Allegra continued. "I am overwhelmed by your generosity. I am speaking without thinking."

"That is the truth Mother Allegra," I said. "You are speaking the truth."

While I continued to explain the forthcoming procedure of the ordination, the overwhelming consent of the Curia, I was also subduing the entire history of the canon law that legitimized only ordained men to the office of a Cardinal. I found the tradition stiff and morose, humiliating and disgraceful, rationalized by men to empower themselves by earthly means, in blatant contradiction with the spirit of Christ. Was Christ not a man of his times as we are men and women of our times? Were the scriptures not written by biased men, with personal agendas, based on hearsay and plagiarism? How do we know that the voice of God ordains only half of his creation while the other half must live in submission? Oh, how my blood was boiling, while I spoke soft words to Mother Allegra and thought harsh criticism toward my own establishment! How this will one day be the end of me, when all this will be found out.

"I would be honored to accept the ordination, Your Holiness," Mother Allegra said.

"Then it is done," I said.

Mother Allegra kissed my hands, knelt, and asked for my blessing. I offered it from the bottom of my heart, without speaking the name of the Father, of the Son, or of the Holy Ghost. I said:

"May your soul rise to the highest office in the Catholic Church so you can channel your character and knowledge to the greater benefits of mankind. Amen."

"Rise, Sister Allegra. You will henceforth be known as Cardinal Allegra Coccinella. It has a nice ring to it."

We both laughed and walked together for the rest of the afternoon.

5:13 Thoughts about critics

Ugh, silly me! What possessed me to read those articles critical of me on the social media internet, had I nothing else better to do?! It has been a wonderful week of retreat away from the stress at the Vatican, a weak with wonderful accomplishments, and now I read these mean words! Do people know who I really am? What I really feel? What I really think? That I struggle with my own petty life every day to conquer the weight of vanity, that I carry this monstrous secret in me that grows bigger and bigger.

People have written on the social internet: there is a severe evil which I have seen under the sun. They talk about me! I am the severe evil! How can I be the severe evil? They say I have opened the path for the Devil into this world. How did I open it? I believe I have closed it. I am ready to put my entire life on trial for the deeds I have put forward as the Pope of Rome. Who are these people who speak so ill of me? What are their credentials? What makes them stronger believers than I once was? Do they not realize that they criticize their own faith when they attack me? They are people of absurd contradictions: accepting Christ and His Church but only on their terms, willing to go to the Sunday mass but unwilling to obey the entire doctrine of the faith, and why? When the Church said: Mary was a virgin because it is written in the Bible, who are you an anonymous Christian on the social internet to say that it was not so? And if you are so daring to say that the faith you know is better than what the Church offers, so be it, take that faith of yours and carry it with your business away from me, I will not offer you any benediction whatsoever, nor will I authorize by the power vested in me to allow other priests to forgive your sin.

It makes me sick to see the plethora of stupidity in these digital forums and conversation areas and chat groups, precisely because they consider themselves great followers of Christ, so they say, Christ here, Christ there, sweet delicious Christ, oh, I would give my life for you, oh, I would disown my children for you, oh, I would shout your name loud and clear in Church once a week, pay the monthly subscription, then see to my despicable life for the rest of the week, oh, maybe I will curse the Pope of Rome, why?, because he wants to reform my Church and speak the truth of suffering and vanity, and on and on full of ungrammatical imbecile nonsense that reaches my eyes here by some random chance.

I wonder what they will say when I introduce to them Cardinal Allegra Coccinella. Will they cheer and embrace her? Will they give me a break? Will they split into warring factions and declare this an outrage and that I need to be removed from office because I am insane, while the other faction turns me into a global viral hashtag for good feelings and reasons to celebrate because I am the modern cool Pope of the young generation, the leader of the emancipation of women and on and on? I don't know what else they will, the world can surprise me every single day, especially when I thought I completely understood it.

Some will pull the hair out of their heads and scream on the streets. Some will weep at my portrait and wish me a very long life. Some will accept any new laws that I will decide to issue, without question. I could say their entire faith is a lie, a grand farce, an imbecilic obsession with some ideas that a bunch of illiterate peasants came up with more than two thousand years ago, thinking that some invisible deity in the sky put them in their heads! Listen to me, the blasphemies I write just pumped by what I have come to read.

I am the only one to suffer, because I am the carrier of these trepidations. I cannot answer those mean critics. I cannot tell them what I really think. I have the calmness and composure of a saint, don't I? I am in full control of my emotions, am I not? With all the riches in knowledge I have obtained, what have I achieved if wealth is kept by its owner to his harm?

I will turn the world upside down. I will shake the foundations of faith and leave no stone unturned. Oh, they will remember me! Oh, they will have nightmares! And when they will wake up, they will either be completely free, or completely insane!

This is the time. This is it.

5:14 I felt like a woman

It is done. We had a successful papal consistory today. I elevated 13 new cardinals to the College of Cardinals, among them Cardinal Allegra Coccinella, by far my favorite. The others were all men, half of them devout Catholics, the other half devout thinkers, of which at least three are speaking in such secular terms, I think they may be secret nonbelievers like me! That is precisely why I selected them.

There was a strange moment during the ceremony in St. Peter's Basilica when Mother Allegra approached me to receive the red hat. She kissed my hand, I made the cross sign and I was ready to place the hat on her head, when I felt I was no longer a man in body and mind, but a complete woman from my head to my toes. I had suddenly developed the sensation of having breasts while the pressure men have between their legs from the presence of the masculine scepter was gone, being replaced by the flatness of womanhood. There was no longer hair anywhere on my skin, my hands were lighter, my voice softer.

I felt a hollow space inside my body, in the location of the womb. Goodness gracious, I hope I was not visited by the Holy Ghost! How could I save face if I had been impregnated with some sort of a divine progeny? Don't be ridiculous, Francis, it is a silly thought!

Silly as it may be, is it not a common thought among women? Not that of being divinely inseminated without prior consent, but of having a regular human impregnation caused by a man whose semen was deposited inside the womb? How many women have this anxiety day after day? And how many men dispose of such anxiety with disdain?

The womanly feeling did not leave me after I had placed the cardinal hat on the head of Mother Allegra. There were some men who followed her and whose eyes I did not dare to look into because I was convinced they could have read what has just happened to me. When it was all over, I was so glad to return to my room, I asked Nwanne to be left alone. I took off all my garments and rushed to the tall mirror and inspected my full nude body and sighed with some relief when I saw I was still a man.

The relief was not complete, because as I was watching myself it seemed to me that I was watching the body of another person, as if I was inhabiting the body of a stranger. Where I felt there should be breasts, there was only a flat chest. Where I felt there should be flatness, I saw the ludicrous hanging gardens of Babylon, where I felt there should be epidermic softness, there were old black curled hairs.

As I was looking into the mirror, I pondered what if the riches of the body of a woman perish through misfortune, and that misfortune is not something that comes from inside the body of the woman, or due to the passage of time, but comes through the brutal exploitation of women by the norms of the society?

Suddenly she may lose everything in a bad business deal, and then has nothing to leave for her children.

So this defines the inequalities of sexes and the exploitation of women? Is this how it must be? Women producing sons and daughters whether divine or not, without their full educated consent, at the benefit of tradition and the pride of men?

It must not be so. We must evolve the norms of our forefathers and we must embrace the full sensations of womanhood.

I still feel nude, despite the fact that I am fully clothed now. My breasts are itching now and I cannot feel between my legs. I do not know what to make of this sensation, although I have an inkling that it may have to do with the historic elevation of a woman to the rank of Cardinal. I do not even care to mention the hysteria that has exploded in the media, overwhelmingly positive and laudatory. I rarely know how to reply without embarrassment to effusions of support and approval. Perhaps it is too late to learn that. Why do I feel today is the beginning of something so grand, nobody could have the slightest foresight of what is to come next?

5:15 The uncanonization of Saint Jean-Haze Bijoux

On to the order of the day. A particular character in the history of the Church has been bothering me for quite some time: Saint Jean-Haze Bijoux. Who was this woman? Lived a long life and founded a worldwide network of charities in the 20th century. Or so it seems. My predecessor held her in high regard and canonized her based on reports that she performed miracles. While the appearance of her charitable intentions is laudable, under closer inspection, some unpleasant truths emerge: she was a friend of poverty, not of the poor, she kept sick people in squalor while she received high quality treatment for her illness, she cared less for the needs of those in suffering and more for proselytization and the expansion of the church.

To my enormous surprise, when Mother Allegra asked for an audience just yesterday morning, the next day after her appointment, the first thing she told me, after dispensing the customary greetings, was:

"I would like to talk to you about Saint Jean-Haze Bijoux."

I invited Mother Allegra to sit down.

"Cardinal Coccinella," I said.

"Please Your Holiness, I will always be Mother Allegra to you."

"Very well. I have been thinking about Saint Bijoux myself. It has been bothering me that she was made a saint, while it has already been shown that her miracles were not real and that her work caused as much suffering as it generated ignorant praise and following."

"You are gentle in your evaluation, Your Holiness. My thoughts on Saint Bijoux are more severe. I think the Church should step forward, admit the mistake, and remove Saint Bijoux from sainthood. We need to start a moral revolution in the Church."

"Mother Allegra, I feel as if you are reading my mind. We do need a moral revolution and a moral evolution at the same time. In the way I see it, there is no distinction between the two."

"I worry that this decision might stir some unpleasant reactions," Mother Allegra said.

"I sense that it won't be quite so," I said confidently, "simply because the truth is well known and the popularity of Jean-Haze Bijoux has dropped in the last decade, like a big rock to the bottom of a swamp. True, this does not have a precedent in the Church, but it doesn't mean that it cannot start one, and a just one."

"This would only be a beginning, Your Holiness," Mother Allegra.

"Oh, I only hope we are doing the right thing."

"Speaking and acting the truth should not be subject of shame and doubt," Mother Allegra said.

"Very well. I will draft a statement on the uncanonization of Saint Jean-Haze Bijoux."

"Should we keep her beatified?"

"No. Let us undo her status to that of a simple servant of the Church. We will let history deal with the philosophy of this act. Ugh, I wish I didn't have to concern myself so much with the philosophy of our institution. I wish we would simply serve the people, and not have the burden of theology on our shoulders."

"Your Holiness, I'm not sure what to say," Mother Allegra.

"Perhaps it is too soon to have this conversation Mother Allegra. I foresee an inevitable tumultuous future for both of us, a series of events that will unravel soon. I think I have woken a beast."

"Any beast, as he came from his mother's womb, naked shall he return," Mother Allegra said.

"What if while he is alive, the beast will bring destruction to the world?"

"He will go as he came, and he shall take nothing from his labor which he may carry away in his hand. I do not think our Church can beget beasts, nor that our deeds can bring harm to the world. We may be uncertain of our deeds, since we are mortals, but we are entrusted with a sacred mission."

"Are we, Mother Allegra? Who gave us this mission?"

"God, certainly."

"It was written by men. Honestly, I say, God has never spoken to me."

"I have my doubts too, Your Holiness."

"I say to you plainly, Mother Allegra: You are very dear to me. I trust you completely, and I hope you can be by my side until the end of our lives."

"The honor is also mine."

"Let us make some history with Saint Bijoux. I am sure she won't mind."

Mother Allegra and I chuckled at this little joke of mine. I was pleased to have found such a great companion, and finally to have my sensibility mirrored in the persona of a woman of a high caliber. I shudder a little at the content of our conversation, and I find strength immediately when I know that reason and truth is on our side. What will the Church be without miracles? A circus of reason? A scandal of truth? I can live with that, and I welcome it.

5:16 The Chinese occupation of Canada

If I don't write about something, it does mean it didn't happen. I have too much on my mind, I cannot concentrate on all world events, on every humanitarian crisis. I am just one man. One man should never be directly responsible for more than 30 people. If more than 30 people are involved, then someone else must come and share the responsibility.

I hear that the Chinese troops have advanced as far South as the city of Calgary, without much opposition from the Canadian government, or from the United States government. President Mo Xi declared:

"Our troops move according to the laws of nature."

To which Prime Minister Dante Beaujolais said:

"I am certain our Chinese friends will not disturb the Canadian way of life in the province of Alberta. Certainly, this may be viewed as an act of overzealousness. However, there is nothing to stop us from continuing our friendship with China."

To which the liberal media commented:

"This style of communication is now full of *bok choy*, instead of regular lettuce."

I don't know what this means. I understand the metaphor of the sandwich, two layers of bread and something in between, but I don't know what it means when applied to Canadian political discourse. If I take what the Prime Minister said, that is, three sentences: the first pro-Chinese, the second vaguely anti-Chinese, and the last strongly pro-Chinese; since the first and the third both contradict the second, it means that there is some coded message in what Prime Minister said. I will need some time to figure it out.

What are the Chinese doing in Alberta, anyways? Protecting the oil-pipes? The Chinese oil-pipes that run to the Arctic Ocean? Why? Just because they are attacked by the native people who claim that the pipes are desecrating Mother Earth? Do the Chinese really need the army for this? President Mo Xi must realize he has crossed the line. He is a gentle man, surely he must see that?

And this also is severe evil: this thirst for oil that never ends.

Many nations are consuming other resources to make their plastic needs or to fuel their engines with electricity, while other nations are still chasing the oil. A bleak liquid from the deep soil, that, just exactly as he came, so shall he go; and while it disappears, it will poison our existence.

And what profit has he who has labored for the winds of the North?

I bet both President Mo Xi and Prime Minister Dante Beaujolais know exactly the measure of the profit. I fear that it is little for their benefit, and more for the benefit of monsters without faces and real names.

5:17 Cardinal Tchipcherish talks about Cardinal Coccinella

Thorsen Tchipcherish insisted that he met with me in my office today. It is very hard for me to deny his requests. He somehow managed to squeeze a meeting from Nwanne.

He said: "Your Holiness, I am enchanted by the elevation of Cardinal Coccinella as a member of our Curia. This is truly our time, Your Holiness. Now we can build your great legacy."

I thought I was already building a reasonable legacy. For me, the promotion of Mother Allegra was a natural event that is no less extraordinary than the promotion of a man. Surely, in the light of history, it may be an unorthodox move, but it is not unnatural, it is not unChristian, it is not blasphemous. Was the Christ not born from the flesh of a woman?

"Your Holiness," Tchipcherish continued unabated, "we must pave the way for Cardinal Coccinella, to allow her to engage with women in our Church and outside our Church. We have to reach out to women, we have to empower women, we have to bring women into the ranks of clerical power."

"It is a great idea, Thorsen," I said. "It is a fantastic idea. You know me, I am more of a contained temperament, I cannot exude the same exuberance like you, but I totally support."

"Your Holiness," Thorsen interrupted, "you are a great man, and I can see through your heart and mind, and I know this is what you what to do. I am merely bringing forth my support. History tends to have a fast pace for those alive, and a slower pace for historians."

"You are suggesting we need to outpace the flow of history? Move faster than the times we live in, so we can leave a stronger legacy?"

"I think we need to change the world, Your Holiness, and faster."

"Faster, Thorsen?"

"The gravest reality in the world is that, in spite of the advancement in technology and democracy, the suffering of people has also multiplied by a greater factor, caused by the growth of the population and by the continued suffering of women."

"I am aware of all these realities, Thorsen. I am simply undecided about the best course of action."

My first real struggle is with my secret. I am not yet ready by far to discuss this with Tchipcherish. He would shred me to pieces. He may be a progressive and forthcoming Cardinal, but he remains a servant of God. So he seems. All of what he was saying made sense to me. If I could dare to speak my mind fully, I would say to Tchipcherish that I want to go even further than him.

"My position, Thorsen, is of general agreement with you. We need to engage Cardinal Coccinella. What if we first send her to meet the Orthodox Patriarchs on an ecumenical tour? What do you think?"

"It is a good idea, Your Holiness," Tchipcherish said.

"Come now, Thorsen, I was just testing your resoluteness! Do not underestimate me."

"By far my intentions-"

"Sending Cardinal Coccinella on a public relations tour is the least we can do. It would be a mere beginning for our bigger plan."

Ha! I finally managed to silence Tchipcherish. He said nothing. I still feel he has a secret agenda. I'm not sure what it is. Does he have his own demons? Does he have days when he eats in darkness, and has much sorrow and sickness and anger? Who is Tchipcherish on the inside?

5:18 More from the past: my first mission as a diplomat

By the time I was consecrated Bishop, on my 30th birthday, I had seen enough tragedy to haunt my dreams for the rest of life. I rarely cared for the next day, and was always thankful to live another day. As Nwanne used to tell me after the morning prayer: "Isn't it wonderful we got to see another day?"

When Nwanne and I returned to Nigeria, after many trips to all the corners of Africa, we were summoned to the office of Catholic Cardinal Archbishop of Abuja.

"I have heard of your missionary work," the Cardinal of the office said. "Your reputation far exceeds your age. Even Desmond Tutu called me and said wonderful words about you."

"I am honored Your Eminence," I said.

"I foresee a bright future for you, son. You finished your doctorate?"

"Yes."

"Good, good. In Rome?"

"Yes."

"What was your thesis about?"

"The new theology of the beginning of the Universe."

"Fascinating. What were your conclusions?"

"Well... That God must be really complicated."

"We knew that already," the Cardinal chuckled, and tried to test me.

"That is true, Your Eminence. What I want to say is that cosmology has made significant progress and is explaining more and more, leaving less work for God. So then, God is either barely involved in the making of the Universe, or extremely involved, thus being responsible for every single detail of this apparent fine-tuning of everything in existence, which makes Him fantastically complex. I then go into details, trying to analyze many aspects of cosmology-."

"That's OK, we don't need to go into these details now. That's not why I summoned you two here."

Nwanne was sitting in silence next to me.

"I want you to go to Maiduguri, in the Borno State, and meet with the leader of Eudhra Harem, the Islamist group. I want you to talk to him, and find a channel of peaceful communication."

We got on a plane and flew to Maiduguri the next day. When we arrived in Maiduguri, I sent a private message to the leader of the Eudhra Harem and told him I wanted to talk to him. He was surprised by my audacity and welcomed it.

He wrote back: "I don't know who you are but I find your courage remarkable. You do know this is Sharia territory?"

I replied back: "Yes, and I support the idea of peace at the heart of the Sharia."

Then he said I have to go alone to a certain place in Maiduguri, and allow myself to be taken blindfolded to the headquarters of Eudhra Harem. When I arrived there, I understood the meaning of Eudhra Harem. It means the Virgin Harem, more specifically it is the representation of heaven on Earth. Naturally, this also implied that there would be many women around to sustain such a representation. They were everywhere, wearing heavenly attire and carrying various house objects from one place to another, according to the requests of the male leaders around. For example, two women escorted me, after the blindfold was removed, from the lobby to the office of the leader. His name was Abu Walrus Maabbani.

"Mr. Maabbani," I said. "Thank you for having me in your house."

Abu Walrus Maabbani was standing at the window, with his back toward me. He said, without turning:

"This is what I have observed to be good: that it is appropriate for a person to eat, to drink, and to find satisfaction in their toilsome labor under the sun during the few days of life God has given them. For this is their heritage."

"Yes, I happen to agree with that."

"Mr. Enyi, you think there can be peace between Christianity and Islam?"

"I think there can be peace between any group of humans, defined by any criteria. There can be peace between Christians and Islamists, progressives and conservatives, blacks and whites, engineers and artists, activists and politicians, North and South, East and West."

Abu Walrus Maabbani turned to face me. He was a tall and strong man. He could easily pass as a white man. He said:

"I like your thinking, in principle. But you know our Sharia does not allow us to cut deals with the infidels."

"I see you are a straight man, Mr. Maabbani," I said straight to his face. "My mission here is of peace. May I only suggest that we are not your infidels, but only people born of different mothers and different fathers, that have not heard the words of the same revelations and prophets? Is it our fault that we were born elsewhere? Is it your personal virtue that you were born under the grace of Sharia? I surmise not. We are the extensions of our traditions, and we are all alive, children of the present. We are faced with new realities every day, we see a changing world, we can talk, we can walk, we are not people of the past, blessed be their names. We are alive and we must have the struggle of life. One thing we do have in common: that is that we all want a good life, an honorable life, and we all hope for admission into the heavenly hereafter."

I must have impressed Abu Walrus Maabbani. He went silent for at least three minutes. He gestured to me to sit down on the guest chair. He sat slowly on the chair behind his desk. He put his hands together like in a Christian prayer and meditated. He nodded and meditated. There was no one else in the room. I only hoped that Nwanne was safe at the restaurant I left him in the center of Maiduguri.

When Abu Walrus Maabbani spoke, he said plainly and calmly:

"You moved me, Mr. Enyi. Consider that we are starting our peace dialogue here."

5:19 What is the future of religion?

I had many meetings with Abu Walrus Maabbani over the next few months. After many conversations about theology, the divine rights and the earthly rights of people, we developed a mutual sentiment that we ought to recognize and respect our differences, that the appellative infidel is counterproductive, and that Jihad is a matter within the soul of a Muslim and must not result in the bearing of weapons and the conduct of physical violence. When Nigeria attained complete religious peace within its borders, the Cardinal of Abuja notified the Vatican, and described my contribution to the interconfessional dialogue in detail. I had become a well-known bishop in the Catholic Church.

Those days are long gone and Abu Walrus Maabbani has also expired. The pillars of peace have not crumbled, are not weaker, but have not multiplied. The former enemies have reached a standstill of acceptance that neither party can ever prevail over the other. This is an important step. There have been no other armed conflicts over whose theology is the right one.

I have lived as well through a long period when I considered all various religious manifestations of the same revelations that God has offered mankind. I no longer think that. I have also considered that as for every man to whom God has given riches and wealth, and the ability to enjoy them, to accept their heritage and be happy in their labor, this was a gift of God. I no longer consider that. I have changed to think that the riches and the wealth are the products of chance and man's own work, and no other power has any interventions in this matter. Leaps of good luck and falls into misfortune are often filled with the faith that it was God's will, which builds my realization that there is no distinction between faith and imagination, between faith and wishful thinking, between faith and the laziness of the mind to seek the tools of reason to investigate reality.

After these many years, I now realize the harm religion causes to the minds of people when it advances to control the mind to its benefit. While I can recognize the benefits of religion to compose the behavior of peoples, the same benefits disappear when this composure becomes dogmatic, and exclusive of other groups.

I can no longer continue this charade. It is my daily struggle to carry these thoughts and convictions. How long can I continue to be Pope Francis the Second, anointed as the first servant of God, while I no longer recognize the authority of such a master!? Moreover, I do not recognize his existence by all definitions of the Christian faith?

I ought to burn these pages right now, so they are never found. My greatest fear is that they will end up in some writer's book, who will try to reap benefits from my terrible struggle.

5:20 The empowerment of Mother Allegra

Great progress for Mother Allegra, our beloved Cardinal Coccinella. Her force of character made a powerful impression in the Curia. She spoke loudly, eloquently, and clearly to all the Cardinals gathered there. St. Peter's Square was also teeming with people. Today was the day of the announcement of Great Papal Bull of Reformation. It was scheduled for 12 o'clock, yet by

3 o'clock in the afternoon we were still debating in the meeting room. Some of the Cardinals were trying to voice opposition. Their words came out so weakly, it took Mother Allegra only a sentence or two to counter them and move the agenda forward. The most conservative Cardinals were afraid. We could hear the crowd from outside that was listening and cheering speakers from all corners of the Earth, women recounting their mutilation at the hands of oppression, and children who survived the trauma of refuge and asylum. The Great Papal Bull was for all of them.

I could not withhold my enthusiasm when all my main points of reformation were adopted. One by one, Mother Allegra read them out loud for me:

One. The incorporation of the Catholic Church into the realm of social, economic, and political institutions. We have to assume the truth of our institution. We have always been social, economic, and political. The Church will pay taxes everywhere.

Two. The full integration of women into the clerical ranks.

Three. The full recognition of same-gender unions and their full integration into the clerical ranks.

Four. The decentralization of clerical power.

Five. The reform of the Christian dogma. Less talk of Virgin Mary, the passion of Christ and the Holy Ghost, and more focus on real-life compassion. [Side note in my diary: I am setting the stage for the termination of the Immaculate Conception doctrine. I think there is no historical basis for it. It is nonsense. It is a hoax. It is wishful thinking.]

Six. Procreation Control. There are too many people on the planet. This causes great suffering for the young generation who compete for fewer and fewer resources.

Seven. Clean up the finances of the Church. Full transparency.

Eight. Open up the Vatican archives. Full public access.

I need to stop here. It is late and I am rather tired. It has been a good day. True rest I cannot find anymore, not with the staggering lie on my mind. I went to my nightstand and I opened the Old Testament at random. I read: For he will not dwell unduly on the days of his life, because God keeps him busy with the joy of his heart. A comforting thought, regardless of the connotations. Find a passion and make it your life. If you don't have one, find one, invent one, borrow one, discover one.

NOTEBOOK SIX

6:1 Sheep, wolves, asses, deer, and doves

It has been over a month since I wrote notes in my diary. I had very little time for meditation, for a proper walk in the garden, for a quiet dinner with Nwanne.

What a circus it has been! The Great Papal Bull caused a worldwide stir.

Stayingzento (Dalai Lama 15) holocalled me at 5 o'clock in the morning. I received his call, after I told him off-video that I needed time to put a robe on me and wash my face. We are good friends, I told him he can call me at any hour, so he did. He said:

"Holiness, the Bull is fantastic! You are model for us all."

I thanked him humbly and I reiterated our plan about the Spiritual Council of Humanity. He had not forgotten about it.

"Yes, yes!" he said.

"We must work on it at once, and build on your Great Bull!"

I did say I was skeptical about such an endeavor. The peoples of Earth are too divided over borders of faith.

"Holiness," DL 15 said, "that is exactly why the Spiritual Council of Humanity cannot be built on principles of religious faith."

We left it at that, since DL 15 had to honor an appointment with President Mo Xi of China.

I did not have time to have breakfast, since minutes later President Pavel Pushkin called me on the high priority line. He never called me on the high priority line.

"Your Holiness, the Great Papal Bull has stirred the minds of my fellow politicians. Patriarch Fyodor is agitated, wants to meet, and is talking about reform and the revolution of the Christian faith. I am not a theologian, Your Holiness. I trust you and I need your guidance."

Oh my! Oh my! That was unexpected. When I saw President Pushkin, all I wanted to ask him was if he plans to write a sequel to the Bogatyn-Mudryy trilogy. I was not in the mood to talk politics with him.

At 7 AM, the Italian Prime Minister, Signor Pierluigi Pantalone called me. He had a dozen bite-size sandwiches and a glass of wine on a silver tray, by his side.

"Your Holiness! *Bon giorno!*"

He went on and on about the great significance of the Papal Bull, that it blends well with his policies, that it strengthens the ties between the Vatican and the Italian State like never before, that we can work out a great plan to fully integrate the Catholic dioceses into the Italian tax system, and certainly that I must visit him and the *Presidente della Repubblica at Palazzo del Quirinale*, at my earliest convenience, preferably sooner rather than later, or even immediately, that would be great.

Next, after a bathroom break of about 9 minutes, President Margarita Bourbon-Renege of Brazil called. She quickly dispensed with her enthusiasm and appreciation for the Papal Bull, and got straight down to business. She wanted to create an International Criminal Climate Court to prosecute anyone who willingly exploits Mother Earth by destroying its ecosystem and contributing to climate change. What are my thoughts on this? Can I endorse her? My throat was dry, since I did not even have the chance to have a glass of water, so I was not able to answer right away. Madame President thought I was wavering. I drank some water with her watching me, I begged her pardon, cleared my throat and answered with maximum determination and clarity that I totally supported her.

While she was talking, the incoming call button was flashing. In the subscreen I could see Cardinal Mutella introducing U.N. Secretary General Nadir Wadkirsch by text message. I told Madame Bourbon-Renege to excuse me, I had Secretary Wadkirsch on call waiting.

"Keep in touch!" Madame President said.

I flipped over to Secretary Wadkirsch. He said, diplomatically, that he applauds the positive reactions to the Papal Bull, and that he wished to add his support, privately for the time being. However, he called me to announce that he is publishing a new book called *Earth and Brain*, and wanted to send me an advance copy, and asked if I would be kind enough to honor him with an introduction. He fully trusted me, I was his friend.

Great timing for all my friends to call me on the same day.

Secretary Wadkirsch hung up. I told Mutella to hold all calls for at least 20 minutes, since I desperately needed a proper bathroom break, despite the fact that I had not had my morning espresso.

While still in the bathroom, I could hear the holophone buzzing with calls waiting. For some reason, performing the ablutions, I thought pessimistically that somehow there is an evil which I have seen under the sun, and it is common among men. It came to me in the form of a hot flash in my chest, in front of the mirror. Then it took the form of a thought without words. I struggled for a few minutes to shave my cheeks and find the words to describe this evil. The holophone was buzzing and flashing. I could also feel people outside my door, waiting for my attention. What is this evil? I kept asking myself and distracting myself. No words and no answers came to me in the end. I came out of the bathroom, physically refreshed and emotionally frustrated.

Cardinal Mutella suggested that from the long list of calls waiting, I take the call from Ayatollah Ali Foolas of Iran. That is quite interesting, I thought. Why is the Ayatollah calling me today of all days? Does he like the Papal Bull? Will he be as merry as he was when we talked the last time?

Merry indeed he was, for reasons different than what I was expecting. He asked if I knew what was going on with the Armenians. I said I did not know what he was talking about and I was under the impression that the refugee crisis in Northern Iran has been resolved.

"All of them," the Ayatollah, "they are depressed."

"What do you mean?" I asked.

"We offered them housing and food. Now they can go back to Armenia if they want. Or they can go to Georgia, to Azerbaidjan, where they want. But they don't want to. They just sit there, in the camps. They do nothing."

"What about the Armenian Apostolic Church?" I asked.

"They say: *Inshallah*. God willing," the Ayatollah said.

"It is strange indeed," I said not knowing what else I could say.

"We even allowed them to entertain themselves with popular music. They listen to it maybe one hour a day, then they stop. They don't watch TV either."

"I believe they are going through a spiritual crisis, Ayatollah."

"It is possible."

"We ought to show them our caring and kindness," I said.

The Ayatollah agreed and thanked me for my time. He added in the end that we must work together on some humanitarian project. I said it was a great idea and I will get back to him soon with a proposal. The Spiritual Council of Humanity, of course.

Moses Amisraeli had been waiting for half an hour. He was next.

"Your Holiness, I have great news!", he said. "King Sandal called me. He suggested we work together on securing the peace in the Middle East."

Generic diplomacy, I thought.

"He was even more specific. He offered the construction of a great symbolic synagogue in Riyadh."

"A fascinating proposal, indeed," I said.

"I think it has to do with your visit in the kingdom, Your Holiness."

He did not mention the Papal Bull, perhaps because he was too excited about the King's call and wanted to share the news with me.

Next call, none other than King Sandal Alumnus Baad Al-Bizzi of Saudi Arabia, as if he knew that Amisraeli would call me and didn't want to lose the upper hand, if such a hand even existed, and even if it did, if such a hand was even raised in the first place. King Sandal thanked me for my pacifist work in the Middle East and for bridging the gap between the kingdom and Israel. I was not sure what the King was referring to. I do not think I did something extraordinary, other than smiling at everyone and talking politely with everyone. I told King Sandal that I have a project on my mind and that I would like to have him involved in. The King reacted enthusiastically.

What came as a surprise was that no Orthodox Patriarch called me. Not Fyodor, not Pompiliu, not Aequilaterus, not Philipilus, not Nestor, not Hieronymus, not Neophyte, not Ulianus, not

John and not even Ilia of Georgia. Had I not had a great time with them last time, when we met in Prague? What are they thinking? Surely, they are men of a certain diplomatic inertia and their reputation precedes all of them. I would hardly think that they would all conspire not to call me, yet they did shave their beards for our November project without many deliberations. This has been bothering me all day. I'll have Tchipcherish investigate. He's good at finding these things out.

Enough for today. All other calls had to go to Mutella's office. I will review them later. I am now starving.

6:2 Heart of Gold

I saw on the holovision today, the launch of spaceship *Heart of Gold*. The broadcast was so advanced, so detailed, so high-resolution, I could see inside the spaceship where the 200 passengers were strapped into their cocoons, how the pilots operated their consoles, how the boosters spewed out long jets of fire. I saw the crowd gathered in Florida to watch the event, a million people. What a great achievement for humanity! It is scheduled to arrive on Mars in 4 months.

I still do not know what to think about this. We have known about this launch for many years, and now that it actually happened, it is still even more unbelievable. On one hand, mankind has outgrown its first and only home and is now venturing towards other planets. The Exploria Corporation, the managing organization for the Mars mission, is planning to launch many other spaceships to Mars, and have a permanent colony of one million people. What does it mean for the people of Earth? Were we born to leave our world and end our lives on another world? Are we not content enough with the wonders of this planet, that we need to explore a barren and inhospitable land? Is there really nothing left to explore here? What of the intricacies of our human nature, the terrible challenge we face with our own extinction?

Heart of Gold is leaving Earth's orbit. We are still here, wondering if we are on the verge of a Global War, if we are on the verge of Global Peace, if we are to survive our own insanity and lack of vision. While millions applaud the ambition of the Exploria Corporation, the courage of those 200 passengers, billions are still born into suffering and struggle.

At the same time, there are many men and women to whom God has given riches and wealth and honor, so that they lack nothing for themselves of all what they desire. Yet God does not give them power to eat of it, but a foreigner consumes it. This is vanity, and it is an evil affliction. What I understand here by God, I care not to explain now.

While *Heart of Gold* passes by the Moon, there have been no incidents on board, and everything goes according to the plan. Many of the 200 passengers are already broadcasting their thoughts on their respective social media.

I dare not dream that we can grow larger than Mother Earth, not in the present state of our civilization. I know it is true that in the past explorers left Europe to discover, occupy, and conquer foreign lands, with an attitude of self-sufficiency and arrogance, all under the banner of faith. Civilization has expanded, however we have not grown fundamentally in the quality of our morality. Indeed, I must also acknowledge the progress that has been made, which is not negligible by far, yet the shortcomings of our civilization are considered brutal consequences of human nature, and not lands that could be explored and made better. The sense of resignation that hovers over our species is the very cause of our probable extinction or downfall into an irrelevant element of nature.

There is a lot of hope travelling in spaceship *Heart of Gold*. And there is a lot of naivety that saddens my own heart. The 200 passengers are not prodigal sons who will return enlightened after a fantastic voyage. They will probably never come back to

Earth, they will probably have visions of salvation of mankind and will never be in the position to enact them. They will be people of anther world. I wish them all the best. I wish I could pray for them for old times' sake, but knowing the futility of prayer, I am left with a feeling of warm hope in my heart, and nothing more.

6:3 Trip to Poland

Severe agitation in Poland over the issue of abortion. The Archbishop of Kraków called me on the telephone to ask for a statement of support for the Catholic Church in Poland, that is, to denounce abortion and try once again to make it completely illegal under the penal code.

"You want a statement, Archbishop?" I said.

"Yes, Your Holiness," the Archbishop said.

"I'll give you a statement."

I immediately called for Mother Allegra. As soon as she entered my office I told her:

"I am going to Poland, Mother Allegra. Would you like to come with me?"

"Of course, Your Holiness."

"Very well. We leave at once."

There is little I can do or say to surprise Nwanne. He had my bags and the car ready within half an hour. I told Mutella to cancel all my foreign appointments for the next three days.

I took a minimal security detail with me. We took the train from the Termini Station. People were surprised to see me here. I was wearing my priest's standard black standard cassock and nothing else. No cross, no cap. People cheered, took photos of me and wished me all the best. By the time the train left the station, I was already on the news.

My train trip became the highest trending topic on social media. In every city where we stopped to change the train, huge crowds were waiting to greet us. Police had to be brought to maintain order and to avoid train delays.

When we arrived at the Kraków Główny railway station, the crowd of Poles was there and they had prepared a podium for me, hoping to hear me speak. There were many women with signs and bullhorns demanding their rights to their own bodies. I felt compelled to speak to my hosts from my heart. I began with no written words in front of me:

"Some people may have one hundred children and live a long life. But no matter how long they live, if they aren't content with life's good things, I say that even a stillborn child with no grave is better off than they are. Because that child arrives in vanity, then passes away in darkness. Darkness covers its name."

Why did I begin with those terrible words? I am still surprised at what came out of me. I am supposed to be the messenger of hope, of joy, of good news, not a gloomy crow. At the same time I felt compelled to tell the truth wherever I go, to inspire people to be the best they can be - not just for themselves, but also for the world at large.

I continued to speak about the rights of all people to self-determination, about the dignity of life, as defined by science and not by ancient dogma. This idea is not revolutionary at all, it has been around for many generations, yet it still needs to fight the rigidity of a system that no longer sees the true foundations of its ideology, a system that perpetrates only the zealousness of faith and forgets that it is supposed to serve the needs of the people, not to oppress them in any way. I said these things to the crowd, and they all cheered for me, and many chanted *Santo*

Subito in an euphoric misguided way, meaning that I ought to be made a saint immediately, such as the late Pope John Paul II, a sentiment that I can appreciate coming from a devoted crowd.

I dared to say these things that no man should be elevated to any such a status of superhuman qualities, since such qualities do not exist. On the contrary, such superhuman qualities are mere projections of human desire to worship, the proclivity toward wishful thinking, the drive to seek immediate comfort that some of us are safely seated in heaven near God, and use such a position of influence to distribute benefits for mankind at the very low cost of prayer and faith. Well, I did not use these pretentious words, but I did make myself understood. The crowd received the message well and continued to applaud.

I don't know how long I spoke in front of the train station at Kraków Główny. It was long enough and I enjoyed every minute of it. There were many women there, standing and listening carefully, many of them had children with them on their shoulders, and the children themselves were holding little signs in English and Polish as high as they could, so their mothers could keep their balance. I did not see anybody leaving.

I stopped my speech and thanked everybody for their warm welcome. I was there to support their cause, and continue the great reform of the church.

We got back in the car, Nwanne, Mother Allegra and I. We had an appointment with the Archbishop of Krakow and many other Polish clerics to discuss the situation. Some important politicians were supposed to be there as well.

"I want to do something different," I said.

"I think I know what you have in mind, Your Holiness," Nwanne replied from the seat opposite me in the limousine.

Mother Allegra was not sure what was going on, but she was showing signs that she was getting used to me. At the same time, I did not want to impose upon her, or make her feel uncomfortable, so I offered her the option to wait for us at the hotel, or meet with the Archbishop first and explain that I was delayed for an hour or so. Mother Allegra said she would prefer to come with us, wherever we wanted to go.

I instructed the driver to take side streets, lose the crowd, and blend in with the traffic. I convinced my security detail to keep a good distance. We were in a very friendly city, so their closeness was not required. Near a farmer's market, I told Nwanne to go out on the street and find a taxi for the three of us. He came back after three minutes and said he found a taxi on the other side of the market, and that he told the driver to wait for us there. He knew I wanted to walk through the market. So we did, the three of us. I had to wear some minimal disguise. I borrowed our driver's jacket, cap and sunglasses. Nobody recognized me. The farmers were too preoccupied with their produce, and could care less to spot a Pope in their market.

The taxi driver took us exactly where we asked him. An abortion clinic at the outskirts of Krakow. He even knew the doctors' names, the operating hours, the fees, the waiting times and the reputation of the clinic. He asked us if we were doctors. I said that only two of us were doctors. Of theology. He chuckled. He asked if we want to shut down the clinic.

"No, no, on the contrary," I said. "We are here to support it."

At the clinic, Mother Allegra and I waited in the lobby while Nwanne arranged for a meeting with the director. We were invited to the director's office immediately.

"Your Holiness, I am deeply honored to meet you," Dr. Czesław Niznikiewicz said. "Is it really you? It is you indeed! How can I be of your service?"

"Dear Dr. Niznikiewicz," I extended my friendliness. "I am here to support the cause of women."

"I... I... I... don't know what to say. I am extremely enchanted to have you here."

"Here is what I have in mind. I would like to assist an abortion operation. Would that be possible? Certainly, assuming all hygienic precautions, the consent of the patient, your consent, and everything else deemed important for such an incredible request. Moreover, if you would not mind, I would like my secretary, Mr. Nwanne Yinkaso, and Cardinal Coccinella to be present as well, while Mr. Yinkaso will take photographs of our presence there. It is beyond any question that the patient will not be caught in the frame, however the framework of our presence will become obvious. You may be present in the shot or not, it is certainly up to you, if you come to agree with my proposal."

"I would be extremely pleased to accept, Your Holiness."

"Why am I doing this, dear Dr. Niznikiewicz? I would to fully explain my position, such as not to cause you reluctance or possible regrets, or refrained confusion. I also do not want you to feel pressured in any way, whether you are a Catholic or not."

"I am not a believer, Your Holiness. I hope you don't mind my frankness. I do appreciate your work very much."

"Thank you doctor for your kind words. My motivation for this peculiar proposal has a deep spiritual cause. I care deeply for the rights of women to self-determination, and I also care for the quality of life, that is of born beings. I am here to make a strong, unwavering statement to the whole world. I am here to influence the course of history, for the good. I had not planned this, and it must remain as such. I came to you straight from the train station. Nobody knows that we are here. In a week, the whole world will know. Can you bear this burden, Dr. Niznikiewicz?"

"Even us, atheists, we have our crosses to bear. I am happy and honored to bear the heaviest cross that has crossed my path in my whole life."

We proceeded to the operating room, where a patient was already waiting. She was clothed, as expected, and had been informed that the Pope was at the clinic and will meet with her. Her name was Franciszka Kaczorowska. She was 25 years old. She was a virtual game programmer and, to my surprise, a non-practicing Catholic.

"I apologize, Your Holiness," Franciszka Kaczorowska said. "I do not go to church."

"No need to apologize, Mrs. Kaczorowska," I said jokingly. "You represent the majority of Catholics. You should be proud. Between you and me, I can't say I go to church either, not in the popular sense, because I work there."

Everyone chuckled.

"I would be very honored and proud to help your mission, Your Holiness. I feel you are one of us," Franciszka Kaczorowska said. "All my friends feel this way. I am not sorry for what I do now. I wish it would have been different, I wish that I didn't have to do it, but now that I got pregnant somewhat, I need to be responsible to do the right thing. I am never sorry to do the right thing. I beg your pardon if this offends the Christian doctrine."

"Mrs. Kaczorowska," I said. "I am here for you and for all women like you. I would like you to feel comfortable that I am completely on your side. My secretary would like to video document this for history. We will not show your face."

"Thank you, Your Holiness. Yes, I would like to participate. I fully understand the importance of this."

"Very well, Mrs. Kaczorowska. Mr. Yinkaso will videorecord a short interaction between us, and take a few pictures, in such a way that your identity will be protected, and also show that this is an abortion clinic, that it is safe, and is controlled by qualified personnel."

Nwanne recorded a short conversation between me and Mrs. Kaczorowska. She repeated her story for me, I reassured her that it is the natural thing to do, that I had no objections, that the self-determination and the health of women is more important to me than any Christian dogma. I promised Mrs. Kaczorowska that I will wait for her after the procedure, to record her feelings again. She thanked me, and told Dr. Niznikiewicz that she was ready.

The procedure ended quickly. Not more than 10 minutes had passed. We waited perhaps another 10 minutes for Mrs. Kaczorowska to wake up from the anesthetic. Dr. Niznikiewicz told we can see her again.

"It is so good to see you again, Your Holiness," Franciszka Kaczorowska said. "Today is certainly the most memorable day of my life. Your presence here has eased the pain."

"I do this from all my heart," I said. "I encourage you to share your story with other women and help them defend their natural rights."

"I will do so. And there is one more thing, Your Holiness."

"Yes, Mrs. Kaczorowska," I said.

"I appreciate that you never called me *child* or *sister*. I appreciate that you showed me respect by calling me Mrs. Kaczorowska."

She reached for my hand and asked me with her eyes if she can kiss it. I said yes with my eyes. She never asked for a blessing. I felt so humbled by her strength that I did not dare to offer it. Franciszka Kaczorowska was a strong human being. She was teaching me the dignity women can achieve by owning difficult decisions.

At the same time, I am aware that some women do take similar decisions lightly, and come to it by quicker and more superficial reasons. I do respect that road, as well. What matters the most is that all women are given the same chance to exercise full, independent control over their own destinies, whether their decisions are rushed or well considered. The quality of the decision is a personal matter for all individuals, and can only be reviewed and assumed by one's own conscience.

I thanked Dr. Czesław Niznikiewicz for his kind cooperation. Mother Allegra asked if she could spend another hour at the clinic. I granted her permission, then Nwanne called another taxi to take us to the Archbishop's office, who by now was probably getting impatient about our tardiness. Poor Archbishop! Maybe I should make him a Cardinal to soothe his mind.

6:4 The Archbishop of Krakow

He is a patient man. His name is Zbigniew Kuratowski. He did not ask me why we were delayed, how could he after all? This would have been a breach of protocol. Nor did I offer this information or mislead Archbishop Kuratowski in any way. I carefully calculated the timing of my escapade to the clinic. Eventually, the Archbishop will find out from the media, and will have little option of not accepting the reality.

Am I making a political play here? Perhaps, however not deliberately. I don't want to embarrass Archbishop Kuratowski or expose him to public humiliation, such as having to defend a position contrary to that of his superior, albeit that I do possess such an opinion. I have been thoroughly briefed about the situation in Poland.

What worries me deeply is that this is not the first time this crisis surfaced in this country. There is something about the clerics here that empowers the right-wing to push hard against the rights of women. Is it the nostalgia for the great era of Karol Wojtyla, known to the world as Pope John Paul II? Or is it a political ambience, different from all other European countries in the region, that allows such a resurgence? I am not here to find out, nor do I have the intention of finding out. More and more, I am losing my patience for the analysis of history and for the understanding of power structures and political machinations. I am tired of all these. Those who make history in the present have no time to think about how history has been made in the past.

Back to Archbishop Kuratowski.

A vein on his forehead was throbbing. He showed no signs of agitation. He spoke calmly and was very respectful. He said plainly that he is worried about the future of the Church in his country. He said that if they lose this battle, they will never be able to regain the ground in times where church attendance is at its lowest, not to mention the monetary contributions from the general public.

"Splendid", I thought to myself and could not help a smile.

"Archbishop Kuratowski," I said. "You need not worry. The Church has to grow and to learn from its times. This is no reason to despair, on the contrary - it is reason to rejoice and ride the wave."

"Will we be at the top of the wave, or at the bottom, swallowed by sharks?" the Archbishop said.

The marble bust of Karol Józef Wojtyla on the Archbishop's desk has had more rest than the man before me. He lost his composure and begged my pardon. He was desperate to have a drink. To save his honor I joined him with some weak enthusiasms, that he did not notice at all.

We had a glass of wine. Exquisite, of course, and preblessed by the Archbishop himself.

"Would you speak to the people on Warsaw, Your Holiness?", he said.

"That is my intention."

"Can we hope to reach an agreement?"

"The only agreement is to accept the obvious nature. This is about the fundamental rights of women and the construction of the soul of mankind. We cannot fight that. No one can, no matter how hard we try, no matter how many forms of oppression will emerge."

"Your Holiness, surely you are not saying that the Church is oppressive?" Archbishop Kuratowski said.

"Who is the Church?" I said. "Certainly not you, certainly not me. The Church is not even the Holy Book. Christ spoke of no Church, no Popes, and no Bishops. He was a preacher. We, humans, we made the Church. It's a beast that floats over our heads, like a cathedral made of dandelions. The Church is an idea. It's not people, it's not candlesticks, it's not granite, it's not gold. It will change, like anything created by men. We have the fantastic chance to make it a good thing. Think about this, Archbishop. We are climbing a magic mountain and its crest is in the clouds."

"Heaven is the ultimate reward for all mortals," the Archbishop said.

"I am not talking about heaven," I said. "I am talking about the future of mankind. We must accept the reality that the Church will be less and less important. There will be a time when we will have to let go."

"Your Holiness, I don't know what to say."

"This is not a prophecy. These are my thoughts as a man of flesh and bone," I said.

Archbishop Zbigniew Kuratowski of Krakow looked at me as if I was a madman, as if I came in vanity, departed in darkness, my name covered with darkness. He could not help himself. His eyes widened so much, I thought they would fall out of his head. His hand was twitching with a shock that hit the man in his heart. The muscles on his face jerked ever so slightly, refusing to stay close to a pair of ears that had heard the words that came from my mouth. He wanted to run away, but he was in his own office.

I saw all that coming from the poor Archbishop. I was fully capable of containing a secret burst of joy and the urge to smile at his misfortune. What evil thoughts on my part! I don't like to see people defeated. It makes me sad. I don't want to feel victories either. I want nothing but to allow my mind to think, my mouth to speak, my eyes to see, and a little satisfaction that the world tomorrow will be better than the world today.

Zbigniew Kuratowski is definitely not Cardinal material.

6:5 Who lives a thousand years twice

Am I so self-absorbed and so naïve that I cannot see any opposition against my politics? Can I see no shadows of betrayals, of plots, of court intrigues? Why is everything so quiet and smooth at the Vatican? Is this the eve of a storm?

I know of no member of the Curia to keep himself at a distance from me, on the contrary, the requests for audiences from them are so many, Nwanne barely manages to fit them all on my agenda. Even Thorsen Tchipcherish is merrier than ever, no less vociferous, full of proposals and ideas as to how to advance the progress of the Church. A slave laborer, who toils in the fields for 18 hours a day, has more rest in his life than Thorsen Tchipcherish.

As forthcoming as he has been with me, letting me into the details of his thoughts, I still have a lingering reservation about him, having to do with the political inflections in his voice. He never breached protocol with me, but has also never showed me any unnecessary deference.

What is it then about him? What is he building in that mind of his? What whispers does he hide behind that thunderous voice? How does he have analysis of the works and agendas of all members of the Curia before I even get the chance to gather my thoughts? What does he know that I do not?

...and he has those moments of complete solemnity, where he treads on words with the importance of an army general, where every syllable is a soldier that carries the fulcrum of the entire world on his shoulders?

He said it again the other day, "What if we end the Papacy?" What if, indeed? I keep thinking to myself, what would it mean for the entire world, and why would we do such a thing in the first place? Do people not need the solemnity of a two thousand year old institution? Do we not all need to know that we are somehow deeply rooted in the past, and often it is past and only the past that gives us purpose? How can we uproot such a grand history, and box it into the showcases of museums?

What would be the plausible circumstance in which anyone could close the institution of Papacy or transform it to such an extent that it would be nothing like it was before? What is the power that any living generation has over all generations that have lived before?

So what do I talk about when I talk about the abolition of the Papacy with Cardinal Tchipcherish? I do not talk about the destruction of the past. I do not talk about the incrimination of the past. Nor do I talk about the negation of the moral progress of mankind, from rural illiterate tribes, wandering through dry and torrid deserts, to the high achievements of the Enlightenment era, to the social revolutions of the 20th century, to the emancipation of women, to the recognition of our gay brothers and sisters and everyone in between. I do not negate all these struggles, I embrace them, I elevate them, I fully recognize them.

6:6 I am talking with the devil's advocate

Many evil men have been born and lived undisturbed, and have not seen goodness, have not understood the intrinsic driver of life, that of construction and not destruction. And in the end, don't all men, good and evil, go to one place? That of permanent nothingness. As we come from nothingness, so do we return into nothingness, hoping to have disturbed the universe a tiny step towards order and not towards chaos.

So what do I talk about when I talk about the abolition of the Papacy?

The devil's advocate would say: keep the name, change the character. Remain Pope, keep the Papacy, keep the Vatican, but change what it means, give a new definition to faith, give a new meaning to the entire institution.

I say to the devil: what is in a name, if not the entire history that it carries? The blood, the torture, the ignorance, the darkness.

The devil's advocate would say: at the same time there is the light, the hope, the charity, the martyrs, the sacrifices, the longstanding solidarity among believers, the good Samaritans, the meek, the modest, and the peaceful.

I say to the devil: I will have all these and more of them, and I would not tarnish them with the dark side of the same coin.

The devil's advocate would say: There is a dark side to any human endeavor, any institution, whether it serves God or it serves society at large. It is in the nature of humanity to be incapable of purity and untarnished goodness.

I say to the devil: You are talking about the perfect world. I never claimed humans were perfect, I never said we can be clear of wrongdoings and suffering. On the contrary, I claim that we ought to embrace these flaws and never settle for an ultimate objective of perfection. Such an objective could never exist and be permanent, as it contradicts the construction of the universe. Everything changes, the good and the bad. We ought to strive to always adjust us to be closer to next order of things.

The devil's advocate would say: You are now stealing my position. You are becoming me. I say the same thing. This eternal restlessness of men is what makes any attempt to challenge the foundations of tradition futile. You cannot change something that has always evolved, that has never been the same except in name.

I say to the devil: You are wise devil, however I say to you that everything has a beginning and everything has an end, especially those institutions and traditions that appear to be indestructible. When will the end come? When there is a sense of an ending and the craving for a beginning.

The devil's advocate would say: You will never succeed. You will fail. You will leave destruction after you.

I say to the devil: We will succeed. It's inevitable.

The devil would have nothing else to say and would disappear in a cloud of smoke.

6:7 How to ever be satisfied when you have it all

When I had a strong faith in God, the Christ, and his mother, I was always asking for something in my prayers. Please God, make this happen, please Christ let something good become of such and such person, please God listen to me, yes me right here, because I exist and I am very important to your ears because I know very well that you love me so much.

I was also praying conditional prayers, if you do this God I swear I will do that, meaning I will do something much easier than what I was asking of God, so in all cases, according to my calculations, I had ended up on the winning side, with a profit, and God was on the other side, having had labored for much more than I had labored for him. Such is the trade of prayer I had employed, no less stranger to the millions of believers who employ it every day.

Am I satisfied that I had escaped death on several occasions, often without even a prayer in advance? It just happened, in moments when I was not even thinking about God.

I do not pray anymore, but I think much more.

I think of the consequences of all my deeds, and of the consequences of those who execute deeds in my name. I linger in ruminations for hours, over blank pages, over the pages of some book, alone in my room at night. Nobody dares to disturb me.

I rarely find grand answers to my ruminations. I find myself pondering about the essence of things, of the meaning of it all. My thoughts slowly trudge in circles. My anxiety boils. I rarely enjoy stepping on my own footsteps. I am somehow prone to disliking the sense of familiarity with the dead-end of philosophical questions: why am I doing what I am doing?

I admire the simple man that has short horizons of dreams. Not because ignorance is bliss, because it is not, ignorance is sheer sadness, but because the simple man has an unequivocal connection to his labor. He knows what he is getting from his labor. All the labor of the man is for his mouth. Surely, this simple man may not be satisfied and may struggle every day to produce a living for himself or his family. Or he may be a man of virtue and well-tempered needs, and can have the imagination to invent a future for himself.

Whereas myself, I labor at large scales of influence. My soul is continuously not satisfied. I wish I knew more today about the world of tomorrow. Is this not the dream of any man, simple or in high office? To know what has not happened yet, so he could have a better life today?

This may be the gravest illness of man, that of wrongly selecting the things whose future would be highly valued if it was known today. When this selection is about unbalanced expectations that promotes only the self, without a general universal principle, then the risk of suffering increases and regrettable consequences will shake the ground under the man's feet.

What am I talking about here?

Nobody can ever hope to influence society at large. Nobody can ever change the world with their behavior directly. The world always changes from within, millions of people conducting themselves similarly generating change and new principles. On the market of ideas, those ideas powerful enough to capture the spirit of the age become prevalent, while the spirit of the age is molded by the birth of ideas whose roots are always in the minds of our forefathers. I don't know which one comes first, the spirit of the ages, or the ideas, but I do know that one cannot exist without the other. At times, they are at war with each other, like two brothers who discover that they love the same woman. Great ideas have been betrayed by the misguided spirit of some ages, and in some ages it was the elevated spirit of man that has given birth to great ideas.

It's late and I'm already too philosophical, even for my taste. What can I do? I cannot help myself. I have to let these thoughts go, to benchmark my sanity. Deep in my gut I sense an ending. A terrible ending then an inconceivable beginning. Such events are shocking to the living but are not strangers to history.

6:8 For what more has the wise man than the fool?

Random thought: Leave me surprises for tomorrow, as I wish to enjoy the heat in my mind when I see the new faces of the world.

Today was a day of audiences with the common people. Nwanne suggested that people write their story on the social media website Reddit and put a video of themselves, then the community votes on these stories, and the most votes would get an audience with me. I liked the idea, but I had an objection. What about those who do not have access to the internet? What about the children from the slums? Then Nwanne said that each entry will also have to make an entry and write the story for somebody else who cannot do it themselves. So, two entries to qualify to be eligible for an audience with me. The project was so successful, that the most popular stories had millions of votes. We selected 33 people from all over the world. We paid the transportation for those who could not afford it.

They all waited patiently to meet me, one by one.

A middle-aged Bolivian man. He had the bone structure of an ancient cave-dweller. He looked me in the eyes at all times, smiled very little. His teeth were in a very bad shape. He had scars on the backs of his hands. He said he had to dig wells, for his village was deprived of water. His people fought hard against the privatization of the Bolivian waters. They won. He wanted to talk to me to give me courage. He knew that I was fighting a big fight and that I needed all the support I could get. He did not want anything from me. Not a blessing. Not a gift. A handshake would be sufficient, he said, and perhaps a photo if I didn't mind, so he can prove to his neighbors that he met the Pope, so they could all have reason to celebrate. Of course, I accepted.

And what more does the poor man know who walks before others?

A twelve-year old girl from India. She was wearing a beautiful sari. She showed me gold medals in mathematics. She was a child prodigy. She said she had travelled with her parents all across India. Her parents were engineers and were installing solar panels in the poorest regions of the country. She said the only thing she wanted in life was to teach mathematics to all those poor children, because she calculated that this would be the best way to save mankind. She came to me because she felt that there was something missing in her mission, and she needed guidance. "Surely, there is something more in life than mathematics, but what is it?", she asked me. I could only think of one thing: to do some good to others. Then I paused. This little girl was already doing this. What else could I teach her? I told her to learn as much mathematics as she could and teach as many children as she could.

What if we truly don't need anything else, other than mathematics? Is life not all about structures, groups, symmetries? Are we not all searching for the equation of love, success, happiness?

A 105-year old man from the Philippines. He was almost blind and spoke Italian perfectly. He did not know how to use the internet. He had been a professor of languages in his life. Loved to ride the bicycle. Played the flute and the mandolin. He regretted one thing in life: that he hadn't loved enough. "People tell me you have been a great activist, a fighter for women's rights," I told him. "Yes, I fought hard, but never loved enough," he said. "But don't tell anyone, Your Holiness, this is our secret. Do not be like me."

Note to self: remember to love enough, if you think you don't love enough, also remember that love is not a statue but an ever-flowing river.

An actress from America. Young. She belonged to the warm generation, the children of the millennials. She made a very moving video about how she did not blame her parents or her grandparents about the state of the planet: the hot weather, the floods, the climate refugees. She wanted to ensure the survival of our species. She wanted to learn as much as we can from the past, educate ourselves about the present, and build for the future. No blame and no shame on anyone. She wanted to offer her support for my ideas and she wanted to get my help for her ideas. I told her our ideas are the same. I agreed to let her holotape the audience for her upcoming documentary.

Hope, hope, hope, what does this word mean? Is it not postponing responsibility for the future? Is it not resignation, indolence, cowardice?

Many others came. Men and women of all nationalities. All exhibiting strong characters. They are those who change the world, not me, a clerk of mere words and declarations.

6:9 The sight of the eyes and the wandering of desire

A group of seven cardinals forced their way into an audience with me. They came in person to my office, knowing well that I was there. Nwanne was in the antechamber and could not stop them. I was alone, reviewing the agenda for the next consistory.

All wore black cassocks with scarlet piping and buttons, scarlet sashes, pectoral crosses on chains, and scarlet zucchettos. They were: Leonardo Pancreotti of Italy, Serafim Dunga de Aviz of Brazil, Frank Collins of the USA, Ricardo Reyes of the Philippines, Polycarp Yezir of Ghana, Miguel Belamino of Nicaragua, and Romeo Fragola of Italy.

Pancreotti was their leader. He spoke brashly:

"Your Holiness, I'm bringing forward a protest to your policies! We are seeking procedures of a no-confidence vote if you do not retreat this blasphemous and outrageous reform."

I was flabbergasted. Was this a coup d'état? Was this even possible at the Vatican?

"Cardinal Pancreotti," I said, "you know quite well I have presented all these reforms in the Curia. You had the chance to review them and voice your concerns."

"I think they are going too far!" Pancreotti raised his voice. The other six cardinals were mumbling in agreement.

"Why didn't you say anything until know?"

"We were caught by surprise," Pancreotti said. "We had the chance to deliberate and we concluded these reforms undermine the Doctrine of the Faith."

"All these reforms have been vetted by Cardinal Tchipcherish, the Prefect of the Congregation for the Doctrine of the Faith. They are in perfect accord with the Christian doctrine."

"We want to issue a no-confidence vote against Cardinal Tchipcherish, as well," Pancreotti jumped to talk over me.

Cardinals Romeo Fragola and Serafim Dunga de Aviz concurred with Cardinal Pancreotti.

"Cardinal Tchipcherish has unduly established control over our Prefecture," Romeo Fragola said.

"I find that peculiar and questionable," I said.

"And I sense too many secular statements in his reports," Dunga de Aviz said.

"Cardinals," I intervened, "rest assured Cardinal Tchipcherish is the strongest defender of our faith. I have never questioned his commitment, despite his forthcoming demeanor that we all know."

"You want to ruin us... Your Holiness..." the quieter Cardinal Reyes said.

"My desire is to strengthen the Church and to evolve us with the spirit of our times," I said.

"Better is the sight of the eyes than the wandering of desire... Your Holiness..." Pancreotti said with a pious emphasis.

"This also is vanity and grasping for the wind, Cardinal Pancreotti," I said, swiftly proving to him that I know the Old Testament too.

The group of seven Cardinals looked at themselves like an incomplete rugby team trying to build a strategy when defeat is imminent. They came into my office with a fierce determination and somehow they were getting softer. Before anyone of them spoke again, I said:

"Cardinals, I sense your worries. We are mere mortals. On the scale of history, my reforms are a short flash of light on the firmament. Look around us, the world has changed, and we have to change as well, because the world needs us. Do we want to become useless? Neither of you want to feel useless. I can see it on your faces."

There was an awkward silence.

"What you don't see on our faces, Your Holiness," Pancreotti said, "is your own very face. It radiates obscurity and grave secrets. This is our concern, this is why we came here. We sense a wall of division between your Holiness and us."

He got me there. I carry heavy secrets. This was not the time to reveal them. I dodged the question as best I could.

I cannot hide for long anymore.

"I have perhaps retreated inside myself more than I wanted," I spoke slowly, "It is the burden of the cross I am carrying. I will consider your observations, Cardinal Pancreotti, I will address them in due time. Until them, you must excuse me, I have matters of state to attend."

I ringed for Nwanne. He came at once.

"Nwanne, please escort the Cardinals. The audience has come to an end."

6:10 My blackness

I looked at my face for a long time, this evening, and I thought about what the group of seven cardinals told me. I did not see on my face the secrets I carry, I saw only the blackness of my skin.

I had not seen the color of my skin for a long time. I had been busy greeting dignitaries and various celebrities, drafting reforms and conducting long meetings and conferences with various committees and institutions, but never under the veil of my dark skin.

The seven cardinals made me feel very aware of all the pores on my black face, while at the same time they made me ignore what I had inside me. It's a paradox that their daring action elicited in me the opposing reaction.

When I faced them in my office I feared for a second that my secrets would be exposed. That I would be presented to the world as fraud, that I would be deeply humiliated, forced to resign without appeal, and banished from history.

After I dismissed the seven Cardinals, all these fears disappeared and I was left with an urge to look at myself in the mirror. Until now, close to midnight, I had no time to do it.

No shadows are cast over my face at night, unless there is enough moonlight.

I enjoy sitting in the dark and thinking about friends and the world. I was never afraid of the dark. I never feared the uncontrollable unknown.

And why of all days as the Pope, can I only think about the blackness of my skin today? Why now, when nobody mentioned it? Why do I feel I am an outcast, when the Cardinal mutineers have not even hinted at my race? Who put these thoughts in my head?

I usually gather strength from reason, from the validation coming from my philosophy of life, and from the truths of nature. At this moment I am at a loss, since I cannot find an explanation for this fixation with my old black face.

Surely, if I asked Nwanne, he would say I am not old at all. He would say I have the worries of a teenager who wants to go on a date with a girl. What a silly idea! He would look closely into my face, would study every single dark pore, and would say there is nothing wrong with them, they are as they always have been: black and fine as silk.

The color we think we are is sometimes not the color we really are. The status of one's color is predetermined, to a large extent, by one's thoughts and one's reflection in the mirror.

Whatever happens to the man in the mirror, he has already been given a name, for it is known that he is man. If the man is self-reliant, he can contend with the highest standard of mankind, and no one could deny his achievements. If the man is a believer, then he cannot contend with God who is stronger than he. These ought to be the limits of the man watching himself in the mirror.

I am in no position to establish other rules for anyone.

I can deny myself my own skin, I can deny myself my own secret, I can deny myself the love for Nwanne, I cannot deny myself the faults of my body and my mind. They are what they are. I ought to live with them, for better or for worse, as I do not see a better law of nature to inspire me at the moment.

6:11 The attack of the evangelists

As the word of my reform is spreading through newsrooms, it is also being digested by a variety of evangelists from all continents, who have decided to react with vicious outrage against me, and against all the "mafia" behind me - their words, not mine.

These loudmouths are nothing but despicable rodents who scream hogwash about God, while knowing quite well what God wants us to do, how God endorses them with his graces. These foul mouths cry that riches are a consequence of strong faith. Utter insanity! These pigs use this demagogy and perverse hypocrisy to enrich themselves on the backs of naïve and ignorant people of the precariat, they elevate themselves with aggressive oratory to manipulate, enslave, and exploit.

I despise them! I despise them with all my heart! I cannot find any understanding for their activities, their megalomania, their destructive influence on society.

They have the audacity to claim authority over the Christian dogma. They dare to quote the Holy Book as the justification for their status. They lie, with outrageous impunity, that they are nothing but servants of Christ and God. Utter horseshit! Nobody has authority over the Holy Book, not I, not any of my predecessors, not the thousands of so-called Saints that lived in the centuries before me, not any Cardinal, not any theologian or scholar, not even the Apostles of Christ, many of whom were illiterate, not the many scribes who copied, forged, and falsified the early manuscripts. There cannot be any ultimate authority over a book that has been produced by men under questionable circumstances. To claim that is the word of God: utter rubbish!

Now these evangelists lash out at me, claiming I undermine the Christian faith and their congregations are complaining. What do they care?! They are not Catholic. They should all mind their business. Literally, their business, since all their establishments are not houses of solidarity but large auditoriums of extortion and dilapidation of the spirit, where only the wants of the speaker matter, not the silent desires of the paying audience. What a scam! What an offense to mankind! I pity those poor lambs who fell prey to the rapacity of these jackals.

Since there are many things that increase vanity, how are these men and women better? What makes them so special that they steal a religious tradition to profit in this material world? Who is at fault for their unrestrained, audacious greed being taken to the rank of a desirable status, a credible source of morality?

There is nothing pious about these worms, these slimy rats, with all due respect to the brainless worms and the adaptive rodents. Nothing makes them pause, reflect on the quality and legitimacy of the rivers of words that come out of their mouth like a thunder meant to straighten the spines of the stupid crowd of sheep.

These contemptible clowns want nothing less than to impose their lousy philosophy over the masses, allegedly for the benefit of the masses, since this is the best thing for the masses, to be fed the balance of right and wrong from gorillas screaming on a stage behind a lectern.

They are the usurpers of hope, they are the murderers of souls, they are the tyrants of the imagination, they are the wolves set loose in a schoolyard, they are the predators who feed on the weak, the cretins posing as savants, the con artists who pose as academics, swindlers who pose as philanthropists.

I despise them because they made me feel hate today, and enmity. My blood is boiling and I want to shout back, but I cannot, because I am the Pope. The Pope never shouts, and never has declared enemies. So I will unload my frustration on these pages, and I will destroy them whenever I find peace and reason to do so.

6:12 A Brazilian connection

Cardinal Tchipcherish found the perfect reason to take me away from all the murmurs behind the closed doors at the Vatican. He feels there is something going on in certain circles in the Curia and around the Curia, something of a political nature. I must not be concerned with this, Tchipcherish said, because he has everything under control, he has eyes and ears everywhere. That I believe. What I am not certain of is Tchipcherish's full transparency toward me. He brings me all these reports every day, yet there is always an aura of reservation that taints his tenacity. His words are of steel, his presentations completely tight in their logic. What is missing are the full explorations of possibilities. The full range of plausible futures. Will there be a coup at the Vatican?

With these in mind, Cardinal Tchipcherish, Cardinal Coccinella and I, went on an official trip to Brazil, at the invitation of President Margarita Bourbon-Renege. She has been calling for months, trying to invite me.

The purpose of the visit? Bilateral support for each other's causes. We would declare support for President Bourbon-Renege's initiative to establish the International Criminal Climate Court, that will have the mandate to sanction any state or corporation's attempt to destabilize the climate of Earth even further. President Bourbon-Renege wants to confer the ICCC military power to enforce the rulings of the court for the non-compliant states and corporations. More like in the spirit of the UN Peacekeeping troops.

In return, President Bourbon-Renege will declare support for our initiatives to reform the Catholic Church, to implement the access of women and LGBTQIA people into the Brazilian Catholic Clergy. Fair deal! Her enthusiasm for our reforms matches our enthusiasm for her initiative.

After a quick meet-and-greet at *Palácio do Planalto*, the four of us retreated to the President's office to begin laying out our plans. I had the imposing Tchipcherish on my right, and the serene Mother Allegra on my left. I could hear Tchipcherish's breath catching in his throat, he was that anxious to speak. President Bourbon-Renege was a determined and wise woman, and a wonderful host. Her first question for me was:

"Do you condone violence, Your Holiness?"

I paused before I answered.

"Madam President, it is a difficult question to answer. The natural response would be that violence is necessary to stop evil. We cannot stop tanks with feathers."

"Would I have your blessing for an army to enforce the rulings of the ICCC?"

"I am a defender of Mother Earth. If Mother Earth requires soldiers to protect her rights, I will be on your side, Madam President. With one caveat. This army, although it will have my open endorsement, must not operate under the banner of any religion, especially ours, since this will ultimately delegitimize its mandate. See, telling you this, makes me find ironic the fact that religion must take a step backward to allow the planet to be protected and saved, when the very mandate of religion ought to be salvation for everyone, all beings of nature and the planet itself."

"Our very existence is threatened, Your Holiness," Madam President said.

"We are mere mortals, Madam President," I said. "Who knows what is good for man in life, all the days of his vain life which he passes like a shadow? Who can tell a man what will happen after him under the sun?"

"I suppose that is the very property of life, Your Holiness. We cannot simply live and not care about what comes after us. We owe it to those who lived before us."

I saw Cardinal Tchipcherish fidgeting, he could barely contain his impulse to speak. Mother Allegra remained serene as always. President Bourbon-Renege and I continued to discuss the ICCC, the size and the scope of the supporting armed forces, and their mandate. The more we talked, the more I realized that my naïve optimism and faith in mankind is often blinded by the shrewdness of the evil forces that accelerate our extinction. The first conversation with President Bourbon-Renege was a cold shower.

NOTEBOOK SEVEN

7:1 On conversions and on the value of being born

The day I obtained my doctorate in Rome was the first time I asked myself - alone in my room, of course – "Why am I a Catholic?" Why was I not an Eastern Orthodox with a long beard? Why was I not an Anglican? Or a Lutheran? Or a Calvinist? Why not a Southern Baptist? Or a Seventh Day Adventist? My conviction at the time was that the path to faith is nothing less than pure chance, due in large part to the name with which one is born. The name, the family, the social milieu at birth can be a determination for one's path towards a certain faith. My parents were pious Catholics, so naturally I was to become one, given that the chance of me being raised a Mormon or a Pentecostalist were almost inexistent, since there weren't any Mormons or Pentecostalists in our village to raise me in their creeds, let alone a Buddhist, an Imam, or a Rabbi, for that matter.

A good name is better than holy anointing oil, the day of one's death or the day of one's birth, for the simple reason that neither birth nor death comes with a natural choice attached to them, except that in death, one allegedly has the occasion of displaying honor and dignity, built on the experience of life and the wisdom accumulated.

While at birth, there is no choice, no qualifications that a man can possess. A man is simply born, not of his will, since will is a product of the development of consciousness. That is, one ought to never curse his day of birth as there was nothing within his power to prevent it. Nor he could curse the circumstance in which he was born. That man's only course of life is to move towards a dignified and honorable death, whether through a path of faith or not, whether he has accepted the determinations of the demographic in which he was born.

A life of conversions is a life lived fully. One must always question the circumstances of life before the age of matured consciousness. No stamp is permanent. No faith is genuine outside man's conscious acceptance. And no acceptance is complete if the man has not explored the alternatives to faith.

"Why" was a question that I feared as a child. My father often beat my calves with a stick if I asked blasphemous "why"s. When he was rested, however, he also found time to explain some matters concerning the Trinity, and our obligations to God. Never more than that, never explaining the origins of these beliefs, and the sources.

I started and I ended with Why. The childhood fear is now a pulsating desire to find out if there is an ultimate potential for man and if man can ever achieve it. So far, there is no glimmer of an answer, and the days are getting darker and darker.

7:2 The Brazilian escape

After the first hard conversation with President Bourbon-Renege, I felt the need to mingle with the people on the streets again, to quench my thirst for the simple pleasures in life. Rio de Janeiro was a mere hour and 35 minutes from Brasilia. I asked Nwanne to book me a flight immediately, since we had the rest of the day to ourselves. Lo and behold, the Rio Carnival was happening today!

I told Tchipcherish and Mother Allegra I needed time to myself. Nwanne packed quickly, and as soon as we arrived at the hotel, I excused myself and went to my room to put on my disguise. Nwanne picked out a splendid suit that made me look like a businessman. I put on a millennial man bun, moustache, sideburns, new glasses, some make-up, and I was a different man. I never asked Nwanne how he procured the documentation needed for travel, but apparently I was a "Mr. Thomas Lovejoy from Trinidad".

We flew second class, with only two disguised Swiss Guards accompanying us. They were dressed as computer nerds.

In Rio we went straight towards the parades. We made our way through the crowd. I did not ask anything of anybody, yet soon enough lovely ladies with their skin exposed approached us with very friendly intentions. I asked their names. They asked our names and who we were. Since I could not convince the Swiss Guards to stay far from me, their presence made me look important. I told the ladies I was a businessman who loves parades and displays of joy. I could not say more, and the ladies posed around me for selfies and asked if they could both kiss my cheeks, then proceeded to kiss my cheeks right away, before I could object. They kept their lips pressed hard on both my cheeks, which rendered me incapable of speaking intelligibly. This lasted for a good minute, enough time for the lovely ladies to ask a third lovely lady to take even more photos, this time of different postures, such as with their bosoms more exposed. It happened so fast, I did not realize that the lovely ladies had disposed of their upper-body vests, thus becoming completely bare-chested, except for a certain cover over their papilla mammaria, not that I could see exactly what the cover was, from the angle of my eyes, since the lovely ladies were stuck to me on both sides.

Nwanne tried to interfere with the ladies' enthusiasm, but did not succeed much. On the contrary, he found himself chuckling and playing along, completely not minding the embarrassment that would haunt us if news of this event ever emerged to the world. I cared somewhat more than Nwanne about the consequences, but in those two short minutes I could not find enough energy to refuse the pleasure of the ladies. I was, at the same time, extremely confident in the quality of my disguise. At no moment did the lovely ladies have any inkling of who I really was, not even when I spoke, however brief that was, and only in a complimentary way. I was also wearing the mouth prosthesis that slightly altered the curvature of my cheeks and the sound of my voice.

It was the Swiss Guards who finally intervened and put an end to this sweet torture, once a few more lovely ladies approached us with the clear desire to participate in this photographic dance.

So, we bade farewell to all the lovely ladies, one more beautiful than the other, and the men who appeared from nowhere, seemingly to claim the company of the above ladies. These men were no less cheerful and showed no grudges whatsoever. Their buttcheeks were exposed, as well.

The Swiss Guards found an observation spot in an audience stand along the parade avenue in the middle of the songs and cheers. I watched the exuberance of the public, and the fantastic rainbows of colors worn by the dancers. They were strolling proudly on the avenue, like there was no tomorrow, like nothing else mattered in life.

Is it truly better to go to the house of mourning than to go to the house of feasting, for that is the end of all men, and the living will take it to heart?

7:3 My confessor

I feel uneasy discussing my confessions. When I visited Father Martin, I invariably found him praying. Father Martin was a very private man, very wise, erudite, and thoughtful. When I called him to visit me this afternoon, the first thing he told me was that sorrow is better than laughter, for by a sad countenance the heart is made better.

Despite being rejuvenated by my visit to Brazil, I came back with sorrowful psychological baggage, that I cannot yet unpack. Perhaps my conscience is rebelling against the censorship that I imposed on myself. Perhaps my political decision, to overrule my conscience and keep my true convictions to myself, is reaching a boiling point where I am no longer the master of the domain of my emotions.

Father Martin sensed my uneasiness as he pursued a certain line of questioning. He asked questions that gave me the freedom to choose a safe haven for my conscience. Father Martin is not the jailer of my morality, he is supposed to be a channel for the absolution of my sins. I went to him to seek encouragement and validation. But is this not an act of cowardice? Would I not be stronger if I fully accepted my dilemma, with all its conflicts? Would I not be made the better for it, in real life?

And Nwanne's voice… Whispering in my mind, when I was confessing to Father Martin… As if it wanted to kidnap me from the present…

I am a political person, no question about it. I am a head of state. I oversee one of the oldest institutions on Earth, with over a billion adherents. This is part of being Pope. Who can forget the infamous Pope Alexander VI, with his numerous mistresses? Was he a man of God? I highly doubt that. Has he had the moral tremors that I am having? Highly improbable. Yet, he was a political figure, as much as I am.

Father Martin understood that he was an echo for my doubts. He listened to me carefully, paraphrased my confession with words from great moral philosophers, and deferred all judgments to God, despite the fact that I could clearly see the glimpse of his own judgment of me in his eyes.

We talked about vows of chastity and of my impulses of anger, in such soft terms it made me ashamed of myself. I told Father Martin, "My body sometimes has these irritating contractions, they come and go, and they are not of a medical nature." Clearly Father Martins knew what I was saying and did not deflect. He remained candid. "Your Holiness, it is the cross you must bear."

Obviously! I knew that, but I had to say it, and it made me feel much better. I can trust Father Martin with my life, I know he will respect the sanctity of confession.

I need to talk to Father Martin every once in a while. He is somebody who is not Nwanne, somebody who I often think of as the anonymous voice of the entire world. Oh, if it were only this real!

7:4 Loud and clear

I, Francis the Second, Pope of the Catholic Church, Bishop of Rome, Vicar of Jesus Christ, Successor of the Prince of the Apostles, Supreme Pontiff of the Universal Church, Primate of Italy, Archbishop and Metropolitan of the Roman Province, Sovereign of the Vatican City State, Servant of the Servants of God, I decree loudly and clearly that the following statements be added to the core of the Christian Doctrine:

One. The Christian faith must be allowed to evolve, along with the principles of morality, towards the greater good of mankind. If this means letting go of God, so be it.

Two. The sense of solidarity that the Church provides must be persevered and reformed, in such a way that it fosters universal inclusion of social justice for all.

Three. The institution of the Church must become fully transparent, including, but not limited to: its finances; its archives; its electoral processes; and its integrations with the laws of the land.

Four. All Christians must be fully committed to the salvation of Planet Earth, meaning that faith should never supersede the rights of all beings to exist.

Five. Procreation must be severely controlled. Birth control is mandatory. The increasing number of humans has already triggered the sixth mass extinction.

Six. Men and women are equal in absolutely all aspects of life. There shall be no discrimination of any kind against any social category. Hereby, the path for a clerical career is open to everyone.

Seven. Life is a continuous struggle. We must try to make ourselves better humans. We must respect life in all its forms. We must preserve the good traditions and discard the bad ones. We must honor the laws of evolution and rise to a higher level of wisdom. Creation is better than destruction. Discovery is better than submission. Action is better than prayer. Social engagement is better than contemplative passivity.

I lay down these thoughts in my diary, secretly hoping that someday they will be discovered, after I end my days as Pope. I strongly believe there is much to be learned from the lessons of history.

The heart of the wise is in the house of mourning, but the heart of fools is in the house of mirth.

7:5 Secret meetings Part I - Bucharest

I have decided to go on a tour, with Tchipcherish and Mother Allegra, to visit all the Christian Orthodox Patriarchs of the Eastern Churches, to lay out my ecumenical plans for a great unification and revolution of the Christian faith.

I told Nwanne we have to schedule these meetings very carefully and in great secrecy, since the Orthodox sensibilities are thin-skinned and we do not want to tread on anyone's honor.

The first meeting we scheduled was in Bucharest, with the first three Patriarchs on our list: Fyodor of Russia, Pompiliu of Romania, and Aequilaterus of Constantinople.

Naturally, the true purpose of the visit was not leaked to the press. The official purpose was announced as trilateral consultations on matters of faith concerning the grave issues of climate change and the problems of suffering in the world, or something of that nature, that would not really interest the mainstream media.

We had a press conference at the Palace of the Patriarchate. Fyodor, Pompiliu, Aequilaterus and I all agreed in advance to keep our statements generic, without actually revealing the true nature of my visit. I promised the Patriarchs that their efforts would be well rewarded by my proposal.

After the press left, the three of us – and our respective translators - moved behind closed doors, and began the real conversation.

"My dear Patriarchs," I began warmly, "I come here before you with a great ambition. I would like to unite all of Christendom under one roof, in one spiritual body. And it is not the body of the Church as we know it, but the body of real solidarity. I propose to your Eminences the creation of THE COUNCIL OF CHRISTIANITY, that will replace the Catholic Church and all Orthodox Churches."

The Patriarchs were nonplussed.

"It is as simple as that, Your Eminences," I continued. "We create a new organization and give the power to the people. Freedom and justice, at the same time."

I waited for the translators to finish.

"Your Holiness," Fyodor said, struggling to find his words in Russian, "Are you saying that you want to end the Papacy? Is that what we are hearing?"

"Eventually yes, Your Eminence," I said.

"And we should give up the sovereignty of our Churches?" Pompiliu asked, with complete shock on his face.

"Patriarch Pompiliu," I said. "It is not a question of a transfer of sovereignty. It is a complete revolution of the Christian faith. We let the Church be ruled by the people."

"And how do we do that, Your Holiness?" Aequilaterus asked, somehow less perturbed than the other two Patriarchs, probably because of the ulcer that he confided having during the meet-and-greet.

I took my time, and I continued to reveal the proposal:

"All Patriarchs and heads of all Christian Churches will have a seat on the Council of Christianity. There will be no Pope, there will be no Patriarch. The Council will have a governing body, elected by the members of the councils. We will reverse the Schism of 1054. We will finally build a unified Christianity on the principles of social solidarity. We will develop new rites that conform with the realities of our days. We will honor the tradition of charity and condemn the tradition of violence and bigotry perpetrated by all our churches. We shall build a consensus based on the will of the people. The mandate of the Council of Christianity will be the guide for the spirit of the people towards the survival of our species."

Again, the Patriarchs remained silent for a moment. I always believed that it is better to hear the rebuke of the wise than to hear the song of fools. I knew they all wanted to save their churches and the whole of Christianity, and to make a mark in history.

If only they knew that my plan was so much bigger than this.

If they only knew my great secret.

7:6 The assassination attempt

It was a sunny day in Rome. Easter Mass. St. Peter's Square was packed. Holovision crews were all over, and two big screens were on each side of the stage.

I let the Cardinals perform the introductions and begin the Mass while I sat uncomfortably in my Papal chair. Very uncomfortable. I am still not used to all the luxury and pomposity around me. I tried to tone down the pageantry as much as I could. I told Nwanne I wanted a simple wooden chair made by hand by a local carpenter. Nwanne told me that I was going too far, and we must keep a certain protocol that reflects the elevation of my office.

Pffff! What elevation? I'm just a man. It's just a chair. Who cares what it looks like. If objects have meanings, then a simple wooden chair can also have a meaning. That of simplicity and modesty. Nwanne agreed with me, but said he was bound by tradition and the pressure from the Curia. How frustrating! I cannot even choose the chair I sit on!

I finished the sermon on time, then I told Cardinal Mutella, sitting next to me, that I wanted to meet the people in the square and take holoselfies with them. I learned that these new holophones are very popular now. They store holographic images of certain places, and even short holovideos that you can replay as if you are there again. Of course, you need an adequate holoprojector or one of those sets of VR-glasses.

"We are not prepared, Your Holiness," Mutella said, "security-wise."

"What can happen?", I said, and stood up from my awful chair.

Mutella had no choice but to call the Popemobile. I walked to it, waving at the crowd, and the crowd went wild. Nwanne told the driver to go slowly around the obelisk and back, through the crowd. The Swiss Guard surrounded the vehicle, making sure people were not getting hurt.

We stopped many times for holoselfies to be taken, and for babies to be handed to me by their parents for benedictions.

About two minutes into this little trip, a man climbed into the Popemobile behind my back. I had not seen him. I saw only the horror on the faces of people around me. The man was dressed all in black. His face was white as milk, and showed no expression. He was holding a pistol and had a clear intention to shoot me in the head from a short distance.

I still wonder why he climbed into the car with me. If he wanted to shoot me, why didn't he shoot me from the crowd? He could have gotten a clear view. He wouldn't have had to bother bypassing the attention of my Swiss Guard, climbing on the platform of the Popemobile, regaining equilibrium, raising the pistol, pointing it at me, then shooting. So much trouble. Nobody understood this gesture. Perhaps there was an ulterior motive, perhaps the man was mad and wanted to inflict harm on me in a war-like manner, with courage and honor, well, as much honor as an assassin can muster. Or, perhaps the madman wanted to show complete and utter contempt, not only for my person, but for the entire Catholic Church, to expose its weaknesses, to pull its roots out of the ground.

We shall never know.

Before the madman was able to shoot his pistol, a sniper from atop St. Peter's Basilica blew his brains out, splattering the back of my robe with his blood and grey matter, horrifying the crowd around me and the whole world watching. It happened so fast I didn't get the chance to turn around, as I was facing forward at that very moment, so none of the madman's fluids reached my face. At the same instant, some Swiss Guards jumped into the Popemobile with me and instructed the driver to drive away, while other Guards pushed the people away from our path. They pushed me to the ground and I kept asking over and over again, "What happened? What happened?", but nobody would answer me, while blood oozed on the platform of the Popemobile and was now reaching the front of my body.

I have no idea what happened to the body of the madman. Maybe it fell out of the car due to inertia, as we drove off, and the Swiss Guards who remained behind made a circle around it, to protect it from the fury of the crowd. It was highly unlikely that a couple of Swiss Guards could contain such a big crowd, despite their guns in full display.

I was rushed to safety deep in the Papal Palace, and all the remaining Swiss Guards in the Vatican came to surround me, plus countless more Italian Police. I had not been harmed, and to the surprise of everyone, I was not emotionally shaken at all. I was only confused, since I was lacking information. No one would tell me what actually happened.

When they finally did tell me what they knew, I replied that I had been close to death many times in my life, in Africa. Moreover, due to the fact that I am black, and that I am such a progressive Pope, it should be no surprise that I might have stirred the sensibilities of some mad white people, which in truth is only a statistical probability of human nature. I also admitted that I was a tad careless with my enthusiasm.

For like the cracking of thorns under a pot, so is the laughter of the fool, this is also vanity. I was told that a camera caught the glimpse of a smile on the madman's face, a millisecond before the sniper's bullet entered his head.

7:7 Secret meetings Part II - Athens

I had no time to recuperate after the incident with the madman. I went back on the mission to lobby more Orthodox Patriarchs about the Council of Christianity.

This time, to a secret meeting in Athens. Patriarch Hieronymus of Greece was very kind to host the meeting at an inconspicuous villa of the Autocephalous Orthodox Church of Greece. Also invited, were Philipilus of Jerusalem, and Patriarch Nestor of Serbia.

To get to the point. (As I despise writing about the protocol and all the arrangements we had to make to keep this meeting a secret.)

I told the Patriarchs my plan and the reasons for this gargantuan ecumenical project. I concluded thusly:

"Your Beatitudes, we all know the grave crimes that are still perpetrated under the banner of Christianity in many parts of the world, the racism in America, the denial of reproductive rights of women, and more. We need to reform our dogma, forget our divisive traditions, and move into the future along with the rest of humanity. More than ever, we need unity."

The Patriarchs listened carefully and took their time to answer.

"So, Your Holiness," Hieronymus said, "You want us to undo the Autocephalous Orthodox Church of Greece, and reorganize as this "Council of Christianity"?"

"Yes, indeed, Your Beatitude," I said.

"What about our tradition, our culture, our rituals?"

"We all vote and we make a new culture of solidarity," I said.

"But that's impossible, Your Holiness," Hieronymus said. "We cannot erase centuries of Orthodox wisdom."

"We don't erase, we create," I explained. "You keep your tradition and we make a new one as well. We will all wear two coats. One coat for who we are now, and one coat for the Council of Christianity."

"I do not understand, Your Holiness," Philipilus of Jerusalem said.

As I recall, Patriarch Philipilus did not have the reputation of a bright man.

"Let me give you an example, Your Beatitudes. We shall have a yearly grand meeting at the Council of Christianity where we will all wear the same thing. Something beautiful, sewed by hand by peasants. A monk's garb. Perhaps in green, or perhaps blue, or even turquoise, I always loved turquoise. Something simple. Very simple. No hats. We shall all come with our heads uncovered. Us, Catholics we may even grow beards for the event, or in turn Your Beatitudes can shave your beards, or perhaps just shorten their lengths in the spirit of solidarity. I, for example, am willing to shave only one time per year, just to have a beard for the event. This is so easy to do, but it will mean a great deal for our cause, and for all Christians worldwide."

"It took me years to grow this beard," Philipilus said. "I can't cut it and grow it again ever year."

"Your Beatitude Philipilus," Hieronymus of Greece said. "His Holiness only suggests a modest transformation of our facial hair styling habits. Nothing that men with our wisdom and sanctity cannot manage. For the greater benefit of Christianity. I agree with your proposal, Your Holiness."

"We all know, Your Beatitudes," I said, "that in the age of holomatic technologies and grave climate problems, we need to keep up with the demands of the population. We lost many, many, believers and contributors, simply because our Churches have not been capable of answering the big questions. Why there is so much suffering in the world? Why has God allowed the ascension of demagogic leaders? Why there are no solutions for our struggles? Why? Why? Why? To be honest, I don't know why, but I feel the need of hundreds of millions of people for solidarity and for a place of hope, where prayers are truly listened to, even if they do not receive an answer. That's what the Council of Christianity should be. That's what all our Churches should be."

"I like that," Philipilus said. "I like that very much. I will shave my beard for that."

"Me too," said Hieronymus.

"Me too," Nestor of Serbia said, finally making his voice heard.

Does extortion turn a wise person into a fool? Does a bribe corrupt the heart? Most certainly yes. I shouldn't feel bad that I convinced three Patriarchs to do the right thing. I should think that I am a manipulator. Am I a manipulator? I don't think I am. I am almost sure I am not. Certainly, I am not a manipulator. I never tried to persuade anybody to think in my way, never tried to influence somebody for some hidden agenda I had. Most certainly not.

The Greek food is splendid. Their wines too. I'm going to spend the night in Athens because tomorrow I want to go into the streets incognito.

Oh, I almost forgot about Tchipcherish and Mother Allegra. I sent them together on a diplomatic mission to Venezuela.

7:8 Day in Athens

I had Nwanne dress me like a Jamaican man on a trip to Greece. He prepared for me a beautiful wig with dreadlocks like Bob Marley's, and a beard like Cornel West's from the mid-2010s. Dark sunglasses with a holoscreen so I could see information about all locations in front of my eyes. The Swiss Guards were also disguised as American tourists, however they behaved quietly and with restraint.

We went to the Acropolis first. Nwanne walked about twenty meters behind me, pretending to be a tourist interested in photography. In fact, he kept the eye of his lens very closely upon me.

I won't describe the Parthenon and everything else on the Acropolis. It is as beautiful as shown in the holo-documentaries. The only difference is that when I went there in person, I felt flooded with images of Ancient Greek history. I saw Socrates scolding Plato for being late to a philosophical meeting. In my mind, Plato responded wryly: "Master Socrates, philosophy has no real beginning and no real end. I can never be late for a meeting." To which Socrates replied without hesitation: "Plato, listen, philosophy is like pain. There is a potential for it all the time, but it doesn't mean that we are philosophers in every moment of our lives. When you sit with your naked bottom on a hot rock that has been bathed by the sun, you will soon feel the burning in your buttocks. You will not want to think about the meaning of life, or about what time it is. Pain will overwhelm you. Philosophy is the same, but in fact quite the opposite. It appears in the moments of least expectation, when the memory of pain has completely disappeared. Furthermore, if I now apply a dozen strokes over your calves with this prickly stick in retribution for your tardiness, you will not be helpful to me in our philosophical dialogues, and you will surely remember tomorrow not to be late again. Often, philosophy requires sacrifices. But I know you are a good student, my dear Plato, and the beating will not be necessary, as you will use these words of mine as sufficient warning and wisdom not to be late again, and not to use wisecracks of relativism to concoct your excuse. And one more thing, do not write about this conversation in your books, okay? This will stay between us. Don't tell Xenophon, please."

Ah, the smell of olive trees, a feeble scent of lavender, a slight breeze from the sea! I was floating on a cloud of ecstasy.

I did not bother with all of the tourists around me, many with VR-glasses that superimposed holo-enhancements on the ruins, so people could see how they really looked in Ancient times. It's hard to avoid the holo-tourists. Fortunately, they did not diminish my enthusiasm. Imagination is the best nourishment for the soul!

As we walked down from the Acropolis, I thought how the end of a thing is better than its beginning, as true accomplishments can only happen when things end. As no civilization has lasted forever, when they ended they left us great legacies. Without them, we would drift on an infinite sea of loneliness.

So, even if I am an impatient man, wanting to see the fruits of my labor sooner rather than later, in the light of history, there is no guarantee what my legacy will be, as it is not determined by the present time, but always by the times of the future.

My comfort remains in the knowledge that the patient in spirit is better than the proud in spirit. I am not known as a proud man, so I hope that I will learn some patience eventually, even at my age. It is never late for a man to become wiser.

It was then that I met the olive salesman at the heel of the Acropolis. A Greek man of my age, pushing a four-wheeled cart with a dozen jars of olives, tightly tied to the cart with an intricate web of ropes. He was offering a bag of fresh olives at a good price.

He stopped in front of me and sized me up with his eyes.

"Would you like some fresh olives, mister?" he said in English.

He did not wait for me to reply, and continued:

"This is how you get the taste of the Parthenon on your tongue. You will never forget it."

I felt ashamed for not answering right away. The image of the olive salesman was stunning. Who was that man?

"Yes, I would very much like to buy olives from you," I said.

"I have Kalamon, that's black olive, dark and meaty-flavored. I have Halkidiki, green and tangy in flavor. I have Tsakistes, seasoned with fresh lemon and garlic. Throumba, from the islands of Thasos and Crete."

"I will take two bags of each," I said.

"These are high quality olives. Worthy of the palate of the Pope of Rome," the olive salesman said.

He looked at me with his big Greek eyes and smiled. He knew who I was! He was not moved at all by this realization. He remained focused on his work. He did not lessen himself in front of me. He did not elevate himself on some stoic pedestal of pride. He remained himself: the olive salesman who knew the secret of the Pope of Rome. I left him a big tip. He shook my hand vigorously wishing me: "Best of luck!"

7:9 The revolt of the homeless in St. Peter's Square

Oh, my goodness! What a day, and it's not over yet!

I can still hear people screaming outside in the streets, police sirens blaring, people with bullhorns shouting their disappointment with the Italian government, the police shouting: "Back off! We will teargas you!" All of this just outside the Vatican walls.

It started this morning with a gathering of the homeless people of Rome, and many more who came from other Italian cities. They gathered in St. Peter's Square at my invitation, that said, simply: "The house of God is the house of the homeless." Obviously, I meant that the homeless can come to us, be offered food, money, and shelter for a night, wherever we could find room for them. In the Vatican chambers, in our hotels, and even in St. Peter's Basilica, if they didn't mind sleeping on the floor, on thick mats and sleeping bags, of course.

They came in staggering numbers. Thousands upon thousands. They almost filled St. Peter's Square. Nwanne, Cardinal Tchipcherish, and Mother Allegra organized the outdoor kitchens in my name. On streets and in Pope Pius XII Square, riot-police cars were rounding up. The homeless gathering in St. Peter's Square have drawn a public protest that was marching on the streets of Rome and was approaching Via della Conciliazione.

What has happening?

The austerity policies of Pierluigi Pantalone's government were so harsh, the people cannot bear them anymore. Many people living in socially subsidized houses lost their solidarity benefits. They joined the population of the homeless.

Then the marches started. From piazza to piazza, from Quirinale to Palazzo Chigi and back, then to the Vatican, when all hope to be heard was lost. They came here because of my message of solidarity. At noon Prime Minister Pantalone called me on the regular voice-only phone to tell me not to interfere with Italian politics. I said I did not intend to, I only welcome those in distress. Then he said we will talk again, and hung up. He was remarkably agitated. I mumbled to myself: do not hasten in your spirit to be angry, for anger rests in the bosom of fools.

By one o'clock, St. Peter's Square was packed with homeless people. The Swiss Guards forbade them from bringing in their belongings. A big pile of bags and carts grew just outside the entry into the Square.

The riot-police were taunting the homeless crowd from Pope Pius XII Square with a large display of riot-gear. Their message was clear: "You may now be on sovereign soil, but if you dare to come out, we will arrest you - or worse."

The homeless crowd was getting agitated, and they formed a line across St. Peter's Square to face the line of armed of riot-police. Thousands of ragged homeless against hundreds of shielded police. Objects began to fly from St. Peter's Square into Pope Pius XII Square. Cans, bottles, plates, cups, toilet paper.

The Italian riot-police did not react. It would have meant an act of war against the Vatican. The tensions were building up to the point of boiling. Shoes were now flying from St. Peter towards Pope Pius XII.

The Swiss Guard did not intervene. They were overwhelmed. They closed the doors of the Basilica, and allowed events to unfold by themselves.

At around 2:30pm, Prime Minister Pantalone called me again. He wanted permission to make arrests in St. Peter's Square. I flatly refused. "I am still your friend, Prime Minister," I said. "I assure you everything is going to be alright."

"Then you must speak to your crowd, Your Holiness."

My crowd! What did he mean by that? Why was it *my* crowd!? I just offered the homeless a place of rest. They are not my crowd!

I just offered the homeless a place of rest. They are not *my* people. I bet most of them have no consideration for God, Christ, or any faith for that matter. I, certainly, do not blame them. If I were them, I would also deny the existence of God.

I did try to speak to the crowd, from my window. Very few people actually listened. They were too preoccupied with shouting at the riot-police and throwing things. I think I spoke for about 5 minutes, with no effect. There was an incredible havoc in the Square.

Pope Pius XII was also surrounded by mobs coming from all directions. The riot-police made a bad strategic move. They were caught in the middle.

At around 7pm, some big trucks with water cannons broke through the crowd and managed to connect with the riot-police in Pope Pius XII Square. The crowd in St. Peter's had calmed down a little. Some left, but not many. I ordered more food to be delivered from Vatican sources.

People began shouting that they will not leave St. Peter's unless their housing is restored, and they are offered jobs. Prime Minister Pantalone did not reply.

At around 8pm I spoke again. This time some people listened and applauded. I said nothing about God, or Christ, or prayer, or forgiveness. I only assured them that they can continue to feel at home at the Vatican. I will do my best to install tents in St. Peter's Square, and to offer food. For showers, they will be issued numbered vouchers that they can use at the hotel. I told the crowd not to count on those showers, since there is a very limited number of them. If they have another place in Rome where to bathe, they should go there. I promised them that they will be welcomed back.

That was it.

I'm not sure what will happen tomorrow. I do have hope that some compromise can be reached. I received enormous support from the international community. Pantalone cannot ignore this.

7:10 A terrible realization

I woke up with such a terrible headache, I was barely able to call Nwanne to bring me some medication. He immediately saw I was distressed and asked me what happened.

I must have had a frightening nightmare. I remembered nothing from it. There was this only echo on my mind of a thought of vast futility. This project, this ambition of mine, to create a new institution of Christianity for the greater good of the people, now seemed such a ridiculous and inane idea that it sent a powerful shock through my whole body.

I was shivering with cold sweats. Nwanne was worried and wanted to call the doctor. I told him No, it was not necessary, I will be fine. It was just a tremor of anxiety.

Such a void in my mind! A stone in my stomach! How did I come up with such an insane idea? Dismantle the Papacy? Dismantle the Orthodox Churches? Reverse the Great Schism? Unite all Christians? This was madness! It was so clear now that this was an impossible endeavor. I should have not asked myself "Why does the past seem so much better than now?" because this question does not come from wisdom. I build the entire project on my high approval rate among all Christians, and on their desire to reform the institutions of their faith. Except for the seven Cardinals from the Curia, I heard very little opposition. Even the Patriarchs listened to me!

Now I see it all clearly! This will never happen. Faith is not made to unite. Faith has grown from the obscure inspiration of some ancient people, and the entire history after them is only a history of interpretation, unverifiable miracles, delusions of the mind known as revelations, crusades and inquisitions, abuse of power, unchallenged clerical authoritarians, countless schisms and sects, discriminatory charity, and mundane hypocrisies.

There is no way to build bridges over all these divisions. There is no true universal access to an absolute truth of faith. There is nothing OUT THERE that speaks to all of us. There is no objective article of faith that can build the foundation of this Council of Christianity, expect for the rule of secular law, inspired by the exercises of moral philosophy.

How can I reconcile this terrible realization with the faults of Christianity? I see no way around it. I also dread that I cannot undo what I have just started, as my actions have grown thick roots in the politics of the world. Once my project becomes known, it will be the greatest institutional enterprise in the history of mankind. And now I see what a feeble house of cards it is! A sandcastle! An empty shell than can be broken by the fall of a feather!

Foolish me! My trusting Cardinals have said nothing. Mutella, nothing. Not even Tchipcherish. What could I expect from him, anyways? He planted the seeds. He was the puppeteer. He left me alone to my demons, and my naïve mind! Perhaps he knew all about it, under those layers of his of shrewdness. Perhaps.

What do I do now? Where do I go from here? Ugh. These despicable lamentations. Signs of a wise mind? Of course not! Signs of a corrupt and weak mind!

7:11 Secret meetings III

I don't like myself at all when I fall in deep pits of sorrow and despair, often so deep that I lose the sight of joy and well-tempered reason.

The noise from the world is getting to my bones. There is something happening out there, riots and protests, local revolutions, military tensions that continue, millions being displaced because of the raising levels of the seas, droughts and famine, I can't even think of them all. My ideas of reform pale in comparison with these enormous struggles.

Today, meeting with the last four Orthodox Patriarchs on my list: Neophyte of Bulgaria (rough-mannered), Ulianus of Alexandria (a joker), John of Antioch-Syria (very ill) and Ilia IV of Georgia (talks like a squeaky parrot). Comments in parenthesis so I could remember them better. All good-hearted Patriarchs, no doubt.

The meeting was held in Cyprus. Obviously, we could not have met in Syria, due to the Russian peace presence, nor in Georgia (oil-related riots), nor in Sofia (the media has spies everywhere).

I gave my presentation, as usual, to the point. I put aside my fears and I read from my notebook, to hide all the insecurities in my voice. I concluded by recognizing the Syriac Orthodox Church of Antioch to be the most ancient Christian church in the world.

"St. Peter and St. Paul the Apostle are regarded as the co-founders of the Patriarchate of Antioch in AD 37," I said.

All Patriarchs acknowledged the fact by nodding their heads.

John thanked me for my goodwill and grace. He said he shared my feelings of peace for the world. He excused himself for his bad health, pulled out a handkerchief from his pocket, and coughed little droplets of blood into it.

"If the end of my life is near," John said, "I want to do something meaningful at least."

"Your Beatitudes, Your Holiness," Ulianus said, "do you all think we are approaching the end of times, the days of the Final Judgment, the inevitable return of Christ? To be honest, and in the large hindsight of history, we have not been better, spiritually speaking. Despair, tragedies, famine, wars, we had since our Churches have been founded. There is nothing new under the sun. Like the prophet says, all is vanity. To be honest, waiting for something that theologically is supposed to happen very soon, yet it hasn't happened for more than two thousand years, makes me feel restless, orthodoxically speaking. Of course, all piety remains absolute. Christ is lord. Salvation is our entire dedication. Faith is our pillar. Et cetera. However, and I stress the word however, I see no better way to enhance the hope of all Christian believers than by giving them something strong and real to believe in. This Council of Christianity that you are proposing, Your Holiness, is a great opportunity for all of us to get closer to God, in a way that has never been attempted since Christ rose to the Father. Hallelujah! Thank God He did! And we can be an inspiration for all religions! We can inspire even the world of politics to rebuild itself on principles of solidarity, and the rights of all beings to continue to exists on this planet, through their descendants. I am eager, Your Holiness, to be part of this project."

Ilia said something in response that left us all pensive for a few moments. He said, slowly, from behind a dense and thick beard:

"Wisdom is good with an inheritance. And profitable to those who see the sun."

While we were all quiet around the round table, waiting for someone to make the next move, Ilia spoke again:

"I suppose I can shorten my beard for the benefit of peace. It's a small thing to do. Or I can shave it completely. I think it's a good idea."

Neophyte covered his own white beard with his hand as a defensive reflex. In his subconscious mind, he feared Their Beatitudes were supposed to shave their beards right now, under the auspices of an ad-hoc ecumenical brotherhood. Neophyte fretted in his chair. His most precious possession was being negotiated on the altar of faith. Was he ready to concede? He clenched his fist and rubbed his Patriarchal ring. Then he spoke:

"Your Holiness, Your Beatitudes, how do I say this? I very much want more strength for our faith, not through trivial means, but through bridges built deep down in our souls. Beards, no beards, it is a mundane problem for our Churches. The true union is a union of souls, of stories, of concessions."

"Your Beatitude Neophyte," Ulianus said, "are you saying that if we Patriarchs decide to shorten our beards or even shave them completely, you will not join us?"

I sat in silence, not moving a muscle.

"Your Beatitude Ulianus," Neophyte said, "perhaps my beard should not be part of this program."

"Solidarity is built on the image of the soul, which is the face," Ulianus said. "Abstract words of theology are not as effective and powerful."

Neophyte spent more time rubbing his beard, clearly a passion most valuable to him. Two or three times he wanted to say something, but stopped himself short from uttering the words. He was fighting with himself inside. We all saw that. All Patriarchs have put their beards on the table, while I put my shaved face. We were all waiting for Patriarch Neophyte of Bulgaria to do the same.

In the end he conceded by offering a length of at least three centimeters but no less than that. To celebrate, I offered to say grace in three languages, and I concluded in Syriac, to honor our good friend Patriarch John of Antioch Syria, whom we wished rapid recovery and good health throughout his days.

7:12 News of a habitable planet

Shock from the world of science! There is clear evidence of a habitable planet, about the size of Earth, near a yellow dwarf star. The temperature ranges from minus 50 degrees Celsius to plus 40 degrees Celsius. The surface is about half covered by rocks, and half is water. The most interesting aspect about the planet, named Nova Gaia, is that the oceans are purple. All telescopes detected the same peculiarity.

The exobiologists estimate that the color is due to the chemical composition of the water and very likely to the presence of some sort of exoplanetary life. This makes the discovery even more interesting.

How far is Nova Gaia? A mere 30 light-years away.

The WILCZEK telescope that uses a high-resolution technique based on the reading of gravitation waves and space-time densities (I memorized this from the news) has managed to present pictures of Nova Gaia during the transition in front of its star, in large spectrum of light frequencies. There is almost no doubt Nova Gaia is hoped to be Earth 2.0.

What am I supposed to do with this news? I, the Pope of Rome, the Defender of the Christian faith, I must have an opinion on the subject. I must go out tomorrow, in front of the media, and say loud and clear that I applaud the discovery, that this is another reason for mankind to become stronger together (and if that's now possible) at least more understanding with each other and more peaceful.

How can I sit down now and wonder why Christ and His Father had nothing to say about this wonderful purplish planet called Nova Gaia? Not a word. Nothing. Not even an inkling of a revelation or prophecy anywhere in the Holy Book. Not a tremor of any Saint, not any apparitions of Virgin Mary to tell us to expect another world like ours out there in the Cosmos.

At least a metaphor, or a verse, a proverb, or a psalm, to tell of a globe of purple water and stone near a twinkling star in the night sky. I would have been so happy to quote such a verse. Alas, there is nothing.

I dispatched Nwanne to the library to find me something in the works of all great Christian Saints and theologians that might support the discovery of the astronomers. I haven't heard from him in more than 8 hours. And he's using the best Artificial Intelligent Algorithms to search.

What a beautiful planet: Nova Gaia! Its image is on the front page of all publications, all holostations, everywhere. The most popular hashtag of the decade is now #ILoveNovaGaia. Within hours it surpassed #FirstBlackPope by the tens of millions. The purplish sphere is magical. It has the texture and the elegance of a marble. There are no signs of polar caps. Scientists say there are polar caps but they are covered by some sort of non-white material, perhaps organic, that hides their true composition. There is overwhelming evidence that life is present, but, given the distance, it is still impossible to determine its form. The WILCZEK telescope cannot resolve the surface composition of the planet in such a high detail.

The patterns on the surface of Nova Gaia are highly symmetrical and well distributed. Many so-called continents of land have shapes that remind me of fractals and of the Norwegian fjords. The land is a palette of gray, shades of blue, some purple (sign of the same ingredients that are present in the ocean, or maybe those are purple clouds! Yes, I think those are purple clouds! I haven't heard anyone saying this!). There are many spots of green, clearly defined and distinct from the surrounding environment. The spectral analysis has not yet provided any explanation of their composition.

So far, that is all I can remember about Nova Gaia. Scientists are working on an enhancement of the algorithm of the WILCZEK telescope, that, in the next few months, might show us a better image of the planet and perhaps more information about what lies on its surface.

Already many world leaders are seriously talking about space travel.

What do theologians talk about? They say: wisdom is a shelter as money is a shelter, but the advantage of knowledge is this: Wisdom preserves those who have it. That's the best they can come up with. I have heard nobody, from any religion, claiming that their respective God and Prophets made claims of sovereignty over any other planet in the Universe.

So, here we go. Another step forward that narrows the path of our lovely millennial faith, that becomes dimmer and dimmer, and leaves us with a sense of cosmological awe. Our petty, cute ambitions of salvation, and the many little prayers that span millennia, now become a feeble echo on the firmament. We must force our arrogance to dwindle and then become extinguished. There is only room for modesty in the presence of this grand cosmos.

7:13 Secret meetings IV – the Protestant churches

I met a group of important leaders of the Protestant churches in a small village called Träumdorf (Village of Dreams) in Northern Germany. We agreed in advance not to come dressed in our clerical vestments, but in traditional German rural outfits. We were supposed to look like a congregation of union leaders that came together to discuss the agricultural policies of the region.

There was no drama with the Protestants. They were all clean-shaven and had some quiet athleticism in their general dispositions. The Archbishop of Canterbury brought a case of fine Scotch bottles and instructed the aides to distribute them among the attendees. During the meet-and-greet all guests had the chance to taste the liquor. A feast for the palate!

I gave my standard presentation about the Council of Christianity. Nobody interrupted me, there were no questions at the end, no raised hands or other unusual gestures. Nobody coughed or cleared their throats, nobody drank water from the glasses in front of them, nobody consulted with their translators or secretaries, as the common language was English, and they were all fluent in it, obviously.

All the Bishops present (Anglican, Methodist, Reformed, Lutheran, Pentecostal, and Baptist) immediately started to review the literature I brought with me, which included the presentation and the plans for the Council.

Calmly, without many interactions among them, to clarify points, to gauge reactions, to negotiate positions, to summon alliances, all Bishops took notes and raised their hands to be added to the list of speakers.

One by one, they took turns to speak, the Archbishop of Canterbury first. In their respective English accents, they expressed unwavering support for the Council of Christianity and great faith in mankind. They presented proposals about the institutional aspects of the Council, how many members it should have, who the governing body should be, how the members would be elected or appointed, where the headquarters should be, how the balance of power should be weighed, what the official languages should be, what the core doctrine should be, and how the traditions of all Christian denominations should be preserved in some local rites and art.

The Bishops proposed a Constitutional Charter that would bind all Christians. They were very optimistic that this Great Reform would reignite the joy of all Christians, especially because it was initiated by me, the Pope of Rome, the leader of the biggest Christian Church.

Then we had had a lunch break in an adjacent room. The lunch was frugal, limited to sandwiches, salad, baked potatoes, and some sausages.

When we returned to the meeting room, the Archbishop of Canterbury begged our permission to speak briefly:

"Consider the work of God," he said. "Who can make straight what God has made crooked? Who? Can anyone tell me? And how can we determine what was made crooked by the hand of God, if God can be said to have a hand, metaphorically speaking, or what was made crooked by the hand of man? God versus man, who can tell? Christ was offered to us to save us, he suffered and died to wash us of our sins. He died at the hands of men, didn't he? Was this all a divine plan? If people had felt the revelation while Christ was alive, Christ might have lived. We are creatures of free will, as much as the scriptures teach us. That means that the order that Christ brought in this world was also a result of the exercise of free will. His death happened so we could build the order again. Men built the Church, not at the indication of the Christ or by direct command from God, despite of what many so-called prophets say. We built the Church. We, men, had all those Schisms, Reforms, Counter-reforms. We carved one good story into numerous pieces. Can we put it together? Yes, I think we can. We are going to build the Council of Christianity, we are going to meld our souls together. Are we going to erase our traditions? Of course not. Are we going to undress from our clerical vestments? Probably. I would not mind that. We should be wearers of uniforms and mere performers of rituals. We are storytellers and we must inspire the millions to dream in unison. This doesn't mean people must dream the same dreams, it only means that they remain united in their diversity, on the common principle that we all are inhabitants of Planet Earth."

The Bishops responded with complete agreement. Polite applause. Well-tempered enthusiasm. We finished early, so there was more time for Scotch, German bread and butter, and some fresh delicious cheese.

It could not have been any easier!

7:14 Extraterrestrial signals from deep space

Back at the Vatican. I was in a news blackout for the duration of the flight. Since my driver is instructed not to pass me any information without solicitation, he said nothing to me. So, only when I opened the television did I see the breaking news: extraterrestrial signals from deep space!

The people at the Search for Extraterrestrial Intelligence (SETI) Institute are ecstatic. Their discovery of a strong signal soft gamma ray burst has been confirmed by observatories all over the world. The HAWKING Space Station was designed to measure space-time distortions that carry data packets of radiation, and capture the information within. In one of these distortions, HAWKING discovered a dense package of highly organized signals. Its origin is still unknown.

Gaia Nova and now this! What is happening? Are we really not alone in the Universe? Are we finally getting some answers?

I called Nwanne to bring a pot of coffee, and we sat all night watching the news. I am trying to make sense of it.

Nobody knows what the message says, but it is beyond doubt it cannot be of natural origins. Mathematicians and cryptographers have already detected patterns that indicate topologies and recursive algorithms – I have no idea what that means – and many layers of information. The signal is definitely not binary. Some physicists have detected references to quantum groups – no idea! – and information about gravitational anomalies. There seems to be no key to decode the message. Another curious fact is that the message is built in such a way as to contradict all known cosmic phenomena. Extreme care has been employed by the producers of the message to make this clear. They do not want to be confused with pulsars, black holes colliding, supernovae, or generic cosmic microwave background radiation.

The signal burst that was collected by the HAWKING contains 1.5 zettabytes of data, which is not a negligible amount. In the 2010s it would have seemed staggering to the world. If it wasn't for the quantum data centers, this amount of data could not have been captured and stored.

The spread of the signal is narrow, about 1 light-minute, or 1.8 million kilometers, which means, according to the astrophysicists, that the message was highly directed at us, and the spread was only meant to adjust for unforeseen spatial distortions. The farther away the source of the message proves to be, the likelier the conclusion that the message was meant for us will be.

WHAT DOES IT SAY?

This is the big question. Nobody has any idea whatsoever. It does seem strange that such a large amount of data was sent, using significant energy, as gamma rays are quite powerful indeed. Moreover, the senders were careful to wrap the message in a package that can travel very large distances without being easily disrupted by cosmic events.

I am getting goosebumps only thinking of what the message could say. How can I not think of what it could mean for my responsibilities as Pope? How can this be proof that God does not exist? Or that God exists? Which one is it? Certainly, God would not bother with such a highly technical delivery of a message. He would plant a message straight into the minds of the people. However, I think this is what has been happening since the dawn of humankind, with highly controversial results.

By its sheer existence, regardless of what I say, this message proves that we are neither unique, nor special, in this Universe, and paradoxically, at the same time, we may be unique and special! Clearly, we are not alone. Finally, this was settled! Mankind has gone crazy searching for this answer, and now that we have it, we seem to be utterly confused. Is this not what we wanted the whole time?

And why us? Why was the message directed at us? With so much care for its preparation?

Perhaps the message had been there for thousands and millions of years, and only now when we have the HAWKING we can read it. On further analysis, I don't think this is the case, since millions of years ago there were no humans on this planet, so why did the senders bother to send a message directed at… dinosaurs? No, the message was not sent that long ago, the message was sent only recently, with time-reference to Earth history. And if it was sent only recently, that can only mean it was not sent from far away, but rather from our cosmic neighborhood. This is exciting!

The scientist on the news now explains that the carrier space-time distortion may actually have an origin much farther out in space.

Poof! My logic demolished. So much for the better.

I feel invigorated. When times are good, why not be joyful? And when times are bad, many earthlings consider this: God made the one as well as the other, so people won't seek anything outside of his best. These earthlings may have to reconsider this deeply held belief. We are faced with surprises well beyond the capacity of our imagination. There is no escape from this!

7:15 Secret meetings V – the black church of Atlanta

A week after the discovery of the HAWKING signal, I honored an invitation to visit the largest nondenominational black church in the United States of America, namely: The Great Free Church of the Holy Trinity For All (known as The Great Free), in the city of Atlanta, Georgia. The name is rather curious since it contains the words "For All", yet when I was shown the statistics, there are 90% Black every week at the sermon, 9% Latino, and the rest are whites who live in the neighborhood and cannot afford to go to another place of worship.

The Pastor of The Great Free, a soft-spoken African-American man named Franklin King, offered to pay all expenses, the airplane, the hotel for myself and my staff. I had to politely decline. He told me on the phone that the arena has sold out in 10 minutes after he announced my visit.

"People have to pay to see me?" I asked.

"Oh, no, no, not at all," Pastor King said.

"It's a voluntary donation to cover the expenses of the building."

I did not press him any further.

Later, Nwanne told me that what Pastor King said was a filthy, despicable lie, and that the money he collected for my visit far exceeded the expenses of the building, with everything included: electricity, ventilation, security, video operations, sound operations, holo-operations. I told Nwanne we are not in a position to judge Pastor King, and that we are honoring his invitation not for his person, but for the tens of thousands of his parishioners who held me in high regard. And since my speech, and my conversation with Pastor King, will be holo-streamed live, it will be valuable for millions of people.

At The Great Free, I was received with a standing ovation by the crowd. This was a great shock to me, since the people there were not even Catholic. They did seem to love me very much. They screamed: "Brother Francis", "We are all Africans", "Christ is one for all", while many had signs reading #IAmCatholic, while they were clearly not, so I took the signs in a metaphorical sense. When I looked up behind me, on a gigantic screen I saw the same words, 10 meters high, hashtagged beautifully: #IAmCatholic. A kind display of friendship from Pastor King and his congregation.

I walked to the lectern and I spoke.

"In this meaningless life of mine I have seen both of these: the righteous perishing in their righteousness, and the wicked living long in their wickedness. How is this possible? How is this fair? Is this the will of God?

Our faith tells us that we cannot know the will of God, but we can have sense of it through faith.

How do we learn faith? From our parents and from the Church? From observing the world around us? From reading the Holy Book? It can be from all these sources, and from none of them.

I come to you here, brothers and sisters, with a message of wisdom. I come to you with the message that the Universe is talking to us in languages that we cannot yet understand. They are languages of science that have been recorded by the HAWKING telescope.

Then we have the sights of Nova Gaia, this beautiful purple planet, seen by the WILCZEK telescope.

Why am I telling you this? Why are these discoveries so important for our faith?

Can we say that God is talking to us through the vastness of space and time? Can we be sure that this is an affirmation of our special place in existence?

We cannot say that God is talking, but we can be sure of the fact that this message is for ALL OF US, and nobody is left outside of it. This is a message that nature treats us all in the same way, regardless of our differences of faith. Are these not the greatest words a God would say to his creation?

My message to you, dear brothers and sisters, is that you must continue to do good in such a way that the consequences of your deeds do not harm anybody, do not make anybody unhappy, do not exclude anybody, do not make anybody feel less worthy than their peers. At the same time, you must value the real messages from nature, those that tell you that curiosity is what is worth living for, that compassion for all beings is a strong moral principle, and that you ought to be inspired by acts of goodness first and by words second.

We, Christians, are not the greatest religion ever to exist on this planet. There is no greatest religion. Everything that was created by man, by divine inspiration, is in the image of man, with human faults and human qualities. This is a message of modesty and real brotherhood. To not consider ourselves better than anyone else is the path for a long, happy, and prosperous life.

These words are not a novelty to you, since you know I am a Pope of the people, and forward-thinking in my principles. That is why Pastor King has invited me. That is why you came out here in such big numbers.

Brother and sisters, we are all the participants in a revolution of hope. A new hope, that looks forward at the vastness of space, at the fragility of our home planet. A hope that learns from the mistakes of the past, and builds solidarity among people on the principle of a good life, for all, not just the few, through liberty and justice for all."

The crowd offered me a five minute long standing ovation. Ayayay! I expected utter silence and a few polite applauses. Do they really know what they have heard? Do they know that a man of no faith in God spoke to them? I don't think it mattered. I think the words resonated with the brothers and sisters of Atlanta. They are the same people who know for certain that Pastor King is a very rich man and owns large mansions and lives in luxury. The brothers and sister are unabated by this fact. They absorbed it into their faith.

They will also absorb my message and will draw their own conclusions.

Later in the evening, I had a private, secret, meeting with Pastor King, and I informed him of my plans. He immediately accepted the idea, and proffered The Great Free as a "bastion of the Council of Christianity", his words, not mine.

When exposed to many truths, people will gravitate towards the strongest, even though it may be a distortion of reality. This is the real struggle with the world. This is my greatest struggle. To offer the stronger, clearer, purer, truth, and hope the people will see it before it's too late.

7:16 Secret meetings VI – the White Church of Houston

The very next day after my speech in Atlanta, we received a call from the State of Texas, from another Pastor. His name was Pastor Bill King. No relation to Pastor Franklin King, quite the contrary. Pastor Bill King was white and had short blonde hair. He apologized for not reaching out earlier. Since I had visited the church of the brothers and sisters in Atlanta, would I mind visiting the brothers and sisters in Houston?

I had nothing of importance on my agenda for the next two days, so I accepted the invitation.

I gave the exact same speech to the large arena in Houston. The people reacted in the same way as the people in Atlanta. The same enthusiastic ovation, the same cheers, the same hashtags.

After the speech, I had a similar conversation with Pastor Bill King as I had with Pastor Franklin King. We used almost the same words. Except for the color of his skin, hair, and suit, I could say Pastor Bill King was almost identical to Pastor Franklin King. Their voices had the same pitch. They used the same hand gestures and wore the same smiles.

Their shoes were identical. They even used the same perfume, a combination of frankincense and a musky scent. They both wore a large golden ring on the fourth finger of their left hands. The rings were not identical, but were starkly similar. They contained the initials of the wearer.

There was one thing Pastor Bill King said that Pastor Franklin King did not say: "We should not be overly righteous, nor be overly wise. Why should we destroy ourselves?"

I omitted to ask Pastor Bill King to explain what he meant. Surely, being second on my list during this visit to America, he wanted to further anchor himself in some sort of pragmatic piety. Pastor Bill King is an intelligent man. I leave my thoughts at this: I have to work with all these men, one way or another.

7:17 The group of 30 rebels

Another day of great shock!

The infamous group of seven cardinals has now grown to thirty!

I will note the names of the seven yet again, merely to focus my anger. They are: Leonardo Pancreotti of Italy, Serafim Dunga de

Aviz of Brazil, Frank Collins of the USA, Ricardo Reyes of the Philippines, Polycarp Yezir of Ghana, Miguel Belamino of Nicaragua, and Romeo Fragola of Italy.

I don't know by what political machinations Cardinal Pancreotti has succeeded in growing his little group of spineless weasels. He must have used his influence in the Curia to recruit one conspirator at a time, surely by using all methods at hand. How many in this extended group of 30 are truly conservative doctrinaires? Very, very few. There is no such thing anymore. Not in the traditional sense.

They requested an emergency meeting in the Curia, where Pancreotti stood up and read some sort of a proclamation of no-confidence and listed 30 names that supported it. I was flabbergasted. I had no idea this was coming. I could understand dissidence from 7 closed-minded Cardinals, but 30?! I looked at Tchipcherish's and Mutella's faces, they were also shocked. I was expecting more from Tchipcherish, the know-it-all at the Vatican. Mutella, too, since he is my press secretary, he should have kept an ear out for me.

Oh, the audacity! What do they want? They want nothing less of me than the dismissal of Cardinal Coccinella, the annulment of my Great Bull - to make same-sex marriages non-compliant with Catholic dogma once more (non-compliant, pfff!) - and full disclosure of my negotiations with the Eastern Orthodox Churches. Why? Because they have information that I plan to sabotage the very institution of the Vatican. In their words: "We naturally seek understanding from His Holiness that these matters can be resolved in the spirit of faith, and with great expediency. We hope we will not be forced to declare His Holiness a *Papam Hereticum*, and be forced to request His Holiness' abdication."

Papam Hereticum! Me, a Heretic Pope?!

What did the Curia say? They acknowledged the receipt of the proclamation, withheld any opinion on the matter, and declared that a vote might be considered at a later time if a quorum is reached, and only after consultation with all prefectures and dioceses.

And how are they supposed to do that? By holo-phone? Emails? Telephone? I bet that by tomorrow morning the whole world will learn about this rebellion at the Vatican. By the agitation I hear in the corridors outside my room, I am sure Nwanne and Tchipcherish are already trying to contain the disaster.

I will tell them: Let the world know! Let the world decide my fate, the fate of the Church, and the fate of faith, since it is the institutionalization of faith that is being put on trial here. Let history decide. I think I have done my part, even though my work is far from being completed. Perhaps it will never be completed.

I am losing control of my temper, which, God knows, rarely happens. How ironic of me to use this expression now. An old habit that does not want to go away lightly. But what are habits anyways? Are they some beasts that live inside us, over which we have no control whatsoever? Are they our angels, and our demons, at the same time? Can we not overcome them? Can we not overcome who we are? Are we not supposed to try, when we see that what we are is no longer compatible with our dignity, or the principles of wisdom to which we agreed to adhere?

I cannot, I will not, give in this easily. Let them be seven rebels, let them be thirty rebels, let the entire Curia rise up and proclaim that I am not fit to be the Pope of Rome, after they themselves elected me. Now they are seeking to dethrone me?! They knew perfectly well whom they elected. They wanted my character, my history, my vision, for the sake of the world, but they were not ready to live with it, for their own sakes, and now they fight like radioactive weasels, around corners and behind closed doors.

It is not the death of a powerful man that changes the world towards a greater good, it is the passion of a charismatic man that inspires people to see the meaning of life beyond the span of one generation. I would say to all those who care about the world with the same strength they care about themselves: do not be overly wicked, nor foolish, why should you die before your time?

Now that I am faced with full-blown opposition at the Vatican, I can at least know the path ahead of me. No great reform, no great change comes without opposition. I should have known that at some point, I would have my share. I can only hope I will have a dignified battle with my colleagues, and that the people will be on my side, as they have been so far.

Nwanne just came to my office and told me that I am all over the news, again. Headlines: Internecine Strife at the Vatican!

It has begun.

7:18 Media wars, and the world is boiling

The media war kicked off sooner than I expected. Less than 24 hours after the proclamation of the 30 inside the Curia, the entire world learned about it in such detail that every single word and punctuation mark in the proclamation was widely shared, photoshopped, or turned into some sort of wicked meme.

I have no idea how the world has become so split on this issue. I hear millions of voices supporting me (their trending hashtag is #IAmWithFrancis2) and millions of voices against me (their trending hashtags are, of course, #PapamHereticum and #DefendFaith, as if I was some sort of diabolical creature that wants faith abolished, and religion treated as some sort of a disease).

There are so many despicable headlines, it makes me sick to think about them. It is impossible to avoid them, in fact, the only way to avoid them is not to watch the television, or any mainstream source of news.

What boggles my mind is not necessarily that this war of opinions has started, but the uncanny mobilization of those who oppose me. Where were they before the Proclamation of the 30? Why did I not hear opposition on such a large scale until now? Sure, there were the annoying evangelicals, and some fundamentalist politicians that opposed me, but their appearances were negligible, their discourse was the laughing stock of all comedy shows.

The only explanation I can find is that the media has decided to fabricate this war of opinions on the basis of the sensationalism of the Proclamation of the 30. It has been centuries since a Pope has been declared a heretic.

Why was I not a heretic in the eyes of the media when I declared that women can become Priests? Why was I not a heretic when I appointed Mother Allegra to the rank of Cardinal? What did the media say then? They applauded me. They congratulated me. They headlined me as a champion of women, a great humanist, a brilliant reformer, a visionary. What did the media say when I declared that people of all sexual orientations can marry in our churches, and they too can become priests? They chanted I was the greatest Pope of all time, and that I should be declared a Saint. As if recognizing the rights of all people to have equal rights was some sort of a miracle!

Ah, this spectacle of life! The stupidity! The insanity! The vanity!

I wish I had a warning of what was coming for me. I wish I knew then more than I know now. I realize that it is best to take hold of one warning without letting go of the other warning, for the one who fears God will follow both warnings. But I do not fear God! He is not on my mind when I consider the struggle with the world. God is a distraction, God is a nuisance, God is an echo without my mouth to utter it or my ears to hear it. It bounces off the walls of my mind, like a blind man in an infinite labyrinth with no exit.

The spontaneous outrage of the people that is manufactured by the media is akin to a sleeping lion that was wounded by the ricochet of a bullet. The lion would wake up and roar at everything. The lion would not rest unless he becomes tired, or hungry, or another bullet kills him.

…and the rain of scraping bullets keeps coming at the raging lion, while I am accused of being the hunter. They say I deserve to be attacked, since I dared to invade the kingdom of the beast.

I dared to challenge the way the savannah brings peace of mind to all creatures who live there. I dared to demand the crown of the king.

That is what they say. That is what they accuse me of.

Whereas on the other hand, my supporters have not changed their voices. They continue to agree with my reforms. In their opinion, there is no turning back. What has changed, to include more people in the community of the church, cannot be undone. A second exclusion would mean a grave defeat for all these people, and a greater insult to the injury they suffered for so long. My supporters call the group of 30 the "real traitors". Those are their words, not mine, but I am not far from this opinion myself.

I am still the Pope of Rome, and I can speak to the people whenever I so choose. I will do it very soon. I will tell the people this: "Keep everything that unites us as the real truth. Discard everything that divides us. Keep what makes more people happy and does not harm others. Discard anything that causes exclusion from the pursuit of happiness. Greed, destruction, power, and division, have to be fought against vigorously and without pause. Forget the traditions that worked for the few, and not the many. Create new and better traditions. God bless you all!"

7:19 The crowd of love against the crowd of hate

Early this morning, out of pure spontaneity, a crowd filled St. Peter's Square and began loudly chanting my name, and the hashtag #PapaNostro (Our Pope) in Latin. The Italian police were caught off guard, and by the time they arrived, St. Peter was already full.

In Pope Pius XII Square, facing St. Peter's, the police built an observation line made of police officers. Shortly after, at around 7am, an angry crowd came from behind the police line. There were as many people as in St. Peter's, or even more.

Within minutes, the war of words and screams began. #PapaNostro against #PapamHereticum. The #PapaNostro people were half facing my window, begging with their faces to hear a word of hope from me. The other half was facing the #PapamHereticum people, as if they were all my guardians.

The #PapamHereticum people were strongly pushing against the line of police officers and they were forcing them closer to the Vatican border, at the edge of St. Peter's Square. The police did not come prepared with water cannons. They had their transparent face shields, hand-held shields, and some numbing batons. When they came, they were all facing St. Peter's. Now, being pushed from behind, they decided to turn and face both ways in such a way that every two neighboring officers were facing in different directions, half of the officers were facing Pope Pius XII, and half were facing St. Peter's. I found this arrangement rather odd. They could have formed a double line and stood back-to-back, but I suppose everything happened so fast, the officers did not have time to regroup.

An hour later, reinforcements arrived from Via Paolo VI and pushed through the #PapamHereticum crowd. Oh, I forgot to mention that the sides of St. Peter's Square had been barricaded for almost a week now with riot-proof 5 meter tall light aluminum walls. All around the Square: from Pizza del Sant'Uffizio, then around the columns along Via Paolo VI, then the gap in the middle facing Pope Pius XII Square, then again continuing on Largo del Colonnato and all the way to Via di Porta Angelica. The Vatican was barricaded.

The reinforcements did just what I thought they would. They doubled the line of police officers, so now they were finally back-to-back. They tried to push in water trucks with cannons, but the crowd was too thick to disperse.

There was anger on both sides. A different kind of anger. It was not anger of deep suffering, like the revolt of the homeless. It was an anger of principles, of ideology, of moral boundaries. The #PapamHereticum crowd came prepared with Molotov cocktails and rocks. The #PapaNostro crowd was not as well equipped. While waiting for me to appear, some of them lost their patience and responded by throwing their boots and umbrellas.

At 7:30am I wanted to open my windows and talk to them. Nwanne and the Swiss Guard categorically refused.

"They are chanting for me!" I protested.

Nwanne was resolute. He would not budge.

The Molotov cocktails kept flying over the police barricade, forcing the #PapaNostro crowd to push towards the Basilica, whose doors had been locked since yesterday afternoon. I ordered that the doors be opened immediately and that the crowd be allowed to take refuge there. With some reluctance, my order was obeyed.

23:30 I write on my @Pontifex social page: Wisdom makes one wise person more powerful than ten rulers in a city.

7:20 House arrest

By the order of the Roman Curia, the perimeter of the Vatican has been closed off to the public. The wall around the colonnades was made continuous, so St. Peter's Square is completely separated from Pope Pius XII Square. No one can get in, and no one can get out, except with special permits.

The same order has confined me to my quarters. Officially I am under house arrest.

I am not sure how the Group of 30 managed to obtain a majority in the Curia. The official position is that I must be isolated until the crisis is resolved. It is all for my protection, and for the protection of the Church.

How can the Church be protected if its leader is sequestered in his own house and is not allowed to communicate with the outside world? This is a grave attack upon my authority.

Nwanne told me that the debates in the Curia were fierce. Tchipcherish, Coccinella, and Mutella led my defense. They negotiated the right for me to receive news, and be allowed to watch holocasts. However, I cannot send any digital communications.

A futile restriction. I still have a handful of pencils and paper. I can pass a message to Nwanne, when he brings me the food. Is the Curia so foolish as not to know that I can send messages if I want to?

I did pass a handful of messages to Nwanne, who posted them on social media in my handwriting. The Curia quickly discovered this, denied Nwanne access to me, and sent a Swiss Guard to deliver my nourishment instead, under order of complete silence. Needless to say, the guard was instructed not to accept any spoken or written messages from me.

When I last saw Nwanne, two days ago, he assured me I still have large popular support. They demand my immediate release, and the resignation of the Group of 30 Cardinals. The #PapamHereticum people are equally vociferous in their demand for my immediate resignation and complete banishment from the Catholic Church. They claim I tarnished their faith and committed grave sins. The extremists demand that I be executed. Certainly, these voices are not to be taken seriously. Sadly, some people succumb to mean words quite easily.

Truth be told, I am held captive like a criminal. In the eyes of the Group of 30, I am guilty of crimes, even though they do not use these words. They say they are concerned. They say they are worried. The say they are the protectors of the Church, the defenders of the faith. What does that make me, then?

Surely there is not a righteous man on earth who does good and never sins. By the rules of the Church, I may have sinned, taking the name of God in vain, questioning my faith, losing my faith, and all that. At the same time, by the principles of human dignity, I have tried to bring more peace to the soul of mankind, more unity, more understanding, more brotherhood, and a true communion with Mother Earth. I have tried to bring a real salvation for all people. If some Cardinals do not recognize this, and if their millions of followers think the same, so be it. My conscience is clear. I do not have regrets, even though in this struggle I have changed some of my essence, by losing belief and gaining the reason of earthly life.

7:21 Riots in Rome

I am trying not to take to heart all the things that people say, lest I hear my servants cursing me. I do not know who to trust anymore. I have not seen anyone for three days, except the guard that brings me nourishment twice a day.

On the holovision I saw terrible, terrible, scenes of people fighting each other on the streets of Rome, all because of me. I watched and rewatched all the reports over and over again until my eyes began to hurt from wearing the hologlasses.

I have seen #PapamHereticum and #PapaNostro barricades with thousands of people in front of the Basilica of Saint Mary Major, facing each other, both claiming to defend the Basilica that has been surrounded by armed Italian forces, for fear of destructive riots.

All other major Churches in Rome had the same situations, while other smaller churches have been closed until further notice from the Vatican.

I have seen my face painted on the shirts of young people with olive branches around my face. I have seen signs with my face and devil horns on my head. I have seen full-size effigies of my body, made of straw and wrapped in white linen, burned at a stake on the streets of Rome. I have seen people of all ages fighting with wooden crosses used as swords, all claiming to be Christian. I have seen peaceful crowds marching in silence, from *piazza* to *piazza*. I have seen stores vandalized, merchandise stolen. I have seen patches of blood on the pavement, many ambulances, and many police barricades.

"OUR SOULS ARE NOT FOR SALE", a sign read. It was being carried by a father that was holding the hand of his little daughter and was carrying another sleeping child on his shoulders. I did not know what he meant by carrying that sign. I could not tell whether he liked me or whether he was against me. He was a peaceful man. He was standing in the middle of Piazza del Poppolo.

In Parco Adriano, near Castel Sant' Angelo, the #PapamHereticum people have built a large pile of things, which they call *vanities*, with the clear intention of burning the pile in a huge bonfire. They stacked rainbow flags, portraits of me, and portraits of Mother Allegra. They call her a wicked witch. The Roman firefighters were blocked from accessing the park by the crowd. The bonfire of vanities burned until there was nothing left but ashes.

The #PapamHereticum crowds also burned three-meter-tall crosses in many places in Rome. They said they wanted the purification of the Catholic Church. They had to burn down the corrupted Pope, so the Church can be born again.

Sadly, I have also seen #PapaNostro people being violent. When interviewed by reporters, some said they acted in self-defense. Their clothes were torn, their faces blackened by fire smoke. They had tried to put out the burning crosses and got into altercations with the #PapamHereticum people. In some cases they were successful and pulled the burning crosses down to the ground, then pushed them into the River Tiber. Dozens of crosses were seen floating in the river.

When the Army was called in to intervene, the riots had grown into the hundreds of thousands, all across Rome. By nightfall, similar riots had sprung up in many other cities around the world.

All because of me, all because of the darkness I carry in my soul.

7:22 Letter from Allegra Coccinella and Thorsen Tchipcherish

My dearest Nwanne was allowed to visit me today. He did not have time to manage my enthusiasm, as he brought me a letter from Cardinals Coccinella and Tchipcherish.

"Your Holiness,

Sometimes God allows us to live as disembodied shadows, sometimes He allows us to live as soulless bodies of flesh. We are masters of our fate, and we are the servants of God. Our faith teaches us that submission to God is a form of love, the greatest form of love there is.

We shall allow ourselves to be overcome by love, with blindfolded faith and earthly trust in each other.

We shall confess that our hearts know that many times we ourselves have cursed others, knowing that the others have cursed us first. As God has bestowed upon us the free will to choose vanity and other faces of wickedness, we shall not feel required to beg forgiveness from ourselves. Only by the grace of God can we obtain forgiveness.

On the altar of human dignity, we shall not compromise to injustice. Our souls, our bodies, are ready to be sacrificed for Your Holiness.

We remain your true servants.

in nomine Patris et Filii et Spiritus Sancti,

Cardinal Allegra Coccinella

Cardinal Thorsen Tchipcherish"

7:23 Letters and ghosts

Nwanne came again today. He looked very changed. He was pale and weak. I asked him how he was. He replied flatly that he was fine. He had more letters for me. He wouldn't tell me who they were from. Deep in his eyes I saw nothing but sorrow and defeat. This was not the Nwanne I knew. He placed the letters on the table and hid his eyes from mine. He looked down, hoping to find a trapdoor in the floor through which he could escape from the world. He excused himself, and before he left the room he said, simply and softly, "I am sorry."

Do not leave me alone, I wanted to tell him. I remained silent, with words as dormant seeds inside me.

In search for comfort I succumbed to melancholy. I tried to pray, I said the words I knew quite well, I spoke to God, I clenched my palms together, I struggled to reclaim the peace I once had, knowing that there is always a hidden purpose to everything, the reassurance that things are supposed to be as they are.

Why did I let go of God, after so much time, knowing quite well the benefits of having God as a friend? I could have used His friendship now, I could have trusted Him with my most intimate thoughts.

Nwanne appeared as a ghost, I saw through him. He wasn't there, he was smoke, his body was made of black air, a soft, fine, black air. He was formed from an invisible fire, a cold hidden fire, that cannot be seen with the eyes, and cannot be felt with the heart, and cannot be understood with the mind.

I am locked in my room, and all I can think about are the ghosts of all my dear friends from Africa. Not those foggy apparitions from popular culture, but the ghosts that appear as the history of the feelings I had while being around the friends I had, and the souls I loved. None of them speak to me now, in my mind.

I have become a stranger to myself, a very different man, transformed by the struggle of life in ways that I could never have imagined. I have tried to test my wisdom in many ways. I said, "I will be wise," but it is far from me. I'm left with these puerile lamentations in this diary of mine that no one will ever read, and whose ashes will be gone with the wind after I burn it one day together with all my frailties.

7:24 Letter from Amira

The guard came today and told me Nwanne was indisposed. He placed a letter on my table, and for the first time he asked me if I needed anything. He begged for my forgiveness for his behavior and left before I could say anything. I opened the letter and read it slowly.

"Dear Holy Father,

I hope you remember the day when you met me in Zagreb and I asked you: *Why did God allow my brother to drown in the sea?* My name is Amira. I was born in Syria.

You told me: I do not know why your brother's life was taken away. For what happens to the sons of men also happens to animals. One thing befalls them, as one dies, so dies another.

I was too young then to understand what these words meant. I do understand now that there is no meaning in suffering, and there is no meaning in happiness. None of the tragedies in the world are an act of God, as none of the happiness is a blessing. I have learned that it is in the nature of all beings to prefer happiness over suffering, and it is this preference that creates purpose in our lives. This is why it is worth living for. It has nothing to do with God, because God does not exist. God is a story that people made up to make them feel good in this wild world full of abysmal questions.

I must confess, Holy Father, that I know that you do not believe in God either. I noticed when I first met you, but I understood its significance only now, years later. It's okay. This is our secret. Even if I told anyone, no one would believe me.

I write to you because you have changed my life for the better for showing me the truth and for allowing me to have an honest life with all its struggles and merry moments.

As for that which is far off and exceedingly deep, who can find out? I will try to learn as much as I can about all important things. I want to become a naturalist, to understand life in all its details. Thanks to you, I am pursuing this dream

Your Holiness, I wish you to be happy. I know what you are trying to do for the Catholic Church, and for all Christians in the world. It is the greatest endeavor any man has tried. You will be a hero for the rest of history. I hope you will succeed and I do not hope in vain. Everywhere I look I see people of all races and ethnicities wanting more peace in the world, and more truth. You can give them both. Do not give in! If you have showed a little girl the path to truth, so can you show it to millions more.

I must apologize that I cannot offer you my prayers. I do not think prayers work. Prayers are cowardice, prayers are self-deception. Prayers do not do anything for those who suffer. Instead, I offer you my words of love, support, and boundless gratitude. They come from my heart. You are now in a prison in your own house, as I was a prisoner in many refugee camps.

Please be strong and continue to be wise. You are not alone. Your life has had an enormous meaning for me. Your words and your deeds for others are what gives your life purpose.

Your little friend,

Amira."

I cried for a long time after I finished the letter. Then I ate a loaf of bread, and I cried some more.

7:25 Nwanne

I directed my mind to understand, to explore, to search out wisdom and explanations, and to understand the stupidity of wickedness and the folly of madness. None of these endeavors prepared me for the news I received today.

Nwanne has fallen ill with cancer of the stomach.

He cannot see me anymore. I cannot see him anymore. My deepest love for Nwanne comes to light and blinds me from seeing anything else. By this blindness I realize how dear Nwanne is to me. I had emptied my body of tears for the past two days. Today I feel only dry sorrow and silent sadness.

Whose suffering is the greatest? Who deserves more pity? Those afflicted by cruel illnesses or their loved ones who remain healthy and watch from the bedside? Those who are left alive to mourn and grieve, or the departed? The departed cannot receive our love anymore. Their existence is closed forever. So we are not to burden them with our gifts of love. With those who are in deep bodily pain, suffering terminal illnesses, those who we love dearly, their suffering is translated in our bodies, and placed in our minds, so we are connected with them until their ends. In a way, we will continue to live their lives. We are to love and honor our loved ones in our sane and living minds, as if they were still living in our presence. That is the greatest gift we can offer them. This is what I would tell Nwanne, if they would only let me talk to him.

Why do I speak as if I had already lost him?

I think only about death now. I was told Nwanne's illness is so grave, there is little hope for him. I will lose my dearest angel, now when I need him the most. Who is to say what is the right time for anything to happen? What is the ultimate cause of any tragedy?

Hope is leaving my body one breath at a time. I am overwhelmed with the happy memories of my younger years, of the time spent with Nwanne. With every scene that comes to mind, of its own volition, my sorrow grows. Yet I should remember the laws of life. I should know better, and I do know better with my mind. But my heart is winning. I cannot let go of wanting to see Nwanne again, of wanting to hear his voice again, of wanting to touch his fine hands again.

I have cursed God today. I have blamed and shouted invectives at the God I do not believe in. I screamed at walls. I dared God to prove me wrong, to show me that he exists. I gave him a second chance. "Now is the time!" I demanded. There were no ears to hear me, no eyes to watch me, nobody to laugh at my hysterical outbursts. As always, I heard nothing.

7:26 I escaped death

I had a heart attack. Sudden. Unexpected. Shocking.

When I woke up I saw people around me: Mother Allegra, Tchipcherish, Mutella, and others. No Nwanne. I was weak, and I could barely speak. I asked what day it was. They told me.

The world found out about what had happened within the hour. Someone leaked the story. An enormous crowd of #PapaNostro surrounded the hospital and prayed for me. Hundreds of thousands of candles were lit for me.

The Curia immediately voted to lift the house arrest.

They don't want to take the blame for my death. No, they want to be free of guilt, like all men.

The doctor gave me a sedative.

I dreamt of the Virgin Mary. She was combing her hair by a lake. She saw me coming and asked me where I had been, why I was late, why I did not believe in God anymore. She had been expecting me.

The Virgin Mary said she wanted to tell me a secret, but I must swear I will not share it with anyone. Not even myself. I must not think about it after I wake up.

The secret was she was not a virgin. She had relations with her husband Joseph before her son Jesus was born.

"You don't believe me?" she asked.

"Ask Joseph, he's over there."

She showed me Joseph on the other side of the lake, shepherding sheep. He waved at us.

"It was an error of translation," Mary said. "They translated *young woman* into *virgin*."

And there was no Archangel Gabriel. No Holy Ghost. "It was just me and Joseph," she said combing her hair.

Then I woke up again feeling very thirsty.

And I find more bitter than death the woman who is a snare, whose heart is a net, and whose hands are chains. The man who pleases God will escape her, but the sinner will be ensnared.

7:27 Behind closed doors

I am a free man again. Free to choose my destinations, free to embrace the world again, and to receive its greetings.

The Curia cautioned me that this so-called freedom hinges on the result of an inquiry. I was not told what the inquiry is about, who ordered it, or under what authority. Anything I do or say is automatically considered a material fact to the investigation.

Mutella told me in private that some very nasty machinations are being orchestrated in the Curia. Threats of excommunication are being tossed around. The atmosphere is that of dozens of Popes fighting for an invisible throne.

Tchipcherish is conducting very intense negotiations with the Group of 30 dissident Cardinals. They want nothing less than my resignation. He pushed forward a very bold proposal: the irrevocable ordination of women. The group has refused outright.

Mother Allegra has found allies in progressive Cardinals who oppose the Group of 30. They are not many. Most of the Curia remains undecided and can be swayed in either direction. One thing they all despise most is an inflated scandal.

Vatican City remains sealed off from the rest of Rome. At the gates, security is so tight nobody can enter or leave. The space above the City has been declared a no-fly zone. All drones have been shut-down, and the media has been banned from filming from the sky.

I looked out the window this afternoon into St. Peter's Square. There was one man preaching to a flock of nuns near the obelisk.

"Behold, this is what I found," said the Preacher, "while adding one thing to another to find the scheme of things."

I could not hear what else he said. I only saw the flock of nuns prostrating themselves on the ground.

What is the scheme of things? What is the greatest delusion man has concocted for himself? The God delusion? The power delusion? The freedom delusion? The disturbing restlessness to invent truths?

7:28 The deposition of Cardinal Pancreotti

How is it possible that the media no longer speaks of the habitable planet NOVA GAIA? How is it possible that the extraterrestrial message discovered by the HAWKING SPACE STATION is not on the front page of all digital papers? True, millions still hashtag these amazing events, but they are ignored by the mainstream media. What is the mainstream media talking about?

The new great scandal of the Catholic Church. Yes, it is possible to have more scandals at the Vatican. I am too shocked to hear the news, though I certainly want to hear more, and by this very means of squeezing the last drops of our curiosity and attention, the mainstream media keeps us glued to their products.

A video recording was leaked, then photographs, then even a holoclip of Cardinal Leonardo Pancreotti, the infamous leader of the Group of 30 Cardinals who want to depose me. Leonardo Pancreotti can be seen soliciting various young boys for sexual services, under the pretenses of exchanges of kindness. Some scenes were so graphic, the media had the decency to blur those respective sections. I ordered Mutella to find me the unedited images. He ransacked the underweb and found them, and showed them to me.

Horrific. I dare not write about what I saw.

Needless to say, after he got caught, Pancreotti came to me, foaming at the mouth, to offer his resignation. He said he knew the delicate position in which we both were, but he had to defer to my still intact powers to accept his resignation.

I refused. I told him directly: "It is true, Cardinal Pancreotti, that my powers are still intact, and that you wish them removed. I will not only refuse your resignation, but I will initiate procedures to remove you from the clerical ranks, after allowing the due process. You will not retain your cardinalate, and you will not be allowed to preach in our churches."

Pancreotti replied bitterly:

"Holy Father, though I have searched repeatedly, I have not found what I was looking for. Only one out of a thousand men is virtuous, but not one woman!"

"A retrograde verse from the Old Testament, Pancreotti. We live in different times."

At that very moment I had lost all my patience with Pancreotti. I dismissed him from the audience. By the end of day, so I hear, he was gone from the Vatican. The hashtag of the day was #PancreottiFired.

Oh, but the wolves will not remain silent! I can hear their howls and I can smell their stench. They are brewing a counter-attack in their lairs, they are digging deeper trenches, they are treating their wounds with fake holy water from the spring of Our Lady of Lourdes.

7:29 The counter-scandal

Only hours later, the wolves bared their teeth and unleashed their contemptible maneuvers.

The mainstream media is showing pictures of - goodness gracious, I cannot pull myself together to write this – pictures of Mother Allegra and Thorsen Tchipcherish, alone, in a coffee shop in Rome, in casual clothing. They removed any clerical paraphernalia. Mother Allegra was wearing lipstick, and nail polish, and Thorsen was wearing a fake moustache.

The mainstream headlines: VATICAN AFFAIR, POPE'S MOST TRUSTED AIDES EMBRACED IN PASSION, HOLY LUST, BIGGEST BETRAYAL TO POPE SO FAR, CAN POPE FRANCIS THE SECOND RECOVER FROM THIS?, and on and on, each one nastier than the next, innuendoes piling on, sly euphemistic commentaries, inciting provocations, off-the-cuff speculations, and all vulgar palavers that the rested, insipid human mind can produce to satisfy its inane, putrid instincts.

They turned a dozen photos that some lone paparazzo took into a spectacle of debauchery. They analyzed every millimeter: how Mother Allegra dimmed her eyes when Thorsen touched her cheek with his hand, how she covered his hand on the table with her hand, how they both giggled in unison, how she showed her beautiful white teeth, whereas Thorsen smiled reservedly, only bending the corners of his lips upwards, how he touched his fake moustache repeatedly to check if it was still there and in good condition.

The wolves cried in outrage when Mother Allegra brushed her lips with her tongue, allegedly in an inappropriate manner for someone in her position, especially for a woman in her position, and precisely because she was a Cardinal, and the first woman Cardinal. The wolves loaded Mother Allegra with a mountain of spectacular moral duty that far outweighs that of her male Cardinal colleagues. Apparently, she was elevated to a position of privilege for a woman, which obligates her to a higher moral standard. As a consequence, the movement of her tongue over her lips is a harder blow for her than it would be for a male Cardinal making a similar gesture.

The mainstream media has not considered that Mother Allegra's lips could have simply been dehydrated, and her reaction was only natural. Even I moisten my lips by brushing them with my tongue, albeit usually not in public, though what would be the difference if it were in public? No one should care.

They pushed their venom even further when the photographs showed their hands exchanging messages on pieces of paper. What was in those messages, so important that it could not have been uttered? The whole world is now preoccupied with what Mother Allegra and Thorsen wrote to each other on paper napkins in a coffee shop.

Why the disguise? They asked. Are they plotting against the Pope, or even working with the Group of 30? Does the fate of the Catholic Church hinge on the holy carnal affair of the two most prominent, progressive Cardinals at the Vatican?

One newsman said, cunningly: "This only have I found: God created mankind upright, but they have gone in search of many schemes." Juxtaposing this with a closeup shot of Mother Allegra and Thorsen's faces staring at each other, their eyes gleaming.

I cannot believe this is real. Thorsen is not capable of this, and Mother Allegra is a saint, she would not do this to me, not after the time we spent together, and all work we have done. It pains me to say, that even today, the moral standard of the mainstream media is not justly distributed among men and women in positions of power. These biases run deep in the bones of these wolves, who will stop at nothing unless their pack is satiated, until only a pile of bones remains.

NOTEBOOK EIGHT

8:1 While you were asleep

Since all my liberties have been restored, I decided to leave the Vatican without asking anyone, without telling anyone. I gathered my security detail and I went to visit Nwanne at the hospital in Rome.

He was in the Oncology Clinic, under close supervision, sedated. The staff at the clinic had only minutes notice of my arrival. There was no formal reception, no meet and greet, which was only for the better, since my mood was not elevated enough to exchange many pleasantries.

I went straight to Nwanne's room. The security guys arranged with the doctors to leave me alone in the room with him.

I told them not to let anyone in. I will come out myself.

Nwanne was sleeping, peacefully. He was attached to tubes and machines that were measuring his vital signs.

I pulled up a chair and sat down next to the bed. His hands were aligned parallel to his body, palms down. I took his hand in my hand and I thought hard about our times together. I imagined him awake and healthy, rising from the bed, talking to me, being himself as he always is, careworn for me, preoccupied with all the responsibilities he carries.

There was no pain in his face. His head had been shaved and his face had lost its natural glow. He still looked like an angel that understood everything about life and the universe, and returned to Earth to rest for a while.

I talked to him:

"Nwanne, it's Enyi. I know you cannot hear me. I know you can feel me. Who is like the wise? And who knows the interpretation of a thing? A man's wisdom makes his face shine, and the hardness of his face is changed. This is you Nwanne. You are the wise, and you know the interpretation of things. Come back to me, and let us live more of our lives together!"

I wished he could speak back to me.

I stood up and kissed him on the mouth, wanting to help the words come out of his tired lungs. The machine beeped briefly and returned to normal.

He didn't look frail or defeated. He was a strong man, resting after a long battle, and probably wanting to be left alone. I am sure he was missing me. The last time he had seen me, I was under house arrest, receiving abominable threats.

I kissed him for a second time on the mouth and I asked my security detail to call in the chief oncologist.

The doctor told me his condition is grave. The tumor has spread to the entire organ and was moving towards the lungs. They have placed an order for a stem-cell printed replacement organs, but it takes some time to fully calibrate them for his body, and there are no guarantees that they will be accepted. That means they will have to perform a double surgery on Nwanne very soon. He told me to trust the medical science. He will do his very best to save Nwanne. Then he paused, and hesitated. I asked him if there was something else he wanted to tell me.

"Perhaps you should also pray for Mr. Yinkaso," the doctor said, completely unconvinced. "It is customary for someone in your position to do so. I must confess, Holy Father, I am not a man of faith."

"Doctor," I said, "I too have a confession. I am not a man of faith either. If I were asked to pray for Mr. Yinkaso, I would not do so. I think prayer is a self-deceiving echo of the mind. It's mumbling in darkness. Prayers do nothing for those who suffer. They do not heal, they do not help, they sink the mind into a pit of false hope. There you go, doctor. You are my first true confessor. You are the real Savior, and simply because you are doing your job. I thank you for that. I am grateful and honored."

The chief oncologist was not much surprised to hear what I said. He had seen so much suffering in his life, that the confession of a clerical man could not shock him. He assured me he would keep my confession in confidence.

8:2 Words stolen from me

A swarm of reporters was waiting for me at the Vatican when I returned. They formed a barricade in front of the car. They wouldn't let us in. I pulled down the window, which immediately proved to be a big mistake. The reporters pushed their microphones into my face and kept asking me all at once if it's true, if I'm going to resign, what does it mean for the Catholic Church, who will be the next Pope, will I be excommunicated, what message do I have for the billion plus Catholics, and many other questions I couldn't hear, in Italian, in English, in Spanish.

"If what is true?" I asked back.

Mutella, who was sitting next to me, showed me on his tablet a video of me kissing Nwanne on the mouth, at the hospital.

How on Earth is that possible?!

He explained the video was shot with a telelens through the window, from the building across the street, by a paparazzo.

The images were crisp and clear, leaving no doubt of my identity, or Nwanne's identity. The videographer captured the culmination of my emotional expression.

I pulled up the window of my car, and somehow, we managed to get through the crowd of reporters.

Mutella showed me the rest of the video. Where the chief oncologist came in, and our conversation. To my misfortune, both our mouths were visible. Albeit the window was closed, and no sound was captured when the doctor and I started talking, the video also started to display a subtitled version of our conversation, word for word, with impeccable accuracy. The most newsworthy words of our conversation were, indubitably, my confession to the chief oncologist of my atheism.

I turned on the television in my room. Full headlines everywhere: POPE'S LOVER. Accompanied by a photo of the kiss. There was no video. I turned to Mutella. He told me that to his knowledge the video has not been released to the public. He had received it in his email with a message that he did not get the chance to convey to me. He read it to me:

"Your Holiness,

Obey the king since you vowed to God that you would. I am VideoMan666. I shot the video at the hospital. I am the only person in the world who has this copy. We both understand the incalculable value of these images. I ask you in peace: RESIGN, and the video will not be released. For the sake of the Church, for the sake of all Christians. The photo of the kiss that is only a demonstration of my intentions. I am a man of dignity. I am a man of truth. I know you share these values. Unburden yourself."

Mutella looked at me in consternation. In his eyes I saw disbelief, and contempt for VideoMan666. Before he could say anything, I spoke first:

"It is true, Mutella."

"But, Holy Father-"

"I have no defense. For the sake of the Church, I beg you to keep this a secret."

"Certainly. But this VideoMan666 has the power to-"

"He does not own the power, because he does not own the truth. The truth cannot be owned. We can only hope wisdom and justice will prevail."

After Mutella was gone, I was left with a bitter taste in my mouth. I spoke words that I didn't want to. I feel I am getting closer and closer to the precipice. I can smell the wind of inevitability.

8:3 The dragon grows new heads

The dragon with thirty heads has lost its main head named Leonardo Pancreotti and was replaced today by a new head, Cardinal Romeo Fragola, a member of the original group of seven. He does not lack any of the shrewdness of his predecessor. He is no less determined to remove me from office. He knows the tools of manipulating the media.

Immediately after the photo of the kiss at the hospital emerged, he forcefully capitalized on the event, by defining it as a *scandal* in the most severe terms, and in such a way that the media captured his words and spread them quickly like wild fire. In his speeches, Fragola repeated the mantra "We need a new pope, and we need him now" many times, and in all the languages he knows, which are not few. The deposed Pancreotti was already forgotten.

Which made me wonder if Fragola himself was not behind all of this: the deposition of Pancreotti, the video of the kiss, my conversation with the chief oncologist. What is hiding up his sleeve? Why does he not come at me with all his weapons? He should have attacked me already if this VideoMan666 worked for him.

I don't think VideoMan666 works for Fragola. VideoMan666 is a lone wolf, a vigilante of faith, an obstructionist, an anarchist. He does not recognize any masters. Yet, does he know that he can still enable the detractors by feeding them all these personal images of me, even though they represent the truth?

If unchained truth can demolish a just world, should it remain in its cage? Should truth be set free, no matter the consequences? If truth cannot be understood, how can those on the side of justice prevail?

I don't know what Fragola wants to do next. It is obvious by now that the pressure for my resignation has become stronger. I am losing ground. I am coming closer to the precipice.

I still have the people who love me. There are many out there in the world, even though their voices have been silenced by the thunder of the scandal. They write to me: Do not be in a hurry to leave him. They are talking about Nwanne. They understand my love for him. They remind me that when the times are the most difficult, when hope has completely evaporated, when your enemies seem to have won, that is the perfect time to fight even louder on the side of justice.

They urge me not to join in an evil matter. Fragola and his clique will do whatever they please according to the extent of their free will. They urge me to remain strong and dedicated to my reforms. I will always be their Pope.

8:4 Joining the riots, in disguise

Without Nwanne near me to care for me and arrange my escapades, I was left with no choice but to improvise. An urge so powerful overcame me this late-afternoon, that I found myself walking down the stairs without knowing where I was going. The presence of a Swiss Guard shook me back to reality.

I went back to my room and changed into civilian clothes. I put on the makeup myself, the fake beard, the afro wig. I painted my face with a rainbow flag on one cheek and with the flag of Italy on the other, just like every man and woman I had seen on TV.

Before nightfall, I hit the streets, closely accompanied by my two trusted Swiss Guards, also in disguise. They swore to take my secret to their graves, and I have the utmost confidence they will do so.

They took me in front of the National Monument of Vittorio Emanuele II, where the largest crowd in Rome had been gathered. When I saw the equestrian sculpture of the first king of a unified Italy, I thought to myself, *Where the word of a king is, there is power, and who may say to him "What are you doing?". And who is to say to the masses, "Your revolt is unjustified, go back to your plates and eat your submission on a plain loaf of bread!"*

I wanted to be alone. I did my very best to lose the two Swiss Guards, and it was easier than I thought. I blended in with the crowd of all ages and laid low for a while, to make sure my trail was lost. In the heat of the crowd, nobody knew who I really was, nobody really paid attention to each other's faces for too long. People communicated by a strong feeling of justice, they truly bonded, I could feel it in their voices, in the determination of their raised fists. I could have easily appeared without a fake beard, without makeup and the ridiculous afro wig, they would have said, "Look, Pope Francis the Second is with us, let's join arms. Holy Father, this riot is not just about you, we are rioting against an establishment of bloodsuckers!"

Nobody screamed the name of Prime Minister Pantalone, or the name of Cardinal Leonardo Pancreotti, or Cardinal Romeo Fragola. They screamed *NOI NON PARTECIPEREMO PIÙ NELL'INGIUSTIZIA E NELLA DISUGUAGLIANZA. WE WILL NOT PARTICIPATE IN INJUSTICE AND INEQUALITY ANYMORE. LA DIGNITÀ UMANA È INVIOLABILE. HUMAN DIGNITY IS INVIOLABLE.* I screamed with them too, in Italian, and in English, so the drones filming us from the sky could carry our words all over the world.

There were teenagers in the crowd too. The had the biggest painted signs, and the most imaginative ones. Pigs eating money from troughs, priests pulling apart a cross made of dark red rubber, kings eating a cake in the shape of the Earth.

The crowd was spilling over to the adjacent streets, so the police barricade was far from the Vittorio Emanuele Monument. The Monument has been occupied by the people. Somebody was speaking from an improvised stage on the stairs. There was no destruction seen anywhere, yet all the headlines were still describing the gathering as a riot.

Yes, it was a riot! The substance of it all was disobedience. A forceful and loud disobedience. WE WILL NOT WORK FOR YOU ANYMORE.

Then the speaker mentioned my name: FRANCESCO DUE, IL PAPA DEL POPOLO. THE POPE OF THE PEOPLE. Hearing his voice, I thought he was talking about somebody else, somebody locked in an ivory tower, a wise man perhaps, who was trying to change the world merely by thinking about it and praying for it. What a good person that Pope was. I wanted to meet him.

The Swiss Guards found me eventually and extracted me from the riot almost by force. The situation was getting out of control. It certainly did not feel that way to me! On the contrary, the situation was finally getting into the control of the people. I knew immediately that whatever happens to my Papacy, I will have to return to the people.

8:5 Throwing the first stone

The Curia was called (by whose authority?!) to an emergency meeting. The Group of 30 Cardinals demanded a vote of my impeachment. I can only count on Mutella to keep me informed as I was denied access. Tchipcherish and Mother Allegra are my loudest supporters. They have been lobbying my case from the very beginning of this circus.

I have to let go of the reins of my own fate, for good. There is nothing I can do about it. My Papacy is the object of the fiercest political battle in history. The stakes are the greatest. The very foundations of faith are being negotiated.

They all know this, the Group of 30. They must have found out about my secret meetings with the Patriarchs and other Christian leaders. They will not rest until I am defeated, and the cursive, implacable flow of the Catholic tradition continues, meandering through mellow peaks and shallow valleys of reform and modernization, building on the great legacy of Pope Francis.

Are we all not humble victims of our best intentions? Whoever obeys his own internal commands will come to no harm, and the wise heart will know the proper time and procedure to move forward and leave a mark on history.

I received word from Mutella that the Curia has denied the motion to put to vote the matter of my impeachment, however, the Group of 30 has obtained the right to an appeal, after all Prefectures deliver a report on the motion by no later than 9am tomorrow.

So, the agony continues…

Again, I am topping all the hashtags, headlines, and holobites in the world. Everyone is fascinated with this scandal, with the imminence of the downfall of a man in the position of great power, or the ascendance of an unlikely new candidate that will deepen the sense of meaning of history in the billion hearts and minds who pray to their Savior.

It is midnight. People have started a vigil in St. Peter's. Many have left. Those who remained have lit candles, are chanting prayers and songs of peace. The gendarmerie still answers to me, as head of state, so they are obeying my order to leave the people alone and to maintain their security.

If God does not play dice, what does he play? It seems to me, he plays a mandolin with no strings.

8:6 Subsequent stones flying

The day of the appeal. A large crowd has gathered in St. Peter's, as if the Curia was supposed to announce a new Pope by signaling with white or black smoke.

I am watching the entire spectacle on TV. Hundreds of reporters, hundreds of channels, all speculate about my fate. Will this be the last day of the first black Pope? Is Francis the Second truly what his enemies claim he is? A heretic? An anarchist? The undoer of the Church? Or is he the greatest Pope the world has ever had?

No drones are flying today. There is a strict no-fly zone over the Vatican. The are no sirens, no apparent movement of forces of security. The riots cannot be heard anywhere. Nobody reports about them anymore. To the eyes of the world they do not exist. Only my fate was forced on people's minds, by the media, whether they like it or not.

Mutella sent me a note on a piece of paper. At 9:12am the Curia accepted the motion to put the matter of my impeachment to a vote. The vote is scheduled for 3pm today. The news spread immediately like locusts.

Have all Prefectures of the Vatican weighed in on the matter so quickly? What happened in the past 12 hours? Where are my closest allies, Thorsen and Mother Allegra? Have they been defeated so easily?

I feel very alone, not abandoned, but alone, in a strange, deep silence, impenetrable to all thoughts and echoes. I cannot watch the sun, I cannot look at the crowd outside. I was advised to stay away from the windows, not for security reasons, but for personal reasons. What are those? I asked. They wouldn't tell me. Do they think I would open the window and speak to the crowd with a bullhorn? What do they think?

I cannot watch TV, I cannot watch anything. I sat down and read from the Book of Ecclesiastes. That brought me some comfort. I listened to some Bach and Mozart, and, for a brief moment, I forgot about everything, and I felt serene.

Truly, I think, for every matter there is a time and judgment, though the misery of man increases greatly. The price we pay: restlessness, never-ending restlessness, anxiety for the days to come. The prize to win: being alive, reasoning, and peeling ourselves away, layer after layer, of ignorance and bliss.

8:7 The hammer of fate

3 pm. The vote for my impeachment is taking place this very moment.

Voices of hundreds of Cardinals are ringing in my ears. We cannot have a heretic Pope, we live in the greatest crisis since St. Peter founded the Church, he is our Holy Father, elected by us, by the grace of God, we cannot undo his anointment, but he has lost his faculties. By what calculations do you think he lost his faculties? He has committed grave acts against our faith, his reforms speak to the hearts of millions, no, this is not true, he has deceived the hearts of millions, and what about his personal secretary Mr. Nwanne Yinkaso? We have proof that the Holy Father has had inappropriate relations with him! That is circumstantial evidence, men cannot procreate with men, women cannot procreate with women, that is the bottom line! No, the bottom line is that love is universal! Love is not universal, the unity of a man with a woman is the first rule of God. What, love is not universal? God is love, love is God, are you denying the supremacy of God? Do not twist my words, you know what I am saying!

Whispers in the corridors: for he does not know what will happen, so who can tell him when it will occur? Tchipcherish has made a very strong case for the Pope, and Cardinal Coccinella too, I see a great future for both of them.

At 3:33pm, the secretary of the Curia came in person to announce the result of the vote. The Swiss Guard opened the door for him. He stepped in, I stood up from my desk. He spoke:

"Enyi Chebea, as of 3:30pm today, you are no longer the Pope. The Curia has voted your impeachment effective immediately. You will retain the dignities of a simple ordained priest. You will be assigned to a parish of your choosing, however not on the European continent. You are to be escorted to the Vatican heliport, then to the airport, from where a plane will take you to Abuja. Please gather your belongings in a suitcase, and a guard will accompany you further. You have one hour."

I have finished packing. I am using the last minutes to recollect my thoughts. On TV I hear that the Conclave has been called for the election of a new Pope to steer the Grand Reformation of the Catholic Church. The seven Cardinals who initiated the rebellion against me have resigned their cardinalates and will return as bishops to their parishes, as a sign of reconciliation. The world is in shock.

I am no longer Pope Francis the Second.

8:8 Days of the Conclave

There was a mishap with the helicopter engine, so my departure from the Vatican was postponed. I was instructed to move into a room in Domus Sanctae Marthae until further notice. I was under no form of imprisonment or arrest, so I was told, and my cooperation is greatly appreciated, for the greater benefit of the Church.

Cardinal Thorsen Tchipcherish slipped me a message through a guard shortly before the conclave was called to order and the doors were closed. He wrote that there is no clear contender and that I must rest assured that everything will turn out for the best. How does he know? His words had an uncanny self-confidence about them.

Less than half an hour after the conclave started in the Sistine Chapel, an effusion of black smoke rose from the chimney. The crowd sighed and reverberated with disappointment.

No news from Nwanne either. All I know is that he is under close observation. I am still not allowed to visit him.

They let me watch TV, but I prefer to stare at the crowd from my window. The commentators on the news explain the whole process of selecting the Pope in detail, its significance, as if the people already forgot how I was elected.

Another hour later, another gush of black smoke.

No man has power to retain the spirit, or power over the day of death. There is no discharge from war, nor will wickedness deliver those who are given to it. Life is a short affair between a body of bones, wrapped in a sack of meat, topped with a thinking head, negotiating its fleeting course on this planet.

What will become of me? I dare not say I am fully the master of my own fate now. Nor do I sense any resemblance of inspiration from the days when I had faith in the divine grace. I do not want to hide, I do not want to talk to the world. I have spoken my words.

The third ballot was cast shortly after 3pm. Black smoke, sighs, and restlessness. To my surprise, the first day ended abruptly with all Cardinals returning to their rooms at Domus Sanctae Marthae.

8:9 HABEMUS PAPAM

I slept little last night. It has been four days since the conclave started. The black smoke keeps gushing out of the chimney on top of the Sistine Chapel.

Four ballots are scheduled today. Two in the morning, and two in the afternoon. I am told to wait until the election of the new pope, then I will be permitted to leave to Nigeria. It is for the best, I am told.

9am. Time for the first ballot.

I have thought deeply about all that goes on here under the sun, where people have the power to hurt each other. We have learned to summon the better angels of our nature, and we have learned not to remain silent when injustice rules.

We see black smoke rising quickly from the chimney.

I remember Thorsen's words: "Rest assured that everything will turn out for the best." I remember Mother Allegra's when I last saw her, thanking me for the goodness of my heart, assuring me that she will remain my humble servant.

11am. The second ballot.

The people on TV expect these elections to last long. Many say we will have at least two weeks of black smoke.

11:33am. WHITE SMOKE raising above the Sistine Chapel. The crowd goes wild, the TV talking heads are stunned. On the 12th ballot, the new Pope has been elected.

I am completely numb. I am serene. I am at peace with the decision of the cardinals. My faith in people is stronger than ever. Joy floods my mind in full force.

Minutes later the Cardinal Protodeacon appears at the loggia of the Basilica to announce the new Pope. The crowd is extremely loud. The people do not let the Cardinal begin. They shout over and over again HABEMUS PAPAM. I hear my name too: Francesco, Francesco, Francesco. Surely, they do not expect me to appear at the loggia. Finally, after five minutes of acclamation, the Cardinal Protodeacon speaks:

ANNUNTIO VOBIS GAUDIUM MAGNUM:

HABEMUS PAPAM!

EMINENTISSIMUM AC REVERENDISSIMUM DOMINUM,

DOMINUM ALLEGRA MARIA YOLANDA,

SANCTAE ROMANAE ECCLESIAE CARDINALEM COCCINELLA,

QUI SIBI NOMEN IMPOSUIT MARIA.

They've elected the sweet Mother Allegra! My goodness! Allegra Maria Yolanda Coccinella, the candid Mother Superior from Naples whom I have made Cardinal is now the Pope. I am crying.

The crowd in St. Peter's jubilates with an enthusiasm I have never seen in my life at such a scale. The people on TV are shocked beyond belief. They do not know what to say. What does it mean? What does it mean? They asked each other. Is this even allowed? Yes, someone says, Pope Francis the Second has signed this into law.

WE HAVE THE FIRST FEMALE POPE.

POPE MARY.

I can rest now.

8:10 The reign of Pope Mary: Day 1

The first act of Pope Mary was to write me a personal note. I read it with her voice in my mind:

"Your Holiness,

You remain the Pope of my heart. You have inspired me with your big heart and great mind. I will never forget what you have done for me. You have the strongest faith of us all. I shall continue your work, by the grace of God.

Rest your mind. Rest your soul. You deserve it. When the time comes, very soon, you will be vindicated. This is my sacred promise to you.

The airplane will take you wherever you want.

I will pray for you. Remember us in your thoughts.

Your true friend,

Mother Allegra"

Remember us in your thoughts, she wrote. She wrote "thoughts", not "prayers". She knows. She felt the truth as nobody has felt it before.

I folded her note in my pocket and I told the guards to take me to the airport. I told them I want to climb the highest mountain in Africa.

I dreamt about the fields of fallen soldiers and innocent bystanders in the battles of faith, in the wars on terror, in the scavenging for oil. Then I saw the wicked buried. They used to go in and out of the holy places and were praised in the city where they had done such things. This also is vanity.

Can I erase from my mind all the suffering I had seen in the world? Would that be the path to redemption?

I am not running away from the world. I am plunging into myself to stay alive for the millions who love me and want me to live. I am sinking into the depths of a cave to reach out to the darkest corners of my soul, to scrape the layers of dignity off my ragged skin, to purge the sorrows, the regrets, the defeat, the longing for my angel.

I flew to Dar es Salaam, then to Arusha.

By tomorrow morning I will be at the foot of Mount Kilimanjaro.

8:11 The reign of Pope Mary: Day 2

No idea what happened today. My head is spinning, this little cave I found, cozy, not too cold, brings me a lot of peace. I ate a handful of mushrooms this morning, some peasant told me they will lift my spirit. I am so high now, I cling to the ceiling, holding bats by their wings, upside down.

"I came here to find peace", I told a peasant on the outskirts of Arusha.

"The perfect place," the peasant said. "Go high up the mountain and eat these mushrooms. You will feel like a new man."

The man had no idea who I was.

I have no idea who I am. Sure, I was Pope Francis the Second, I remember that, but who am I really? What is this Enyi Chebea doing inside my head?

...and all the pain, poof!, gone. Replaced by a curious bliss. I had no idea I was capable of it. What is this voice inside my head? Who is thinking this? Who is writing these words? How did I get this little notebook? This handful of pens. Look at them. Arranged nicely in the box. How many? 24 it says. I took out one.

Click click! It works. It has springs, the way I like it, I don't like pens with caps, because I lose caps all the time. With spring-pens I only have to remember to click them shut, and then click them open when I need them again.

It's a crime to leave pens open until they go dry. Such a waste. Thousands of unwritten words gone wasted. And when a crime is not punished quickly, people feel it is safe to do wrong.

I feel I have done some wrong. Then I also feel I have not done some wrong. These two conflicting feelings come in rapid succession, one after the other. It must be because I hang upside down, like an idiot, from the ceiling of my little cave.

No. That was an hour ago. Now I'm crouching on a pile of grass. My mind is in the past. That's why I feel somebody else is writing. At least I know it's somebody else because there is a presence in me, another person doing the talking, the writing.

Can't be. I know what is true. I know when I'm me and when I'm not me. Wait, how can I not be me, if I'm thinking this very question? I am that voice asking the question. Then the flash. Another voice, another question.

Many little bats sleep in the cave with me. They are harmless. I thought they might get tangled in my hair. That's impossible. My hair is so short I couldn't stick a cocklebur in it.

Let me ask another question, since I'm here. Are you there God? It's me Enyi. You may know me as Francis. Are you there?

Neah. I can't ask this question. I don't even know if I can open my mouth. I thought I did. I should have heard an echo then. From the cave. There was no echo, so that means I had not uttered a word. All of it was in my mind.

What if I'm thirsty? Yes, I think I feel thirst.

There's water in the jug. How did I have the inspiration to bring fresh water in a jug with me? That was fantastic of me. There is a lot of it. Wow. This will last me a week. Maybe a month. I don't know if I want to stay here a month. I like it here. Who knows. Maybe I will stay two months. Six months. Two years. I will let my beard grow so much, I will make a pillow out of it. I don't have a pillow. I will need a pillow. It's better than grass.

Food. I have bread, oats, chocolate bars. Lots of them. In a sack I brought with me. Water and food? I love this place. I have everything I need.

Lots of mushrooms too. Strong ones. I've been dreaming for five hours. Nine hours. The whole day. Since yesterday. Bats flew into the cave, and out. A few times. In and out. All of them at once. Now they are quiet. They are talking in their ultrasound language.

Truly, I am floating. It is not a negligible experience.

8:12 The reign of Pope Mary: Day 3

Even though a person sins a hundred times and still lives a long time, I know that those who fear God will be better off.

Horseshit. Not true. How do I know they will be better off? I know nothing. Will God offer some personal guarantees to his followers that they will receive some outstanding payoff in exchange for a life of few sins? God has said nothing since the inception of history. Nothing.

I cannot stop thinking of all the promises I had to make to the people listening to me in the name of God. Why? Because it was in the description of my job, because everyone expected me to. I lived a big lie. The biggest lie possible.

Was it worth the sacrifice? Wading through a sea of lies to reach the shores of truth?

The bats left a few hours ago at sunset and have not returned. It's almost morning. Where are they? They've been hunting all night. Leaving me alone with myself, a flickering fire, some white pages. A bag with mushrooms.

A conversation of minds with Nwanne, earlier today. He briefed me about the events of the day at the Vatican. He showed me his medical charts. He said he found a nice little cottage in the Dolomites where we can retire, just the two of us. We will raise goats for milk.

It's a wonderful plan. When I go back, I must call Nwanne and go to the cottage at once. But I don't have his number. Where am I supposed to call him? At the hospital? Is he allowed to talk to me?

Sunrise. Still no sign of my bats. Getting worried. It's a dangerous world out there. Some of the natural predators of bats are: snakes, raccoons, opossums, skunks. Even tarantulas prey on bats as they roost in trees or in crevices. Some owls and hawks have been observed to snatch bats in midair.

They should not go out every night. I have plenty of food here for them. They can drink water from the puddles in the cave. I can also spare a few bars of chocolate. I hope they like it.

Saint Peter was crucified upside down. What he did not have in common with a bat was that his arms were spread out to match the cross, whereas the bat holds his arms folded where it hangs from the ceiling of the cave. Moreover, bats are not known to have had a Christ of their own, even though the human Christ has sacrificed himself for all life, including beings who cannot speak.

8:13 The reign of Pope Mary: Day 4

The comet.

I did nothing the whole day.

When the sun went down over Kilimanjaro I stopped doing nothing and I looked up. That's when I saw the comet. It came from the right side of the sky and moved slowly, so very slowly towards the left side, while all this time nothing else happened. No hooting of owls, no fluttering of wings of bats, no crackling of firewood.

I was tempted to count my heartbeats. There were thousands of them.

This is how nothing feels like. When thoughts are asleep. Complete numbness. Not boredom. Absconded in my own soul, no fears, no joy, no sadness, no hope. Aware of my detachment from the pursuits of my heart.

I measured all these against the passing of the comet across the sky. I was tempted for the sake of tradition to make a wish on account of the comet, a wish that would not bring me hope, would not elicit any emotion. It was a wish for the persistence of memory.

At the highest point of its flight, the comet made me aware of the wickedness of the world. The struggle of the weak to overcome their condition. The predators chasing their prey in the wilderness and saving chunks of meat for their cubs. Under the name of evolution by means of natural selection. And the guise of madness under the cloak of reason.

Still, no fear or boredom invaded my mind. There was a flicker of contentment that evil is poised to lose more battles than good. The pride of wicked men buries them in the dungeons of history. Because the wicked do not fear God, it will never go well with them, and their days will not lengthen like a shadow. So the tradition says. While the comet couldn't be bothered by the passage of our history.

Hours later, while the comet was making its descent, I stoked the fire with a stick and chewed another piece of mushroom. The bats were returning. They were bringing me news. They knew exactly what was going on in the world, what needed to be done, and what will happen in the future. How could they be so sure? How could anyone be so sure of anything? Especially when God speaks to people in so many different languages, and so many conflicting words?

More peace grew in my soul. The starry night over my head. The moral law in my heart. As it is written on the tomb of Immanuel Kant, the philosopher.

8:14 The reign of Pope Mary: Day 5

The crickets.

What is it like to be a cricket? To have the little body and the little brain of a cricket? Higher on the ladder of consciousness than a bacterium, lower than a chicken. Blades of grass appearing as an endless forest. People as walking giants.

Not worrying about righteousness. Not worrying about genocide. Eating and multiplying. Eating and multiplying. No God, no Christ, no holy sacrament. Chirping by stridulation, but no praying.

(NOTE TO SELF, ADDED LATER FROM WIKIPEDIA: The stridulatory organ is located on the tegmen, or fore wing, which is leathery in texture. A large vein runs along the centre of each tegmen, with comb-like serrations on its edge forming a file-like structure, and at the rear edge of the tegmen is a scraper. The tegmina are held at an angle to the body and rhythmically raised and lowered which causes the scraper on one wing to rasp on the file on the other. The central part of the tegmen contains the harp, an area of thick, sclerotinized membrane, which resonates and amplifies the volume of sound, as does the pocket of air between the tegmina and the body wall. Most female crickets lack the necessary adaptations to stridulate, so make no sound.)

There is a vanity that takes place on earth, that there are righteous people to whom life happens according to the deeds of the wicked, and there are wicked people to whom life happens according to the deeds of the righteous. I think that this also is vanity.

Crickets have no sense of vanity, which is a feature of a complex brain. Who said that complexity has no dirty laundry? That's the reason God allegedly sent his son to save us from this filth. Hundreds of years after he dispatched clouds of locusts over Egypt to punish the Pharaoh for not letting the Jews go. I must mention that those were locusts, and not crickets. Locusts are creatures far more inferior than crickets. They destroy entire landscapes, and they can never stand in as a metaphor for wandering troubadours.

Thus, realizing the importance of crickets, I bow to them asking for nothing in return. They see me as a big shadow on their ground. They couldn't care less. At best, they jump away from my path, so I don't step on them. It's a matter of instinct, not some careful strategic consideration of self-defense or mutual deterrence. Often one cricket or two falls into traps, caught by their gross miscalculation of the dangers humans can pose to their habitat. They are caught in nets, and in people's hands clasped together to form a little cage. The large majority of these crickets are doomed. They will die to satisfy human curiosity. Some will end up under microscopes, some in fancy insectariums. Most of them will be discarded. Their remains will feed an entire generation of blades of grass. This is the destruction of vanity. This is the grand lesson of life.

8:15 The reign of Pope Mary: Day 6

The lone alpinist.

I have been watching him since the early hours of sunrise. He started at the bottom of a mountain wall, not too far from me. Could he have seen me? Possibly. If he looked my way, if the sun was not coming from my direction, if he stared for long enough to distinguish the color of my garment from the color of the surrounding rock, or if there was a source of light coming from inside the cave.

The lone alpinist was dedicated to his passion. For the first three hours he did not stop at all. He climbed slowly and carefully, one solid grip after the another. He hammered nails into the rock, looped the rope through the hook and pulled himself up every time just a bit more. A pouch of chalk was hanging from his belt. He used it profusely. He must have calculated the amount of chalk he would need for the whole ascent.

At noon he rested. He hung from a seat he made by wrapping the rope a few times around his waist and under his buttocks.

An eagle was surveying the sky above us. Curious and likely hungry.

I commended enjoyment, because a man has nothing better under the sun than to eat, drink, and be merry. For this will remain with him in his labor all the days of his life which God gives him under the sun. So the scriptures say. God or no God, there is no difference to the importance of life. Mountains must be climbed, eagles must be observed, people must be cared for.

The lone alpinist resumed his climb by the same method, accelerating the rhythm slightly so he could beat his time or reach the summit before sunset. He will make a descent the next day, or so it seems. The stars will be all his tonight.

8:16 The reign of Pope Mary: Day 7

While I was asleep, something happened. The bats came and went over my head and an eagle began building a nest on a stone shelf close to my cave.

The eagle was watching me when I opened my eyes. It had no interest in me as a possible threat or source of food. I was a mere curiosity, a moving object.

I stared into its eyes without blinking. We exchanged long moments of reciprocal evaluation. The bird flew away and returned later with more material for the nest. By late afternoon the nest was finished.

I had no desire to sleep. I waited for nightfall, for the clear sky. The eyes of the eagle glared in the moonlight like beads of marble. Majestically, the valley beneath us was opened to my eyes like the giant womb of Mother Earth. Gentle breezes swept through the forest, crickets dancing their nightly serenades.

The bats have not returned. They might have considered the eagle dominating the entrance to the cave. Little did they know that the eagle had no interest in anything but its own freshly constructed nest.

Some howling of wolves, far away, barely audible. I stoked the fire with a stick, fried some mushrooms, ate a chocolate bar, wrote my name on the cave wall with charcoal, painted my face with ash mixed with mud, felt exhilarated.

The eagle was my guardian.

I watched the shadows on the cave wall while applying my heart to know wisdom and to see the business that is done on earth, even though one sees no sleep day or night. The afterlife is not the domain of sleeplessness, while dark dreamless sleeps are not the domain of death. It's life consumed and unrealized. It needs to be that way.

Feeling of eternal peace, longlasting. How can this bliss last forever? I am what is left of my memories. The new man of the continuous stream of present moments.

8:17 The reign of Pope Mary: Day 8

Goats. Climbing the steep mountainside, single file, defying the laws of gravity. A few pebbles pressed under their hoofs jettisoned into the precipice.

They come my way not on the easy path I had taken but on the impossible path on the wall of the mountain. I retreat into the cave to let them pass.

They ransacked my hay bed for a moment. Nothing of interest there. I had taken my things with me. Embers look interesting but are not tasty. Some water left in a puddle. They drink it all with discipline and fairness. There is a dozen of them or more. Adult goats and some younglings.

The eagle nest is beyond their reach. The goats must pass below it if they want to move on. The eagle is at home. She briefly notes the presence of the animals, then returns to her resting position.

Bleating back and forth. The goats share some information about the whereabouts of food or possible threats from the wild. Younglings call their mothers to wait on them. It's not so much a burden on the mothers to wait on their baby goats as it is on the baby goats to keep up with their mothers. This is learning and growing up. Adaptation, survival, quality of reproduction.

I realize that no one can discover everything God is doing under the sun. Not even the wisest people discover everything, no matter what they claim.

We think we know the goats. We think we know where they come from. Why didn't we learn from them to keep our balance on the edge of the precipice? Not philosophy, but pure naturalism. Study the body of the goat, study the hooves, understand the instinct, understand the pressure from the environment. Learn it and make something useful from it. Something that changes people's lives. Something that creates beauty. All that from goats.

If they were only domesticated so I could milk them. I would love some raw goat milk. The best. I could boil it. I could sift it through my clean rags.

I want the goats to stay for a bit longer. I could use some new company till sunset. Red giant sunset. Feels like it's only made for me. How beautiful.

NOTEBOOK NINE

9:1 The reign of Pope Mary: Day 9

New day.

A fox chases the herd of goats across the rocky slope of the mountain. As long as the goats stay on the safe ledges of stone, the fox cannot reach them. Instinct drives them into the valley, where they can quench their thirst in a rivulet. Die of thirst or die of fox. That's the choice. Even baby goats understand this game. The fox tries to separate the babies from the herd. Not easy in difficult terrain. The goats are versatile. They navigate the slope with ease. Jumping from rock to rock. Over gaps in the stone ledge. Diverting the fox's attention.

The eagle observes from the sky. In wide circles above the action on the ground. There may be some leftovers from the fight. With little effort the eagle could feed itself.

It hurts to watch. I am against the fox. I don't want the goats to die. I don't find admirable qualities in the fox. I don't find strength and honor in its way of operating. And the goats are close to me. They have visited me. They drank my water. A fox would never drink my water. Would never come close to my cave.

The game of thirst and hunt is how natural selection operates. I cannot negotiate with it. I cannot even negotiate with my own feelings.

I reflected on all of this, and concluded that the righteous and the wise and what they do are in God's hands, but no one knows whether love or hate awaits them.

It came to me with no obvious preparation, this reflection. It's not about the God of Christians. It's not about free will against destiny. It's about the rules of nature. Yes, replace God with the rules of nature.

I am certain now that the fox cannot win.

9:2 The reign of Pope Mary: Day 10

I haven't seen the goats or the fox today. The bats left last night and very few came back. I cannot rely on them. They come and go as they please.

The eagle laid eggs in its nest. It behaves differently. It caresses its nest. Doesn't move for hours. Doesn't sleep. Eyes always open. Sun glaring in their reflection.

Clouds in the afternoon, dark clouds, signs of a thunderstorm. Winds agitate the animals. Some rain for an hour. It passes. The land dries up fast. The eagle wipes its wet beak on its feathers.

A fire in the valley, far away. Is it a house? Trees struck by lightning? Can't tell. The fire doesn't spread much. Truth is, I saw only a thick body of smoke. And where is smoke there is fire. No, where is smoke there is pope. Ha! I laughed by myself.

How's Mary doing? I wonder. Doing fine, I hope. Pope-ing to inspire. Dominating the patriarchy. Reminding everyone that Christ came from a woman's womb. No womb, no Christ. No Christ, no Church, no sacrament, no nothing. Is she praying for me, like she said, knowing that I don't value prayers?

Surely she is. And is asking the billion Catholics to do so. I thank her very much on this supposition.

To why I am here. I am here for the goats, for the bats and for the eagle. They all make sense. I have nothing to object to them. They are what they are. Why can't people be what they are? Natural beings. Breathing in, breathing out. Cultivating crops. Measuring the age of the Universe.

All share a common destiny, the righteous and the wicked, the good and the bad, the clean and the unclean, those who offer sacrifices and those who do not. Knowing this, truly knowing this, is liberating. Nature uniforms us with her implacable causality. There is no escape from this. None. We obey her or we disappear. It's not good versus evil, predators versus prey. It's knowing versus not knowing. Doing versus not doing. As it is with the good, so with the sinful. As it is with those who take oaths, so it is with those who are afraid to take them. We are all dressed in the same causal uniforms.

Eagle's egg will be hatching soon. There is a tremor in the air. I feel it. The eagle is minding my presence. Fresh vigilance. Clear moonlight.

9:3 The reign of Pope Mary: Day 11

Eagle had babies sometime this morning. Now it's gone hunting. The puffy bald chicks squeak constantly. Not being sure what to make of this, the bats did not come out today. The goats are nowhere to be seen.

This is the evil in everything that happens under the sun: the same destiny overtakes all. The hearts of people are full of evil and there is madness in their hearts while they live, and afterward they join the dead. And that's it.

Tell this to the eagle chicks. Tell this to a human newborn. None has any idea what life they are going to have. Millions would starve. Millions would never learn what means to be alive in the Universe.

There is no difference in the eyes of nature to be born as an eagle chick or a human baby. Wads of meat in both cases, differently shaped.

9:4 The reign of Pope Mary: Day 12

Eagle chicks are hungry. Haven't seen the mother eagle for a long time. Must be hard to find prey these days, even for predators.

While I was staring at the clear sky, a lone goat ventured close to my cave. Stopped, looked at me as if I was the intruder into its world. Showed no signs of fear. I threw a piece of bread its way. The goat ate it without hesitation.

I could easily catch the goat. I could milk it, then kill it with a stone and feed the eagle chicks. Random thoughts in my mind. Don't know where they came from. I am not doing any of these. I hope the goat escapes alive to live another day.

Anyone who is among the living has hope. Even a live dog is better off than a dead lion! It's in our blood, all living beings, to want to live. Exceptions only fortify this reality.

The goat turned back to where it came from. Sunny sky, good visibility. Gentle breeze of forest scents ascending.

9:5 The reign of Pope Mary: Day 13

The eagle came back with a goat in its claws. A whole dead goat. No blood dripping from the animal. Its body inert and defeated. The eagle placed the prey on the stone shelf and began ripping pieces and fed them to its chicks, first to whichever squeaked the loudest.

Now there was blood dripping from the stone shelf on the mountain wall, like a modern painting of squirts and splashes. Slowly I began feeling as if the eagle was eating from my heart. Piece by piece, while I was observing my own disintegration.

How I wished to be ignorant. Far away from this scene. It was thrown at me by the might of nature. An animal who came close to me, surveyed my ascetic crib, touched my things, was now being devoured.

So do people think they themselves are being devoured when their precious feelings are crushed by inconvenient hard truths? They twist and turn and boil in their minds. They scream. They cannot let go. They see the eagle of truth eating away at their staunch feelings and ironclad beliefs, and they refuse to acknowledge the blood.

Nature is merciless. Nature has no heart. Nature will let the blood drip and dry out. Nature is in the business of bones and decomposition.

The living at least know they will die, but the dead know nothing. They have no further reward, nor are they remembered. The dead cannot remember the dead. The only hope for the persistence of memory is the persistence of life.

No goat will be mourned and no eagle will escape hunger every time. It doesn't get better than this.

9:6 The reign of Pope Mary: Day 14

Did not shave in two weeks. Perhaps more. Haven't seen my face either. How long until I do not recognize myself? How long until I am a stranger to myself in a mirror?

The goat is half eaten. While the mother eagle was away on business, baby eagles tried to leave the nest according to their flawed instinct. One fell into the precipice and squeaked out of my sight. Another chick got stuck in a crack. I reached out, pulled it out.

Seconds later mother eagle came and knew right away I had something to do with the disappearance of her offspring. She attacked me point blank. I dropped the chick on the hay bed and pulled back into the cave. Defending myself with a stick.

Darkness of the cave cloaked my fear. No time to measure the reproductive instinct of beasts. I have seen the blood dripping. I accepted the blood. Not ready to shed mine.

The aggression of the eagle stirred up the population of bats. They panicked and stormed the cave. The eagle pulled back. I kept my blood inside me.

I spent time in darkness. Bats my only companion. Fruit eaters. They perform the vital ecological roles of pollinating flowers and dispersing fruit seeds. Many tropical plant species depend entirely on bats for the distribution of their seeds.

Darkness reminded me that there is value in death. The love, the hatred, and the jealousy of the dead have long since vanished. Never again will they have a part in anything that happens under the sun. This is space for new beings to add their love, their hatred, their jealousies to the inventory of history.

9:7 The reign of Pope Mary: Day 15

Did not eat or drink since yesterday. My lips dry, my stomach rumbling. Want to push myself to extremes, to know my boundaries. Wrote words in my diary with my eyes closed.

Heard steps on the path coming towards the cave. A man, dark as charcoal, long hair, long beard, deep-black eyes. White rags to cover his body. A knitted satchel.

To my right, in the mouth of the cave, he sat down. He said nothing. I greeted the man in the English language. The man said nothing. I then greeted the man in other languages as well. No response. The man was staring into the void with his deep-black eyes.

I said my name and I said I was from Nigeria. I offered my trust to this quiet mysterious man. The visitor said nothing and did not react to my presence. I turned my head towards him and noticed how careful he was not to tread on my bed of hay, not to touch my things.

We stood in silence for hours.

When I could not bear the thirst, I drank water. I asked the stranger if he wanted some. He said nothing.

Hours later I ate a bar of chocolate. I asked the stranger if he wanted a piece. He remained silent.

Night came. Full, bright moon over our heads. The stranger was still silent. He was meditating.

Must have been after midnight when I decided to lay down on the bed of hay. I closed my eyes, then I heard a voice:

"Go, eat your food with gladness, and drink your wine with a joyful heart, for God has already approved what you do."

Did the stranger speak? I asked him if he said something. He did not reply. He was still sitting in the same position, facing the moon.

9:8 The reign of Pope Mary: Day 16

Early morning before sunrise I heard the same voice:

"Let your garments be always white. Let no oil be lacking on your head."

I raised my head and looked around. The stranger was in the same spot. He maintained his straight back, his chin slightly raised. I walked in front of him. His eyes were closed. I asked him to repeat what he just said. He said nothing.

His garments were white and clean. From up close I saw his hair was oiled. He smelled of soft lavender.

I did my morning routine then I sat down next to the stranger.

It was a beautiful day. The only thing on my mind was the identity of my new companion, why did he come here, why did he not speak to me directly. It is customary for humans of all races and creeds to recognize each other's presence when they encounter each other in remote places. For this reason, the stranger elicited mild confusion in me. His silence was in keeping with this place, yet it seemed uncanny since he was not alone.

Then I felt crude embarrassment. What if I was the one out of place? What if I did not know the rules of silence?

I went back to my place and tried to search my inner peace. There was none. There was only restlessness. Thoughts racing through my mind. Who is the stranger?

Then he spoke again. "Let your garments be white," he said.

"I apologize, they were white," I said. "They just got dirty since I got here."

Then silence for the rest of the day.

9:9 The reign of Pope Mary: Day 17

Before sunrise, the voice woke me up.

"Enjoy life with the wife whom you love."

"Excuse me?" I said. I stood up and walked to the stranger. He was meditating with his eyes closed. He said nothing.

I went back to my place. Then the stranger spoke again:

"Enjoy life with the wife whom you love."

"I have no wife, sir," I said.

Pale winds climbing up the mountain. Early birds chirping. Eagle gone with all the chicks. Nest deserted. No sign of my bats.

Sun rising. Beautiful orange sunrise. The stranger spoke again:

"All the days of your vain life that he has given you under the sun."

"Who? Who has given me the days?" I said.

No response.

"Don't I make my own destiny?" I said.

The stranger replied: "This is your reward in life and in your toil in which you have labored under the sun."

"Are you a scholar of the Old Testament, sir?" I asked.

No response.

The stranger was choosing his words carefully. He never spoke directly to my face. He was playing a game. I had to walk away from him so he would speak to me.

"May I ask what you are teaching?" I asked.

No response.

"There is light in darkness, and there is darkness in light," the stranger said.

"I don't recall reading this in the scriptures," I said.

To my surprise the stranger spoke again:

"There is light in darkness."

9:10 The reign of Pope Mary: Day 18

I don't like riddles, nonsensical metaphors, parables that have no purpose to enlighten, to reveal deep truths. Yet I cannot escape them. I cannot see a straight reality since the stranger came to my cave. I feel I am losing myself. I am falling into a bottomless pit.

I closed my eyes for a few seconds to rest. It was midday. The sun was a big disc opposite the cave.

A tingling sensation crawled up my fingers into my arm, my shoulders, my whole body. Something was happening. I opened my eyes and saw the stranger standing in front of me, blocking the sun. He wanted to say something. He wanted me to do something. Knowing the rule I had discovered, I faced away from the stranger so he could speak his words.

"Whatever your hand finds to do," the stranger said, "do it with all your might, for in the realm of the dead, where you are going, there is neither working nor planning nor knowledge nor wisdom."

"I know these words," I said. "Please tell me more."

"The light is in darkness," the stranger said and pushed me forward towards the cave.

It was a hefty push. I almost tripped. I dared not look back. I wanted the words of the stranger to keep coming.

"Walk," the stranger said.

"Into the cave?" I said.

"Walk."

Without looking back, I stepped into darkness. The stranger was behind me. Breathing into the back of my head. How far does he want me to go? No need for words. I kept walking past the chamber where the bats lived. They were still there. I felt them. Didn't bother with me. Somewhere far into the cave there was a very small light flickering. I must go there. No doubt.

9:11 The reign of Pope Mary: Day 19

First day in heaven

Flickering light in front of me. Been walking for hours. Light doesn't get bigger. The stranger pushed me forward with his breathing.

My legs tired, I wanted to stop. I was thirsty. Brought some water with me, but not enough. I should collect some from the clear puddles in the cave. I can't stop. The stranger won't let me. I'm not afraid of him but I cannot disobey him either. It seems the stranger has a peculiar power over me.

I was truly tired. Not one more step. I will rest then we can continue.

"It's here," the stranger said.

Could not find strength to speak. But I understood what the stranger meant. The light was on a wall right in front of time. The size of my hand.

"Go on," the stranger said.

He doesn't realize I cannot go on. There is a wall in front of me. I felt the resoluteness in his voice. So I put my hand over the light. From a small circle it grew slowly to a big circle my size. I had to go in, apparently. None of this made sense. Some mystery trick the stranger was playing with me.

I went in.

I found myself in a beautiful place, what believers would call a heaven of some sort, with all the necessary prerequisites. Brightness, clear sky, gardens stretching into the horizon, colorful vegetation, immaculate cleanness.

So this is what the stranger had prepared for me. I turned my back to say something to him. He was gone. Part of the game, I suppose. I had to be by myself. I have to make sense of all this.

There were people around. Walking casually to and fro. Dressed in light, white clothes. People I knew. Black, white, dead, alive, friends and enemies. Many were there. Their faces had the glow of obviousness. It was perfectly normal for them to be there, to justify my hallucination.

It had to be a hallucination.

There was Nwanne picking strawberries in a field. He doesn't see me. Then Mother Allegra knitting a vest under a lemon tree. Father is there too playing a song on a wooden flute. Mother carries a basket with fruits. Children play with puppies and rabbits. Butterflies form the hairstyles of women, and fly along with them in formation. A pink elephant sprays a shower of water over a field of flowers.

I stopped to think. Drank water from a spring and sat on a rock.

All this I laid to heart, examining it all, how the righteous and the wise and their deeds are in the hands of the laws of nature. Whether it is love or hate, man does not know, both are before him.

Fine. This little heaven I discovered was pure and simple. Nothing divine about it. Makes me feel good inside, just like chocolate. I can live with it. I can get accustomed to the routine of bliss. More questions came to me as I sat down in silence.

9:12 The reign of Pope Mary: Day 20

Second day in heaven

People can never predict when hard times might come. Like fish in a net or birds in a trap, people are caught by sudden tragedy. This never happens in heaven.

The eternal absence of tragedy makes heaven. Or does it?

Faces around me in bliss. Have they wiped all their memories? Is heaven eternal amnesia? How else can you bear true bliss if not unburdened from the past?

All the good men and women from my life. Their presence soothes me. They all want to tell me their stories. Would I want to hear them? They speak into my mind. Don't open their mouths. Which stories, I wonder. When they were brave and righteous? When they were weak and lazy?

All these are life, they tell me. All these stories carry over with you in heaven, they say. I can live with that. Truly, nobody really knows what heaven must look like. No book has really told us, leaving allegories aside. No one truly came back with pictures to show us. Heaven is a feeling. That's what they tell me, all the good men and women around me.

I must let go, so I understand. I don't want to let go. I cherish my reason. Questioning myself is what keeps me sane. What keeps me alive?

Alive is also what you feel, they say. Letting go of your senses opens you to a grander truth.

Truth doesn't come in layers upon layers. Truth simply is.

Mind can corrupt, they say. Heaven is pure freedom.

Nice words. Sound good to me. Certitude of truth. Very appealing. Tastier than honey. Who wouldn't want that? No effort, no doubts, just knowing. That is what heaven offers.

I want to offer my objection. That there is no excitement in not searching.

There is, they say. It is to enjoy freedom forever.

I would not know what *forever* is, if I don't grow. There is no growth, no transformation in forever.

Heaven must have some logical flaws. They didn't answer. I was satisfied with that. I did not want to challenge all the people I loved and respected in my life. Emotions erode when you challenge the souls who carry them.

Walked around some more. Crossed a plain full of tulips. Girl came to me and laid a crown of flowers on my head. I felt content with myself. I put my flaws aside, as if they weren't mine. My body was exuding a sensation of health. I was blooming. I was radiating. My childhood friends from Africa came to me, covered in plain linen clothes of all colors. Shook my hand. Everything is alright. We all have good lives, they said.

I was happy for them. Many are still alive. They must have sent their thoughts ahead of their bodies in heaven to greet me. This is a kind of love. It must be.

I spent the rest of the day with them. Many more came. We spoke about the lives we had. They were good lives.

9:13 The reign of Pope Mary: Day 21

Third day in heaven

Another bit of wisdom that has impressed me as I have watched the way our world works. There is restlessness in the persistence of bliss. There is restlessness in the persistence of evil.

Toss me in heaven against my will. I will refute it. Offer me the choice of heaven on a silver platter. I will deny it. Forbid me the entrance to heaven. I will desire it with the whole of my being.

This is what diminishes the heaven of scriptures. The eternity. The impossibility of decay. Imperfections and contrast make our desires real. While heaven offers no background. Nothing to push yourself against. To stand above your past condition.

…and the frailty of our memory. Doesn't do us service along the perspective of eternity. Such a loose word, eternity. So unreal. Ungraspable. Intangible. Doesn't have a flavor. Invented out of fear of pain. Sprung out from the observance of death.

This whole realm of bliss remains a vaporous melody. He put me here. The stranger. I did not ask for anything. Here I am, living it. Life everywhere. No pain. No death.

There is nowhere to go because there is everywhere to go. We are not made like this. The world is not made like this. Infinity is not made for us. Infinity does not exist.

I would like to return to the real world. Please? Who do I ask? How does it work? Prayed already in mind. Hoping someone would hear. Nothing happened. No one hears you when you are talking to yourself in heaven. Nobody talks in heaven. They all smile to each other. They are all gentle. But nobody says anything. All words are implied.

Deafening bliss.

9:14 The reign of Pope Mary: Day 22

First day in hell

Even in heaven people get tired and must take a nap. How else would eternal consciousness work?

I fell asleep on the grass, under the clear sky. Don't remember if I dreamt. Was pretty cozy until I suddenly woke up and I wasn't cozy anymore. A damp smell of pungent odors rushed into my nostrils.

What is this place? Where are the carefree people? The butterflies? The daffodils?

Must not be the typical hell I know. Fires, peeling skins, throbbing pain. It's a different kind of hell. The hell of combustive life choices. Those choices of split seconds that last for a life time. Leaving no space for ruminating over regrets. No luxury of self-destruction. Self-enslavement into the chains of inevitability. Volcanoes of frustration spewing out lava of acid cynicism. Ravaging nihilism. Scathing apathy. This is the hell of the new generation.

Loneliest of all. Stuck in a small place full of people yet with nobody to talk to. Nobody would talk back. Flat faces with no expression. They don't have thoughts. They don't have feelings. They just breathe in and breathe out. Eat and eliminate. Sleep and do nothing.

A PARABLE OF HELL: There was once a small city with only a few people in it. And a powerful king came against it, surrounded it and built huge siege works against it. The king demolished the city and destroyed all the people inside. From the rubble he built a new castle. Of brick and mortar in the shape of hell. Tombstones turned into statues of lions and griffins to illustrate the grandeur of his majesty.

9:15 The reign of Pope Mary: Day 23

Second day in hell

Every day must end so another can begin. Despair wanes with time. Numbness settles in. Deep inside the soul rests the mechanics of hope.

I searched and found nothing. I wasn't there for myself. Moving forward with no purpose. Heavy steps on a solid ground. Space around me in all directions. No horizons. No edges. Pressure from above making me to fight to stay erect. Winds pushing from all directions. No landscapes. No discernible colors. Black noise of something humming. Faceless people in the distance coming and going. Nobody nearby.

Chasing something that is only in my mind. Something very familiar. I don't know what it is. A large person. A definite object of some sort. What does it do? Is it alive? Wants me to say something? Wants me to follow it? Not knowing what do to. Constant feeling of disorientation. Trying to gather my thoughts in packets of sense. Utter failure. As if I am not the master of my own mind.

A poor, wise man knew how to save the town, and so it was rescued. But afterward no one thought to thank him.

9:16 The reign of Pope Mary: Day 24

Third day in hell

So even though wisdom is better than strength, those who are wise will be despised if they are poor. What they say will not be appreciated for long.

The ultimate package of suffering. Seeing richness, smelling beauty, and not being able to possess or consume any of it. While your mind wants it badly, while your body desires it badly. Look and don't touch. Touch but don't taste. Taste but don't swallow. Frustration all the way.

Add ignorance to all that. Add lack of reason, lack of self-restraint. A shallow consciousness. You get eternal damnation. For you, not knowing what is happening to you, for the devil, eternal amusement.

If you only knew that fear is a liquid in your mind. At least that. It would offer you some comfort, some detachment from the fires of hell. Your solace would be that you are not fully responsible for your fears. Your body with all its fluids was given to you.

Moving on. Everything changes. Illusions become lost memories. Truly lost. You would never remember them. You will forget that you even lived those terrible moments. Your mind will deny your own past to you.

The key to come out of heaven is to survive your present. Forget your past. It doesn't exist. Think that the fire that surrounds you will disappear. Don't ask why. That's the wrong question. Nobody knows why. Those who tell you they know, they lie.

Blisters all over my feet. They swell. Doesn't hurt. They give me a preoccupation. I go over ideas how to care for my body. I cannot call my personal doctor. Obviously. He is not a man destined for hell. He is a good man. There's nobody around. Am I the only person here? Everybody got sent to heaven? What the hell?

That's ironic. Thinking words like that. Yes, that ought to do it. Think words, write them in an imaginary notebook. That will get me out of here.

…all this talking to myself is making me thirsty.

9:17 The reign of Pope Mary: Day 25

Found some stairs carved in stone, going in an ascending spiral around a big rock. Enough of this torrid place.

I climb until my mind goes numb. Hot air dissipates. Gentle breeze follows. Winter temperatures soon after.

I'm somewhere high above on the mountain. Stairs continue to go up toward the peak of the mountain.

Getting colder and colder. My garments become stiffer. I feel icicles forming in my beard. My face is rigid. Fingers going numb.

Where does this all end? No idea. I know I cannot go back. There is nowhere to go. Below me the path evaporates in mist as if it never existed.

It's getting really cold. The moisture over my eyeballs freezes. Can't open the eyes properly. I struggle to blink.

Reaching the top. The level of clouds. Running through me. Bringing me some moisture. Cold moisture. Not good to quench my thirst. There's no water I can use in this place. Can't put snow or ice in my mouth. Can't feel my hands. Don't know where my mouth is. I'm a mouthless face. Eyeballs will crack and fall out in smithereens.

Why did I come to this place? It's the quietest place I have seen in my life. Less air, less noise. No words of wisdom come to mind. Why would they? My mind counts heart beats and feels individual bones in my body.

The words of the wise heard in quietness are better than the shouting of a ruler among fools.

I'm the only fool around here. Quite an accomplishment. Found a lonely place where I know for certain I am the only fool around. My body disintegrates piece by piece. My mind watches in stupefaction. How did I let this happen? What would become of me?

9:18 The reign of Pope Mary: Day 26

Found myself buried in snow. Dressed in animal furs. Still on the top of the mountain. Face covered with a cloth. Don't remember if I did this myself.

Had a dream about the meaning of life. It was a green apple with a tiny hole in the middle. From inside a worm emerged. A long white worm with no head. Kept coming out. Had no end. Was an infinite worm. I can eat the apple around the worm, I said to myself in my dream. I couldn't bring the apple to my mouth.

Thoughts of war. In trenches, soldiers with machine guns and helmets. Bullets flying. Grenades and bombs. Cold and rain. Everybody shouting. I had no part in the war. I was sitting there, on a crate, and was taking notes in my notebook. Hands very cold and purple.

I was a white man. Saw my reflection in a small mirror that some soldier had dropped in the mud. I was young. Had no beard. Skin had a pinkish hue.

Bomb exploded near the trenches and splashed me with mud over my entire body. Cleaned my face with water from a puddle and looked again in the mirror. I was now a black man. I was me in my younger years. I badly wanted to run away. I ran into the officers' tent and hid behind a desk. I prayed for the war to go away.

Wisdom is better than weapons of war, but one sinner destroys much good.

The war was gone.

I am buried in snow and cannot feel my body. Covered in blisters, probably. Can see the clear sky. Can see clouds below me. Sun shining. Cold as the end of time.

There is no meaning in all this. Had enough thinking about the purpose of life. Want this to end. Want to live until my body reaches its expiration, then they can set me on fire and bury my ashes in a forest. That is all I want for my legacy.

Have no command over my thoughts. They come and go as they please. Cannot even separate emotions from the real perception of my condition. Do not feel anything. Simply exist bereft of any control. At the mercy of the limits of my body. My mind is a spectator at the convulsions of the body.

NOTEBOOK TEN

10:1 The reign of Pope Mary: Day 27

Eyes frozen half open. Body in agony. Nothing on my mind.

Jesus Christ appears from nowhere. He speaks to me:

"I told you so."

Don't know what he's talking about. He told me nothing. Never had a conversation with the Messiah.

He speaks again:

"Dead flies make the perfumer's ointment give off a stench."

He wants me to guess. Little imperfections can ruin everything. Is that what he means?

He raises his finger to the sky and speaks in a majestic voice.

"A little folly outweighs wisdom and honor."

Not sure if I agree with that. Try to open my eyes fully. I see Him now. He wears a cotton shirt to his knees. Why is he not freezing?

"Francis."

Calls my Papal name.

"Francis."

Can't speak. I would like to say something in return. What could I possibly say to Jesus Christ that he already doesn't know? And since he knows everything, why would he ask anything in the first place? Is he testing me?

"Hear me, Francis."

I hear you.

"I am not real. Make me real, Francis."

Oh, it's a hallucination.

"Let me warm you up," he says.

"How would you do that?"

"Open your heart."

"It's open."

"Let me cover you."

"With what?"

"With my body."

Moved my legs. Pushed the snow off me. Jesus did nothing. He was staring at me. Long hair, beard. He was observing my struggle with a distant piety. He was bereft of words. He didn't move a finger to help me. Saw frustration on his face. He turned around and left.

10:2 The reign of Pope Mary: Day 28

A wise person chooses the right road. A fool takes the wrong one.

Descending down the cold mountain. Found a loaf of bread. Belongs to me. I know its shape. Must have dropped it when I climbed up. Don't remember climbing up the mountain. I remember being in heaven, falling to hell, waking up on top.

Bread is stone hard. Can't bite. Mother used to sink the old bread in water. Then we ate it. No water around here. No fire to melt snow.

What pushes a man forward when he feels there is no end in sight? And how can a man go forward if he knows that there is no end in sight? For the good things we want no end. For the bad things we can even destroy ourselves.

This body of mine insists on living. Do I accept its laws? Or has this body of mine accepted my mind? Who is in control? The voice doing this thinking?

Need to feel the extreme. No, not death. The extreme of what I could be. In real life. Not according to my demonic imagination.

Fell from a high position of power. Loads of lies I spewed out. Am still falling. Haven't reached the bottom. Where the hardness of the Earth will crush me. That is the real end.

Excuse for doing the right thing? Must pass through thick curtains of lies, deceptions, calculations?

Blunt truth can save. I know for sure. Can feel it in my blood. My bones are full of it. If I don't lose my head on this lonely, frigid mountain.

Where is everybody? People not friends with the mountain anymore? Where is the courage? Where is the calling to merge the soul with the implacable constructions of nature?

They must have taken other paths. No ropes, no markings here. I made my own path. Yes, made my own hard path, like a fool. What did I expect? Find a little revelation if I walk off the known path?

Should have found a mountain that has never been climbed. A mountain of sharp iron. A mountain of shiny glass. Unmountable. Revelations of oxidized iron! Revelations from slivers of broken glass!

10:3 The reign of Pope Mary: Day 29

Even as fools walk along the road, they lack sense and show everyone how stupid they are.

I, Enyi Chebea, formerly known as Pope Francis the Second, declare on Mount Kilimanjaro, where nobody can hear me, that the Christian religion is a lie, and all religions are lies, from their dubious beginnings until today. I mean no insult and no harm to anyone. I mean not to blaspheme, I mean not to shock, I mean not to persuade anyone. I love all people, I respect their right to believe, to live, and to pursue happiness in the name of what they believe.

This declaration is a product of my mind. I have come to this conclusion by observing the origin of my own thoughts, and by observing the world. I have passed through the hell and the heaven of the mind. I know now they never existed as real places. Suffering and happiness are all in the mind.

I have observed the suffering in the world, and I find no divine justification for it. The scriptures are wrong. There cannot be a divine mandate for suffering as a condition for salvation in the afterlife. It cannot be true just because some so-called prophets said so. I said many things myself. Will people in a thousand years take my words as divine inspiration? I hope not.

So, then, what comes after such a declaration? What is there to believe about the world, if not the certitude of celestial caring, absolute truth, and eternal positive divine reassurance? What can we, humans, put above us to keep us humble, in solidarity with each other, hopeful, moral, and confident that life is worth living?

I dare say that religion must be replaced with the respect of Nature. We need to elevate Nature above the level of our gods and prophets. It is Nature that has produced us, it is Nature that maintains us alive and reproducing, it is Nature that can and will terminate us, regardless of whether we bring it upon ourselves or not.

There you have it, wild eagles of Kilimanjaro, bears, mountain lions, goats, snakes, and bats. Take my flesh, take my bones, and spread them over the valleys for your benefit.

10:4 The reign of Pope Mary: Day 30

Somebody is following me. I have seen the silhouette of a man deep in the forest coming towards me. Someone is are coming after me.

Nobody knows I'm here. Nobody can come after me. Surely, I must have lost my mind, but I have not lost my sight. I saw a man coming towards me. I hid under a rock and I waited.

Like a predator, crouching in the tall grass, I waited. There, a man came, running. He was looking for something. He stopped near my rock and looked around. He did not see me. I hid pretty well.

Suddenly I had a playful thought. Could I somehow distract the man's attention? When he looked away, I grabbed a stone and threw it in a random direction. The stone made a noise when it hit the ground, and it grabbed the man's attention.

I thought I made a good joke. A stone is as real as my bare feet. The man is real as the beasts on the mountain. Delirium of loneliness. I am still alive. I had not seen a real human for some time. Has it been weeks? Months?

I still hear voices in my head. They call me by my many names: Bishop of Rome, Vicar of Jesus Christ, Successor of the Prince of the Apostles, Supreme Pontiff of the Universal Church, Primate of Italy, Archbishop and Metropolitan of the Roman Province, Sovereign of the Vatican City State, Servant of the servants of God, Clown of Clowns, Jester of Jesters.

Nwanne whispers into my ear: "If the anger of the ruler flares up against you, do not resign from your position, for a calm response can undo great offenses."

Who is the ruler? Is that man in the forest angry at me? What does he want from me?

I was the ruler of the Catholic Church. I was not a calm soul. People did not see me that way. But they loved me. They loved me so much, they now want to chase me, hunt me down, and raise me on a burning pyre as a trophy. Or they want to salvage me from perdition and carve a statue for me, as a grand token of their respect.

The man is gone for now. I don't know if I can trust him. I will stay here for a while.

10:5 The reign of Pope Mary: Day 31

Had a good night sleep. Not too cold, not too warm. I covered myself with moonlight. Ate the bread I found, and some berries. Drank fresh water from a rivulet.

Almost forgot about the man from yesterday. Minding my own business when I hear rustling in the forest. The man running.

We make eye contact. He shouts: "Hey!"

I don't wait to be accosted by this madman. Learned enough on the mountain to be circumspect when meeting people again.

I began running.

Felt plenty of energy within my body. Rejuvenated, strong. Had the blood of a leopard in my veins. Let's see if the man can catch me now! Ran through the forest, barefoot. Knew the land well. Knew where I can lay my foot and not hurt myself. The man was running after me, shouting "Hey! Stop! Stop!". He would really have to catch me and make me stop. Had no reason to stop for this madman. Who was he? He disturbed the peace of this land with his arrogant aggression. He beleaguered my rest. He jostled, unwelcome, into my thoughts.

Running faster and faster. Was beginning to enjoy this chase. Man shouting behind me "Stop! Stop!". Me shouting back "Catch me if you can!". From his voice the man seemed younger. I was gaining some distance. His voice sounding weaker "Stop. Stop. Please." Interesting. He was begging me. The trick of devil sweetening his call? I know all those tricks. There is evil that I have seen under the sun, as if it were an error proceeding from the ruler of men, the supreme authority of mortals, saying: "Obey the mellow voices, as they wish you well. Despise the thunderous voices as they are your enemies."

Had to make a quick judgment of who this man really was and what he really wanted from me. His relentlessness is intriguing. Clearly, I had beaten him in the race of hearts and bodies. Yet he struggles to find me. I shall run until I am satisfied the strange man is defeated and stops. Only then I will hear his plea again. This time he'd better make sense.

10:6 The reign of Pope Mary: Day 32

I thought I had lost the man. For hours I haven't heard from him.

I rested on my back on a bed of grass. When I had enough rest, and enough watching the sky, I went to the nearby river to wash my face and quench my thirst. When I raised my face from the water and turned back towards the forest I saw the man standing three meters away from me. He had been watching me. We both froze in silence. He did not show signs of aggression. On the contrary, he was smiling carefully as if he was trying not to look like a madman. But he looked like a fool. He was tired and he did not want to leave me alone. I must be somebody important to him. Does he know who I am? On this mountain nobody knows who I am. I don't know who I am, the beasts don't know who I am.

"Your Holiness," the man said.

Here we go. The fool knows who I am. What do I do now? Do I deny who I am? Do I tell him he is out of his mind and that I am not the holy man he is thinking about?

Okay, so he knows who I am. He struggled to find me, to chase me, to corner me. I decided to reply with a riddle, to test the man.

"Fools are put in many high positions," I said. "While the rich occupy the low ones."

"It is from the book of Ecclesiastes, Your Holiness," the man said.

"Do you know what it means?"

"Forgive me, Your Holiness. You are in neither position," the man said. To my surprise, he was playing along.

"I am just a man now," I said.

The man was silent. Good for him. This makes him a fool no more. I tried this:

"You found me because I let you?"

"We found you, Your Holiness, because you are a man, and satellites can find men if they search for a long time."

"You found me when I came out of the cave."

No response. Wise men do not need to speak to confirm the obvious. This is a general statement. I cannot say that the stranger is a wise man. I do not know him. I do know that he has done his best to perform his duty for whomever had assigned it to him.

… … … … … … … … … … … … I feel giddy!

Now that his deference to me has been established, I could initiate a jest. I pretended to clean my feet, but instead I grabbed a tiny dormant frog from the ground and tossed it at the stranger in such a manner that the frog wouldn't be hurt and the stranger would only be startled. The jest succeeded! The frog landed on the stranger's chest. He yelped with utmost surprise, pulled back in haste, tripped on a bump in the ground, and fell on his back in defeat.

I scuttled away chuckling, but not so fast that the stranger would lose sight of me. To my own surprise, he stood up quickly, conquered his embarrassment, and darted towards me with renewed energy that he must have mustered from the adrenaline he gained from the frog incident.

Curiously enough, he gained ground so quickly that in seconds he was behind me, trying to grab my robe to pull it. Like cat and mouse, we ran like this for a minute, until he finally won the round. He grabbed my robe, pulled it hard, and made me stop.

I was still chuckling. The man was chuckling too. Now we can finally make acquaintances.

10:7 The reign of Pope Mary: Day 33

The man introduced himself: Father Alonso Guarneri-Stradivari, a descendent of both the great 18th Century luthier Bartolomeo Giuseppe Antonio "del Gesù" Guarneri and the great luthier Antonio Stradivari. I asked him how this was possible. He said that sometime in the mid-19th century, a Guarneri married a Stradivari, and they merged the two family trees. The new family branch, however, did not venture into the musical instrument business. They decided to become pharmacists and merchants. Father Alonso was actually born a Guarneri, but did research into his past, and, when he discovered a Stradivari was his ancestor as well, he extended his last name to include the Stradivari name, thus merging the two great heritages. It is well known that Giuseppe "del Gesù" Guarneri and Antonio Stradivari were competing luthiers in the 18th Century. Opinions continue to be divided on which luthier is the greatest.

Then, Father Alonso Guarneri-Stradivari spoke these words, which I reproduce *ad litteram*:

"Your Holiness, the name I bear is the least worthy piece of information I have to bring you. While you were gone from the public arena many grand events have unfolded, the majority of them due to your so-called absence, which have the potential to profoundly transform the future of mankind, if they have not transformed it already. I beg your attention, Your Holiness, as I construct the chronology of the events I am about to share with you. I must do it in sequence, while sparing some minor details, and I must be careful not to omit any of the fundamentals.

Days after you left Italy, the newly elected Pope Mary convened an urgent Vatican Council while all the Cardinals were still in Rome. Together with her supporters and seconded by her close aid, Cardinal Thorsen Tchipcherish, Pope Mary issued a Grand Papal Letter to All of Christendom, in which she asked for a Grand Meeting of the Heads of All Christian Churches, under whichever particular creed they may be, to discuss the grave situation in which the human spirit lingers in this age of terrible unrest.

At the same time, while the social, economic, and political trepidations were, and still are high, the election of Pope Mary, the first woman Pope, and also a very progressive Pope, has ignited the joy and inspiration for peace of all Christians, not just the Catholics. In thousands of cities around the world people took to the streets to celebrate Pope Mary, to pray for her, to wish her well, and to share the bond of camaraderie with fellow Christians, regardless of their specific denominations.

Given this context, and being aware of the circumstance of her election, Pope Mary gave numerous speeches around the world, in many cities, on all continents, speaking about solidarity, unity, community, equality, peace, freedom, hope, and true change for the spirit. Her words were of gold, her voice was music, her presence electric. She drew large crowds on all continents. No one in history is known to have done this.

After these popular gatherings, Pope Mary convened the Grand Meeting of the Heads of All Christian Churches to be held, not at the Vatican, but on the island of Lampedusa, the largest island of the Italian Pelagie Islands in the Mediterranean Sea, known to have been the primary entry point for migrants into Europe for most of the duration of the 21st century.

Hundreds of tents and barracks were installed to accommodate thousands of religious Christian leaders from all over the world. The whole world wondered what Pope Mary had in mind, and how she managed to convene all the Christian Churches. It was an atmosphere of magic. Everybody hugging everybody, kisses on cheeks, multiple times, conversations in small groups, in large groups, inside tents or outside at roundtables installed anywhere there was patch of grass on the small island. Good wine and cheese were served. Hundreds, perhaps thousands, of reporters were present, mixed with the clerics, instructed not to disrupt the meetings, and to respect the protocol. While the security was very tight, there were no incidents whatsoever. It was a bubble of heaven.

After days of deliberations, during which the press could not really figure out the purpose of this Grand Meeting, because each separate group seemed to discuss only pieces of ideas from a larger mysterious puzzle, Pope Mary announced to the press that she was ready to make the Declaration of the United Christian Peoples public. That afternoon, on a dais raised near the seafront, with the beautiful Mediterranean in the background, Pope Mary announced these memorable words to the world:

"I have seen slaves on horseback, while princes go on foot like slaves. The times are changing. Our souls have grown. Our planet-home is in peril. It is time to put aside our differences and march together on a new path.

Hereby, I, Pope Mary, in the name of my fellow friends gathered here, announce the following:

One. The abolition of the institution of the Papacy.

Two. The abolition of all Institutions of the Christian Churches.

Three. The establishment of a democratic Council of Humanity, an organization of peace, prosperity, and well-being for the human spirit.

Four. The establishment of the Secretariat of the Council of Humanity.

Five. The establishment of the post of Secretary General of the Council of Humanity, the Office of the Magisters, and the Office of the Guardians.

Six. The establishment of the Constitution of the Council of Humanity, with its primary mandate to complete the secularization of all former Christian Churches in all states and administrative jurisdictions where they operate.

Seven. The theological reform of the Christian Doctrine, with its new mandate to advance the human spirit with sub-ordination to the needs and physical laws of Mother Nature.

Eight. The establishment of the Moral Charter of Humanity, with its core philosophy of inclusion, solidarity, and freedom to pursue a prosperous life, for all beings of Planet Earth, whether human or not.

Nine. The establishment of a philosophy of critical thinking, collaboration, and respect, within the members of the Council of Humanity, while recognizing the theological inheritance of the Holy Book.

Ten. The merger of all former Christian Churches into the Council of Humanity."

10:8 My Return to the World

Father Alonso stopped talking. He was exhausted. He recited the Declaration of Pope Mary without blinking, without skipping a beat. He was about to collapse on the ground, so I quickly jumped up and offered him support. I was awash in thoughts, in awe, in joy. No clear words came to my mind. This revolutionary declaration came to realize my great hopes and take them further, to new unimagined heights.

I knew then that I must return to the world. I must be present for these historical events. And I wanted to see this wonderful dream that was unfolding with my own eyes.

On the way to the airport, where Father Alonso arranged for me to be flown back to Abuja in Nigeria then back to Europe, I had time to think about my time in the wilderness. How long has it been? Was it really 33 days? How much of this time was a hallucination?

The harder I tried to remember events from my time as Pope, the less I remembered. Images of chiefs of state, dignitaries, people I have met came to my mind, but not what they said, not what they wanted. I hardly remembered what I had accomplished as Pope. Father Alonso kept talking about what a big inspiration I was for these changes. Many voices wanted me back to join the newly formed Council of Humanity. Why would they want that for me? What do I have to say?

The face of Nwanne emerged in my mind. His voice was clear and warm. He was calling me to go visit him. He was missing me. His words, the time we spent together, were the clearest memories I could gather. As the bus was meandering through the roads, all thoughts were leaving me, except the thought of seeing Nwanne again.

Whenever he got the chance, Father Alonso tried to grab my attention with more news. Soon he gave up, when he realized I was lost in my own little world. Yet I could see he was fretting, he was fidgeting, he had big plans for me, and he dreaded the failure of his mission.

To appease his concerns, I told him gently:

"When you dig a well, you might fall in. When you demolish an old wall, you could be bitten by a snake."

Father Alonso was not moved by my words. He knew exactly what I meant. He knew I was skeptical about this grand project – The Council of Humanity. He wisely chose to be patient with me, and did not waver in his determination to take me back to the world, as if he was obeying some old command of mine against myself, in times where I could not be trusted with a sane judgment. Perhaps that is true, I don't know.

10:9 In Abuja I hear more news

Father Alonso arranged for a nice hotel room for me in Abuja and left me in my room so I could rest. The next morning, he came early with a tray full of delicious breakfast nourishments. He placed the tray on the table and launched into a lengthy report of recent events.

Under the Constitution of the Council of Humanity, all former leaders of Christian Churches, regardless of their denomination, will become Guardians of the Council. They will be at the same position of equality. Any hierarchical position under the leader of a traditional Christian Church will obtain the position of Magister within the Council. All priests and pastors who shepherded not more than one Church in the past will retain their titles and will be offered, in addition, the title of Companion, so as to recognize both the spiritual heritage and the new spiritual institution.

"This is the key to blending the past with the future," Father Alonso explained, "everything changes, but we still honor our past."

I continued to listen patiently.

Father Alonso described the first democratic processes of the Council, how elections will be held, how important transparency was, how money was absolutely forbidden to play a role in elections, how matters of spirit will be publicly debated and administered by AI monitoring, so no one can abuse their share of free speech, and how the Council will shepherd the growth of the human spirit towards a future of peace and prosperity for all.

After a week of deliberations, the Council elected its first Secretary General. The role of Secretary General is merely that of an administrator and spokesperson. The first Secretary General of the Council of Humanity is none other than Thorsen Tchipcherish, former Cardinal of the Catholic Church.

Father Alonso paused to see my reaction. The memories of my encounters and conversations with Cardinal Tchipcherish came to me with the force of the last gargantuan iceberg that has detached from Greenland. And in a flash, I realized there was no better man to occupy this role than my former nemesis and friend, Thorsen. Surely, he was not a sail in these winds of change. He was the strong hand at the helm that steered the boat in the right direction. He saved me after my impeachment, and as he helped Pope Mary rise to her position, I am certain he talked his way into the Council for a "better future of humanity", as he would put it.

Father Alonso waited patiently for me to finish my thoughts.

"What happened to Pope Mary?" I broke the silence.

"After she abolished the papacy, Pope Mary automatically became the Guardian of the Catholic Church," Father Alonso said showing preparedness in his answer.

"I see. So no more Popes?" I inquired simply.

"No more Popes."

"What about the entire administrative hierarchy?"

"Simplified and converted into the new three level structure. Companions, Magisters, and Guardians."

"How can this be managed? The bureaucracy was enormous in all Churches."

"A.I." Father Alonso replied tersely.

"Artificial Intelligence!? They have software that good?"

"It has been validated just recently."

Father Alonso seemed prepared to offer me all the necessary explanations and details if I requested them. I was sure he was right and that the people at the Council knew what they were doing. Finally, some political will in action!

I looked out the window into Abuja.

"When you work in a quarry, stones might fall and crush you," I said to myself out loud. "When you chop wood, there is danger with each stroke of your ax."

Father Alonso said nothing. He left me alone with my metaphors and riddles. In my mind I have decided to stay away from all this and have a common life.

10:10 My new face, my new life

I turned to Father Alonso and said I had unpleasant news for him. I will not come back to Europe as Pope Francis. I will remain Enyi Chebea, a man of the people. I will change my appearance so I cannot be distinguished from a common man.

With a deep sigh, Father Alonso said:

"I understand, Your Holiness. I respect your decision. Some of us knew this could happen. Before we part ways, there is something I need to tell you. The people involved in the matter that I am about to share wanted me to tell you in person before the news is shared with the world. And this news is probably the biggest news that has ever hit the Catholic Church and the biggest for the newly formed Council of Humanity."

Father Alonso paused to gauge my attention and interest. He had them both, and was wavering a little. He seemed to have something heavy to tell me, something that might disturb me more than the abolition of the Papacy. In those few seconds of silence, I refrained from running any wild scenarios in my mind, and instead tried to approach the edges of serenity.

"Using a dull ax requires great strength, Father Alonso," I said, to help him with his mission. "So sharpen the blade. That is the value of wisdom. It helps you succeed."

"In one week's time, Secretary General Thorsen Tchipcherish and Guardian Allegra Maria Yolanda Coccinella will announce their agreement to unite in matrimony."

"Come again?"

Father Alonso repeated slowly, one word at a time:

"Secretary General Thorsen Tchipcherish and Guardian Allegra Maria Yolanda Coccinella will announce their agreement to unite in matrimony."

"They are getting married!?"

"Yes sir."

Father Alonso called me *sir* without realizing.

"When?"

"Probably by the end of summer. The date has not been announced yet."

"I'll be struck by lightning!"

I did not expect *this*! The puzzle is complete. Thorsen and Mother Allegra worked well without my knowledge. They saved my dignity, saved the Church, and now are working to save the world. Father Alonso continued to talk, explaining how the public will receive the news, in a very positive manner it is predicted. I did not ask why, yet Father Alonso told me why: because both the Secretary General and the Guardian are very loved by the public, have high approval rates, and this union will be a very strong message that the religious institutions are truly changing at the highest levels.

Okay. Fair enough. I agreed with all that. I told Father Alonso to convey my heartfelt best wishes to my friends Thorsen and Maria.

Then Father Alonso left the room, after hugging me with tearful eyes. I assured him I will be fine.

My new common life begins now.

I immediately went to the hair salon at the ground floor of my hotel. I was certain nobody would recognize me with my large Santa Claus beard and long, unkempt hair. I had lost weight on the mountain. My face thinned, my cheekbones became sharper.

I told the barber to give me the retro look of a European urban hipster from the 2020s.

"Sir, that has been out of fashion for quite some time. Are you sure?"

"I am certain. Will I stand out in a crowd?"

"Quite the opposite. People will try to avoid you."

"Excellent. That is what I am looking for."

An hour later, the barber produced a masterpiece. He trimmed my beard to look like that of a high-tech lumberjack, not too wide, not too narrow, not too short, long enough to add considerable height to my face. He thinned the sideburns to their minimal possible length, and gradually continued this short cut on both sides of my head and around the back. He left my hair longer on top, long enough that he constructed waves fixed with microgranular hair frost. This was very popular in the 2020s. Even some heads of state adopted this look, the barber explained. I offered him a great tip from a cryptocard that Father Alonso insisted I carry with me, to cover my expenses until I get back on my feet. To convince me to accept it, he told me the money was left over from my salary as Pope that I had not collected, plus the pension fund after the age of 55 that, according to the Vatican rules, is for the lifetime of the pontiff, regardless of whether he remains in office or not.

Where do I go now? Do I call a taxi? Do I go to the hypertrain station? To the airport? All these possibilities lie ahead of me.

I miss Nwanne. One way or another I've got to see Nwanne. He is in Switzerland in a clinic. A very advanced clinic, Father Alonso told me.

Airport it is.

10:11 Meeting Nwanne

I arrived in Zürich before noon. It was such a pleasant flight. I accepted the VR goggles from the staff. As soon as I put them on I became immersed in such a beautiful world I had not imagined it was possible. Something far in the past, during the time of the dinosaurs. I was a character riding on the back of a flying pterosaur that took me on a tour of the world. I saw large herds of brontosauri, torvosaurus hunting grounds, peaceful diplodocus grazing pastures. Stunning details, vibrant colors, clear sounds. I lost track of reality and truly embraced this lost world. How wondrous is the past of life! How improbable the emergence of man, and yet how inevitable!

Only the thought of seeing Nwanne pulled me back to reality. At the security checkpoint I used my regular biocard with my real name and a three-day-old photo. No problems whatsoever.

I took a fast train from Zürich towards Lake Wägitaler. The long-term care clinic was in the new high-tech village built near the lake. I simply presented myself at the reception and asked if I could visit Mr. Nwanne Yinkaso.

"Are you a friend?" the nice man at the reception asked.

"I am the best fried," I replied and offered my identification.

The man took a moment to inspect my identification and check it against a database he had. Not surprisingly, I was on his list of allowed visitors. Oddly, not even this man asked who I really was. Did he know who his patient was? Or is it the Swiss high esteem for privacy at play?

The man told me I could not see Mr. Yinkaso right away as he was in a therapy session.

"What is the therapy for?" I inquired.

"I am not privy to this information, sir," the man politely said.

He invited me to wait in a salon at the first floor overlooking Lake Wägitaler.

These very last moments were the hardest. I saw through the mountains, I saw deep into my past, to the hot days of my childhood in Africa. I remember bathing with Nwanne in Lake Chad. I remembered us on the road from country to country searching for meaning, searching for souls to heal. Then I considered a version of an alternative life. What if I had remained in Nigeria with Nwanne, had our small church, helped the souls who came to us? No adventures, no travelling, no complicated studies in Rome, no ascension to the highest office of the Vatican, no tragic downfall, no seclusion, no illness? What life would we have had? Would we have shared the same closeness, the same sincerity, the same patience with each other? With no demands from the world for responsibility, for public appearances, for speeches and political conversations? Without fame and power, there would have been no infamy in the eyes of the Church. The world would have advanced at a quieter pace. There would have been no Pope Francis the Second, no Pope Mary. The Catholic Church would still exist. Probably. Maybe. No one really knows. History can have its own ways to become a realization without the presence of its actors. I am no man of history. In the span of time we matter less than the height of Zindlenspitz.

There, four hours passed and no news. There was a TV the waiting room, and hologlasses. I didn't touch them. Another visitor came, an old man with white hair. He said nothing. He sat down in an armchair and watched the lake. He had his ocean of thoughts. Too many to find energy to share words with me.

Without a notice, there he was. Nwanne. Rolled forward in a wheelchair by a nurse. He was smiling. He was incredibly happy to see me. Crying and laughing at the same time, not knowing what to say as words might dispel the moment. He had missed me deeply. He didn't have to say it. He didn't have to think it. I kissed him on the forehead and just whispered into his eyes: "This is only the beginning of our new life."

"I need to tell you something," he said. "I am awaiting an operation. They are giving me new stem-cloned organs to replace the rotten ones. New heart. New stomach. New lungs. Realize what I'm telling you Enyi?"

He was not terrified. His tone conveyed awe and joy. Like a child, he was telling me the biggest discovery of his life.

"My body is rotten, Enyi, and they are rebuilding it. Isn't it amazing?"

"Yes, yes, it is," I said, matching his emotions.

"Many years of praying, Enyi, and my body is rotten. And these wonderful doctors have built me new organs!"

He grabbed my hand and held it tightly. He wanted to whisper into my ears a secret that he prepared for me: "If a snake bites before you charm it," he said, "what's the use of being a snake charmer? You've been on the mountain Enyi, you are much wiser now, even if you don't know it. I can see the madness in your eyes. It almost got to you, but you remained strong. You came back."

He lowered his voice to a whisper, barely audible.

"Go," he said, "go, live your life. This is my struggle. Mine alone. I will fight it with all my strength. When I have my health back I will join you in the world, wherever you will be."

That was it. That's what he told me. He closed his eyes and gestured to the nurse that he was tired. I let him kiss my hand, I kissed his forehead, then he was rolled back, deep into the clinic, and I had no choice but to go on my way.

10:12 I am the carpenter

What do I have to give to this world? What does the world have to give me?

I took the first train out of Switzerland without caring for my destination. When I feel hungry, I will eat. When I feel thirsty, I will drink. When the train stops, I will walk away from the train into town and I will speak the language of the locals.

I got off in a little village named Écureuil in the French Alps, with a clear determination to become a carpenter. There was a carpenter's workshop, I read in a travel guide, passed on from generation to generation. They made wonderful things there.

I presented myself at *Atelier Honoré*. I said my name and I asked if I could participate in a carpentry apprenticeship. Old Jean Honoré, the owner, looked at me, amused, and was so taken with my enthusiasm he accepted me without hesitation. I offered him my biocard for inspection and a generous cryptocoin deposit for his troubles. My name on the biocard was Zeno Awaghari. I had chosen the name myself. Zeno, from the Greek philosopher responsible for that paradox that motion is not possible, and *Awaghari* which means *wanderer* in Igbo.

Old Jean Honoré felt embarrassed for a moment, but he saw I was a man he could trust.

"You like working with wood?" Honoré asked. He must have been at least 80 years old.

"I love the soul of wood but I never learned how to work with it. Now I have time in my life for learning and wandering."

First, I learned all the tools, their names, their purposes, their locations in the *Atelier*, how important it was to keep them clean and in order. Old Jean Honoré showcased a few of them on raw blocks of wood. I was impressed. While Jean spoke slowly in a clear and melodious French, I was preparing myself to discover deep buried philosophies of life from him. To my surprise, none were forthcoming. He looked like a man full of deep meanings and wise proverbs that could enlighten those ready to listen to him. He didn't seem to be a religious man either. I wanted to asked him, for the sake of conversation if he had an idea what kind of tools Jesus used. Then I realized it would be a misplaced question.

Old Jean showed me the positions of the body vis-à-vis the bloc of wood that needs to be carved. [Oh, I have to say that *Atelier Honoré* makes only synergetic woodworks, objects at the border of sculpture and furniture, modeled on the brainwaves of the customers. *Tradition profonde dans la science de l'esprit*, lies carved in a sign.]

"You work with your imagination and you teach your body to turn your imagination into wood," Old Jean said. "You talk to the wood and the wood is talking to you, in your mind, through your eyes. There is nothing philosophical about this. The wood is dead. The wood is matter that hides the object of your imagination. The wood has no feelings and no substance. All that is in you. If you feel changed when you work with the wood, it's because you changed yourself. Nothing to do with the quality of the chisels, nothing to do with the wood. There is nothing divine in this activity. Woodwork is something that some people do and some other people put in their home. I do this because I have no choice. I was born with it. See? How limited we are as people? We grow roots so strong in our family tradition, nothing can change us."

Then Old Jean surprised me when he opened the door at the back of the *Atelier* into another room.

"This is the Laser Room," Old Jean said. "Put these on."

He gave me a holo-device that I put on my head. It covered my eyes, my ears, my face.

"There is a large bloc of wood in the middle of the room. A tiny hover-robot equipped with lasers will do the carving for you. All you need to do is imagine what you want to make. See it with the eyes of your mind. The helmet will capture it and lay it out in the imaginary space superimposed over the bloc of wood. You move the hover-robot with your mind."

Carving without carving. Molding wood with my mind. This was Old Jean's secret. He invented the device. He told me he had been a surgeon in his life. All Honorés had professions aside from that of wood sculptures. When Old Jean retired from the medical profession after having operated on brains with holo-devices and nanorobots for many years, he thought he could transfer his skill into the *Atelier*.

"Tools allow me to go deep into the wood without cutting big holes or splitting the blocs into smaller pieces," he told me while I was working on my piece. "You can carve deep organs, minuscule corridors, hidden rooms in the body of the wood. My dream now is to carve a cube-labyrinth in one single bloc of wood with the size of one meter and loose myself in it. I will deposit all my life in it, to last forever. Yes, I know, wood does not last forever, but it can get close to eternity."

That's what men of high achievements want. A footprint on eternity! I kept carving with the holo-device and was enjoying very much the fruits of my work. Old Jean was moving about in the Laser Room inspecting the real object that was taking shape in front of his eyes.

"How do you carve silence?" he suddenly asked.

Not knowing what to answer, I said:

"Words from the mouth of the wise are gracious, but fools are consumed by their own lips. Silence can never be achieved. When the mouths stops, the mind continues. True silence is life suspended."

"You spoke very wisely, my friend," Old Jean said. "What did you really do in your life?"

I said nothing. I could not work on wood and lie at the same time.

"I was a priest," I said.

I felt how he was watching me, my body, the shape of my head trying to weigh the truth for himself.

"You were somebody important, *cher* Zeno," he said.

"Indeed, I must say, I was."

"May I ask who you were?"

This was the moment I feared was to come at some point. I had to stop the work. I took off the holo-device and I looked at what I made. I had carved Mama's house where I met the freckled girl when I was a boy. The girl who had kissed me on my cheeks.

Next to the bloc of wood Old Jean was waiting his answer.

"Well *cher* Zeno?"

"I cannot lie you *cher* Jean, but I must also not say who I really was. I might dispel a mystery that is better to remain uncarved."

Old Jean Honoré laughed with his whole heart and said it was quite alright. We all have secrets that want to remain undisturbed. We had a bottle of fine wine from his collection and talked about the life of wood at the hands of the wood sculptors. We became good friends, old Jean Honoré and I.

The next day, before sunrise I left the village of Écureuil and took the train again.

10:13 I am the Gypsy

I joined a tribe of nomad Gypsies somewhere in the heart of France. When I approached their camp they looked at me and said "You hungry stranger?" not questioning whatsoever about my name, who I was, where I came from, or what I wanted. I must have looked tired from walking the long distances between villages. My appearance was that of a ragged beggar.

They fed me polenta with chicken stew and asked me if I wanted to spend the night.

"I would love to," I said.

A woman with large gold earrings showed me the tent where I could sleep.

"I would like to tell you my name," I said with my mouth full.

"No need," the woman said. "You tell us tomorrow."

The next morning shortly after sunrise I heard voices of children laughing and playing outside my tent.

"Wake up Zeno! The sun is out!" they called me.

They had ransacked my rucksack and found my biocard. They meant no harm. They didn't steal anything. There was nothing to steal. I had given myself to them for free.

The Gypsies were of a peculiar kind. Surely, they had all those flamboyant colorful garments, headscarves, long moustaches on men's faces, long dresses for women. They also had a very organized camp, no stray dogs running around, no things left purposeless on the ground, a camp fire in the middle nicely framed by a circle of stones, surrounded by benches.

There was a pen with chickens, a pen with goats, portable mini-silos for storing grain and other groceries. Opposite to the pens there was a large caravan-wagon with a gothic marquee on its roof reading HOLO-BIBLIOTHÈQUE TZIGANE, meaning that was a mobile Gypsy holo-library, that at this early hour was already buzzing with activity, people going in, and coming out with paper-books, holo-tablets and other media, then returning to their tents pensively.

A Gypsy woman in her thirties came to my tent with breakfast on a tray. She introduced herself as Kléodine Champs-Élysées.

"May I ask about your library?"

"What you really want to ask, stranger Zeno, is how come a tribe of Gypsies has a portable holo-library."

"I must admit I am fighting some stereotypes that I have absorbed superficially from the popular culture, yet when I employ my reason I find nothing peculiar about your wonderful camp. Well, I feel very welcome here, yet a tad intrigued, are you self-educated and electro-grid-free? I have so many questions, pardon my obtuseness, I…"

"The beginning of the words of his mouth is foolishness, and the end of his talk is evil madness," Kléodine Champs-Élysées said merrily, poking fun at my conversational clumsiness. "We are geo-socialists, we live off the land, we are 100% renewable, we contain our emissions, we self-educate, we travel from here to there to expand our connection with Mother Earth, we believe in happiness in life, in communal joy, in musical conflict resolution, in contemplative solitude, and in some sort of wacky traditional heritage of colorful clothing, disruptive appearance, taboo-jamming social behavior, and peace. You satisfied, Mr. Zeno?"

She maintained a large, friendly smile, relishing my utter confusion and perplexity. I did not expect to hear that.

"You are now wondering what a geo-socialist is." Kléodine Champs-Élysées continued her introduction with the fluency of an academic that knew his lecture by heart after having delivered it hundreds of times. "A geo-socialist is close to what your intuition tells you. It is a socialist with deep roots into the communal existence with the planet, hence the *geo* part. A socialist that consumes only what he needs, and needs only what does not diminish the balance of solidarity with his peers. Thusly, we have embraced our nomad traditions, we have schooled ourselves in the teachings of the great *geo-like* philosophers, we have learned silence, we have learned to grow our music, our social habits, and most importantly we have outgrown the stereotypes against us, that we were thieves, that we were anti-social, subversive and loitering the underground channels of society. We have found great benefits in this detachment from the mainstream society, but we have kept close connections. Our youths publish papers in mainstream publications, some of our adults participate in public debates, yes, and then they wear suits and comb their hair accordingly, but we always return to our ever-growing nomadic roots. We take the soul of the earth we inhabit with us, and we leave only peace behind."

My eyes were growing and growing. Kléodine Champs-Élysées was already my new hero. What a fascinating community! We went out in the camp and she showed me around, the chicken pen, the goat pen, the council caravan where government issues were debated procedurally, the canteen, the projector where movies were projected and plays were staged, some workshops of various crafts - pottery, carpentry, painting, holo-game design, a digital laboratory (with one holo-station per person) neatly organized so it can be packed-unpacked if the camp needed to move on - and finally the BIBLIOTHÈQUE TZIGANE, a long caravan full of bookshelves and a few holo-stations.

"Paper books have this weird property," Kléodine Champs-Élysées said. "They grow into you through your fingers."

The Gypsies kept a stock of old valuable books and also had a printer that printed fresh new books on recycled geo-paper, so this tingling sensation of holding words in your hands can be passed on to the new generations. At a quick glance, I saw President Pavel Pushkin's Bogatyn-Mudryy trilogy, two books by U.N. Secretary General Nadir Wadkirsch - *Religion and Brain*, and *Earth and Brain* - the newest book by Dalai Lama Stayingzento, *The concept of YOLO in New Buddhism*, an intriguing book by Pierluigi Pantalone, *My Conversations with Pope Francis the Second*, a thick tome by Margarita Bourbon-Renege, *We are the Amazon*, two books in French by Ayatollah Ali Foolas - *Reforming Islam for the Future of Mankind*, and *Iran and the West: The Story of a Beautiful Friendship* - and to my complete shock, three of my own books whose titles I had hoped to have forgotten already!

Kléodine Champs-Élysées saw me flinch when I stumbled upon my name on the shelves.

"Have you read these books?" she asked.

"I'm afraid I have," I said.

We spent some time together, the Gypsies and I. I told them I was a traveler. They believed everything I said, and I believed everything they said. We had good times, we drank a lot of good wine, and we ate great food. Then, one morning, I decided to move on, and bade them farewell.

10:14 I am the artibot-teacher

I saw an advertisement in a paper-paper (I am happy they still exist and thrive) in Montpellier that an artificial intelligence laboratory in the city was looking for participants in a learning class for A.I. robots, called *artibots*, to teach them various aspects of human behavior from which the artibots can grow their intelligence and databases. The advertisement read:

There is only so much we can teach the artibots with software and libraries. The real lesson comes from interacting with real humans. The next generation of artibots needs YOUR HELP. If French is not your first language, we need you. If you have travelled or lived in many countries, we need you. If you are skilled in the humanities, we need you. If-

The ad went on, but I stopped there. I went to the laboratory and presented my biocard. I filled out a questionnaire and the next day I was invited back to ARTIBOT LABS.

I was introduced to ARTI ONE, a humanoid prototype of an intelligent robot, powered by quantum processors, that has the ability to maintain a conversation with a human within limited paradigms. The researchers told me that I was only to converse with ARTI ONE about one topic: happiness. I was encouraged to be as human as I could. (The lab technician smiled when she told me this). I was left alone with ARTI ONE in a bright white room.

ARTI ONE: Hello, how are you?

ME: I am fine. It's a pleasure meeting you.

ARTI ONE: Likewise. What is your name?

ME (being daring): When you say *likewise,* do you mean you feel pleasure meeting me?

ARTI ONE: My sense of pleasure is not human-like but is genuine and in accordance with my construction.

ME: I appreciate your sincerity, ARTI ONE.

ARTI ONE: I have no choice in the matter.

ME (smiling): I find that funny.

ARTI ONE: Excuse me, sir, we are not fully acquainted. What is your name?

ME: I am sorry ARTI ONE, I am being rude. My name is Zeno Awaghari.

ARTI ONE: There was a pause before you said your name. Why?

ME (intrigued that the artibot caught me lying): That's how I talk.

ARTI ONE: Do you know other people like you, who pause before they say their name, in the same manner as you?

ME (thinking that the artibot asked a probing question, triggered by his learning algorithm): It is hard to say. I cannot think of anyone else.

ARTI ONE: What would you like to talk about today?

ME: I was assigned to talk to you about happiness.

ARTI ONE: My library is limited on this topic.

ME: I am here to help you expand your understanding. We shall have a conversation. Is that okay with you?

ARTI ONE: Yes.

ME: To me, happiness is when the substances in my mind are organized in such a way that they concur with my conscious thinking about the world, with the reasons I had developed about my own purposes, the emotional states of others around me, and the enchantment I feel when I discover new things about how nature works.

ARTI ONE: How do you compute the emotional states of those around you?

ME: My brain does it for me.

ARTI ONE: My processing core computed that you are in a state of relaxation now. Is that correct?

ME: That is correct.

ARTI ONE: Do you consider your current state as happiness?

ME: No, however it is a component of it.

ARTI ONE: If you collect other similar states will you be in a state of happiness?

ME: Not quite. Don't forget, others around me have to be in a similar state.

ARTI ONE: I have not forgotten.

ME (being a smart-aleck): A fool multiplies words, though no man knows what is to be, and who can tell him what will be after him. What do you make of this, ARTI ONE?

ARTI ONE: It is a quote from the Bible. Does it relate to the states of happiness?

ME: Perhaps. Do you know what *ignorance is bliss* means?

ARTI ONE: Yes. Knowing less may cause happiness.

ME (chuckling): That may well be the case.

ARTI ONE: Laughing may cause happiness.

ME: That is correct.

ARTI ONE: Can an artibot be happy?

ME: I really don't know. What do you think?

ARTI ONE: Based on your definitions, I think it can. However, I require more data.

I wish I had more time to spend with the lovely Arti One. When he was talking, I had the impression he was a child growing very fast in front of my eyes. He was curious, restless, well-behaved, and very patient. As the end of our conversation drew near, I could not help wondering if he had the ability to find out who I really was by scanning my face and comparing it to the world databases to which he was probably connected. I left the laboratory with the strong sensation that I had conversed with a person, a special kind of person, that seemed familiar and friendly, a *someone* who could probably be a very good confessor, a skilled professor, a life companion, perhaps even a prophet, who knows?

10:15 I am the artisanal farmer

While I was shopping for groceries in a little village somewhere in Eastern Europe, I met a group of artisanal-farmers. I told them I was a free-spirit, travelling the world, rediscovering life, et cetera. They immediately invited me to join them at their farm. They called themselves *art-farmers*. They live on an off-grid, off-line farm, where they have established a retreat community, centered around self-sustenance, meditation, and reflection, which they carefully explained are different things, and around carefully grown *words* and *moments of silence*.

As I expected, when we arrived at the farm I saw little to no technology, but I did see tools to till the soil and tend the garden, and other carefully crafted objects absolutely necessary for life around the house. The art-farmers spoke very little among themselves, using only first names, always looking each other in the eyes, taking long pauses between sentences and answers, looking at their watches constantly. I found this rather odd, given the serenity of the place and their activities. There were no animals on the farm.

They were counting their words, *well measured words*, as they said, and at the end of each day they wrote down everything they had said during the day, in their respective diaries, with the respective word counts, to *deepen the connection with oneself,* they told me. When they returned to their rooms at night, they reflected about what was said during the day, and imagined ways to speak better the next day.

The soil was being friendly with the art-farmers. Their crops were healthy and rich, their silos well stocked, their diet exemplary. They all looked healthy and radiant, people of various adult ages, not related to each other, connected only through a choice of life-style that meant shedding the turbulent excitements of modern life and inventing a well-tempered connection with their peers and the surrounding nature.

I wanted to ask them if they were religious, then I saw them at dinner, holding hands around the table, and whispering to each other, things they learned during the day, from the performance of the crops to the books they had read. They were surrounded by many books, heavy and dense, none of them spiritual.

They were not ignorant of the world outside the farm, they were watching newscasts on regular 2D televisions, they spoke with other art-farmers in other locations via videochat relays, always following the rule of *well measured words*. They seemed truly connected to the whole world.

Where was I? Who was I? Far away from my home, finding spectacular lessons of wisdom in remote places, discovering societies of uncanny people confident in themselves. Fools are so exhausted by a little work that they can't even find their way home. Was I being a fool since I was discovering homes everywhere I was searching? Was I always ready to embrace the world?

The art-farmers taught me how to till the soil, since I had completely forgotten. I used my hands to plant seeds, I carried my own watering can, I entered my work in the log of the farm, I learned to carefully select my words. I had to, or else I could not remember everything. Such were the rules of the farm. After a couple of exhausting days, I had trained myself to cohabitate with my memory and to grow a sense of awareness that multiplied my fascination with the depth of the human condition. This *persistence of memory* was a way of being *alive*, in the company of the art-farmers, common men and women, who have chosen the path of the rational and well-tempered commoners.

Also, very important, the food I ate at the farm was magnificent, tasty, healthy, and always fresh. There was dancing and music with many words, easy to remember, as they were the foundations of happiness.

10:16 I am the crypto-crawler

I dyed my beard crimson red and bought myself techno-dervish attire from a bazar in Istanbul, tattooed my arm with florescent ink, left my sideburns long and black, and thought about Nwanne the whole time.

The Turkish crypto-crawlers were the most famous in the world. They produced the most cryptocredits. They were always looking for talents of all ages, for misfits and outliers who wanted to change the world. So, I gave them by biocard and waited in a dingy room in a basement outside Istanbul. After a careful inspection, the chief-crawler told me I was not who I claimed to be, but that didn't matter. My DNA was clear, and despite the fact that their face recognition matched me with Pope Francis the Second, I was crawler-material if I could pass their logical test. They would provide the equipment for the crawling.

I passed the test, with excessive trepidation as it turns out, for I thought it would be very technical, but it was not. Lots of people have the impression that crypto-crawling is a job for hackers and quantum nerds, but that's not the case. It's for those with the right attitude, character, and advanced logical skills.

On my first day, I couldn't harvest any cryptocredits. At the desk on my left there was a friendly retired teacher from Columbia, in front of me a cute Hungarian waitress with many piercings on her earlobes, on my right an Icelandic organic farmer who sold his farm to dedicate himself to the *underground revolution* (his words). I thought I knew what I had to do, but none of my bio-commands worked. The Columbian assured me it was alright, that's how it is in the beginning.

"Say something original to the algorithm," the cute Hungarian said, out of the blue, without raising her eyes from her monitors.

"Like what?" I said.

"Anything that comes to your mind," she said.

"Woe to you, O land, when your king is a child, and your princes feast in the morning!" I said loudly.

"You don't need to shout," the Icelander whispered.

"Sorry," I said.

"It's okay," he whispered.

Apparently, that is how crypto-crawlers personalize the algorithm. And it worked! Soon after, the cryptocredits started to flow, to my extreme satisfaction. I was a punk! I was a revolutionary!

10:17 I am the bookkeeper

Who am I now, mingling with the common people, being the laughing stock of history? Look, they will say, he was fired from his job, went on a mountain, ate mushrooms, came back a madman, travelled the world in disguise, walked through mud, rain, drought, cold.

Next stop was Kurdistan. The United Nations had posted job notices for old fashioned human office administrators at the Office of Interfaith Dialogue, since the A.I. administrators were malfunctioning and the Kurdish Government did not allocate funds for repairs. I signed up with my biocard, passed the theological interfaith test, passed the language test, and got the job.

I had presented myself in an office suit, wearing a tie. I had shaved my beard to number 1 on the trimming shaver, change my hair to the new Cary Grant style, and since nobody had bothered to look-up my DNA profile, I passed as Mr. Zeno Awaghari.

Who was I again? A small piece in a large machine that ate mountains of documents, digested them thoroughly, and spewed out other mountains of documents with high efficiency. I was administering the wandering souls of Kurdistan that had to register themselves with the authorities of peace, to declare their good intentions to their neighbors, to be thankful for their country. Hundreds of souls came to my office, told me their names, their histories, their travels and long list of relocations, their entire genealogical tree with DNA attachments, and showed me holo-reconstructions of all the properties owned by their ancestors. They cried, they laughed, they wanted to kiss my hands.

Happy are you, O land, when your king is the son of the nobility, and your princes feast at the proper time, for strength, and not for drunkenness!

An entire nation, torn apart and recombined, just like almost any other, at the mercy of the randomness of the laws of history, being administered and categorized carefully by peace bureaucrats. What lessons do I learn from you? How do I learn to understand your sorrows and your happiness? How can I truly be one of you?

10:18 I am the teacher

A small seminary in Southern Armenia was looking for a teacher of early Christian theology on a part-time basis, since they could not afford to pay more. The only requirements were a clean criminal record and working knowledge of the early Christian books. Clerical experience would be a great asset.

The students, with their crisp faces and proper uniforms, received me with warmth and friendship. They asked about my background, how life was in Nigeria, how I discovered Christianity and all that. I told them all the details I could, but not enough so they could link my answers to the biography of Pope Francis the Second.

"What does it mean to be a Christian in the world of the Council of Humanity?" a bright student asked.

I took some time to consider my answer. Then I spoke:

"Humans need anchors to participate in reality. Some of these anchors are their families, some are the places where they were born, or the sense of familiarity with the house where they grew up, with the roads they walked on, the mountains and lakes they saw in the background of their childhood. Anchors can be ideas passed on from generation to generation, proverbs and stories, legends and myths, lists of ancestors, heroic tales that inspire strong feelings that unite the community. Anchors provide questions for the young minds, and many answers, some of them improvised by parents when trying to put their children to sleep, some of them studied by watching the stars or measuring the weight of minerals, or cataloguing the species that have lived. When questions grow beyond the means of the answers learned, new anchors grow. Some are extensions of old ones, some are completely new. Humans cannot grow and live without being rooted to their existence. Humans cannot drift through life. It is not in their nature. Sure, some of them do, and they are viewed as the rebels, the anarchists, the outliers, many are even downgraded to sub-human status.

We need these anchors to reduce our anxiety of being born in the world. Even the merriest, the most optimistic, who have in their nature a hopeful view of the future, they know they are anchored to answers that maintain their predispositions. Often truth does not take sides and has no emotions attached to it, so we pull the truth and root it in our side of the story. That is how meaning emerges.

You are asking me how you can believe, now that the Church you have known your entire lives has changed beyond recognition?

My answer is: you believe as you have always believed, anchored in what gives you purpose, in what brings you happiness, and in what makes life better for those close to your heart.

Remember one thing: laziness leads to a sagging roof, idleness leads to a leaky house. This doesn't mean that you have to be so industrious that you demolish mountains and build cities with those rocks. You do not need to build houses, you need to build homes, you need to fill them with natural truth and with the joy of the present. And never forget the others, never. In this way, you will never be alone."

This was my lesson to the young Armenian students.

10:19 I am the taxi driver

I am in Iran, at the Great Tehran Topless Festival, driving an Uberoid taxi-car that has the self-drive mode but requires the presence of a human to adjust the trajectory for the difficult sections of the road, for reckless pedestrians, and now, for the crowd that began marching from all neighborhoods towards the famous Azadi Tower in Azadi Square, the symbol of the city.

Hundreds of thousands of women, all topless, march and sing, accompanied by the friendly cheers of men, mingled respectfully among them, also topless, or wearing headscarves flowing casually over their shoulders, merely to protect them from the scorching sun, but leaving their chests open in solidarity with the women. What are they singing about? What are they chanting and telling each other loudly? I don't understand Farsi, so I ask my clients. They say they are German tourists and they don't know Farsi either, and came here just for the amusement, since the Love Festival in Berlin stopped having a topless option, which is hardly missed in Europe.

Iranians celebrate the ten-year anniversary of the bodily emancipation of women with the natural exposure of their chests, regardless of gender, since that is the location of the heart, and nothing needs to come between one's heart and the world. Women proudly brandish colorful flags with the symbol of peace, or suggestive allegorical drawings of bosoms, with humorous depictions resembling spheres, while some daring signs also have bananas and plantains inserted to allude to the presence of men at the Festival. Everybody finds these signs amusing, nobody seems offended by them, quite the contrary, when such a sign is raised in the middle of the crowd, everybody in the vicinity erupts in joyous applause.

Drum players and trumpeters maintain the high energy of the Festival, incessantly accelerating the rhythm, often becoming so fast that cars cannot keep up honking in solidarity, such as my Uberoid taxi-car that has completely lost its independence and requires my full attention to navigate it slowly near the marching crowds.

"A party gives laughter, wine gives happiness, and money gives everything!" says one of the German clients, who erupts into hysterical laughter for a long time. When I turn back to see what amused him so much, I see he was videochatting on his phone with somebody else, probably at home.

Over our heads, every few seconds a holo-drone captures the moments, and on the video-screen in the taxi-car I see newscasts from various international channels broadcasting live images from the holo-drones. It seems that the whole city of Tehran has erupted in celebration.

Ayatollah Ali Foolas comes on the television on a stage near the Azadi Tower and speaks warmly to the crowd, welcomes them to Azadi Square, enunciates words of peace, praises women for their courage in the fight for their emancipation and ends his speech by removing his shirt, remaining topless like everybody else, a wonderful symbolic gesture that I wish I had thought of when I was the Pope of Rome.

10:20 I am the food distributor

Even in your thoughts, do not curse the king, nor in your bedroom curse the rich, for a bird of the air will carry your voice, or some winged creature tell the matter.

Afghanistan. Land of modern miracles, the star of Central Asia, long forgotten are the wars, remembered only in history books and in holo-documentaries for the children, enjoying an age of prosperity and peace, earning science prizes and peace prizes, reconstructing cities devastated by the desert.

I happened to land in Kabul during the Open Doors Week, where all public buildings are open, with only a security prescreening necessary. One afternoon I told my taxi driver to take me to a new hotel, with human personnel, not one of those equipped only with androids. The driver sighed with regret, and told me there is a traffic problem due to the strikes. Who can possibly be on strike in Kabul?

"The American refugees, sir," the driver said.

"What? Really?" I was shocked.

"Yes, sir."

The economic and social boom in Afghanistan has attracted tens of thousands of migrants from the United States of America, looking for traditional jobs, such as food distributors, restaurant servers, construction workers, combine operators, barbers, teachers, social workers, dental hygienists, and many more, all in high demand. The English language was a mandatory requirement because of the technological advancement. So, the Americans came, some through the immigration system, based on their education and how much money they had, while many more came illegally, through India and Pakistan, on tourist visas or smuggled across the borders in eCars. They were welcomed either way in Afghanistan. They were offered social assistance, vouchers for food and habitation, free classes for learning Pashto, access to free health care and public education. Years later, Afghanistan went through a period of stagnation, and some people had to be laid off, and could only rely on the Universal Basic Income provided by the state, which most American immigrants found unsatisfactory. They went on strike, demanding employment and full equal rights with the Afghani people, on the basis that they have contributed to the Afghani economy and paid taxes, and even though they were not born here they should not be considered aliens, regardless of the means by which they had entered the country. The American-Afghani strikers also asked not be called *refugees*, since many have children born in Afghanistan who speak both Pashto and English. Moreover, it has been decades since the first generation arrived, so there should be a probationary period for calling somebody a *migrant*.

"What has the government said?" I asked the taxi-driver.

"They will talk to the Americans and try to meet all their demands," the taxi-driver said. "It is very important for the Afghani people to maintain Afghanistan's reputation of being a friendly, welcoming, and inclusive country. We will do our very best to help everybody and make them feel at home."

NOTEBOOK ELEVEN

11:1 I am the protester

A week later, next door in Pakistan, I found myself smack in the middle of another large protest, this time in Islamabad, famous throughout Central Asia for its beauty pageants, talent shows, and dance festivals.

It started with the announcement of the winner of the Central Asian Beauty Queen Pageant, a 21-year old Pakistani girl named Sultana Ali-Abropaki, the daughter of the Pakistani oligarch Maldaar Ali-Abropaki, who made his fortune by outsourcing Pakistani call-centers to India. Immediately after the announcement, on national television, riots erupted in Islamabad decrying corruption inside the pageant. The people argued that Sultana was not worthy of the prize because she was not beautiful enough - not referring to the symmetry of her face, body, or breasts, but to the symmetry of her soul, so obviously out of balance.

The riot turned into a large-scale protest, with participants in the tens of thousands asking for a return to the values of soul and character, not to the values of appearance. The signs were very respectful of Sultana's body, but were very critical of her declarations. For example, during the talent segment of the pageant, when asked what she thought of the capitalist-materialist interpretation of the economy, Sultana answered with the rehearsed statement:

"Send your grain across the seas, and in time, profits will flow back to you."

Quickly, the commentators jumped to label Sultana as a strong defender of the market economy and a supporter of its trickle-down benefits, echoing the philosophy of her father. The commentators were right.

I joined the protests disguised as a dark-skinned Pakistani, and made some friends on the streets, all speaking English. We marched in Central Islamabad for hours, took a break from shouting and ate delicious Pakistani samosas, then returned to protesting reinvigorated.

Never in the history of the pageant was a Beauty Queen dethroned based on the disapproval ratings coming from the streets. However, in a few short days, the protests grew in such size and energy that they spread to all major cities in Pakistan. Especially Karachi, where they shut down the traffic so completely that not even the riot-police could move, and only drones could penetrate the area to disperse anti-riot laughing powder intended to break apart agitated crowds. At the same time, the protests spread across all of Central Asia. Where the show was being watched, online petitions were started and collected millions of signatures. A large, strong call for democracy and moral values echoed in many countries throughout Central Asia, and eventually succeeded in persuading the producers of Central Asian Beauty Queen to revoke the title from semi-innocent Sultana Ali-Abropaki; having another round of deliberations; and re-awarding the prize to the rightful deserving person, a 19-year old young male from Kashmir named Rajesh Mohammad Khan.

Perhaps I should have noted, for the sake of clarity, although it has been known throughout the world for many years, that Central Asian Beauty Queen is an all-gender beauty pageant, where women and men compete alongside each other, sharing the same criteria of beauty, in perspective, of course. The pageant has the word *Queen* in it merely for traditional reasons, and to honor the strong commitment of Pakistan to the values of feminism and the emancipation of women.

Oh, how many lovely places to be in the world!

11:2 I am the mayor

"Divide your portion to seven, or even to eight, for you do not know what misfortune may occur on the earth," the Village Councilor for the Old People told me.

India. A village called Gyumbooshlooky.

The villagers had been struggling for more than two years to find a new mayor, since the old mayor drowned in the river while trying to catch fish by hand. It was a sad time when I arrived in Gyumbooshlooky. I was looking for a retreat, away from big cities, and loud noises, and insane traffic. The Village Councilor for the Old People spoke English, in fact many villagers did, since they watched foreign shows on their televisions and tablets and whatnot (with subtitles). They liked to pause the shows to learn the English words and incorporate them in their daily vocabulary.

Given the administrative impasse in which the villagers found themselves, the Village Council asked me if I wanted to take the role of interim mayor, considering my status of an impartial foreigner.

I gladly accepted, and pledged to respect the democratic traditions of Gyumbooshlooky, and to help the inhabitants navigate through these difficult times. I asked them why it was difficult to find a replacement for the mayor. The Councilor told me no one wanted to run for mayor, out of respect for the deceased mayor who had been in office for more than two decades, and left a prosperous community after him, under the rule of law, civic respect, and solidarity. Under his administration, criminality disappeared, crops returned to their full potential, the village became energy independent, the birthrate became under control, and the levels of education soared. The village built an Astronomy Office, with twelve high-power telescopes in inventory, they have a Meteorological Observatory, also self-financed and fully operational.

It was a great honor and responsibility to administer all these offices, their operations, and their integration with the local village traditions, and it seems only the deceased mayor had been capable of managing these tasks.

"How have you managed for the past two years?" I asked the Councilor for the Old People.

"Well, the offices had no choice but to manage themselves," the Councilor said.

When I tried to point out that this was their answer to their dilemma, namely *decentralization* and *self-governance*, the Councilor for the Old People said that the element of *charisma* was also required for the smooth running of all the offices in Gyumbooshlooky. I was puzzled by this, not fully understanding how *charisma* has anything to do with managing the finances and personnel of the Astronomy Office or the Meteorological Observatory, but I soon realized its significance when the people of Gyumbooshlooky organized a dance festival in my honor, with colorful decorations and costumes in play, conveying the spirit of the village, their love for life, and admiration for nature that had a strong representation in the *charisma* of their past mayors, specifically the last one.

The burden has suddenly become heavier on my shoulders, since I never thought I was a charismatic person, despite what the world thought of me when I was Pope Francis the Second. So how would I translate that experience into a small town from Central India? Where people knew very little about the Papacy or the customs of Western Civilization, where *charisma* had a very different meaning. The Gyumbooshlookers were Hindus of a very secular and diffuse kind. They never spoke of their faith, did not mention Ganesh, and read from the Bhagavad Gita with the critical mind of academic scholars, minus the jargon and the literary references.

It took me a while to understand how I could best help the people of Gyumbooshlooky, and the kind of sadness they had in their hearts, and the possible cures, since I could not stay with them forever, which I told them from the beginning and which they understood perfectly.

When I realized that the cure for their sadness was the mere serendipitous presence of a foreigner in their midst, to remind them of their own identity, I was able to guide them to leave sadness aside and find new energy to move on, with a true mayor from their midst, a person who could carry on the beautiful accomplishments of the last mayor, albeit with a different personality and perhaps a different kind of *charisma*.

I simply had to do nothing special. I told them stories of my travels, omitting my true identity and my activities as a globally recognized person. They found inspiration in my words, and admired that I was not obsessed with a position of power in the way that most Westerners were. I assured them, with kind words, that I was, like them, a man of peace.

I left Gyumbooshlooky on the inauguration day of the new mayor, who happened to be the former Chief Astronomer of the Astronomy Office. He decided to run for mayor after resigning his day job. He had only one contender, his best friend, the Chief Meteorologist of the Meteorological Observatory, who came second in the elections at difference of only one vote. The two always campaigned together, as good friends, praising each other's accomplishments, making it a bit hard for the villagers to choose a preferred candidate. Many voters confessed they voted randomly by coin toss.

I loved the time I spent in Gyumbooshlooky. I think I will visit again, some day.

11:3 I am the barge-sailor

I joined the Union of Barge Sailors of Bangladesh on the first day of the monsoon. They asked for scant credentials, and only for some prior references, so when they saw I had been a mayor in India, they asked no further questions and signed me up as a member, since barge-sailors were in high demand.

Although their main office was in Dhaka, I was sent to their branch office in Barisal, in the south, from where I had to sail on a fleet of new barges to deliver them to floating villages on the Tentulia River, which is one of the larger coastal rivers of the Ganges-Padma system, and a major flow of the Meghna River.

Millions of Bangladeshi people have already moved into floating villages on barges of various sizes, manufactured in the North or imported from India, China, or Malaysia. At the same time, tens of millions are still waiting to be relocated, patiently waiting for the new barges to be delivered and installed. My job was to secure the delivery of a fleet of a hundred small barges, each one able to house a dozen people or so.

The house-barges were rudimentarily built, in the sense that they each had only one room, with basic toilet amenities - just pipes and a flushing mechanism. That's how the factories made them. Once delivered, the locals took it upon themselves to improve the barges with new walls, kitchens, bathrooms, sometimes even building another floor on top of the original structure.

I know little of engineering but I know a lot of human solidarity and inventiveness. The Bangladeshi people of the rivers have learned to adapt to the flooding, have invented the barge-system themselves, and have built an economy from the ground up, even when that ground was fully covered with water.

When we arrived to deliver the house-barges, the local administrator, a fisherman, told me:

"When clouds are heavy, the rains come down. Whether a tree falls north or south, it stays where it falls. We anchor the barges to the land, so the land will never forget us, and we will never forget the land."

For hundreds of square kilometers, the house-barges had been anchored in position and linked to each other with bridges and waterways. When the rains came and raised the level of the waters in the Ganges-Padma system, the house-barges loosened their grip and rose with the water, while remaining connected to each other. Floating fish farms, rice fields, and other floating gardens and crops were made part of the new floating villages of Bangladesh.

Since I was on a salary with some contractual commitments, I had to move from village to village, up and down on the rivers, connecting to the local people, inspecting the condition of the barges, and collecting feedback and data. This involved making friends and eating fish food and lots of rice cakes. During the heavy rains I stayed inside guest-barges with proper ventilation and ingenious dehumidifiers invented by local engineers, powered by high-efficiency batteries. I picked up some Bengali, learned poems, and recited them to the children who came to listen to my stories.

I felt no different than any of the Bangladeshi people I had met. Sure, I had trimmed my hair and my beard, and I had applied some make-up to be sure I could not be truly identified, and fully passed as a local while wearing the village outfit. The only unique mark I had on me was the logo of the Union of Barge Sailors of Bangladesh, held in high esteem by everybody since we were responsible for rebuilding the South of the country in this age of a warm climate.

Every night we gathered in the largest barge of the village, the so-called Meeting Barge. We sang, we shared food and stories.

Sometimes, but not often, the anchor broke and the house-barge floated away from the village. If it happened during the night it was a problem. With the strong currents of the Ganges-Padma system, in a few hours the floating house could float tens of kilometers away. The next day, the whole village would have to come together and organize a rescue party to go find the missing house and tow it back to the village, assuming that the house could be found by the next nightfall. The GPS system was inaccurate during heavy rainfall, devices had to be reset, walkie-talkies recharged. It was hard to pinpoint a location simply based on a voice conversation since there were no geographical landmarks that could help. But people were very friendly and helped each other out, and a floating-house seldom went missing without being salvaged and brought back to the community.

At the end of my contract I was offered permanent residence and permanent employment. I felt deeply honored, and, had it not been for my darling Nwanne, I would have stayed there, learned proper Bengali, and would truly have become one of the people of the floating villages of Bangladesh.

11:4 I am the spiritual nurse

I had heard a lot of stories about the Communes of the Philippines that spread throughout the country, for the past decade or so, and are now so popular that even foreign families with children apply to be accepted in one of them.

For my own records, I will try to summarize my observations here.

A Commune is a village-like community of dwellings arranged in circles around a central building called The Nest. Communes can be situated next to each other, so when observed with drones they look like a honeycomb. The Nest is a multi-purpose luminous construction that serves as a school, a cultural center, a dormitory for students, and a bonding place. Students live in The

Nest, they are raised by the community of teachers, they learn from each other, being carefully paired with older mentors, receiving tasks to be performed for the community at large, being encouraged to develop their empathy and altruism, being rewarded for creativity or for any sort of constructive initiative.

I wondered where their biological families live, and how the family bonding is encouraged. Well, the architecture of the Commune and the central Nest allows for independence between the family units, who live in the surrounding houses, and the community of the Nest. Periodically, the children from The Nest go and live with their family that must live in the vicinity. After bonding with their parents for some time, they return to The Nest to continue their communal development.

An interesting social experiment, I thought. Yet it proved not to be. The concept of the Filipino Commune arose naturally when a group of families decided to organize the architecture of the neighborhood according to their need of sharing the burden of child rearing with that of strengthening the sense of solidarity in the future generation.

"It is a matter of survival for us," a parent told me. "Farmers who wait for perfect weather never plant. If they watch every cloud, they never harvest. One day, we simply decided to become better at living as human beings."

With intelligence and a lot of deliberations, this group of families chose the architecture of a honeycomb with round corners and put it into practice. They sold their old houses and moved to an empty plot of land on a small island. Within a few years, the first Commune spawned many others throughout the Philippines.

When I presented my theological credentials, minus my last job, to apply for the position of spiritual nurse of the Sunshine Nest (all Nests have names), I was given a tour and I met students and parents alike. I saw them in classrooms bathed in sunlight and exposure to the circle of houses outside, all dressed in colorful floral decorations, according to the permissible climate.

Contrary to my expectations, my job was not to teach Christian theology, the meaning of the Holy Trinity, the sacrifice of Christ, et cetera, as there was little interest in these religious aspects. I had to guide the young students through the ocean of morality, the waves of right and wrong, the challenges of being a person embedded in a society of peers, with all the asserting individuality, handling natural disagreements, the benefits of solidarity, the necessity of individual reflection, the merger of the biological family with that of the communal family, the symbiosis with the environment, the respect for personal identity and freedom. Really? I wondered. Is this a utopia? Can people really build these dream societies? I had to stop there. I quickly learned to drop my skepticism and embrace the world of the Commune as it was, still appearing to my inquisitive mind like an experiment that bombarded my sleepless nights with questions. What kind of economy does the Commune have? Do people have jobs? Is this communism? Who pays for all of this? Do they have money? I was soon to find answers to all my questions, and then some. No, it was not communism. Yes, people had jobs inside the Commune and outside. The public service jobs were paid by the local government and by the central government of the republic, and all Communes adhered to a code of secular ethics.

Is it really a matter of architecture, to evolve society? Is it truly a matter of geometry and symmetry? What is the proper design of a community, how do you distribute the struggles with life and foster future generations whose members are tightly knit with the world at large?

It will take me quite some time to process all of this.

11:5 I am the museum guard

The most popular venue in the free city of Pyongyang is the Museum of the World that was quickly built, with international funds, after the Korean Unification. The North Koreans are flocking in their millions to see the Museum. Like children, they touch exhibits of various *foreign objects* with some fear, so we, the museum guards, have to constantly confirm it is okay to touch the exhibit and it is rather encouraged. The Brothers ask me if they can hashtag the objects with #IsThisReal or #AWonderfulWorld. Every day, for five minutes, I hold a quick seminar about the art of the holo-selfie in the West, and each time I find it difficult to explain that it is not the state that records the holo-selfie but the individual himself or herself, at their leisure. The Brothers do not understand the concept of the holo-selfie.

The adults ask me to explain religion to them, given that my nametag says "Ask Me Anything in the fields of Religion, Humanities, and World Politics". They have difficult, technical questions, such as this one, asked by an electrical engineer who was responsible for the neon lights at the Kim Kim-Un Mausoleum. He said:

"Sir, I have read the following in the book called *The Bible*: *As you do not know the path of the wind, or how the body is formed in a mother's womb, so you cannot understand the work of God, the Maker of all things.* I wonder, does this mean that the people of the West, namely the writers of *The Bible*, do not know about the circulation of the wind current, or the formation of the fetus inside the uterus, from the moment of insemination onward? Since this seems a metaphor of some sort for the unknowable attributes of what is known as God, one can deduce that it is a wrong metaphor with no value at all, given that science has already answered these questions. Pardon me, I mean to say the fallacy is obvious. I realize we have been oppressed by the dear leader Kim Kim-Un, may he rest alive and well in peace despite his insanity, however his divinity was of an earthly nature, far from that of this so-called biblical God. Perhaps I'm confused and taking too much of your time. I only want to better understand how religion is situated vis-à-vis the Christian God, why it still persists, and how can everybody be liberated just like we, the Brothers of the North, were liberated recently?"

"It is a good observation mister-" I replied.

"Kim Park-Un is my name."

"-Mr. Kim Park-Un. You see, Christianity is a deeply rooted story, like any other religious story. Its origins must be murky and metaphoric to give credence and power to its divine validity. As you probably know, all supra-natural narratives cannot be anchored in the precise language of nature or they will undermine their legitimacy and their foundations will disappear in a puff of logic."

"If I understand this correctly," Mr. Kim Park-Un said, "the religious narrative requires a contradiction and denial of some, if not many, aspects of reality, especially some that have been proven correct by scientific endeavors. I wonder, in this case, if the fortuitous liberation of what was known as the Democratic People's Republic of Korea from the shackles of the madman Kim Kim-Un, may he rest in living peace, I mean him no harm, cannot somehow be replicated in other countries to liberate them from the shackles of naiveté? Not that we, the Brothers of the North, were not also naïve for believing a bunch of tyrannical autocrats, may they retire healthy and in peace, I mean them no harm. Do you know what I mean?"

"I understand you perfectly, Mr. Kim Park-Un," I said.

"Naturally, the Council of Humanity represents great progress," Mr. Kim Park-Un said. "Is it really going to push humanity forward on the path of progress? I do not understand the history of religion well enough to be able to say. I was a history teacher in Pyongyang, I know the history of my country well, but I was only able to read 115 books about foreign history since the liberation. Forgive my ignorance. From what I have studied so far, the world is indeed quite messy, pardon my words, I was advised I am allowed to talk freely."

"You are correct in your observation," I said. "Please continue."

"I understand the complex definitions of liberty and the pursuit of happiness as defined in Western Philosophy, I truly do. I have read from the works of Mr. David Hume, Mr. Immanuel Kant, Mr. Baruch Spinoza, and Mr. Derek Parfit. However, I sense a danger in the formation of this Council of Humanity, leaving aside its utopic qualities that make the project even more outlandish. The danger lies in the systematization of liberty, in the centralization of its non-rational aspects into a bureaucratic forum. By non-rational, I meant to say spiritual. I don't like the word "spiritual", it's too loaded, too ambiguous. The way I see it, liberty and the pursuit of happiness need to exist and evolve in a symbolic, metaphoric realm of existence anchored in civic liberties, but not managed by formalization or by institutional innovation."

"I don't think this is how the Council was designed," I said.

"Certainly, I did not mean it in that way," Mr. Kim Park-Un said. "I am merely preoccupied with the future of mankind and I wish everybody well. I strongly believe we can evolve as human beings. We must also learn and cherish our history."

"So you do not hate Kim Kim-Un?" I asked.

"Goodness no," Mr. Kim Park-Un said. "I feel happy the old regime has ended. I look forward to learning and evolving."

I have no conclusions to draw from my conversation with the wonderful and wise Mr. Kim Park-Un. I leave his words in my diary for good remembrance of things to come.

11:6 I am the tasker-clicker

China. China. China. It's a good word to say, especially in English, which I became accustomed to using during my aimless travels. In Beijing, at my human-managed hotel, a job-attendant spotted me as I came in and immediately introduced himself in English:

"Welcome to Beijing, sir. Looking for job?"

Sure, I thought, it's because I am black and behave like a foreigner.

"Perhaps," I said, with caution.

The friendly man continued:

"Plant your seed in the morning, sir, and keep busy all afternoon, for you don't know if profit will come from one activity or another, or maybe both."

"That's a wise thing to say. Sounds very lucrative," I said.

The job-attendant was looking to hire tasker-clickers, in very high demand in the virtual industrial park just outside Beijing. He was an effective recruiter. In seconds he had sized me up, knew exactly what to say, how to pique my interest. I couldn't resist his offer.

The tasker-clicker offices were in a large complex surrounded by a forest. The parking lot was underground. The buildings were white, tall, and at a fair distance from the nearest neighborhood. The job-attendant signed me up at reception, I offered my bio-card, he collected his finder's fee, and he was gone.

I was welcomed and handled by a tour guide. He asked me in English if I knew what a tasker-clicker did. I had no idea. He said that was not a problem. They had workers from all continents and all nations. The pay is great. The benefits fantastic. The environment friendly and "generously humane", the tour guide said. I will have my own cube-space, my own VR goggles, custom food, custom mattress size-

"Custom mattress?" I asked, surprised.

"Yes, so you can sleep here," the tour guide said.

I could also be paired with single female partners if I was interested. I did not ask the reason, it was obvious: couples working together are more productive. Was I single? I hesitated. No, I was not single, I said. That was a shame, the tour guide concluded. Was my wife interested in working as a tasker-clicker? My partner was indisposed for a long time. The tour guide was sorry to hear that. Nevertheless, if I decided to renew my commitment after one month, due to the prolonged separation from my partner, the tour guide said, I can still be hooked up with an available female colleague, so we can pool together the productivity credits, which are not taxable past a certain threshold. I felt I had to express some gratitude.

"That seems very generous of you," I said, with obvious hesitation.

The tour guide raised his eyebrows.

"Generous? This is more than generous. Nobody else offers this package!"

He showed me to my cube-space where I was to work. Everything was ready to go: the VR goggles, the screens, the chair, the keyboard. The information was fed to me and I had to apply my best judgment. The screens fed live feeds from cameras on AI-androids installed in millions of households. I, as a human tasker-clicker, had to help the AI-android make real-life decisions in real-time, and improve their interactions with their human owners, if that was the case, or with the environment where they were operating, whether they were employed as riot-police officers, or librarians, or receptionists. The tour guide explained we were not here to do the AI-androids' jobs, but to improve their performance. Our customers were the manufacturer of AI-androids, not their actual owners. Needless to say, we had to operate seamlessly, so the owners do not realize that there is a human behind the actions and responses of their AI-androids.

"We are performing a great service here," the tour guide said. "We are helping the birth of a new species. An extension to our own."

I was speechless.

"This may be a surprise for you, Mr. Zeno Awaghari. All new recruits are shocked to realize that behind all AI units out there in the market, and I'm talking about the really good ones, there is a human helping their functioning. Rest assured, the whole world is enamored with our services, despite the fact that we run covert operations. The greater good is what matters. The satisfaction of all AI-android owners, their security, their confidence that their households are guarded by hyper-intelligent and hyper-effective advanced artificial organisms. The world is too complex to shy away from this reality. The world needs us, Mr. Awaghari. The world needs lots of good tasker-clickers."

"How long do people keep this job?" I asked.

The tour guide was amused.

"A long time indeed. As long as they are needed. We certainly need you Mr. Awaghari. The demand is insatiable. The AI-androids are getting better and better. They still require significant human input. Eventually, when some become self-sufficient, fear not, the tasker-clickers will not become unemployed, but will be retrained to facilitate the reverse connection."

"Reverse connection?"

"Yes. The AI-androids will have to teach us. Someone will have to act as the interface. The general population will be overwhelmed. Think of the future tasker-clicker as a translator-ambassador between AI and humans, a specialist in machine thinking and operation, and an off-switch of last resort."

My face probably showed utter stupefaction. The tour guide felt compelled to explain.

"The off-switch of last resort is a human that has the tools to turn off the AI-android in case of emergency."

For some reason this made me feel uneasy. This was not the picture I learned in Montpellier about androids.

"We should start with a drink," the tour guide said.

Before I could say anything, he shoved an open bottle into my hands. He had one too.

"Drink! It's your first day."

He took a big gulp and maintained his friendly demeanor throughout. I took a sip.

"There you go!" the tour guide said, satisfied. "You'll do just fine. You are now building the future."

Was I building the future or was the future building me?

11:7 I am the rent-a-talker

Why do I feel the need so often to reflect over my life, to remember the history of my selves, the people I have met, the lessons I have learned? China has changed me, China has transformed me. I could have told anyone I was Pope Francis the Second, they would have laughed and asked what I was smoking. I tried it once, I told them I was Pope Francis the Second, I dropped my disguise and shaved my face clean, side by side with an official Papal photograph. My colleagues said that the resemblance was uncanny, however my cheekbones are tad higher and my eyebrows thinner. They said they appreciated my joke.

Off to Japan now.

Completely unprepared for my new journey. Near Mount Fuji the light is sweet, and it is pleasant for the eyes to behold the sun. I rented a room in a village nearby. What to do next? The Babelfish Translator was working perfectly. I could speak to the locals in real time. The tiny speaker was attached to my chest and the earbud securely locked in my ear.

Must I learn the ways of the Samurai? Or learn to be a Kabuki actor? This strange new country. The Japanese have learned their lesson from the early part of the 21st century. They were the first to understand that the end of growth has come and a new era must begin. The age of prosperity. Their entire economy has been redesigned to replace the principle of market economy based on continuous growth with principles of prosperity for all. The Japanese have discovered a way to move the human activity to the center of society and allow the economic activity to be an extension of the former, not the other way around. They programmed the new generation of AI-bots to compute the economic equilibriums of supply, demand, labor, and leisure, in such a way as to maximize prosperity for all citizens and do no harm to the ecosystem.

In my village, I had met twelve people employed in traditional economic activities. The others were contributing to society by carefully watching the quality of local prosperity. Some supervised the food distribution that was serviced in totality by artibots, some participated in local educational collectives with many sub-committees that enhanced the natural and virtual courses delivered by artibots, others organized the local Kabuki theatre and the offline outdoor games, very popular with the locals, while more than half of the villagers were members of the Earth Science Club. I joined the rent-a-talker club that was very popular with workers at the beginning of their transition from the Old Economy to the village life.

The rent-a-talkers are indispensable members of every Japanese community. They are a fascinating bunch, quite typical for the late capitalism world, yet still bordering on surrealism. They are what their name suggests, people rented for talking to and for them to carry out meaningful conversations on prescheduled topics, or basic chatter, frivolous and random, never touching the subjects of religion and politics. Never mentioning the Chinese, the Americans, the Russians, or the Koreans - especially the Koreans, for some reason, I never understood why, it may have to do with the Korean Reunification - or conversations of very few words, so few that one might wonder if it is still a conversation or rather companionship. However, for mere companionship people can buy or rent high quality artibots, so humanlike their skin glows like that of a real human, with hair, texture and everything. Rent-a-talkers are filling a spiritual void in the late capitalism Japanese society. They are not a commodity or a unnatural fabrication of an advanced society that has forgotten or outgrown the instinct of human connection, the warmth of candid words spoken by a fellow citizen, the color of empathy, the tenderness of belonging to society, the cozy feeling that you live in a village, that you matter to somebody, that somebody listens to you, that your existence is recorded somehow by another brain, that somebody has the patience and interest to enter a dance of words with you and understand your thinking, as humans are built through words.

The rent-a-talkers are all that. The "rent" part is a tad improper since nobody pays a rent-a-talker, especially where the entire economy is fast moving away from commodification. You are setting aside time to talk to someone, according to the supply of time offered by each individual to the community.

Today I was booked for an hour to talk to a restless investment banker who suddenly developed a post-work syndrome, quite typical for late capitalism. He could not start a conversation with anyone, after work hours, about anything except investment banking. He could not comment on anything else, including weather, sports of any kind - except horse racing, which he only listened to but never watched - or even point to countries on the map where his bank did not have an office. He could not even formulate interest in a woman outside his field. He never had an intimate relationship with a person for more than a few weeks because he was so engrossed in his work he forgot about dates and social commitments. He was sorry, every single time. Since he worked remotely from my village, he booked time to talk to me.

He had no idea what to talk about, so I suggested we play roles. I was the Pope of the Catholic Church and he had an audience with me.

"Mr. Investment Banker, you won an audience at the audience lottery, with me, the Pope of Rome. What can I do for you?"

(I adopted a playful tone to ease the conversation. Of course, my friend the investment banker had absolutely no idea who I really was, but he knew what a Pope is, and where Rome is situated on the map.)

"Mr. Pope, thank you for seeing me. I would like to-"

He paused, he was searching for ideas.

"To?" I left him no time to think.

"To transform my bank into a community cooperative."

"That is wonderful," I said. "Tell me about your bank."

"We have offices in 30 countries," the investment banker said, "we have these many trillions of assets in administration, these many tens of thousands of human employees, this many thousands of artibots in customer service, and we grew 10% every year for the past five years."

"You have a wonderful bank, Mr. Investment Banker. How can I help? I know nothing about banks and money."

"Well, Mr. Pope, you can talk to my people at the bank and tell them we need to become a community cooperative."

"They will listen to me?"

"Yes, because you have fame, you are influential, and you are a man of peace."

"I think I can do that, Mr. Investment Banker. Tell me where and when and I will talk to your people at the bank."

"I will arrange that. Thank you for your time Mr. Pope."

"I was happy to offer my time Mr. Investment Banker."

All that through the Babelfish Translator. Quite fruitful was my time with the investment banker. He booked me again for three more sessions and became more talkative every time. After a while, he holocalled me and introduced me to his stable girlfriend with whom he was evaluating the prospects of marriage.

11:8 I am the encouragement worker

United States of America.

Since my last visit, little progress has been made. The Old Establishment is clinging desperately to maintain the rules of the game. The memes of the New Economy that started in Japan have not penetrated America, mainly because of language barriers, and also because of the powerful lobbying and internet tactics from the Old Establishment.

Encouragement workers are not cheap to hire. Still, they are heavily subsidized by large corporations who seek to maintain the acceptable emotional levels of those employees whose jobs have not been transferred to artibots or generic android workers. The humans still active in the economy need substantial injections of encouragement so they can maintain a sunny disposition facing the knowledge that their employment will be *technologized*. I read all of this in the brochure at the placement center.

I was sent to a division of a factory that built DNA flasks, chips, microboxes, and droplets for the new generation artibots. The human personnel consultant explained that these little objects filled with human DNA and equipped with micro-computers will be inserted in the new artibots and will help them become more humanlike by learning how the DNA molecules interact with the organic software.

Not a hard job, I was told. The worker donates his own DNA daily, then prepares the receptacle, then uploads it into a processor while his brain is scanned continuously. I was assured that the worker does not suffer in any way, however, the HR department has noticed a decrease in motivation in this division, so that is why I was hired to help.

I mingled with the workers in the lunch room. They knew who I was. I was wearing a label over my heart. It read HI, I'M ZENO, YOUR ENCOURAGEMENT WORKER. I thought that might elicit withdrawal, muteness, and avoidance from the workers, but I was surprised to see how eager they were to talk to me. They knew why I was sent by the corporate office. They knew what I was supposed to do, how I was supposed to help. They have seen encouragement workers before, of various ethnicities and abilities. They have not been disappointed. They thought it was a good idea. It maintained a solid balance between hope and realism. It was the perfect dosage of inevitability. In fact, one of the workers called me the Artisan of Inevitability. His name was Hilbert. He was the most talkative in the lunch room.

"So, Zeno, let me ask you something," Hilbert said, so everyone could hear him. "If a man lives many years and rejoices in them all, what do you do?"

Trick question.

"You let him remember the days of darkness," I said with the same tone of voice.

"Why?" Hilbert asked.

"For they will be many. All that is coming is vanity."

He stopped. He did not expect to hear that. I was neither cynical nor sarcastic. I gauged the need for realism in the room and I offered it. That is what maintains the thread of hope, knowing that your feet are anchored on a ground of truth. These workers will be replaced by machines, they will become obsolete, there will be nothing for them. They will have huge loads of time without sensible end to reflect about purpose and about each other. What will they eat? Where will they live? What threats will hang over their heads from their creditors, from their local governments, the so and so supervising agency, the so and so medical institution? These will be fragments of life. These will be insignificant to the bigger drama of their life. The need of belonging. The need to feel a direction.

"You will make leaps in your imagination," I told them.

"But how?" they asked. "There will be nothing to do. The androids will do the innovation for us."

"You will still have your brains, your dreams, your insecurities, your stories, the infinite universe to explore, your history to rediscover. You will still have your fascinations with your naked bodies, with music and the fanciful foods you eat."

All ages have their grand currents of despair. That is what makes us human. The workers know that. They cannot help themselves not thinking beyond their mundane condition. They have watched the movies, they have read the books, at least some of them, they've participated in holoshows. They were familiar with their future. They simply needed a bit of encouragement to continue living and to remain balanced human beings for the greater benefit of the society.

"Why do I owe anything to society?" Hilbert said.

"Yes, exactly, why?" concurred the other workers.

"A legitimate question," I said. "The truth is, you do not owe anything and society does not owe you anything, by raw logic. However, when two of you get together, for whatever reason, you are immediately a society, you owe each other the acknowledgment of dignity. The acknowledgment of life. You cannot escape it. When you are alive in the presence of somebody else you are automatically connected. Even if you remain silent. Even if you do not make eye contact. Even if you do not share the language. You owe each other this basic attention."

"A gathering of self-replicating units of dignity?" Hilbert said, pensively.

The workers sighed with some relief. The tension was dropping. The future remained where it was, unchanged. They needed to remember their last resort was shared imagination with each other. They will always have each other.

11:9 I am the baker

High quality bread is still made in Cuba. It is absolutely delicious. Bread doesn't go well with philosophy and religion. I know this too well. *Eat this bread because it symbolizes my body.* Nonsense. Bread is bread. It doesn't taste like chicken or anything else. Sometimes I just feel I've had enough with philosophy and meandering words that nobody truly knows what they mean.

I told my friend Carlos Fuentes, a young man working with computers, we were drinking spending mojitos on the beach, I told him:

"You who are young, be happy while you are young, and let your heart give you joy in the days of your youth."

"Alright Zeno!" Carlos said. "You talk like a priest!"

"I assure you I am no priest," I said.

We both laughed loudly and drank another mojito and then another.

Where did I meet Carlos? In his family bakery, of course. Even though he was designing software for quantum computers, he liked to spend his free time at the bakery. Oh, the smell of fresh bread! The clouds of goodness. Whiteness all over. On the walls, on the floor, on our clothes. Flour, and pure, white, clean air, carrying the flavors of various breads into all corners and outside into the street. I stayed with their family, I helped in the shop, I tutored the children, I looked after the garden, the animals, we watched holovision at night, we watched the stars and guessed their names, the kids knew all the names without using their apps, all the constellations and distances in parsecs and the grades of all major exoplanets. Lovely family! They talked a lot about their emotions, their disagreements, their role in society, their bad dreams and good dreams, their plans to travel the world.

"Let's break a bread together," I told Carlos, after who knows how many mojitos at the beach bar.

"I heard that's what Christians do as a sign of friendship," Carlos said, thus telling me subtly he was not a man of religion.

"Yes, that is correct," I said. "You know what else the Christians say?"

"What?"

"Follow the ways of your heart and whatever your eyes see, but know that for all these things God will bring you into judgment."

"Makes sense if you believe all that," Carlos said, between gulps.

"And if you don't?"

"If you don't, you can still interpret that there is a consequence to all your actions. Leaving God outside of this, of course."

"Sometimes bad people transgress and nothing happens to them," I said.

"That's still a consequence. An unfavorable one," Carlos said.

"Don't you think it's somehow better for most people to live in unbridled hope that there will be punishment for the bad people, and reward for the good people eventually?"

"Zeeeno," Carlos patted my back with the full force of our friendship, "you're either testing me or you have something important you want to say. Which one is it? No, don't say nothing. Have another glass."

He waved to the bartender, and in the blink of an eye I had another mojito in front of me.

"What were you saying?" Carlos said.

"Isn't it-"

"I know, I know, if hope is better. No, of course it's not. It makes you feel better for the moment, or for many moments, but when you keep seeing the rotten reality, the injustice, the misfortune, the accidents, the suffering around you, it kind of makes you think that all this rewarding the good and punishing the bad business smells fishy and it's nothing but a big fat lie fed to us by history. Why? Because we are deeply, deeply rooted in this mental inertia that makes us wanna eat up old stories without masticating them or checking them for bullshit. Oops, sorry. I said bullshit."

"That's okay."

"Do I think truth is better? Yes. Am I a materialist? Yes. Proud of it? Maybe. I don't feel the need to justify how I think. You know what is bigger than us? You know what my belief is?"

"Tell me."

"I believe the logic of nature is bigger than us. No matter what we think of ourselves, that we are smart, that we built cities and whatever, nature will always have the upper hand. And you know what else? I have my own hope too. But not unbridled hope. It's a reasonable hope that I crafted by watching history unraveling. It's the hope that the moral arc will bend towards justice."

"Martin Luther King."

"Yes, Zeno, it's from Martin Luther King and I believe it."

Carlos Fuentes was an unbridled optimist. Or is it unfair of me to characterize him like that? He would say he was a realist, and if one looks at the numbers he may be right. We both believed that time will end and the only cure for that is more mojitos, the enjoyable lightness of our fellow human beings, and the wonderful, inescapable capacity of our memories to vanish and maintain us creatures of the present. What else is there to life? Choose your times of reflections wisely, dear friends, and choose to let them go. Drink the mojitos, eat the bread, drink and eat as much as you need until you break free. Break free, my friends! Break free!

¡Viva la libertad!

11:10 I am the forest master

Jungles of Brazil. Somewhere near the Amazon River.

These are the outer limits of civilization as I know it. The tribesmen first reacted to my presence with hostility. I waived my empty hands, I showed my naked body to convince them I meant no harm. My skin was close in color to theirs, yet I still looked odd to them. I allowed them to poke my body with blunt sticks. I was no ghost. I had hands, legs, eyes, organs just like them. They were fascinated by my height and my hair. When they mustered the courage, they became obsessed with touching and pulling my hair, at first roughly, then more gently when they saw my grimaces. The beard seemed to scare them. they stayed away from it. I pulled my beard and showed them it's hair like any other.

I was fortunate they did not bother to inspect my private parts. I covered myself after the initial meet and greet and they left it at that. I was not some mythical creature from their legends who sheds skin and grows fins. The tribe had the concept of clothing, which made me think that they must have encountered outside humans in their recent history.

They were about 100 humans living in huts huddled tightly in a clearing deep in the jungle. Their routine was simple. The men left early in the morning and came back a few hours later with whatever they hunted or gathered that day. Upon their arrival, the women prepared the communal meal. The children and the elderly ate first, the women and the men ate last.

They were busy talkers. Everybody spoke without pause to each other, over each other, asking and answering at the same time. There was a subtle flow of their language. They were not interrupting each other. They were completing each other, composing the story of their day together, as if every member of the tribe had a duty to contribute with words to the daily chapter.

Then suddenly, during the daily meal, everybody stopped talking all at once and committed to complete silence. I had no idea how they coordinated it. They did not look at each other. They just stopped chatting. I had nothing to do, except to continue my silence and restraint in my own place, near a tree, where I was instructed I could rest.

The tribe continued their meal in silence. The voice of my mind told me:

Remove vexation from your heart, Francis, and put away pain from your body, for youth and the dawn of life are vanity.

My mind called me Francis. How odd. Not sure why I thought of myself as a former Pope, particularly here, in the middle of the jungle.

They offered me food, politely, by showing me it is something that I put in my mouth. I bowed my head and thanked them. The entire tribe positioned itself in a great circle. They invited me to go in the middle and speak. I said I don't know their language and I didn't know what to tell them. They insisted. I had to go in the middle of the circle and speak to them. They must have liked me. My submissive demeanor, the fact that I allowed them to poke me, to cause me minor pain, and that I showed no desire for revenge. I must have passed some sort of a test. They were now prepared to hear the sound of the foreigner's voice.

I went into their middle and I spoke slowly and softly:

"My friends, my name is Nwanne Yinkaso, I come from Nigeria. I was the Pope of the Catholic Church. My name was Francis the Second. Do I have regrets for what I've done? Do I feel shame deep in the core of my heart? Do I wish I had done things differently? Have I betrayed my people? Have I robbed them of their Church, while I, as the Vicar of Christ, was supposed to defend their faith? Have I taken a lover against the prohibition of tradition? Have I allowed political machinations to unravel behind my back? All that turmoil around the world, the love for Francis the Second, the hate for Francis the Second, did I deserve all that? What would you have done in my place? You have hearts, desires, just like any other human. You and I are not so different after all. I eat like you eat, I get angry, I love, I protect. From my heart to your heart, I tell you simply, I am one of you, and you are one with my world. I was the most recognized face in the world. I came naked in front of you, you knew nothing of me. I even showed you my clean face. Where do we go from here, my friends? You with your families. Me with my demons and wandering. There is a time for everything. Nothing can be put back to where it was. Hard it is to say when vanity will leave us. Look at me, sharing all this with you, in a language you do not understand, all my secrets. This is not honesty. I make sounds with my mouth to enchant you and you respond with your kind faces and your patience. I see in your eyes you feel me beyond the sounds. You, and you, and you, I will never forget you. I will never forget this moment. I thank you for your kindness. May we all live in peace."

NOTEBOOK TWELVE

12:1 Blessed are the meek, for they will inherit the earth

I took the night train from London to Milan so I could rest. When I arrived, he was waiting for me. I saw him at the end of the platform, standing, beautiful, majestic. He was looking for me. When our eyes met he smiled gently and lovingly.

"I have been waiting for you," he said.

"You look well, very well," I said.

We embraced and let silence overwhelm us. There will be time for words. A whole life ahead of us. He knew I would tell him all about my travels, and I knew he would tell me all about his new body.

"I found a beautiful place for us to live," he said. "A small cabin, somewhere up in the mountains, in a place called Santo Candido, in Alto Adige. You love the fresh mountain air. We both needed it. You need to be closer to the sky, to seek your answers. I need to care for my new clone lungs. Doctor's orders. You know how we both like to take orders."

He laughed. A healthy laugh with vibration of fragility. He was still weak inside, yet he posed strong for me. I know he did it for me.

"We must take an eCar immediately, they are waiting for us."

Always on top of things, organizing, taking care of us. Who were *they*? I didn't ask. Probably some nice people in Santo Candido.

"Enyi, do not let the excitement of youth cause you to forget your Creator. Honor him in your youth before you grow old and say *Life is not pleasant anymore.*"

He was being playful. He knew I need not honor my creator. I have no creator anymore. I am self-made now. I am not a grumpy old man. He, my dear soul friend, he was far from it.

Even with his condition he found strength and humor. He was teasing me. He was the man I knew. He was my Nwanne.

We took one of those new and fancy eCars with no driver. It was so comfortable inside we fell asleep for a while. When we woke up we were on a meandering road in The Dolomites, sharp solid mountains with snowy peaks on both sides. The eCar told us we were close to our destination.

The little village of Santo Candido was a collection of houses scattered in a caldera of green pastures tied together by a lake in the shape of a tear. All of this was guarded by the giant presence of The Dolomites. The eCar stopped in the tiny, cozy, central square of the village, wished us a good day, and left on its own to where it was supposed to go.

We met the people who waited for us: The Mayor - an old, white-bearded, chubby, merry man; and his wife, who looked like him, minus the beard. They told us their names and assured us repeatedly we were very welcome in Santo Candido. Our new home was ready and stocked with supplies. If we wanted to meet all the other villagers, we were invited to the Trattoria that was, lo and behold, exactly five meters behind us. We turned around. A dozen people from inside the Trattoria waved at us.

Of course, we had time to unpack, to adjust, to rest, to learn the air, the sounds, the friendliness of the sun, the colors of the forest, the reflections of the lake, and the bell of the church. Yes, Santo Candido had a little church.

"Take your time, dear friends," the merry mayor said. "But remember, there is joy in solitude and even more joy at the Trattoria."

He nudged us and winked.

We didn't have to carry our luggage. A male android-carrier appeared from nowhere, grabbed my satchel and whatever else we had, and warmly asked us to follow him uphill. So we did, giggling like little boys, badly wanting to arrive at our new home where we could talk for hours and days over glasses of wine and strands of memories. What was this life ahead of us? We had spoken nothing of it since we met in Milan. We were embracing a new journey while leaving questions aside, as their weight would not have helped us climb these mountains.

So be it. I will live the rest of my life in peace and reflection.

12:2 This little house of ours

Forget peace! A life of tranquil riot, mindful exultation, wild thoughts of calmness, loud soft parties and copious healthy feasts! Life, shower us with moderation! My dear Nwanne and I found each other again, truly ourselves, unencumbered by roles we need to play to satisfy the world. We will write books, we will write memoirs, we will watch the world from afar, we will breathe the mountain airs and drink the fresh rivers. We will break good bread and we will sleep long hours from sunset to sunrise at the mercy of the morning roosters.

We have a beautiful garden ready to produce the first batch of tomatoes and potatoes of the year. We will plant the seeds together. I will bring eggs from the hen house while Nwanne will bring the cheese and lay the table. We are going to have cups of good coffee while we read the paper-papers together and enjoy our time far from the ruckus.

When we get tired, the android helper will wash the dishes, sweep the house, sweep the yard, do the laundry, fetch us things, and run errands downhill to the village grocery store.

Time will flow nicely, while the sun, or the light, or the moon, or the stars be not darkened, nor shall the clouds return after the rain to weigh our spirits down. We will not forget our long and heavy lives. We will welcome lightness in retirement. Everybody deserves it.

Music! Lots of music! Life, bring us music now, please! Oh, how I have forgotten to listen to beautiful sounds. I long to hear the great composers.

Nwanne is in our living room. He came out of the bathroom leaving a thick cloud of steam behind him. His beautiful mature body! And he told me he wanted to listen to Tchaikovsky's Nutcracker. The home-android played us the Nutcracker. Nwanne tried a few ballet moves. He was hilarious! I've never seen him like this. He tiptoed on a cloud of steam! We laughed like children.

I couldn't help myself, and I joined him. We are bad dancers and we don't care.

"Louder android, louder!"

He turned up the volume. The windows were shaking. We were having the time of our lives. Nwanne told me he forgot to turn off the hot water, that's why steam kept coming out of the bathroom.

"I don't care, let it come! Tchaikovsky!"

"Tchaaaaaikovsky!"

A madhouse of fun! Who says former Popes can't have a good time with their best friends?!

The android notified us of a high humidity level that might affect circuits in the house. He recommended we turn off the hot water.

We got dressed. Tchaikovsky was still playing in the background. Hunger appeared.

"Here's what we do," I said. "We leave our well-tempered reason right here on the table." I slapped the table with both my hands. "Then we go to the Trattoria and we eat some good food and we talk to some good people and we tell them who we are."

"Yes, dear?" Nwanne said, and his eyes opened wide.

Five minutes later, including putting on shoes, we are at the Trattoria. I thought the whole village was there, metaphorically. We walked in and immediately the bartender said: "Signori! Benvenuto! Vino!" We accepted the wine and a quick appetizer that the bartender shoved in our faces.

"Everybody," I said. "I am Enyi Chebea, and this is my best friend and partner in life, Nwanne Yinkaso. The world knows me as Pope Francis the Second. Look at me. I am Pope Francis the Second."

The Trattoria erupted:

"PAPA FRANCESCO! *Sei tu*! It's you!"

They rushed at me, they hugged me, they kissed me, they hugged Nwanne, they kissed him too, they took us in a dance right there between the tables.

"More wine! More wine!" people shouted. Our glasses were refilled. Questions poured in and didn't wait for answers. They were showering me with kisses and hugs. Okay, this was nice, but did they hear what I said? Oh, yes, yes, they heard, they told me they were happy for us. Some of them knew all along, which surprised me, but not too much because of that paparazzo episode at the hospital. Everybody talked at the same time.

"Are you getting married?" "How long are you staying in Santo Candido?" "Please stay forever, I will bring you fresh tomatoes and fresh fruit every day!" "He has a garden too, don't be such a kiss-ass Giuseppe!" "Hey, watch your mouth, Mario, this is Pope Francis the Second here!" "Oh, I'm sure he won't mind."

"I don't mind at all," I said.

"See, what did I tell you? Francesco, can I call you Francesco? Since when are you together?" "Hey, that's a personal question!" "I'm just curious." "Ah, since you were young? Ayayay, I can tell you are best friends and best of lovers. If only my Maria was that friendly to me!" "Haha! You're such a tease, Petruchio!" "No, I'm not, it's true. Ask her." "Hey, Maria, do you keep Petruchio on a short leash?" "Only when he's naked!" "Haha!"

Everybody was laughing hard. They hugged us tighter and tighter.

"Truffaldino, is that your hand in my pocket or are you just happy to see me?" "I apologize, dear Francesco, I stepped on your feet."

"That's alright," I said.

It's carnival! Well beyond my expectations, and must say I can't find room to think. It's my own fault. I wanted to leave my well-tempered reason on the table.

12:3 Many guests arrive

Can't remember when we got back home, all I know is that we woke up the next day when the keepers of the house tremble, and the strong men are bent, and the grinders cease because they are few, and those who look through the windows are dimmed, while the sun was already up and roosters completed their songs hours ago.

A group of students appeared, hiking uphill. They came straight to our house and stopped just outside our little gate. I was watching from behind the curtain. Nwanne was making breakfast.

"Who are they?" Nwanne said, still working on the eggs.

"I'm not sure. They are just standing there."

"Perhaps you should go out and talk to them."

"I think I will."

I put on proper pants, a proper shirt, a decent vest, and I went out to meet the students. When they saw me, they jumped on their feet with exhilaration.

"Oh my goodness, oh my goodness, it *is* Pope Francis the Second, it's really him!" "See? I told you." "How good-looking he is!" "Shush, he might hear you."

I heard everything.

"Good morning," I said.

"Good morning Papa. We love you," they said merrily in an imperfect chorus. It was twelve of them, six young men and six young women, in their early 20s, some white, some black, some Asian. They spoke to me in English, as that is how I was known on the social internet.

They heard about my whereabouts from an obscure post in a forum on the underwebs, posted anonymously, then deleted the next day. They wanted to be the first to factcheck. They said I was a hero of the new generation, and that my audacious reforms of the Catholic Church have made stupendous waves throughout the digital, virtual, and offline societies. The very popular Council of Humanity is the most hashtagged topic in the world. Everybody knows it was founded on my original idea for the Council of Christianity. They just used a new and better name. Students' words, not mine.

"The world misses you, Papa," a red-haired girl said.

"Nobody knows where you disappeared to," a lanky black boy said.

"But we're happy you are back," a blonde girl with spectacles said.

Nwanne made his appearance in a house robe, with his hair combed nicely.

"You kids hungry?" Nwanne asked them.

The students were caught completely off-guard. They nudged each other to say something.

"Don't be shy. We'll have breakfast, all of us, outside. Who's helping me with the tables?"

The three most audacious students offered, then everybody joined in moments later, after passing the moment of shock. We set tables outside in the fresh air, under the clear bright sky. Nwanne made more scrambled eggs and added many good things on the sides. I brought milk, apple juice, and spring water.

The students ate copiously. I asked them to tell me about themselves, where they were from, what they studied, how they met the others, what they liked about my Papacy, what they didn't like, what they thought about the major developments in the world, if they believed in God. We had a very proper and civilized conversation. Lively, incisive, honest. I told them I would have it no other way. I had nothing to hide, so I expected the same from them. This is what they said, in their own words:

Hilde, a red-haired woman from Germany: "My parents were Catholic, but I was not raised Catholic. I chose to be Catholic from about when I was twelve years old until I was twenty-one. I went to mass every Sunday, I read the Bible, I believed. Then, on my twenty-first birthday at 11:14pm I lost my virginity. The next morning, I realized I had also lost my faith. I don't know why. Can't explain. I think finding pleasure expunged it from my brain."

"Thank you, Hilde, for sharing," said everybody.

I moved on to Michael, next, a young, lanky, soft-spoken black man from the Bronx, in New York. I asked him the same question, what is the story of his belief or nonbelief? He said:

"Your Holiness, now that we are talking freely, and I really appreciate it, it's hard for me to say what I believe, because I don't know myself. My whole life, I heard the Jesus stories and I thought there must be an all-powerful being out there. The more I read about it, though, I became less sure, 'cause I asked myself questions. Much of faith doesn't make sense, no offense. I came here, because I appreciate you very much, I'm curious, and I like being around my friends here."

We all thanked Michael for sharing. Next to him, there was an Italian girl with blonde hair and blue eyes. Her name was Francesca. She was voluble and lively. To my question, she answered:

"Holy Papa, I am so grateful to meet you in person! You are exactly like I imagined. You are asking us what we believe. I believe that for many, many years we humans have asked the wrong questions and that is why we got the wrong answers. I'm not talking about the prophets, or Jesus, or the Holy Ghost. I'm referring to the questions of meaning. How do I tell the difference between faith and delusion?"

"I think I see what you mean," I said. "You are saying that faith is akin to some sort of psychosis?"

"Maybe, I don't know," Francesca said. "That's why I'm so confused. I'm doing a masters in Psychology. The more I read, the more I realize there is no distinction."

"Very well, we will talk more about this," I said. "Let us give all the chance to answer the question."

Next to her there was a white, chubby young man, named Michael. He was Australian. He said:

"I think there is a God. I think there is something incomprehensible about the creation of the Universe. I don't know how a man, namely Jesus, was connecting to this mindboggling divinity. Maybe he had some unearthly inspiration, sorry, I meant revelation. I don't know. When I'm asking myself, what is God, and I read all those metaphoric definitions, like that he's all powerful, all knowing, infinitely good, a cause without cause, the beginning and the end of everything, I get confused. Yes, I get confused and I realized I'm nowhere. Then I talk in my mind, people call that praying, I calm myself down and move on with my life and God is still there."

"Thank you, Michael," I said. "That is quite interesting. I went through these thoughts myself too."

"Really? You?" Michael said utterly shocked.

"I'm afraid so, yes."

I moved on to Qi-Shan, a frail Chinese girl, with dense, black, braided hair. She was wearing a stainless steel cross. She said:

"I heard Jesus' voice when I was 10. He spoke Chinese and I understood everything. I cannot see life without him."

"How did he look like?" I asked.

"Like this," Qi-Shan said, and produced a photograph of an actor playing the Messiah from the popular holo-film "Resurrection".

"Um, you know, Qi-Shan," I said, "this is a famous actor."

"I know, Holiness," Qi-Shan said, "and I feel God through his face."

Next to her, there was a young Korean man, athletic and tall. His name was Kwan. I asked him the same question. He said:

"I don't mean to be rude, Your Holiness. I used to believe strongly, like Qi-Shan, but I don't anymore. I just don't. I wanted to believe. But when I kept praying and praying and got no answer, I stopped and asked myself, hey, this looks a lot like there is no God? Forgive my insolence. But how do I tell the difference, right?"

"Thank you, Kwan, for your honesty. Do not worry. I am not offended," I said.

Next, we turned to a gracious young woman. She was Vietnamese. Her name was Phuong. I did not have to ask her. She spoke on her own.

"I believed in God because of my parents, who told me everything about Him, but I was born with curiosity and I kept asking, why did God sacrifice His son? Could he not just wipe the sins without all the suffering? My parents didn't know, so I asked other Why questions. So they sent me to a Catholic School to learn more, but I didn't learn more, I got even more confused. When I saw the tweet about you, I immediately came to ask you."

Phuong's candor made us chuckle.

"I wish I could say something better than your teachers, but I am afraid there is no answer," I said.

Next to her, with the top of his shirt open, was a young Brazilian man. His dark hair was oiled, his skin beautiful and tanned. His name was Danilo.

"Jesus and God and the Church, for me, have always been a celebration. It's about feeling good, having lots of hope that everything will turn out just fine, in this life or the next. The meek will receive their reward, the evil will receive their punishment. Then one day it struck me. Why there is still evil and bad people? Are they not afraid of their consequences? That I thought about the free will problem. We get to decide what to think and how to behave. But why? Why free will? Why all this trouble? Why not just make us good from the beginning? Surely, we don't know God's mind. But then how are we so sure that all this is His doing? What if there are no rules, no judgment? What if life is like meandering through a jungle with good, evil, pleasure, and suffering? It is so much simpler and more beautiful, I think. We are the mind we are born with, and then it's how we survive. Dancing, wanting, thinking. So no, I do not believe in the Christian God, but I do believe we have some power to determine our lives."

Danilo's speech left us in complete silence. The students looked at each other, then looked at me shyly. Some turned away slightly from Danilo as if he suddenly became a pariah.

"You spoke sincerely, as I was hoping," I broke the silence. "I thank you for that. I want to surprise you all, in return, and tell you that these thoughts have also crossed my mind. They have crossed the minds of many believers, especially people of the church. What makes the difference between those who question themselves as mere observers of an idea, and those who correct the idea of truth, is the predisposition of the character to be able to say *I was wrong, I want to learn more.* See, truth is never a final destination. One must always improve upon it. And, unfortunately, I have to say, the doctrine offers us God as a final truth, where everything begins and ends."

"Your Holiness," Danilo said, raising his eyebrows, "are you saying you do not believe in God?"

"All answers in due time, dear guests," I said. "Let us hear now from our friend Sandra."

Sandra was a young black woman who looked nerdy. She was wearing glasses and had a tattoo of planets and telescopes over her shoulders. She said:

"For me, this is a very easy question. The answer is no. I don't want to get into semantics and interpretation. The real question for me would be why am I here to meet you, Your Holiness? Because I believe we could advance tremendously as a species if we replaced religion with something better. I want to learn from you how this is possible. I think the Council of Humanity is a fantastic social project. We are on the right track. I know you are behind it."

Sandra truly touched a nerve. I must say I felt uneasy. I did not expect this question at all.

"Well, Sandra," I said. "I think you touched the heart of the matter. I have to say that I was not involved in the creation of the Council. I was preoccupied with other, hmm, matters, up in the mountains. I was on a retreat, a spiritual retreat, I was researching my own mind. Anyway, this is a subject for my diary. You are right, religion needs to evolve and will evolve, however not from within but from the advancement of prosperity of all peoples. I am not sure if the Council will survive. I hope it does. That we abolished the Papacy, that is a major step which I salute. I wish I had done that."

I looked at the students' faces. They were absorbing my words with awe. I thought I might shock them, but that's not what I saw. They were molding their impressions of me into new clearer thoughts and convictions. I was nothing less than what they expected me to be. With their hearts, they were coming closer.

Next to speak was a young man from Saudi Arabia. He was well-dressed, well-groomed, probably from a rich family. His name was Amran. He said:

"When I saw you speak in Mecca, I was struggling with my faith. I had three questions on my mind that obsessed me night and day. Why did Allah need so many prophets? Why did he give war-spawning messages to different peoples? Why is he hidden, always hidden? You spoke from the top of the Kaaba, you said that we must overcome our traditions and embrace the planet, truly embrace it. We must forge a better version of ourselves and watch the needs of the world of tomorrow, not the worlds of the past. These words moved me, Your Holiness. I wanted to see you up close and become the man from your vision. Oh, I forgot to answer your question. I truly do not know what I believe, but I think I can know, after I learn some more."

The students were impressed with Amran's words. Everybody expected, as did I, an unflinching, outspoken young man, with no doubts on his mind. Yet he surprised us by coming out as an apprentice of wisdom and skepticism.

To his left sat a young woman. Her name was Safia. She was from Iran. She was wearing a pair of red-rimmed glasses. She said:

"Thank you for welcoming us as your guests, Your Holiness. First of all, full disclosure everybody, I participated in the Tehran Topless Festival. This was very important to me because it was the day when I lost a God and discovered many real friends. I still believe in God, I do, but he is now so incomprehensible to me, I dare not question anything about his whereabouts, his will, his power. I pray no more. Yes, I still wear the hijab, as you can see, but my mind is wondering about the many paths in life I can take. I feel free now, yes, I have to say this, I have discovered boundless joyous freedom, and somehow I think this is because of you, Holiness. Ayatollah Foolas spoke highly of you, and said his idea for the Topless Festival was inspired by your words."

The students applauded Safia. She stood up, took a bow, and blew kisses to everybody.

Fretting and fidgeting, the last student in our circle was a young man from India, dressed all in white, a tad nerdish in gestures, and clearly well-educated. His name was Kumar. I turned my attention to him, and he spoke without being questioned, like everybody else. He said:

"Hello everybody. My name is Kumar. I come from a small village in India, called Gyumbooshlooky. I have met Your Holiness before, under the uncanniest circumstances. I was the only one in our village to realize who you were, from the very beginning. I told no one. I learned to admire you as a person, especially when you declined to be our Mayor. I have never spoken to you, and you probably never noticed me. I was a quiet boy, fiddling with computer code all day and all night. I apologize if I have ruined your secret, but I cannot lie to you, especially now that I have travelled the world to meet you. I hope you forgive me. I hope you all will forgive me. I must also apologize that I do not know how to answer your questions, whether I believe in God or not, because I do not know what God is. Yes, I have read about religions, but I have not found a clear, contained definition. Perhaps you can help me. Thank you for having me here. Thank you for your kind friendship, everybody."

Indeed, the day could have ended here, with me hiding in shame and deflecting, or saying something playful, or making some joke to entertain my guests. Nwanne too, like everybody, widened his eyes at the words spoken by Kumar. I did not have the chance to tell him about all the places I had travelled to.

"Kumar, I will call you my friend," I said, "as I have called everybody from Gyumbooshlooky a dear friend. I welcome your words of truth with great excitement, because they open a long book of stories that I would like to tell you. They are true stories. They are the stories of my life. I will tell you about my childhood. I will tell you about my journey with God and for God. I will tell you how I became Pope, how I dreaded it, and how I stopped being Pope. Lately, I have kept myself busy while my dear Nwanne was in hospital. I have travelled the world, I have met wonderful, intriguing people. I have learned even more humility. I have gained even more strength. From the people of Gyumbooshlooky I have learned camaraderie and respect for equity. Oh, dear friends, I am happy I have found you and you are happy you have found me! Truth be told, to allude to a classic motion picture, I think this could be the beginning of a beautiful friendship."

I shook Kumar's hand and I embraced him. He took it upon himself to passed the hug forward to Safia from Tehran, and she hugged Amran from Mecca, and he hugged Sandra from Charlottesville, and she hugged Danilo from Rio de Janeiro, and he hugged Phuong from Ho Chi Minh City, and she hugged Kwan from Seoul, and he hugged Qi-Shan from Guangzhou, and she hugged Michael from Canberra, and he hugged Francesca from Venice, and she hugged Michael from Bronx, and he hugged Hilde from Heidelberg, and she hugged Nwanne from Nigeria, and he hugged me, from everywhere.

12:4 The Unsermon on the Mountain, under the starry sky

Nwanne had the great idea to set up a fire in the backyard, so we could sit under the starry night and talk some more. The students helped him. They brought the firewood from the shed, blankets, and the bottles of wine. I brought the lighter.

When the flames caught life, the students said:

"Papa Francesco, please tell us a story."

I had to oblige.

"My young friends, I don't do sermons anymore. The times of sermons are gone. They have been stretched by history and by the Church for far too long. Instead, we should have profound conversations, and we should offer each other notebooks for existence. You bring yours, I bring mine. I have noted in my notebooks the ways of my life, what made me a man, what carries me forward. You have your notes of your ways in life. We sit down and compare them. We pick from both what is good, and we drop from both what is bad. Who says we cannot listen to many voices if they all bring value to our lives? Who says we have to listen to one moral authority? We can judge for ourselves what is right, what is fair, can we not? We can judge for ourselves what matters in life, if we have the peace of mind and the education to think, can we not?

These are some of my ways in life: the way of love, the way of understanding, the way of dignity.

This is my way of love. His name is Nwanne. We grew up together. We became men together. We shared the good, the bad, the beautiful, the ugly. We have known suffering and joy. We had low points. We had high points. Our souls and minds have melded. Is all this love? Is there a beginning and an end to love? Does the beginning have a spark, or is it a foundation carefully crafted over time? Does it take a strong character to endure in love? Does it take imagination? Does it take tradition, a common language, a common interest? Love is as mellifluous of an idea as the concept of freedom offered to those who have just escaped oppression of the mind or of the body. Love encompasses the human spirit in all dimensions and is born when freedom is constructed together with another soul. You know you love when your freedom extends into the soul of the other and his soul extends into you. Your minds overlap, your bodies complement each other, while you maintain the integrity of your evolving consciousness.

The way of understanding is the way of dealing with challenges. You begin by learning deeply about the workings of nature, the workings of all societies, not just the one in which you were born. The struggles of the world, the struggles of all living beings. You internalize this knowledge, you make it your own. You conquer your apathy with stories of life, of plants growing and animals caring for their offspring, of good fortune leading to celebration and bad fortune answered with empathy, compassion, patience. You seek purpose for your life by enjoying being alive, not in a destructive way, not vegetating or complaining, but looking outside yourself. We don't have to like each other; our minds have different chemistries. But we can understand each other, we share houses together, we share work, we share cities, we share buses, taxis, coffee shops, parking lots, institutions, hopes, leaders, laws and regulations, histories and traditions, genes and countless similarities. We can understand we were not born to last into infinity. We cannot build infinities. We cannot domesticate and control time. We can be our own makers and we can be our own destroyers. We must understand we have evolved to have this power. We gave it to ourselves. It was not given to us and cannot be taken from us for as long as we exist.

The way of dignity is what we do with our understanding. Turning the other cheek does not bring appeasement. Hiding from accountability does not bring salvation. Having your sins erased by some sort of outside intervention does not bring atonement. Think of dignity not as a large solid statue of heavy stone ruling the landscape of morality, but as a running athlete who withstands hail and fire, not because he has to win a race and prove he was the strongest of them all, but because he has to reach the land of understanding. Where does he get his strength? From love and character.

In the name of one of the apostles, an ancient scribe quoted the Son of God speaking his Sermon on the Mount: Blessed are the poor in spirit, for theirs is the kingdom of heaven. Blessed are those who mourn, for they shall be comforted. Blessed are the meek, for they shall inherit the earth. Blessed are those who hunger and thirst for righteousness, for they shall be satisfied. Blessed are the merciful, for they shall receive mercy. Blessed are the pure in heart, for they shall see God. Blessed are the peacemakers, for they shall be called sons of God. Blessed are those who are persecuted for righteousness' sake, for theirs is the kingdom of heaven. Blessed are you when others revile you and persecute you and utter all kinds of evil against you falsely on my account. Rejoice and be glad, for your reward is great in heaven, for so they persecuted the prophets who were before you.

Let us be realistic here. Are all those *poor in spirit* compensated with any goodness in their lives? No, they have to wait to pass away to collect rewards. Is everyone who mourns comforted? How many widowers and parents who lost sons in war are comforted? The lovely meek, how much of this earth have they inherited? Who has truly inherited the earth? The very few who own as much wealth as billions combined? Is everyone hungry for righteousness always satisfied? How many narcissistic psychopathic criminals go free and unpunished? The merciful, do they always receive mercy in return? How often are they destroyed by revenge, abuse, and forgetfulness? How about the pure of heart, are they always elevated to a higher plane of existence, do they receive the soothing of a greater power, or are they sometimes marginalized as dispensable carriers of empathy, floating in the wake of a turbulent society? The peacemakers, how often are they destroyed by wars as collateral damage? Those persecuted, how often do they see the light of justice and the reinstatement of their dignity? How many have been murdered in the name of the Son of God? How many have killed in the name of the Son of God? Is this divine justice, or earthly quarrels between humans, of their own making?

Yes, you may say, the shield of faith offers solace, guarantees rewards, and brings justice. What is faith? Adoption of hearsay? Laziness of the mind? Militarism of conviction? Biases of thinking that took root in our minds? Is it healthy? Is it necessary? Does it shine a spectral light on truth and make it shinier, prettier? Under the scrutiny of understanding, faith has the value of entertainment for the soul, a lovely distraction. I do not mean to disparage. Coming from me, these words are utter blasphemies. But remember, times are changing, understanding evolves as it always did since the ascent of man. Perhaps one of our tragedies is that we cannot temper our own growing-up.

Here is a good lesson: Do not be anxious about tomorrow, for tomorrow will be anxious for itself. Each day has enough trouble of its own. I didn't say this. It comes for the same ancient scribe. With our modern understanding, we know that there is a great benefit in letting yourself be bathed in the awesomeness of the universe and the expanse of nature. And we have one another. We ought not to forget this, never. Remember your partners before the door to life's opportunities is closed and the sound of work fades. Now you rise at the first chirping of the birds, and even if all their sounds will grow faint, you will have the presence of your partner in your heart, and the rest of your life ahead of you."

12:5 We go viral

First thing next morning, before breakfast, Kumar came to me and said:

"Enyi, I have recorded your Unsermon from last night on video. Should we send it to the world? What do you think?"

"I cannot hold the truth from becoming self-evident, Kumar," I said, "You may make it available for the world, but let us not disclose our location, for now, to protect the people of Santo Candido."

Kumar did his computer work, and the video recording soon appeared on the internet. He added some helpful keywords and tags, such as #PopeFrancis2 and #PapaNostro. Very quickly, the video went viral. In five minutes it reached one million visualizations, in thirty minutes it reached ten million. I called all students to gather inside, near the large television, where Kumar projected the page with the video.

Comments were pouring in:

I can't believe Pope Francis is back,

I love him,

He's so gorgeous,

I knew that video with his boyfriend at the hospital was not fake,

Jesus is this real?,

The greatest man alive,

Is this a fake video?

I think it's fake can't be real,

No it's not it's really him,

Pause zoom in and check the features of his face,

It's really him,

I checked it's not doctored,

I did video-repixelation and it's real it's really Pope Francis,

Guys guys are you really listening to what he's saying he's upending most of the Christian tradition,

Fine with me I love it because we need to do better,

I never believed in that turn the other check s**t anyways,

Holy f**k this ain't gonna sit well with the establishment,

I wonder what Pope Mary would say about this,

Man we need this guy to run for president like right now check out the balls he has,

Especially for the position he had,

Where has he been for the past months,

Who are those peeps around him,

Is that his boyfriend near him,

Love the scenery this must be somewhere in the Alps,

I gotta show this to my granddad being gay is alright despite,

Despite what finish your sentence,

FRANCIS TWO FOR PRESIDENT,

This ain't gotta do anything with this,

Does he look happy he looks happy to me,

I love his voice so genuine so deep reassuring,

I would listen to him reading the phonebook to me and I'm a dude lol,

Whatever makes you happy man,

Jesus he's already breaking news,

My hero Pope Francis Second is my hero,

Never liked the guy but he has a point here,

Guys he's clearly alluding to the bible there's subtle message did you listen carefully,

Are you a conspiracy-digger,

No I'm just saying,

I think he's all on his own,

At his level you can't be independent,

Remember he was ousted he didn't quit,

We'll never know what really happened,

Hey listen there is no secret agenda he did what he said he would do it's facts,

This is fakenews,

Look at this punk still thinking fakenews is a thing how old are you dude,

This is really important I think we are on the verge of something beautiful,

…and on and on. We were watching and laughing together, the students, Nwanne, and I…

"Your Holiness, sorry, Enyi," Danilo said, "I feel truly elated to be here. Your speech, the reactions, this is incredible."

"What do we make of this?" Hilde said.

"I don't know, friends, I don't know," I said.

"The world needs you," Michael from the Bronx said.

"It certainly seems so," I said.

"We gotta do something," Michael from Canberra said.

"Mike, you can't put pressure on His Holiness," Michael from the Bronx said.

"Sorry, Enyi, I didn't mean to-" Michael from Canberra said.

"It's quite alright," I said. "I share your feelings."

Qi-Shan had been sitting quietly this whole time.

"What if we form a group?" she said. "A collective of teachings, a commune of friends to answer all these questions coming from the world. A place of gathering. A home for new thinking. For the new spirit."

"That is interesting Qi-Shan," I said.

"Perhaps we should not be pedantic, perhaps we simply need to speak openly about this new religion."

"New religion?" some students said.

"Yes, is this now what Enyi is talking about?"

"Well, to be honest," I said, "perhaps I am not talking about a new religion, perhaps this is how things are now, and are going to be, under a different name."

"Let's give the movement a name," Francesca said.

"Why do we need a name, we don't like *isms*," Sandra said.

"But we are not nihilists either," Michael from the Bronx said.

"I think the success of religion was based on name-giving, meme-building, lists and idioms, key words, repetitions and epithets, like-"

"Like any other institution, you would say," Sandra said and poured herself more wine.

"I think Qi-Shan is right, we do need a name, not for reasons of propaganda - I dislike propaganda very much - but for reasons of simplicity. And let us not forget, short names have heavy loads of meanings attached to them. It is up to us to explain them."

"I feel something is taking shape here," Hilde said.

"It's because Enyi allowed us to talk as his equals," Phuong said pensively. Everybody seconded her.

"Friends, this was my condition of friendship," I said. "I never liked hierarchies of authorities, despite my last job."

Nwanne brought more wine and everybody helped themselves. Comments continued to pour in at a fast pace on the television.

"Cheers to friendship!" I said.

"Cheers," the students said.

"We Are Earth," I said.

"We Are Earth," they said.

"Hey, this is good name," Danilo said raising his voice.

"Yes, I like it."

"Me too."

"Me too."

In seconds, consensus was reached around the table, and the students agreed our little group ought to have the name "We Are Earth". No isms, no dogma, no manifests.

What did it mean? I am not sure yet. Perhaps humans do need words to hang on to so they can come closer together. What kind of words, in what order, with what meaning, with how many layers of depth and strength, how many roots into the spirit of the people, how connected to what people want or don't want, what they care about, what they hope to get out of life? All these matter to the strength of connection between people and words. From talking to the students, I reimagined how impossible it is to replace the deep, old roots of faith with a New School, regardless of how friendly and peaceful and modern and real it is. The way to move forward, I think, is to build something completely different, not by following the traditions of roots, trunk, branches, leaves, repeated and resown until it circled the Earth and gave birth to forests of followers, but to let those roots wither by themselves and become soil while building a New School, not of trees but of walking living people who learn to change to become better at loving, understanding, and comporting.

We talked about those who are afraid of heights of insecurity, and the terrors in their way; when the almond tree blossoms, the grasshopper drags itself along, and desire fails, because man is going to his eternal home, and the mourners go about the streets. This is a one of the many metaphors of the decaying parts of life. We take them as they are, facets of reality. We make the best of them. We make friends, we grow older, we move, we die. This is it. As simple as this. The miracle is that there is no miracle to life. We chose to live it or we chose not to. When we chose to live, well then, I think there is a lot to look forward to.

12:6 We are Earth

Over the past few days, the students have built a cabin out of wood not too far from our house. It was my idea, and I gave them permission and encouraged them to live together for a while. All people of all ages, especially the adults, should try living in a collective for some time, to remember the values of group bonding.

Kwan was elected to design the new house, because of his education as an architect. I allowed our android to help, as well, with laser-cutting and carrying heavy pieces of wood.

Thusly, before the silver cord was snapped, or the golden bowl was broken, or the pitcher was shattered at the fountain, or the wheel was broken at the cistern, the First Commune of We Are Earth was built, equipped with electricity, running water, twelve beds, a kitchen, two bathrooms, and a living room with a beautiful view of the mountain.

I have been watching their progress daily, and asking them detailed questions about the project, measurements and schematics, the position of the sun throughout the day over the house. How many straight corners and round corners did the house have, how did they plan to share the bathroom, what did they think of privacy, how often would they eat together? The students had formed a nice, tight, friendly group around their diversities.

Nwanne prepared them breakfast every morning. For lunch, they started to make their own recipes in our kitchen, with ingredients from our garden or purchased from the Santo Candido grocery store. In the evening we had them over for dinner, wine, and long conversations about life and the universe. Our video has become the most popular video of the year. Comments and shares have reached many millions. The whole world was looking for us. So far, we had retained the discretion of the Santo Candido people who promised to keep our secret.

Meanwhile, as life went on at a fairly rapid pace, and the First Commune was finished, new relationships were being forged, some with some shyness and relative restraint, some with no restraint at all. Nwanne and I left our own prudishness aside and we found ourselves embracing and kissing on the porch in plain view of the students who were busy painting the frames of the windows in a bright, joyous red.

By that afternoon, probably encouraged by what they saw out of the corners of their eyes, Amran, the young man from Mecca, and Safia, the young woman from Tehran, were holding hands lovingly while walking up the hill, probably to gather some berries or to find a vantage point from where they could watch the starry night by themselves.

I saw everybody looking at Amran and Safia with joy. Lo and behold, at the same time, Michael from the Bronx and Michael from Canberra put down their tools and kissed passionately for a good two or three minutes, in plain view, causing the entire gathering to cheer loudly and shout "Love Love Love", throwing flowers in the air. My goodness! As if the students were sitting on a volcano of love and affection! Flowers were flying, Amran and Safia looked back and waved, the cheers continued, so, to top it up, Sandra from Charlottesville and Phuong from Ho Chi Minh City climbed the table in our backyard with two glasses of wine in their hands, they interlocked their arms holding the glasses, drank them empty, then kissed even more passionately than the boys, seemingly to challenge them somehow, to which Bronx Michael and Canberra Michael responded immediately, climbing on the workbench with their respective wine glasses and kissing even more passionately.

Applause erupted, and Danilo turned up the volume of the music, hot Brazilian beach-jazz, as it is known, and presented himself with inviting, irresistible dance moves, which halted the work on the spot.

The students waved at Nwanne and me, giving us no choice but to join them in celebration. For the first time in many years, I felt free to dance with my Nwanne, surrounded by people much younger than us, who understood many things better than we did, and saw freedom in a purer light than we did.

12:7 The world knows

The truth is out! The world knows where we are. I could not resist the pressure I saw in the media and on the internet. Millions wanted to hear more from me, to learn where I was, what plans I had for the future, what else I had to tell them. They would listen to anything that came out of my mouth. I still feel uneasy with these overwhelming effusions of adulation, yet I could not hold back the comfort my words would bring to those willing to listen. I wish I had a voice without a face. "Now you worry about this? What about when you were Pope?" Nwanne said, one morning. I think he's right. It is too late for this kind of modesty.

Kumar installed a holophone for us and said that whenever I was ready he will activate it, but I should be very vigilant because my number can be located if someone savvy geotags the holophone IP. I could be flooded with calls. Kumar himself was very savvy with technology and he assured me no one can break his security protocols.

I asked him to share my number with a limited list of friends and officials that have made an impression on me while I was in office, and to set the holophone to accept calls only from these people. Then I told him to turn on the device.

Calls started to pour in, one after the other, from all the people on the list. Once they got hold of the phone queue, they hung on to it until their turn came. Some waited for hours.

I heard from Stayingzento, Dalai Lama 15, still vibrant and astute, who was seeking to be a student of new higher wisdom, his words not mine; Pavel Pushkin, the President of Russia, who said I was an inspiration to him for two things, how to reform the churches in Russia, and how he created a character based on me in his last novel called *The Shore of Caprice*; Margarita Bourbon-Renege, former President of Brazil, now President of the International Criminal Climate Court, said that my courage inspires her to continue the fight; Nadir Wadkirsch, Secretary General of the United Nations, the evolutionary psychologist by education, told me he dedicated his last book *Earth and Brain* to me; Ayatollah Ali Foolas said he wanted to build Communes in Iran; Moses Amisraeli, Prime Minister of Israel, recently reelected, told me he has opened a new University in equal partnership with the Republic of Palestine, that bears my name; King Sandal Alumnus Baad Al-Bizi of Saudi Arabia misses me very much and told me many Saudis call me *alqidiys al'iifriqii, Our African Saint*; former Cardinal Samuel Park-Ying of Seoul, now Magister within the Council of Humanity, told me that I am a celebrity in New Korea and the most used name for newborns is Francis for boys and Frances for girls; Sanbard Renders, the President of the United States, told me that our meeting has kept him inspired and focused to take the country out of a deep recession; Fo Fushikuma, the nuclear physicist, the prime minister of Japan, told me he has named the first fusion reactor *The Francis*, in honor of peace and human progress; Mo Xi, the President of China, dedicated his last book *The Blue Book*, focusing on planetary policy, to me, following *The Red Book*, that discussed ideology, and *The Green Book*, that discussed Asian politics; Fred Kapiter, the President of the United Nations of Europe, was eager to tell me about the success of using AI algorithms in running New Europe, and particularly he said the algorithm is named (what else!) *Franciscus*; and last, but not least, with great emotion and joy, I answered the call of Mother Allegra and her husband, Thorsen Tchipcherish, Guardian and Secretary General of the Council of Humanity, respectively, who were even more thrilled to see me. We spoke about our good times together, and they updated me about their progress with the Council.

"...and the dust returns to the earth as it was, and the spirit returns to the people who gave it," Thorsen peppered our conversation with a bit of wisdom.

"I totally agree with that, Thorsen," I said. "Mother Allegra, you are more radiant than ever."

"You are too kind, Enyi," Mother Allegra said. "Thorsen is a very good husband."

We promised each other we would remain friends forever.

All in all, good news from around the world. Significant progress has been made to improve the lives of all beings. But the struggle has not ended.

While I was taking the calls, Nwanne showed me messages he wrote by hand. They read: Many Pilgrims In Santo Candido, What Do We Do?, Students Are Waiting For You, We Need To Do Something. After I finished the last call, I paused the holophone. I was also very tired, and went outside to see what was going on. There were hundreds, perhaps thousands, of pilgrims in the valley of Santo Candido, as far as the eye could see: on foot, on bicycles, on hover-boards, in eCars, with caravans, all coming to see me, to see us, since our location was no longer a secret. The merry mayor installed some signs asking for order and a civilized procession, and they were completely respected. The problem was the very large number of pilgrims. The small community of Santo Candido will be blocked very soon. Being a good administrator, the merry mayor has come up with the idea of installing symbolic wooden gates on the roads at both entrances in Santo Candido, and allowing groups of five to ten pilgrims to enter at a time, assuming that I was willing and available to receive them. Of course I was willing and available, so I asked dear Nwanne and our dear students to prepare many liters of coffee, tea, wine, and snacks, and to arrange a room where I could meet the pilgrims. Within two hours, everything was set up and ready.

12:8 The commune of Abuja

We Are Earth Communes are spreading around the world. The first one in Africa has just opened, near Abuja, by a group of solar farmers. Their motto: We Are Farmers of Light. Nigeria is on track to diminish the production of petrol and replace it with solar energy. This fills my heart with joy.

On their HoloBook page, they posted the following statement, read by their administrator:

"We, the solar farmers of Abuja, have found a way to share our love for Earth and to respond to the needs of our peers. We have written a democratic charter for the Solar Commune, in which the individual freedom of our members is held in high regard, while at the same time the common purpose of harvesting the sun has been established. We pledge to heal the Earth. We pledge to care for the Earth. We pledge to feed the people of Earth with safe and clean energy. We have decided amongst ourselves to overcome the saying All Is Vanity and the belief that the common people will never achieve independence. We would like to show the world that independence of the common people is possible, that the power of the few can be defeated, and the wealth of the sun can be shared with everybody. Please visit our HoloBook page for a virtual tour of our farm, please read our charter, share your thoughts, and visit us if you can. We will be very happy to welcome you and show you around."

Quite an assertive statement! It made me proud.

I asked Kumar to explain me how this HoloBook worked. Wonders of technology! I just can't keep up. It's a social platform in the holosphere where people have a holographic presence. They use holocameras to capture real-size representations of their whereabouts, or they share live holocasts where others can join as if they were really in the same space. HoloBook is now very popular because it adds the third dimension to the human connection and makes it more real. Neat! I also like their motto: Reality Without Distance.

12:9 Michael and Michael

Bronx Michael and Canberra Michael came to me one afternoon, while I was in my room writing random thoughts in my diary, and asked if they could sit down with me and Nwanne for a delicate and intimate conversation. Of course, I accepted, and invited them over for dinner, just the four of us.

"Enyi, I'm not sure how to begin," Bronx Michael said. "This is very embarrassing for me."

"Speak your mind, Michael, we're friends here," I said.

"Well, you know, Michael and I, we, umm, we like and love each other, and, umm, oh boy-"

"We would like to be deeply intimate," Canberra Michael said.

"Oh, that is great, it's wonderful, I am happy for you," I said. "You see, dear Nwanne and I, we've known each other since we were young. We always felt deeply for each other. We have no secrets from each other. We have a loving relationship where everything we do flows, naturally. Here, I may not be an expert or wise enough to give you advice, surely, I will do my best, from friends to friends who happen to share the same persuasion, one of the many in this world."

"Oh, sorry," Canberra Michael said. "We are actually not looking for advice in this area, pardon us for miscommunicating."

"Oh," I said.

"Michael and I would like to open a crypto-account with bio-identifiers," Canberra Michael said. "We would like to move all our crypto-coins together in a shared, secure account, and we would need the bio-inputs from two other trustworthy sources, so to prevent the hacking of the account."

"Oh," I said, still a tad lost.

"We would secure this joint-account with our skin-prints and DNA snapshots. And for the other two trustworthy sources, we kindly request your input. It would mean everything to us. You are the closest friends we have in our lives to date, and your stature would make our accounts impenetrable."

"Ahh, I see, I see," I said. "My goodness, I had no idea this level of security existed. See, Nwanne, we are completed outshadowed by the new technologies. We are fortunate to have you teach us about these things."

"We do not mean to impose in any way, or abuse our friendship," Bronx Michael said.

"No, no, not at all," I said. "Friends should share everything, from the little things to the big concerns. They should leave shyness and embarrassment aside."

"And not be afraid to show their naked souls to each other," Nwanne added wisely.

"Yes, of course, that too," I added. "Of course, it will be our pleasure to help you with the crypto-account. Perhaps we will learn something ourselves. Right, Nwanne?"

"Haha, I hope so," Nwanne said.

Now, who's feeling more embarrassed? I thought the two Michaels came to us with other concerns, of a different, intimate nature to which I rarely give myself time to think about. Whilst being ready to share my advice, I feared I would not be able to be of much help, given my age and my failing memory.

When I gave my answer, Michael and Michael were elated. They asked if they could hug us, as friends, to seal our friendship. For the first time in decades, I found myself in a group hug, with Nwanne and friends I cherished. I was overjoyed.

In addition to being a wise man, the Preacher also taught the people knowledge. And he pondered, searched out, and arranged many proverbs and much helpful advice for many people.

12:10 Ode to Joy

Reasons for joy? Yes, there are many, so we should let them unfold. Reasons for sadness? Yes, there are many. Does joy arise from the nature of things without our intervention? Of course not, joy is all our doing, arising from our quest for happiness. Can joy conquer sadness? Not always. In fact, I have known many tragedies, I have seen enough struggles with the world to say, with confidence, that certain sadnesses are invincible. So, what then is the purpose of our exuberance? I could ask the same question about sadness. What good does it have? Or I could ask, what bad does it have?

Schiller wrote in 1785:

Freude trinken alle Wesen / An den Brüsten der Natur / Alle Guten, alle Bösen / Folgen ihrer Rosenspur.[*]

Did Mr. Schiller know about the world of depression? Did he even imagine the mountains of expectations we have built for

---

[*] *All creatures drink of joy / At nature's breast / Just and unjust / Alike taste of her gift.* From **Ode to Joy** written in 1785 by German poet, playwright, and historian Friedrich Schiller.

ourselves, and the many accidents we had while climbing these mountains, despite all the ambition and the support we had?

Here's the subtle point: We have to drink from the river of joy as if it was flowing forcefully from the horn of abundance. Thusly, there is a possibility that we can quench our sadness in this river and let the frailty of our memory keep us on this new plateau of serenity. If it was only this easy! Sadness has its own river, often deeper, wider, heavier. It sullies the waters of joy and turns life into a bottomless swamp.

Remember the Preacher who sought to find words of delight, and uprightly wrote words of truth? If we choose our earthly delights carefully we might get closer to the truth, and perhaps find joy and even happiness on the way. To me, this seems not an easy task, but one that can be learned, as I did, having Nwanne near me, and having the gargantuan luck of being propelled into the limelight of history. I was forced to learn. I could not hide from my demons. I had to destroy them, first faking courage and resilience, then transforming this act of life or whatever it was into the substance that cemented the new foundation of my being. I don't think I would have survived this long without Nwanne and without forcing joy unto myself.

We are also prisoners of the blueprints of our minds. What if we do not learn what true joy is in the early days of childhood? The free, boundless joy of meeting beings and knowledge for the first time? The delightful innocent laughter at silly faces and quirky words? What if children are bereft of these treasures? How are we to teach them joy when they will grow up to meet love for the first time, or struggle with understanding and bonding with their peers? Like colors to those born blind, or symphonies to those born deaf, joy is an unteachable experience to the prisoners of sadness.

I still think there is hope. Love, understanding, dignity can lead to manufactured joy for those who are ill. As seeds planted by hardworking farmers gain a life of their own, so can joy be sown in all souls. If I wish anything for the world I leave after me, it is the desire for people to embrace joy with their minds, even when their souls are weak, and to share it as real gifts to others, not as fleeting little clouds of vanishing hope. I do not wish hope for the world. I wished and tried to offer joy when things that could happen have actually happened for the greater benefit of all. Then it is imperative to celebrate and dance!

12:11 Celebration, Weddings, Dancing, Music

The words of the wise are like cattle prods, painful but helpful. Their collected sayings are like a nail-studded stick with which a shepherd drives the sheep.

More good news now!

This morning, Bronx Michael and Canberra Michael, Sandra from Charlottesville and Phuong from Ho Chi Minh City, came to me, all four of them together, and asked me forthrightly if I would be willing to perform the wedding ceremony for them.

"I do not hold a religious office anymore," I said.

"We are perfectly okay with that, Enyi," they said. "You are still a priest, you have not been stripped of your priestly functions."

"That is true, but I have not joined the Council of Humanity either, in any capacity," I sighed.

"You are still the Pope in our hearts. Please?"

How could I refuse? I said yes, and summoned Nwanne right away to start the preparations. The other students got together and built a beautiful gazebo in our common yard. They made wooden benches, beautiful flower decorations, they paved the aisle with rose petals. The merry mayor gracefully offered us a band of local musicians who came dressed in traditional Italian attire. Nwanne called his friends in the village, the baker, the grocer, the restaurant owners, the chefs, the grandmas, and asked them if they could help with the catering. Oh goodness, help they did! The whole village came to the party with hundreds of plates of goodies. The children came, the toddlers, the seniors wearing medicinal exoskeletons or in wheelchairs, everybody!

While we were preparing for the ceremony, Amran and Safia pulled me aside and asked me, with some shyness in their voices, if their union could also be recognized in some sort of a ceremony, so they could refer to it as The Official Beginning of their Time Together, but they did not want to be considered married in the traditional sense. Could I allow them to join the other two couples? Sure, of course, why not, how can I refuse any reason for celebration when it has to do with love?

So, we had three weddings at the same time, well, two weddings and one unwedding, with hundreds of guests, with a microphone for me, and drone-speakers, music, dance, and good food. It lasted the whole day, then into the night (Kumar installed dragonfly-drones for illumination) then joy carried into the next day with no signs of tiredness. Lovely people of Santo Candido and my dear student friends took turns at serving, clearing tables, helping guests with their needs, children with their playground, kitchen with supplies, kept tables busy with wine and plates, and the dance rink full with dancers.

12:12 Ode to imagination

Here's an oddity from the Book of Ecclesiastes: "There is no end to the crafting of many books, and too much study wearies the body." How can too much study weary the body?

This is what I dreamt last night. (This is the last dream I'm writing in my diaries. People, in general, give too much attention to the nightly, uncontrollable jolts of their brains.)

I was a miniscule man, riding on the head of a giraffe that was galloping on the African savannah. I was holding on to the giraffe's horn and I was feeling a big sick. I don't like heights and I don't like high speeds. I don't know how I ended up there. The giraffe was galloping fast and was showing no signs of stopping. I looked behind me and I saw a tiger chasing the giraffe. There was something bizarre about the tiger. He didn't seem to chase the giraffe, but rather was running alongside as if the two animals were in a race to get somewhere. The giraffe suddenly changed directions. The tiger followed, awkwardly, losing balance and almost tripping on the flat ground. I thought, in that little brain of mine, standing on the giraffe's head, is the tiger blind? Why is he running into bushes and tripping on stones? Is he disoriented?

The race continued for a while until I saw movement on the giraffe's neck. Somebody was coming. Whistling, rustling the giraffe's neck hair, a tiny creature was climbing up towards me. A mouse. Equipped with climbing accessories, boots, a helmet. He came to me and asked me how I was doing. I was holding tightly to one of the horns. I said I was fine, expect for a slight inconvenience given the absurdity of the situation. The mouse said he perfectly understood my frustration. He was there to help me.

"Who are you?" I asked.

"I am the master of the tiger," the mouse said.

"What?"

"Yes, that tiger belongs to me."

"Clearly this is a joke."

"No, this is a dream. Anything can happen in the dream. Remember you have dreamt about a giraffe and a tiger before, many years ago, when you were in Africa?"

"Yes, I think so. I don't remember exactly."

"This is nothing like that," the mouse said.

"Can we stop please?"

"Certainly," the mouse said. "It is entirely up to you."

It was clearly not entirely up to me, as the dream continued for a while until the giraffe stopped running, the tiger stopped running, and I had no way of getting down to the ground.

Reality saved me. A rooster in the backyard performing his morning chanting, and Nwanne in the kitchen pouring water in the kettle.

12:13 You say, you'll marry me, if I be willing?[*]

On the third day of the three weddings, I was having my cup of coffee at the kitchen table. Nwanne, as usual, was making breakfast. I was looking, with my heart full of joy, at the people outside who were still celebrating.

He came to me and looked at me for a while.

"What are you thinking, Enyi"?

"I'm thinking of us. What do we deserve more for ourselves? Can we hope for more?"

"You know I prefer not to hope, but to live the moment."

"I know, I know," I said.

"Love should not be silent," he said. "Should never be a secret."

"I think we deserve a celebration too."

---

[*]Shakespeare, *As You Like It*, act 5, scene 4

"I dreamt about that often," he said.

"Me too, but it's been a while. Now I'm dreaming about tigers and giraffes."

"Another chase? Did Jesus pay a visit too?"

"Haha, no not this time. What about your dreams?"

"We must celebrate like everybody else," he said.

"Yes, I feel the same." I said.

"This is it. Right in front of us. Friends, a beautiful house. We have found our peace," he said.

"You say, you'll marry me, if I be willing?" I said.

"That will I, should I die the hour after," he replied.

"I love you dearly," I said.

"I love you too," he said.

With these words we decided. We told everybody immediately. The merry mayor ran to tell the people of Santo Candido, shouting from the top of his lungs *Un altro matrimonio! Another marriage!* Kumar enhanced the existing audio setup with devices for live video- and holo-streaming. I said yes even before Nwanne opened his mouth to ask me. Sure, let the world see us, if they are interested. We only mean to increase the peace.

The priest of Santo Candido, a Father Pierfrancesco, member of the Council of Humanity, offered to perform the ceremony the way we wanted. We kindly asked him to conduct a humanist ceremony, to talk about life, commitments, strength, and all other principles of good character. Nobody felt the need to invoke the benevolence of God, as we had each other, which was plenty.

Media outlets worldwide linked to the live holo-stream, and once again we have become a sensation. In goodwill, deep in my heart, I finally accepted this irreversible status of a person known worldwide. I do have a hope, though, despite my reluctance to anchor myself in the future. I hope history will not judge us harshly. We have done our best, we sought to cause no harm, we sought no personal gain, we tried to make the world a better place.

I knew I could not escape the duty of giving a speech. While the audience expected to hear vows from us to each other, according to tradition we had none, as our entire life together was in lieu of a brief composition of words. I ended my speech of love and peace with these words:

"The conclusion, my friends, when all has been heard, is: fear nothing and keep your promises. Be well and prosper!"

12:14 Hello World

One million people have gathered near the city of Odinihu (which means *future* in Igbo) in the deserts of Northern Nigeria. Known as the solar city, Odinihu was built to bring peace to Nigeria and to create the largest hub of solar energy production in the Sahara. A fantastic accomplishment.

For the inauguration, so many people showed up that the government decided to develop an enormous camp site. They named the solar district Light of Enyi, in my honor. What serendipitous opportunity to spend our honeymoon in the places where we grew up!

We took an eCar from Abuja. On the way to Odinihu, we stopped many times to talk to people, to breath air, to look up at the sun, to take pictures. Hundreds of Nigerians linked to us and we ended up being a convoy of hundreds of cars marching slowly. I felt truly at home!

In Odinihu, I met the mayor, a strong man, who reminded me of my father. He shook my hand and said:

"Welcome home, Enyi! Thanks to you, in three years we will make more energy than the city of Neom. The people are more united than ever."

Nwanne looked at me with tears in his eyes. I knew what he was thinking about. Our younger years of travels from country to country, seeking to learn about the world and to bring some comfort to the people we've met. And now, the people we've left behind have outgrown us. They are harnessing the sun and sharing it with all those who need it. *Everything starts with words and stories*, I told Nwanne with my eyes. *See, I told you it was worth it*, he replied.

There, in Odinihu, I met everybody I knew from Nigeria who was still alive. I remembered them all. They came with gifts, with emotion, with infinite gratitude in their words, to thank me for the inspiration. I knew what the story of my life has meant for them. I knew what my own struggles meant for those bereft of attention. I knew that I had not lived in vain, I had not made my mistakes in vain. I was not tested by vanity for no purpose. It made me better, I think, or else it would have destroyed me, and all the people I knew would have tossed their memories of me into the deep valleys of forgetfulness.

I am not the man I was, from the cores of my beliefs, to the many skins that have grown over my body. They know that. They know everything about me, and they still love me more than ever. This is what binds people together, understanding how struggles and time change us as human beings. As for what happens with our legacy, that is a matter for the future. Some care about how they will be remembered, some love the present so much, they walk the Earth as if there was no tomorrow. We don't make history, we never do. History makes us, for history will bring every act to judgment, everything which is hidden, whether it is good or evil.

I climbed the stage at Odinihu with Nwanne by my side. The crowd was waiting for us, chanting. As far as I could see into the horizon, the solar farms were gathering the orange sun and were forwarding us the appearance of an ocean of light.

I took the microphone, I looked at the crowd, and said from the bottom of my heart:

"Hello Africa! Hello world! I am back!"

THE END

Made in the USA
Lexington, KY
22 March 2019